Bridge to Normal

A Novel

© 2014, Wilhelmina Fitzpatrick

Canada Council Conseil des Arts
for the Arts du Canada

Canada

Newfoundland
Labrador

We gratefully acknowledge the financial support of the Canada Council for the Arts,
the Government of Canada through the Canada Book Fund (CBF),
and the Government of Newfoundland and Labrador through the Department
of Tourism, Culture and Recreation for our publishing program.

Printed on acid-free paper
Cover Design by Todd Manning
Layout by Amy Fitzpatrick

Published by
KILLICK PRESS
an imprint of CREATIVE BOOK PUBLISHING
a Transcontinental Inc. associated company
P.O. Box 8660, Stn. A
St. John's, Newfoundland and Labrador A1B 3T7

Printed in Canada

Library and Archives Canada Cataloguing in Publication

Fitzpatrick, Wilhelmina, 1958-, author
Bridge to normal / Wilhelmina Fitzpatrick.

ISBN 978-1-77103-051-9 (pbk.)

I. Title.

PS8611.I895B75 2014 C813'.6 C2014-904700-2

Bridge to Normal

A Novel

Wilhelmina Fitzpatrick

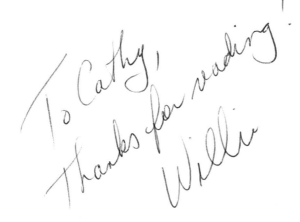

To Cathy,
Thanks for reading!
Willi

killick press
an imprint of Creative Publishers

St. John's, Newfoundland and Labrador
2014

This book is dedicated to my sisters,
Joan, Geraldine, Madonna, Georgina, Sharon, Deanne, and Pippa.

Special thanks to the following people:
Michael, Ian and Keith for filling my life with love.
Madonna Fitzpatrick for sharing her professional knowledge of,
and insights into, issues of mental health.
Cecelia Frey, Dixie Baum and Sue Hirst for their always-honest
and always-helpful critiques.
Pam Dooley, Amy Fitzpatrick, and Todd Manning for all their help.
Marnie Parsons for her excellent editing and generosity of time.
And last but never least, Donna Francis.

1

Normal. That's all I ever wanted to be. A normal family, all I ever wanted to have. My family owned a funeral home. Dead people were our business. We also sold life insurance.

"They gets you one end or the other, them Ashes."

I was six years old when I heard that. I had no idea what it meant. Maeve Mullins, the owner of Mullins Meats and Mercantile, Exile Cove's only store, was weighing and packaging portions of salt fish while talking over her shoulder to Lizzie Gordon, the town's beautician. Lizzie, who also cut men's hair, wore Coke-bottle glasses and had to squint to see anything much past her reach.

Lizzie placed a can of shaving cream and a box of Red Rose on the counter. "That Andy Ashe always got that look, like he's measuring you for a box."

"Yes, and that hawk nose of his points right at me. I swear I can feel the cold in the ground." Maeve exaggerated a shiver and, having finished meting out the fish, turned around.

That's when she saw me standing behind Katie Dollmont at the far end of the counter, each of us squeezing a nickel in our palms. We had been hoping to go unnoticed while we waited for Carol, Maeve's younger sister, to return from her dinner break. Katie claimed that Carol always gave her extra candy.

Maeve studied me for a long moment before focusing in on Katie. "What can I get for you, Katie, my dear?" Katie's father was the mayor, as was his father before him.

"Hi, Mrs. Mullins," Katie said in her false sweet voice. Moments earlier she'd called Maeve "a goddamn biddy." "Could we get five cents' worth of mixed up candy each, please?"

Maeve – we only called her Mrs. Mullins to her face – looked a little sheepish, which boded well for us. Sure enough, she filled the small brown bags.

Katie beamed, all teeth showing, except one missing at the front. "Thanks, Mrs. Mullins."

We were near the door when Katie drew me past the "Ladies Linens and Lace" sign and into the women's section. She ignored the hot pants and mini skirts and bell-bottoms and went directly to the rack of underwear. After rummaging about for a few seconds, she poked her arms through an extra large pair of panties, then pulled a pair of pink bloomers over her head and tugged a patch of her curly red hair through each leg opening. I was trying to stifle my giggles when we overheard Lizzie's voice. "...them are a strange lot...never has folks in... size of that Josephine...300 pounds if she's an ounce," to which Maeve responded,

"...and them dolls she does dressed up like brides of Christ...don't know why, mind you...never darkens the church door, she don't..."

Katie's mouth tightened. She yanked the underwear off and started to turn.

I grabbed her arm. "Come on, Katie. Let's go." She hesitated. "Please," I begged.

She dropped both pairs of underwear on the floor and stomped on them. "Cunt."

Katie had been my best friend since the first day of school a year earlier. Students were required to be six years old to start Grade 1. Josephine thought I was five. We all did. "You can already read, sure," she'd said, hauling me down the street. Josephine was short and wide and round with big bones that had lots of fat on them, except for her hands which were unexpectedly small with thin fingers, although there was a puffy layer on the back and palm. "Why wait another year when you could be spending the whole day in the school room?" It wasn't until Grade 11, when I requested a copy of my birth certificate from the government, that I discovered I was a year older.

I was enrolled in the combined Grade 1/2 class that morning. I sat at my desk, shoulders hunched, head down, as the other students teased and tormented one another. Their families had deep roots and connections throughout the area, a history of permanence and long-standing habitation that everybody recognized. We'd only moved to Exile Cove a few years before, and had never become involved in the community. Josephine said we'd best keep to ourselves, that we didn't need strangers looking in on us, nosing around. Best stay inside, she told me. We were private sorts, she added, her tone smug. Being private was a lonely state as far as I was concerned.

"Bridgina Ashe." Even though there were 32 of us in the room on that overcast September morning, I was the lone pupil Mrs. Flynn singled out during roll call. "So you're one of them Ashes-From-Away? Josephine and Andy Ashe's girl?"

There were other Ashes in the area, all quite possibly related to us somewhere along the line – the Ashes-By-The-Beach, the Mrs.-Jack-Ashes, the Taxicab-Ashes, among others. For lack of a better distinguishing feature at the time, we became the "Ashes-From-Away." I don't think people were aware that it made us, or me at least, feel set apart. I noticed it sometimes when I was served at the store or went to pick up the mail, that quick up-glance, that moment of hesitation reserved for someone not as well known as everyone else in the room, those who had first-hand history there. It wasn't always something you could pinpoint, it was that small.

Mrs. Flynn removed her glasses. "Stand up now till I get a look at you."

Feeling more insignificant than usual, I stood. My face burned. There was a tingling sensation behind my eyes. I pressed my hands against my cheeks, pushing the skin back like I did to stop myself from crying. Josephine hated crybabies.

"What are you doing to your face, child?"

Katie's hand shot up. "She's not from away. She lives right down the street from me, sure." Katie nodded extra hard as if that would prove her point.

Mrs. Flynn seemed about to protest, perhaps to say that where I lived wasn't important, that what was important was where I was born, and where my parents were born, and their parents before them, and so on, when Sylvia Mercer nodded as well.

"Yeah," Sylvia said. "They lives near us too. They're not from away."

Looking exasperated, Mrs. Flynn motioned for me to sit down. She was calling the roll from back to front and the only student left was Billy Abbott. She dispensed with him and proceeded to write the alphabet on the chalkboard.

The Ashes-From-Away. I hated being called that. Still, it was better than the alternative.

Josephine was the one who'd decided Dad would open a funeral home. This was after our neighbour, who was rumoured to have died of some horrible disease that was never spoken of above a whisper and that nobody put a name to, was waked in his living room.

"It's disgusting, Andy." Josephine bent to take out the leftover roast, her backside obstructing all views into the fridge. "Think on it. In that little house, they got to eat in the same room pert near. They're frying up a bit of meat and he's not 10 feet away, dead from God knows what. I could hardly stomach that cake and biscuits they had laid out."

Dad lit a cigarette and plugged in the kettle. "But sure that's the way it's always been done." He measured rum and Coke into a tumbler and passed it to Josephine.

"So what? It's 1965, for God's sake. Get with the times." She took a swig and grimaced. "How many times I got to tell you? I likes the diet stuff. This is too sweet to drink," she said, taking another swallow. "Bridgina, get me a can of Tab."

I slid down off my chair and went to look in the cupboard. "None left."

Dad frowned. "I thought it was the other way with the Coke and the Tab. Anyway, people round here not going to change. They can't afford it, girl."

"Don't be minding half them what got the poor mouth. Some of that crowd got loads of money." She took the big knife from the butcher block and swished it up and down three times on the sharpening stone.

"I don't know, Josephine. Lot of work starting a new business." He blew his nose and took a moment to study his handkerchief. "I'm not sure. Like I say, I don't know."

The steel glinted as she tested the razor-sharp edge against her hand. "Well, I do."

The next June, Ashe's Funeral Parlour opened in St. Paul, five miles down the road. St. Paul was larger than Exile Cove and serviced all the surrounding towns when it came to necessities like lawyers, doctors, dentists, and now, death.

From the outset, Dad hated the funeral business. Josephine said too bad, that was where he'd put his money so he was stuck with it. According to Dad, the worst part was trying to get people to pay their bills. "You can't get blood out of a turnip and you can't get a dollar out of a corpse," was how he put it, with a little chuckle, as if it was the funniest thing he'd ever said, which it may have been. He was not known for his wit.

Four years later the funeral home burnt to the ground. Dad had gone home for lunch so no one was in the building at the time, except for Theo Sparrow who was already dead. His family had been expecting a traditional burial.

With nothing left but ashes, the exact cause of the fire was never determined. Dad had plenty of insurance and when the money came, he bought the Sparrow building down the street from our house. It had been for sale since shortly before Theo died because all his children had left town and none showed any desire to return. There was an ice-cream shop and an office on the main floor and two small vacant apartments above. Josephine immediately took over the ice-cream shop and Dad, happy to be done with the funeral business, and relieved not to have to make the long drive to and from St. Paul every day, relocated his insurance agency to the office.

My older sister, Melinda, apparently held the same view as the Sparrow offspring. She'd lived away as long as I could remember, visiting Exile Cove twice a year. However, when I was in Grade 5, she surprised us all by taking a nursing position at the hospital in St. Paul. Although I didn't know her well, I was thrilled to have someone else, someone almost young, in the house, even if at first she and Josephine engaged in frequent shouting matches. I would always leave the room but I still heard snippets of what they said. It was confusing. "Home-wrecker" sounded like a big job for Melinda, who had a few extra pounds around her middle but was otherwise small. I had no idea what a slut was either, but Katie said that her mother had washed Seamus's mouth out with Lysol when he'd said it. Fortunately, Josephine and Melinda must have reached some sort of truce. After a couple of months they just stopped arguing.

Two years after that my family grew once again when the government resettled Lost Harbour, the outport community where my grandmother had spent her entire life. Dad convinced her to come live with us. Now we were five, which, although small by Exile Cove standards, was far more respectable than three. Gran was a tiny stubborn old woman who reminded me of a bird, pecking at her food without ever eating much, her head bopping about on her scraggy neck like the chickens in the Mercers' backyard as she fretted about the noise from all the traffic and the general lawlessness of Exile Cove, about how she could only catch sight of the ocean if she craned her neck to see past the neighbour's shed. She was nice to me, though, nicer than Josephine, that's for certain. Gran had one flaw, however, that outweighed any other. She was a teetotaller. From the beginning she and Josephine crossed swords, and within a week she'd moved into one of the Sparrow apartments. Six months later, she died in her sleep. I missed her for a while.

Dad's funeral business had only been open a few months before I started school and I hadn't given much thought to it. But that first day when Katie walked home with me, she was full of questions. How many dead bodies had I seen? Did I get to see accident victims? Were their arms and legs ever cut off? How about their heads? Could she come over to my house?

Finally, a question I could answer. "Sure." Josephine would not be pleased.

"Let's walk home together every day." Katie tucked her arm into mine and started us off on a skip down the road.

My heart leapt with excitement. I generally played alone in my room, creating stories and plays, acting out all the parts by myself.

"Let's do everything together, just like sisters but better." She stopped in mid-skip. "Oh my God, you can marry Seamus. He's older but that's okay. Girls are supposed to marry older boys, right?" She didn't wait for an answer. "I wish you had an older brother, then I could marry him and we'd be like double sisters. Oh well, we'll just have to be best friends for now."

I forgot all about Josephine and dead bodies. Katie was a tomboy with wild red hair and a great deep laugh that seemed too big for her little body. The other kids had been hanging around her all day, but for some reason she wanted me to be her best friend.

"You have to show me your room," she said. "Best friends have to know everything about each other."

Katie talked the rest of the way home, about her brothers and sisters, her aunts and cousins, her dog and two cats. I marvelled at how many people there were in her family. Mine consisted of Dad and Josephine and Melinda, who I decided I could count even though at the time she was still working up north, wherever that was. I hadn't yet met my grandmother. The one time Dad went to visit, he went by himself, so it didn't seem right to include her.

"Josephine, I'm home," I called out when we entered the house.

I heard Katie gasp. The floral sofa, which was fitted with a thick layer of plastic, was covered with dolls, each decked out in either an elaborate wedding gown or a plain black uniform, the brides' heads covered with veils of stiff lace, the nuns' faces protruding from black and white plastic habits. Each doll had been positioned to face forward, looking toward the door. Sixteen sets of glass eyes gaped at us.

The remaining furniture in the room consisted of four chairs of different shapes and sizes, one for each of us. Mine was the small rickety rocker with the bed pillow on the seat, Josephine's the oversized partner to the sofa with a big butt dimple sunk into the centre. Unlike the sofa it wasn't covered in plastic, which was unfortunate because, like Josephine, it had absorbed more than its fair share of rum and Coke. My sister had a chair, too, for when she visited. It was part of some long dead aunt's old settee set and positioned next to a small bookcase filled with Melinda's romance novels. Melinda always had one of those on the go. They were the only books in the house besides Dad's Mark Twain collection, which he said was mine now since I'd started reading it. The black office chair was Dad's. It had wheels so he could push himself back and forth to the television. There was also an oak-stained coffee table to hold the TV guide and Dad's favourite ashtray, and Josephine's drink.

Josephine, who always had an afternoon nap, thumped down the stairs in her housecoat. "For the love of God, I'm sick of telling you to keep the noise down." She pointed at Katie. "You're that Dollmont girl." Katie turned to stare, speechless, at Josephine, who grunted, "Keep quiet," and headed back upstairs.

Katie grabbed my arm. "How come you got so many dolls?"

"They're not mine, they're hers."

She moved towards the dolls. "What does she want dolls for?"

I followed close behind. "She makes them and sells them. These ones are ready for the fair this weekend." As Katie reached out, I stepped in front of her. "We're not allowed to touch them."

Katie laughed and tried to go around me.

"Please," I said, so afraid that my new best friend would get me into trouble, or worse, not want to play with me anymore. "Josephine will know if we touch them."

"You've never played with them?" Her voice sounded sorry for me.

"No, but I saved some of the ones she was throwing away when she stopped making the nurses. They're in my room. You want to see?"

I led her down the hall to my room, which was actually a large pantry that Dad said he had converted because it was small like me. When I was really little it had scared me to sleep on the main floor by myself, but Josephine said there were only three bedrooms upstairs and Melinda was too big for the pantry when she was at home. "Be glad you got that," she said. "Folks round here sleeps six to a bed. Quit squawking."

My windowless room was pitch black. I turned on the light.

"Holy shit!" Katie ran the three steps toward the refrigerator box along the opposite wall. "It's like a real house."

When we'd bought the new fridge the year before, I had begged Josephine to let me keep the carton. She was adamant that it was going into the garbage until Dad made her a deal that he would get her a new sewing machine to make her dolls' dresses. I had spent weeks colouring the cardboard with flower boxes and lace-curtained windows and a white cat and a black dog, then surrounded it with a white picket fence I made out of construction paper. Unfortunately, I kept stepping on the fence in the middle of the night when I woke up to go to the bathroom, or worse, had already gone and needed to change my pyjamas and bed sheet.

Katie and I crawled inside and sat on the cushions I had set up in front of a smaller box that served as a table. We pretended to drink tea from the toy cups and eat make-believe cookies with the nurse dolls. Katie put on a British accent and pretended she was the Queen of England. I was laughing and holding my stomach when she put down her cup and switched back to her own voice.

"How come you calls your mother Josephine?"

"That's her name, sure," I said, biting into my imaginary cookie.

"Don't she get mad when you call her that?"

"No. Should she?" I lifted the pretend plate. "You want another one?"

"Well, yeah, she's your mother," she said, her voice rising. "You can't call her by her real name." She looked at my hand. "No thanks."

"What do you mean? Why can't I?"

Katie screwed up her nose. "Your family's different."

"We are? How?" If she told me maybe I could fix us.

"You hardly got any brothers and sisters and cousins and stuff, and your mother plays with dolls, and you got a funeral home. Weird stuff like that. You know."

I had never thought about it, yet I knew she was right. I also knew that I didn't want to be different or weird. I wanted to be normal like everybody else. More than anything, I wanted Katie to keep on being my best friend.

"I like different." She crawled out of the box. "Got to go, see you tomorrow."

As she danced out of the house, I heard her mutter, "Agnes," under her breath.

"Dad whacked me across the arse, said not to be disrespectful," Katie told me the next day on the way to school. As soon as she'd arrived home she had tried the name out on her mother. I don't know what made the bigger impression on me, that I'd actually had an influence on someone or that her father had hit her and she was laughing about it. I never laughed when Josephine hit me.

From that day on, in an effort to be respectful, I tried to call Josephine "Mom" when I spoke of her, though not to her face. She would find that odd. It took several months to muster up the courage to ask her about it. Melinda had come for a visit and I'd noticed that she didn't call Josephine "Mom," either. When she was talking to her, she didn't call her anything, and when she was talking about her, she called her "Her" or "Herself," with the sound of a capital at the beginning, as if that was her name.

We were eating breakfast after Mass. Dad went to the first Mass every Sunday, and if I was up I went with him. Melinda had cooked the porridge, which was good – she added more raisins than Josephine. Christmas music was coming from the TV.

"How come we don't call you 'Mom?'" I asked Josephine.

She glanced uneasily at Dad, who looked uncomfortable all of a sudden. Melinda did too, her spoon stopping part way to her mouth.

Josephine bit into a slice of blood pudding. "No reason."

"But Katie said – "

"What did Katie say now? That brat always got something to say, no matter – "

"Come on, Josephine," Dad cut in. "She's a good girl."

I smiled at him, pleased that he'd stood up to Josephine for me. "Katie said – "

"Never mind what Katie said." Josephine sprinkled brown sugar onto her toast.

"But you just asked – "

"Now, Bridgina," said Dad, butting out his cigarette. "Don't be talking back."

"But Dad – "

"Youngsters today," Josephine spat out, her mouth spraying half-chewed crumbs and grains of sugar. "No respect at all."

"But that's respect, to call you Mom, isn't it?"

There was a tense silence. Josephine glared at Melinda, then at Dad.

Melinda put down her romance novel. "Let it go, Bridge." There was a dead-on look in her eyes, a look that said not to argue. A warning.

So I let it go. For 10 years, I left it alone. Yet every once in a while, I'd remember that look, that conversation, and wonder what they all knew that I didn't.

2

"Hello?" I waited half a moment. "Hello?" Louder this time.

I'd been in the bathroom when the phone began to ring. I hated when that happened. Rushing to force the zipper up my too-tight jeans, barely washing my hands, sometimes not at all if there'd been too many rings already, running down the stairs, racing to the phone, grabbing the receiver off the hook, trying not to sound breathless.

"Katie? Is that you?" Too late. I slammed the phone down.

Dad lowered the paper from where he would have raised it to hide behind on the first ring. Melinda, who had by some miracle managed to burrow further down into her stiff settee chair, sat up straight again. Josephine was likely in the kitchen with her head in the fridge. She didn't trust the telephone and rarely spoke on it.

How had I ended up in such a family? We had nothing in common. Nothing. I loved to listen to Disco music or the Beatles; they liked Don Messer. I wanted to watch *Laugh-In*; they thought *The Andy Griffith Show* was the height of comedy. I read everything I could get my hands on, except for Melinda's romances; Dad and Josephine struggled to make it through the local weekly paper. I treasured my friendships with Katie and Sylvia; they didn't have friends, although God knows my sister could have used some, especially male friends. The woman seemed to have no interest in the opposite sex.

Not me. I was very interested in boys, although hopeless around them, tongue-tied, awkward, a complete introvert. Katie and Sylvia talked about boys all the time, especially Jed Power, who they both liked, and Simon Connors, who Sylvia had zeroed in on from the day we entered Grade 9. Both were on the basketball team with Katie's brother, Seamus, and they were all two years ahead of us in their last year of high school. Jed had a bronze complexion that made him look exotic next to all his Irish-skinned schoolmates. With his curly brown hair and stocky build, he was easily the most handsome boy in high school. His eyes, a little on the small side and close together, were his one flaw, but they were always smiling. His father owned the gas station down the street from our house. Jed had worked there since elementary school and apparently planned to stay on after graduation – in my opinion, a far bigger flaw than his eyes. Why would anyone want to stay in Exile Cove when they could move to St. John's?

If Jed was the most handsome boy around, Simon was the smartest, which was interesting given the rumours about his father's shortcomings. Simon was tall and gangly, and his features were sharp, with a long nose and thin lips in a long thin face. When Katie asked Sylvia why she was so obsessed with him, Sylvia gave a sly grin. "It's all about the size of his brain, or something." Then she laughed, "I hear it's huge." Everyone knew Simon was brilliant. Still, once you got past all the angles and edges, there was something about him. It might have been his eyes. When Simon looked at you, he really looked at you, not at your chest the way other boys did. At least, he didn't look at mine.

Simon was my partner in debate club, which was great because he was one of the few boys I was comfortable around. He had been Seamus's best friend and I had been Katie's for so long that we were both part of the landscape at the Dollmonts'. From the very first debate meeting, when something funny happened, Simon would catch my eye, a tiny smirk on his face, one corner of his mouth a tad off-centre. And while he had a sharp tongue, he also had a subtle way with words so that he could slip in a bite of sarcasm without the recipient realizing it. I appreciated that. It was how I spoke to Josephine if I thought I could get away with it.

Once Sylvia got wind that Simon was in the club she developed a keen interest in debate. "More tongue than brains, that one," Simon whispered to me when he heard she was trying out. When she didn't make the cut, she made fun of the club in that derisive way she had, saying it was best to keep all the nerds together. She didn't laugh when she saw the team picture in the school paper, though. Being short, I was in the front. Simon stood behind me, his hand on my shoulder. Sylvia accused me of flirting with him, which was ridiculous. I didn't know how to flirt. She flung the paper across the cafeteria table. Seeing her so aggravated, Katie piped up in her most innocent voice, "Must have been something interesting on top of your head the way his eyes are glued to it," grinning conspiratorially as she stirred the pot. I tried to tell them that he'd lost his balance just as the camera clicked but Katie was too busy laughing at Sylvia storming off. Sylvia switched her attention to Seamus then, and a few other older boys.

I didn't have a crush on any boy in particular, except Jed Power because, after all, who didn't? Simon and Seamus were the only boys I talked to, and they were more like brothers. But I would gossip along with Katie and Sylvia to fit in. All we did was talk. We were "good girls" – at least Katie and I were; we weren't so sure about Sylvia – girls who would never dare do anything more than kiss a boy. Not that I'd had the opportunity. I wasn't exactly popular. I was not a party girl like Sylvia, and I wasn't pretty and outgoing like Katie, who had gorgeous red hair that fell in waves to her shoulder blades and small soft freckles fanning out from the bridge of her nose. My freckles were big and brown. My skin was too white, my cheeks too big. If I didn't tie my hair back on a windy day, my face all but disappeared in a brown tangle. But it wasn't just that.

It was my family. Josephine, who was as famous for playing with dolls as she was for the size of her arse. My father, the ex-funeral-home owner who had cremated his own business. And my sister, a 32 year-old recluse no one wanted to marry, who preferred reading about romance to the real thing and spent night after night at home in polyester pants drinking Fresca and eating salt and vinegar chips.

I looked at the phone again now, willing it to ring.

"Who was that?" Josephine's suspicious voice shouted from the kitchen.

"I wouldn't know, would I?" I stomped across the room, threw myself into my chair and pulled my book up to my face.

Mel's sigh, short and loud, blew over at me. "Shut it."

"Now, Bridge," Dad said in his mild mannered way, "watch that temper of yours."

"Why can't any of you ever get the phone?" I yelled into the page.

"Why can't you stop being so melodramatic?" Melinda shouted back.

I slapped the book shut. "But how come I always got to answer it?"

Melinda's voice hardened. "Because it's always for you."

"It is not." An empty denial. On the rare occasion it was for one of them, they would motion for me to say they weren't there, or groan as if it was the worst news in the world that someone wanted to speak to them.

I briefly considered the possibility that I was adopted. Hope faded when I added up the physical traits we had in common. We were all short and we all had thick knotty hair, except Dad who had been grey and balding forever. But I did share his and my sister's pointy nose and fair skin, their long skinny toes. And Melinda and I had the same wide-set grey-green eyes. As for Josephine, other than the height and the hair it was hard to find much else in common because her facial features all blurred into each other.

Living in our house was like living in an old folks' vacuum, with two legitimate elders and one heading there prematurely, all shuffling around in slippers, back and forth from the green, white-flecked shag carpet in the living room to the blue and grey linoleum in the kitchen. One day wormed its way into the next with no joy or enthusiasm, no desire. If you happened to stop by for a visit, not that you would, you'd never guess that four people lived there. The air had an underlying hollowness, like an echo that refused to sound. Perhaps the empty resonance came from the televisions that were on from morning till night, the brand new colour console in its shiny walnut cabinet in the living room and the smaller black and white at the end of the kitchen table. But TV voices lack the energy of live voices. They lack power, strength. They are not real.

The prevailing mood was sluggish and glum, unless Melinda was pissed off at me, or if Josephine had something to say. The woman had no grasp of her own volume, although mine was another matter. "What are you making so much noise for?" Josephine would bark. "You'll be waking the dead with that racket." "I wish," I'd mutter, careful she didn't hear. I didn't want to feel her hand across the back of my head. For a small hand, it packed formidable force.

Having no social life themselves, all three seemed baffled by my need to interact with the outside world. Getting a ride to a school dance was like pulling a wisdom tooth. I couldn't wait for my 16th birthday. With my licence in my wallet, I would rack up the miles on our underused car, soaring away from the Ashe morgue and into the freedom of the open sky.

Our house was the polar opposite of the Dollmont and the Mercer houses, where people were always coming and going, and where, compared to everyone else, I was the quiet one. I loved the chaos there, kids fighting and playing, adults arguing and yelling and laughing at the children and each other. We didn't laugh a lot at our house. We didn't cry a lot either, not like at Sylvia's, where a discussion about politics or religion wasn't over until someone ended up in tears. Never Sylvia. We didn't play cards and have drinks with family and friends like Mr. and Mrs. Dollmont, and we certainly did not wrestle like Katie and her sister and brothers. The Ashes didn't touch much.

Mrs. Dollmont passed Katie a steaming bowl of fried rice to put on the table. It was the beginning of June of our last year in high school. Katie was worried she might fail math and chemistry and not be able to go to St. John's in the fall. I'd come over right after breakfast to help her study.

"You staying for supper, Bridgina?" Mrs. Dollmont called out to me where I stretched contorted across the Twister mat.

Katie's mother was a short round woman with a soft belly and motherly curves that brought to mind warm cuddles and endless hugs. With silver streaks in her ginger hair, she was still attractive, even though her face was usually red and flushed because she was always busy, kneading dough, running the clothes through the ringer washer, on her knees scrubbing the floors. Yet she never complained.

I spent most of my time at Katie's, and would have stayed there permanently if I could have. Everyone treated me like family. Her mother was a great cook, too, and it wasn't the same old fish and brewis or baked chicken or salt beef and cabbage. She made things like lasagne and curried chicken and sweet-and-sour pork, food that perfumed the house with mouthwatering aromas.

Katie, who had lost early at Twister, spooned mashed carrots and turnips from the pot into a large bowl. "'Course she's staying, right, Bridge?" she said, shoving the cat off the counter. "We're having one of your favourites, Simon-says-chicken."

"Great. Thanks." Mr. Dollmont had named it Simon-says-chicken years before because Simon would always say it was the best chicken he'd ever tasted. Mrs. Dollmont used to make a point of inviting him whenever she made it.

Ten-year-old Greggie chose to make his move just as the cat jumped over me. I toppled over onto my back. Greggie landed flat on top of me, his hand pressed against my left breast. Before I could scramble away he pushed himself off me as if nothing had happened. Which was true, really. In a one-bathroom house with six brothers and two sisters, touching a breast in a game of Twister was no big deal.

In our house, breasts were taboo. No one brought attention to them in any way. I'd only started wearing a bra the year before because Katie insisted. "Some of the girls are talking about you, Bridge," she said. "A few boys too."

I had never been so embarrassed but I couldn't talk to Josephine about it. I took to wearing baggy sweaters until the right moment came to raise the subject with my sister. Finally, one night I was at the kitchen table doing homework when Melinda came in. She was working the late shift and wore a shapeless beige cardigan over her nurse's uniform. After plugging in the kettle, she leaned against the counter, her arms covering her chest, her hands holding a book to her face while she waited for the water to boil.

"Mel?"

"Yeah?" She continued reading.

I focused on her feet in her sensible white shoes. "I was wondering…"

After a moment, she glanced over. "Wondering what?"

I checked to make sure we were still alone. "It's…well, Katie said – "

Melinda raised her eyebrows in much the same way Josephine did when Katie's name came up. "What now?"

"She thought…well, that I should be wearing…you know…"

The floor creaked as overburdened feet trundled across the linoleum. The empty space between Melinda and me disappeared as Josephine's rum-and-Coke breath puffed out over her massive breasts, those blobs of wobbling flesh that seemed to start at her armpits and stop at her waist. Her hand held an empty glass.

Melinda shifted sideways to see past Josephine. "What should you be wearing?"

"A bra." The word sounded odd, the "b" too loud, the "a" too long.

"Shut up, Bridgina." Josephine's eyes skimmed the room, stopping on the doorway. "Your father could hear."

The next evening Melinda opened my bedroom door and threw a bag onto my bed. "Herself said to get you one."

The bra was too big but it was a relief to have those tell-tale strap marks across my back. Once home for the night, I'd rinse it in the sink and hang it from the bedpost. After wearing a damp bra to school for several days, I bought a second one that fit better.

I hopped up off the Twister mat as Seamus, fresh from a bath after a day working on the dock, vaulted the last four steps down the stairs.

Katie looked up from the stove and sniffed the air. "Jesus, where's the dead fish?"

"Go on, girl." He nuzzled his nose to his armpit. "Fresh as a flower, I am."

"Yeah, a pissybed." She moved our books off the kitchen table and onto the sideboard. "I don't know why you don't go back to school. You're after wasting the last two years on the docks when you could have got an education by now."

He pretended to consider. "A university man? Sure, I'll go meet up with Simon in Montreal. What do you think, Bridge? Should I be a doctor like Simon?"

I hadn't seen Simon since the summer after Grade 9. He had come into the ice-cream shop where I was working, although "work" was a relative term seeing as Josephine rarely paid me. He was with Jed and Seamus, and they all ordered double scoops. Even though I was used to being around Seamus and Simon, I was self-conscious with Jed being there and couldn't banter the way I usually did. After Jed joined Seamus outside, the heat ebbed from my face and I relaxed. Scooping up Simon's order, I readied a translation of pidgin French in my head: "Ici ton crème glacée," I said, presenting him with a triple scoop. Our eyes met, mine laughing, his not so much. It was a different sort of look, not the encouraging nod he gave me in debate, not the sarcastic smirk when somebody did something stupid. His eyes were serious, intense. They made me uncomfortable in a way I couldn't put my finger on. But then he said something about enjoying the rest of high school and left. The three boys stood out by the road where Seamus appeared to be giving Simon heck about something. They all looked in and caught me watching. I waved and looked away. Simon left for Quebec the next day and had been going to university year-round ever since.

"Sure, why not?" I said now to Seamus. "Dr. Dollmont has a nice ring to it."

Katie waved her hand at him. "They wouldn't let you darken the door of McGill. I'm talking about a trade, like a plumber. Get something decent so you don't stink to bejesus the rest of your life."

"Well, all I can say, it don't stop the lasses." He leaned close up against me. "Come on, Bridge. Tell her how good I smells."

Blushing, I pulled back and away.

"I knows someone got his eye on you," he teased, tapping my nose.

My face reddened further. "Give over, Seamus."

The front door opened. Katie's eyes widened. "Dad!" she squealed.

Everyone was up and running, the dog barking, the cat scurrying for cover. Mr. Dollmont stood inside the door, obviously pleased with himself. Tall and solid like Seamus, but with salt and pepper hair, he was always ready with a joke or a laugh, often at his own expense. He'd spent the last six months working at a place called Fort McMurray out in Alberta, and hadn't been expected home for another week.

The kids crowded around, everyone talking non-stop, while Katie's mother rushed to put dinner in the oven to keep warm. As she was bending over the stove with a plate of chicken, Mr. Dollmont pulled her up to him and kissed her hard on the mouth in front of us all. After a moment I looked away. I had never seen Dad kiss Josephine. Katie laughed while Seamus gave a mock groan and said, "God help me, they're at it again." Blushing, Mrs. Dollmont wriggled out of her husband's grasp but she looked ever so pleased.

"And how's our Bridgie?" Mr. Dollmont said. "You're after getting prettier every time I sees you, sure."

Mr. Dollmont was like Katie and Seamus that way, always trying to make people, or me at least, feel good. Katie was forever moaning about how she hated being a redhead and how she wished she had my dark hair and big eyes. Katie's eyes were as emerald a green as an eye could be, whereas mine had too much grey to have any sparkle.

It was his first day back, but I hated to leave and I didn't feel unwanted. Mr. Dollmont had long teased me in the same manner as he did Katie. She was his "Katie- Kitty" and I was "Bridgie-Bee." As everyone started to calm down, he patted my back, tormenting me about the non-existent boys in my life and nudging me towards the table. Seamus moved down the bench to make room for me, much as he would have for Katie or Greggie. We said grace and then everyone was talking and laughing at once as the food was passed around.

After dinner, I washed the dishes while Katie cleared the table and set up our books again. Mrs. Dollmont started a batch of figgy bread, Mr. Dollmont's favourite. Then she called Katie's aunts and uncles to tell them he was back and they should come over later for a drink and a game of 45's. Katie and I made chocolate chip cookies to help us study. The younger kids devoured them as soon as they were out of the oven so we made a second batch. With all the commotion it was impossible to study anyway.

It was like being part of a normal family. Then I went home.

"It's ready," Josephine yelled. "Bridge, Andy, get in here."

I bounced out of my chair and followed Dad into the kitchen. Melinda, who'd been home two minutes and had already changed into her fat pants and slippers, was at the table. She looked old and frumpy, what a fishwife – whatever that was – might look like. I, on the other hand, had been feeling light and care-free all afternoon. I'd written my last exam that morning. High school was over.

Unfortunately, supper was not.

We were having our standard Friday feast of fish and brewis, dried up old leathery bits of salt fish mixed with rock-hard bread, all boiled up together with scales and crusts and rashers of fried fat scattered throughout. The smell of it turned my stomach. Josephine knew I hated fish and brewis, yet every Friday there it was piled extra high on my plate. She was never so generous with the Sunday chicken.

Her eyes scorched me as I poked at the food.

"Bridgina. Eat your goddamn supper."

I pushed my fork around another minute. "What do we have to have fish on Fridays for, anyway?" I was beginning to feel as grumpy as Melinda looked.

Josephine rolled her eyes and took a swig of rum and Coke. "Not this again."

"Christ's sake," Melinda said. "You knows darn well why."

"Now Melinda, she's –" Dad stopped as a fit of coughing overtook him. We all waited until he spit into his handkerchief and wiped his mouth.

Melinda wagged her finger at him. "Them fags are going to kill you. You'll end up with lung cancer if you don't quit smoking."

I dropped my fork onto my plate. "Just 'cause God was crucified on a Friday doesn't justify making us eat this crap. What were they all, cannibals or something?"

A familiar look passed between Dad and Josephine, the one I called the here-we-go look.

"Andy, will you shut that youngster up." Josephine slathered a thick coat of butter onto a hunk of bread and stuffed the whole piece into her mouth.

"It's like the whole Mary Magdalene thing, was she a prostitute or not?" If they were going to make me watch them eat slop, I would not do it quietly.

Josephine's cheeks swelled with the effort of trying to take a smack at me while dealing with the overload of food she hadn't had a chance to chew. She swallowed, then started to sputter and gag. Her eyes bulged. She staggered to her feet.

Dad reached up and tapped her back. "You okay, Josephine?"

She gasped for breath. Dad stood and tapped harder. Nothing. He took a good whack, his face crossing the line from concern to dismay in an instant. When she didn't protest or come to her senses, Melinda put down her book, went behind her and did a Heimlich. Food shot out in chunks. I grabbed the dishrag from the sink and pressed it to Josephine's face. She looked disgusted and pushed it away.

Dinner was over for me. I went to my room and curled up on the bed, hands tucked under my cheek, the sour stench from the dishrag wafting up my nose. I rolled onto my back and lay dreaming about September when I would start university in St. John's. I couldn't wait to go to MUN, couldn't wait to move into an apartment with Katie and Sylvia. For the umpteenth time I pictured it, this exciting life that would soon be mine. Friends, new and old, would drop by unannounced, just walk in the door and hang out. We would have rousing conversations and intellectual discussions about every topic under the sun. We would stay up late and play loud music. We would have parties. I so much wanted to throw parties and go to parties, to live in a house and belong to a group of people who did those things.

Josephine's voice carried down the hall, the words muffled and indecipherable, the tone angry as always. Lying on my bed I tried to remember if we had ever had a party, had ever had cause to invite family or friends into our home to share our good fortune. I could not recall the last time we had something to celebrate.

And then, one day, we did.

3

The late June sky put up a constant cry, tracking trails and streams down the living room window. Everything, inside and out, looked uncared for, unloved. No one walked the streets. Only an occasional car, its windows steamed up, wipers thrashing, passed by the house. I was drowning in a river of boredom.

At five o'clock, we sat down to supper. The grey and white Formica table, as colourless as the rest of the world, gave a jolt as Josephine leaned forward on her elbows to retrieve her drink. It was a Friday. I'd had an extra peanut butter sandwich at lunch.

Across from me, Melinda's jaw clicked as she chewed, the only sound other than the muted static from the TV. Reception had been poor all day and Dad had lowered the volume on both sets. My sister's fork moved from plate to mouth and back again at a steady pace. She spooned another load of mush onto her plate from the pot in the middle of the table. Oddly enough, she wasn't reading a book. In fact, she had what appeared to be a smile on her usually bland face. Something was up with her lately. She wasn't as cranky. Several times she'd been late home from work. One day she'd gone in early, wearing pink lipstick!

Melinda scanned the table, Josephine to her left at the head, Dad and I on the other long side to make room for the TV at the end. She made a show of clearing her throat, then waited until we were all looking at her.

"I'm getting married," she said.

"You're what there, Melinda girl?" Dad had a cigarette halfway to his mouth. Without taking a puff, he placed it back in its little curved groove in the ashtray.

Melinda smiled at him. An unfamiliar lightness in her eyes made them seem more green than grey. There was a rosy tint to her cheeks, and her hair, which had been curled, had lost its mousy tone. Had she been using the lemon dish soap to wash it?

"I'm getting married." She winked at me.

Oh, so she was kidding. Although it was not like her to wink. Or kid around, especially about such a sensitive subject.

Josephine gave her an exasperated scowl, puffing out her already bulbous cheeks. I swear I could read her mind. "Girl's gone and lost it. Just like a spinster, inventing a love life, then cracking up altogether."

Melinda scooped up a forkful of food. She paused before placing it in her mouth. She chewed, swallowed and licked her lips. "Banns'll be in the bulletin Sunday."

We snapped to attention. Banns were serious business. Banns were real.

Josephine demanded to know what she was talking about, and more importantly, who. Dad looked nervous, afraid to be happy, already preparing for the inevitable disappointment, either it was all a joke, or the groom was a poor catch, although at Melinda's age any catch was a good one.

"Victor Brennan." Melinda's voice was self-assured, challenging.

We each took a few seconds to match a face to the name.

"Who?" Josephine shook her head as if to clear her ears.

"Victor who?" I asked.

Dad turned off the TV. The fuzz faded to a white dot. "Victor Brennan?" he said, glancing at Josephine. They both turned doubtful, yet hopeful, eyes to Melinda.

Melinda answered me rather than them. "Dr. Brennan down at the hospital."

Dr. Brennan? But he was ancient. And he was a doctor. Melinda was marrying a doctor? Could she still be a nurse if her husband was her boss? And would she call him "Doctor" or…what? Would she be rich? Dr. Brennan's kids were the best dressed in school. I had long envied Charlotte, who was a year ahead of me and always decked out to the nines. If they got married, did that mean that I might get Charlotte's old clothes? But everyone would know they'd been hers. No, I did not want Charlotte Brennan's castoffs, thank you.

"Sure he's an old man," I said.

Melinda's face, which a moment before had been happy, bordering on joyful, looked like someone had let the air out of a happy-face balloon.

"Compared to me, I mean."

She recovered quickly. "He's only 44. I'm nearing 35, not that big a difference."

By this time, Josephine and Dad had come to life, her voice rushed and breathless, his boisterous with belated confidence in his older daughter's prospects. How did it happen, they asked, and when and where?

According to Melinda, she and the doctor had been friends since she'd helped care for his wife throughout her long illness. Victor had been a good husband and spent much time trying to ease her passage from one life into the next. He'd talked to Melinda of his family and his children, of how hard it was for them to lose their mother so early in their lives. Patsy had been a dedicated mother and homemaker. How would he be able to cope with four children working doctor's hours?

Melinda crossed her arms, causing her plump white flesh to press against the short sleeves of her blouse. She leaned back in her chair. "After she died, it seemed natural to keep on talking. Then last week he said, 'Why don't we get married?'"

"But did you ever go out on a date or anything?" Although yet to have a real date myself, I was becoming outraged as she described how the relationship had evolved.

"Well…yeah, sort of."

"What do you mean, sort of? Either you did or you didn't."

She sat up straight. "We eat lunch together lots of times, or supper on the night shift."

I pictured them in the hospital cafeteria, gazing into each other's eyes as the boiled cabbage and mashed turnip grew cold on their plates, bedpans and supper trays clattering in the background. "Oh. Well then."

Josephine held up her hand. "Just one minute here. Are you knocked up?"

Melinda eyes narrowed. "Shut up, Josephine."

That was something else I'd noticed recently. Ordinarily, Melinda didn't bother to talk back. If Josephine was rude to her, she stuck her head in her book and ignored it. Lately, however, she was likely to tell Josephine where to go.

"Don't bother with an attitude, missy." Josephine picked up her fork and pointed it at Melinda. "We both know it's a fair question."

Melinda shoved her plate away and spat the words at Josephine. "I'm not pregnant."

"Good. So, Dr. Brennan, eh?" There was wonder in Josephine's voice. In her book, being a doctor was as near to being God as a person could get. "When is this –?"

"July."

"What's the rush?" Josephine let out a little snort. "I mean, if you're not."

Melinda gave her an icy stare then turned to Dad, who had two cigarettes on the go, one lit, the other not. "Victor took a job in Toronto, starting the end of August. He wants to get there in time for the younger ones to settle in before school begins."

Josephine started to comment but Melinda talked over her as if she didn't exist.

"He's such a good father. He asked me if I'd mind not going to work, if I could stay home till the children get used to things." There was a rare excitement in her voice. "So that's what I'm going to do. Take care of the house, make sure the children are okay, and, you know, take care of the family." Her voice held an aspect of wonder, as if it was all something that, up until then, she'd only read about in one of her novels.

None of that mattered to me in the moment. "You're leaving Exile Cove?"

Melinda nodded, blatantly happy.

"But…what about me?" Melinda and I had never been buddy-buddy, but she was the closest thing to a normal family I had. Dad tried. He really did. But it was such an obvious effort for him that it was just sad. And Josephine? From what I could tell, Josephine did not like me. So even if my sister and I didn't gossip and share clothes and inside jokes, I didn't want her to leave me with them. "I'll be all alone." My voice sounded small, tinny.

Josephine's hand flew out to smack me upside the head. "Goddamn selfish."

"Ow!" I cried out.

"Aw Josephine, don't do that," Dad said.

"Oh shut up, Andy. Miserable brat should be happy Melinda got a husband." Josephine rummaged through the leftovers in the pot. "And Dr. Brennan, at that."

"I didn't mean it that way. It's…I don't know…"

Melinda patted my arm. I wanted to grab her hand and hang onto it but she didn't let it rest there. She glanced sideways at Josephine, then at me. "Believe me, I know."

Josephine blew out an annoyed breath. "How we planning a wedding that fast? And who's going to pay for it?"

Melinda sat back. "Not much to plan. Victor's been married before – "

"You haven't," Dad cut in. "It's your first."

"Didn't Dr. Brennan's wife just die?" Josephine said.

Melinda reddened. "It wasn't 'just.' It was ages ago."

"Ages? Since when is six months, ages? A big wedding won't look too good."

"For God's sake, never mind. Besides, I don't want anything."

Josephine snorted. "Suits me."

Dad's pale eyes settled on Melinda. "Now honey, I want to do right by you. First off, you'll need a dress. Josephine just got a whole bunch of new material."

Josephine turned on him. "Not for her, I didn't. Besides, she already said she don't want nothing."

Dad took an extra long moment to fish a cigarette out of his pack. "We got to remember that she's marrying a doctor. He's an important man. Think how it will look to the neighbours." He lit up. "Unless you think you can't make a full-size dress," he said, the cigarette bobbing up and down in the corner of his mouth.

"'Course I can make a full-size dress. But I'll be ordering replacement material, so don't think you're getting off with that." Josephine's lips puckered into a tightly ridged bunch. "I'll call Maureen in to help."

Maureen McCarthy was widely regarded as the best seamstress in town, which didn't necessarily mean much. The town wasn't that wide, more a handful of streets running parallel with a few offshoots. Maureen was also known as the crazy dog lady of Exile Cove, and could be seen every day walking her five Chihuahuas, "Mexican purebreds," Maureen insisted, "alien rats," Josephine called them, their pointy triangular ears sticking straight up as their skinny little legs trotted along.

"Well that's right good of you, Josephine." Dad's smile bordered on smug.

"Yeah, well, it *is* her wedding day." Her tone was odd, almost wistful.

At that point I left the room. I felt like crying, for myself because I was going to be left home alone, even if I was moving to St. John's soon, and for Melinda, having to settle for an old man with four children, one of whom was older than me. And now Josephine wanted to dress her up like one of her dolls. No wonder Melinda didn't want a big wedding. What was there to celebrate?

Later that evening we were in the kitchen waiting for Maureen. I was looking through an old Christmas catalogue, trying to ignore Josephine's voice while I made a game of comparing the number of gifts on odd and even pages. Josephine was organizing her sewing supplies along the counter, which was a similar blue and grey to the linoleum on the floor, covering it with bolts of fabric and lace, tubs of shiny buttons and pearls, crinolines and hoops for petticoats and veils. When it was all laid out, she pointed a finger at Melinda.

"Your father got a point about having people in. We'll have a doctor in the family now. A real live doctor!" Her voice had risen as she repeated the word with added reverence. "We got to have something, else it wouldn't look right."

Real doctor or not, I was surprised she was pushing the idea. Having people in to eat your food and drink your booze cost money.

Melinda peered over her book. "Like I told you, I'm not having the whole big wedding thing."

Josephine perched her sewing glasses on her nose and stuck several pins in her mouth. "You're marrying a doctor," she mumbled. "The neighbours will expect –"

"Who cares about the friggin' neighbours?"

"I do." She spat the pins onto the counter. "And you got to have a witness, too."

Melinda glared at her. "Fine. Bridge, then."

I looked up from the catalogue.

"You're going to be my bridesmaid." Melinda said. "Or maid of honour, or whatever you call it."

"Can't you get one of your friends?" I was still sulking from finding out she was leaving.

"I don't know, Melinda, having your own…" Josephine paused, "…your own sister standing up for you?" She eyed Melinda over her glasses as she took the last swig from her second after-dinner rum and Coke.

There was an uncomfortable silence that I attributed to Melinda's embarrassment about her lack of friends. Still, there was something in the way she held her breath for a moment, in the hateful eye she cast on Josephine before turning to me.

"You'll do it, right, Bridge?" she said. "You'll stand up for me?"

"Maybe. What do I have to do?"

"Get gussied up and sign the marriage certificate. You can pick out your own dress." She held up her hand to Josephine. "I'll pay for it."

"What about his family?" Josephine squinted as she lined the thread up to the needle. "Any of his crowd going to get home for it?"

"Doubt it. There's only his brother and sister, and they're both living out west somewhere. They got families of their own, so I don't think they got the time to be traipsing down here for a second wedding."

"How did Dr. Bre…how did he ever end up working here anyway?"

"His folks grew up out in Trinity but they left before he was born. Victor used to visit his grandparents every summer, and then he went to MUN after high school and never left again."

"What about his parents?" I said, joining the conversation. "Are they coming?"

Melinda shook her head. "His mother's dead and his father just went into an old-age home in Toronto. That's why he took the job there, to keep an eye on him."

"Come here," Josephine ordered.

Melinda sighed and placed her book on the table. On the cover a woman, her blouse torn, her striking face smudged with dirt, held a small golden-haired girl in her arms. Behind her, some distance away, rode a man on a horse. A cloud of dust framed the scene behind him as he peered across the void towards the woman and child.

Josephine draped a swath of silky material around Melinda's waist. "The way you talk, you wouldn't know but it was an everyday event."

"Well, it's not the end of the world. And watch out with them pins."

"No, it's not the end of the world," Josephine parroted.

Dad, who was in the living room in front of the television, had obviously been listening in. "It's the beginning of a new one for you, isn't it, Melinda honey?" he called out. "The start of a new life, what?"

Melinda and I glanced at each other. It wasn't like Dad to be romantic, or to pose introspective questions to himself or anyone else.

"Well, yes, I suppose…" Melinda paused when there was a knock on the door. She whispered quickly, "I don't want nothing fancy – "

"Talk to your father," Josephine said on her way to let Maureen in.

Melinda took a few steps towards the living room but at the sound of the front door opening and closing, she turned and sat back down at the table.

"Wonderful news…at her age…can't get over it…" Maureen's nasally voice preceded, then announced, her arrival into the kitchen. She stopped in the archway, her jet-black hair piled high on her head, her lips a red gash in her thin, powdered face. "There she is, the blushing bride." She pressed her hands to her chest. "Melinda, my poor dear girl, you finally had a bit of luck, what?"

Melinda poured Maureen a drink and topped up Josephine's, rolling her eyes as Josephine preened and talked about the coming wedding, throwing out words like "fiancé" and "engagement" and "betrothed."

"Victor Brennan!" Maureen exclaimed when she discovered who the fiancé was. "Not the doctor over at the hospital? Not that Victor Brennan?"

Josephine assured her that Victor would soon be part of the family. She hardly flinched when she said his name.

"Poor Patsy. Didn't take him long, what?"

"Get on, girl, she's been in the ground for ages," said Josephine.

Maureen looked at Melinda. "I hear the oldest girl's been a right case since her mother died. I say you'll have your work cut out for you there."

Melinda pursed her lips. "I can handle a teenager."

"I'm sure you can. Well I must say, you done well for yourself in the end, didn't you?" Maureen took a large gulp of her drink. "Better than my Loretta, that's for sure."

Melinda had gone to nursing school with Maureen's oldest, Loretta, who'd quit two years in to get married. Loretta was now a single mother of four living on welfare.

Josephine raised an eyebrow. "You don't know the half of it."

"Half of what?" Maureen looked confused.

"Nothing, don't mind her." Melinda's dirty look was lost on Josephine.

Maureen shrugged. "So, you having a big wedding?"

"No – " Melinda started.

"We'd like to," Josephine tutted. "Herself here don't want a fuss."

Maureen pondered this for a moment. "You could do hors d'oeuvres."

We all looked blankly at her. Josephine tried to recover with a mindful nod but it didn't fool me.

Or Maureen, apparently. "You know," she added, "no big sit-down. People stand around with a drink and a bite to eat. You can do it casual-like, informal."

"Yes, well," Josephine said, "I'll have to think about that."

"Now what kind of dress do you want, Melinda?" Maureen asked.

"Plain and simple." Melinda looked directly at Josephine. "Nothing poufy."

"Hope you don't mind my saying, Josephine," said Maureen, "but she's right. There comes an age when plain is better than fancy, don't you think? For the food and the dress, what? And it'll cost a lot less, too."

Josephine promptly agreed, about the food anyway. No need to get all hoity-toity, she said. Just because there was a doctor in the mix didn't mean they couldn't have regular food, even if it did have a fancy name. Plain food was fine with her.

Plain food, plain dress, plain man. Poor old Melinda.

4

The guest list consisted of Victor's four children, some hospital colleagues, the neighbours on either side of us even though we didn't have much to do with them, the Smith spinsters across the street, a few Ashe relatives we rarely saw, and Maureen McCarthy. I had wanted to invite Katie but Josephine said there were already more people than the house could hold.

Guests may have been scarce but the food was not. Fish cakes and fried chicken, turkey and ham, potato salad and coleslaw, all laid out along the kitchen counter on silver platters I hadn't known we possessed but which Josephine dug out from a cupboard high above the fridge and which took hours of scrubbing and buffing to get the shine back on. A side-table had been set up near the wall outlet and two new-fangled electric crockpots simmered away – one with moose stew, the other with fish and brewis.

The house was sweltering. My new outfit, at Melinda's expense, had far too much material for such a warm day. A full-length blue floral peasant skirt and matching long-sleeved blouse, it had seemed perfect on the mannequin at Angie's Boutique in St. Paul on a cold rainy Saturday the week before. By contrast, Charlotte Brennan looked cool and classy in a sleeveless sundress that showcased every curve. Who could have guessed that on Melinda's wedding day the sun would shine like there was no tomorrow?

I moved closer to one of the fans that Dad had set up to circulate the air, hoping to cool off, and to get further away from Charlotte who, when she'd breezed into the house, had acted as if she had never laid eyes on me before, which might have been the case. The smell of fish wasn't as strong there either. Dad was not much of a drinker, but he'd laid on plenty of booze – rye and rum, vodka and beer, even wine. People were thirsty. The mass had been at two o'clock, and by four everybody had downed a few. As the liquor continued to loosen people up, guests took turns eating at the four chairs around the kitchen table, which Josephine, who was well lubricated herself by then, said was casual and informal enough, especially for "oderfs."

Melinda and Victor appeared to be enjoying themselves. Melinda seldom drank but had obviously decided that her wedding night would be an exception. Her eyes were shining and her flushed cheeks stood out against the soft white of her dress. When she'd come downstairs that morning, I'd been unable to speak for a moment. She looked almost beautiful. A small veil of embroidered lace covered her hair, which was arranged in a simple up-do. Her neck and shoulders were bare, emphasizing the top of her dress, a silk V-cut trimmed with tiny beads. The smooth material hugged her bodice and midriff down to a flattering empire waist that flowed to just below her knees. No frills or flounces. The dress was elegant.

Victor, who had been reserved at first, had removed his tweed sport coat and rolled up his shirtsleeves. He still looked old, though. His hair was greying and there were lines around his mouth and eyes, not big gouges like my father's, smaller ones, but lots of them. On the other hand, he didn't have a potbelly like most men his age. He might have been handsome once upon a time. And although he didn't look like a typical groom, or Melinda the typical bride, they did look happy.

I was smiling at the thought that maybe it would work out after all when I saw Maureen trying to get up from the sofa. Her tight miniskirt had risen high on her thighs, and her legs, which were bare because she'd taken off her nylons earlier when they'd gotten a run, were stuck to the plastic covering. When she spread them apart to try to get to her feet, I was shocked to see a red garter trimmed in black lace. One of the doctors from the hospital had noticed as well. His plate had crumpled and the gravy from the moose stew was dripping to the floor. If his wife hadn't drawn his attention to it, he would have lost the lot, so caught up was he in what was happening over her shoulder. Maureen had managed to get one thigh free but had put it back down to work on the other. She leaned forward and placed her hands, one of which was holding her drink, onto the sofa to push herself off. One leg released but the other didn't. The drink toppled over onto the plastic.

As I rushed to bring a towel, Josephine, in a rare moment of drunken tolerance, told Maureen, "That's why the plastic is there, don't worry about it." Maureen nodded as if that was common sense.

After I finished wiping the sofa, Dad took the towel from me and gave me a big hug in front of everybody. He smelled of rum and cigarettes. "That's my girlie." His words were slurred. "Such a good lass you are." After planting a slobbery kiss on the side of my head, he steered himself towards the bar set up on the end of the counter.

I was contemplating getting another beer myself when Victor caught my eye.

"Bridgina, I do hope you'll come see us in Toronto. I suggested to Melinda it could be our way to thank you for being our bridesmaid."

"Yeah, that'd be great." Was he offering to pay my way? Could I ask him that? I had never been at ease talking to adults, especially ones I hardly knew. Still, I had to make some sort of effort. "Good party, what?"

"It certainly is." He looked around at the guests, most of whom were in varying stages of drunkenness, including his oldest daughter. "So, how was school this year?"

"Good, I hope."

"You're in your final year, aren't you?"

I nodded. "The marks should be out soon."

"What will you do after?"

"I don't know. I'm sure somebody'll have a party."

"A party?"

"Or we'll go out somewhere or something."

There was an awkward silence before I grasped what he meant.

"I'm going to MUN in September," I rushed to add.

"Excellent choice," he said. "I attended Memorial. Years ago. I was hoping Charlotte might have gone there last year."

I didn't have much to say to that. Charlotte Brennan was a spoiled brat who did nothing but drink and smoke dope and mess around with one guy after another.

"So," he tried again. "MUN. Those were the days. I'm sure you'll love it."

"I'm sure I will." My eyes roamed the room.

"Oh Victor," Melinda's voice trilled from the kitchen. "Can you come here?"

We nodded at each other. He seemed as relieved as me.

Overall, and considering the ragtag nature of the guest list, the evening turned out far better than expected. By the time the last of the guests staggered out the door, including Charlotte, who was too drunk to drive her sisters and brother home from their father's wedding, it was nine o'clock. Who knew the Ashes could keep a party going for so long?

Not used to drinking, I was mellow from the three beers I'd had. Melinda was standing at the hall window, keeping an eye out for Victor, who had driven his children home. As I watched her waiting for her husband to return, it occurred to me how much everything had changed, how our lives were veering off in different directions. I went over and put my arm around her shoulders. Though I had never done it before in my life, it felt natural.

"That was a friggin' good time, Mel."

She smiled a tipsy smile and put her arm around my waist.

"I like what you did with your hair, by the way."

"Thanks," she said. "Beat's what Lizzie Gordon would've done."

I leaned in. "Katie says she's got a collection of earlobes hidden in the shop."

Laughing, we looked out the window together. It was a clear night, the stars extra bright in the sky.

Melinda pointed upwards. "The Big and Little Dippers." She swayed to the side and held onto me tighter. "Oopsy," she giggled.

"And a crescent moon," I said. "I bet you could curl up inside it and go to sleep."

"Such a sleep you'd have, all snug and safe." All those 's'es were giving her trouble.

We watched the sky for another minute before turning and walking toward the living room. I slowed at the entrance, not wanting to end the closeness. Melinda stopped too and leaned against the doorframe. Content to stand there, we looked into the room. Full drink in hand, Josephine sat on an old wooden chair brought up from the basement for the party. Her elbow rested on a side table where Melinda's paperbacks were displayed between two bookends. Josephine's backside, sheathed in polyester floral, bulged over the sides of the seat. She leaned forward to put her drink on the table. The chair legs creaked beneath her.

"That poor chair," I whispered.

Melinda started to giggle. Before long, we were holding each other up and laughing to wet ourselves.

"Melinda!" Josephine shouted. "Sober up, for Christ's sake."

Dad was laughing with us, the unfamiliar sound sweet to my ears. I hadn't known he was a happy drunk.

It was then I saw that the chair legs were no longer straight. I think Melinda noticed too. Neither of us said anything. The legs tilted further sideways at a wider angle. Josephine must have felt the shift. She looked puzzled. Drunk and puzzled. And then, with a crack, the chair collapsed into the side table. Josephine landed on the floor, arse up, splattered with rum and Coke and surrounded by romance novels.

Melinda and I burst into a fresh fit of laughter. After a stunned moment, Dad moved to help Josephine but she ended up pulling him down on top of her. I should have turned away from the sight of them, him sprawled sideways across her, her dress up to the top of her great lumpy thighs, but it was gruesomely fascinating.

"Christ, Andy," Josephine yelled. "Get rid of the goddamn cigarette."

As the stench of singed hair drifted over to us, we rushed to help. Melinda grabbed the cigarette and put it out. With much straining and tugging, the three of us managed to heave Josephine up and plunk her onto the sofa. The plastic cover squeaked against the sudden weight. Dad retrieved her upturned glass and headed to the kitchen.

Josephine sat, her bosom heaving with such force that I was concerned for her. Finally, her hand almost steady, she wiped her forehead. "Andy, where's that drink?"

Dad rushed in with two full glasses and a new pack of cigarettes.

Josephine took a long swallow and turned to Melinda. "I'd watch it if I was you, missy. You haven't consummated this thing yet." She set down her drink and shifted about on the sofa, lifting one cheek and then the other, trying to pull her dress down. "Fine man like Victor won't be putting up with no drunk for a wife. Don't forget how lucky you were to get him, 'cause it ain't like you had a lot to offer."

"Right," said Melinda. "Unlike you. The widow bride."

Josephine's eyes narrowed into mean little slits in her flushed face.

Dad raised his hand. Cigarette smoke curled upward. "Now Melinda…"

"No way. I'm sick of her always making snide remarks."

"Melinda honey," he said, removing his handkerchief from his pocket to mop the sweat from his head and neck. "That's not true."

"Sure it is. Ever since I was little she – "

"She what?" With a mighty push, Josephine stood up. "Took care of you? Your own mother wouldn't do it, but I did. And what thanks do I get?"

"Thanks? You want thanks? Thanks for being a miserable…"

"You ungrateful bastard…"

They noticed me then, standing there watching them, my family, each one drunk to some degree, and not making a whole lot of sense.

"What are you all talking about?" I asked.

"Nothing…" Dad said, stopping to cough into his handkerchief. "…nothing at all. It's time we all went to bed…"

"Whose mother wouldn't do it?" I persisted. "Mel? What's that about?"

Melinda shook her head. "Not now, Bridge."

"Oh for Christ's sake." Josephine picked up her drink. "Just tell her."

"Tell me what?" I shouted.

"Nothing," Melinda shouted back. "Let it go, Bridgina. It was nothing."

I folded my arms across my chest. "I don't think so, Mel."

Melinda moved toward me. "Listen, this is not the time. You hear me?"

I backed away, studying her face, trying to decipher what I'd heard. I swung around and faced Josephine. "You're not her mother, are you?" Then it struck me. "Oh my God, you're not mine either."

Josephine waved her hand dismissively. "Talk to them two. It got nothing to do with me, thank God."

I had never disliked her more than at that moment. "'Thank God' is right. You made a rotten mother." I said it viciously, wanting to hurt her, but was rewarded with a dismissive grunt. Josephine did not wound easily.

She downed the last of her drink and weaved her way into the kitchen. "Useless cowards, the lot of you."

Dad crushed out his cigarette. "Bridge, don't say things you don't mean."

"I meant every word. But now I want to know the rest. Who's our mother?"

He leaned forward in his chair, hands between his knees, his face downcast as he looked at Melinda sitting limp on the footstool in her crumpled wedding dress. When Josephine returned, Melinda stood and smoothed her hand down the front of her dress.

"You know what?" she said to Josephine. "For once, you may be right. It's time she knows the truth."

"The truth?" Josephine placed her drink on the table and pulled the folds of her dress closer together to begin the process of settling herself back onto the plastic. "Your side of it, you mean."

Her voice ice cold, Melinda hissed, "Fuck off, you."

Josephine tried to whirl around but she was too drunk to pull it off, and finished with a wobble and a backward flop onto the sofa. "Fuck off, yourself."

Melinda raised her arm as if to strike. Josephine stiffened, her eyes glittering like sleet under a streetlight.

"Melinda, that's enough. Now sit down." Dad's gravelly voice cut the silence with an authoritarian tone that made both women stop and look at him. He reclaimed his glass and took a long swallow. He turned to me and pointed to my chair. I sat down. "Bridgina, there's some things you should know and I'm going to tell you. From the beginning," he said with emphasis. He set himself down onto his own chair and took another pull at his drink. "And the both of you," he pointed his nicotine-stained index finger first at Josephine, then Melinda, "can bite your tongues till I'm done."

Melinda crossed her arms and sat. Josephine waved at him as if he was a pesky fly. Neither said anything though.

"When I was 36," he began, "I married Susan Walsh. She was 16. Now that might sound young but them were different times, and there wasn't many women in Lost Harbour not married. Anyway, a year later we had a baby." Dad's eyes teared up as he looked at Melinda. "She was the prettiest baby, and some good too, hardly a peep out of her. Which is why I could never understand Susan for the life of me. She wanted nothing to do with her, her own baby." He spoke as if astounded by his own words. "She wouldn't feed her, or change her, or anything at all. Hardly got out of bed, just lay there staring at the ceiling all day long. Can you fathom that? So I took over, and I gave her a name, one I heard tell of on the radio and that no one else had in the whole town. Melinda, such a pretty name. I didn't mind tending to her, I was that proud. I'd walk her around in her stroller showing her off, and I'd hold her and sing her to sleep at night. She was the loveliest little girl."

Josephine's voice rose from the depths of the sofa. "My arse she – "

"No, Josephine." Dad held up the hand holding his half-empty drink, which sloshed about but didn't spill over. "You can pipe down till I tells it."

My mind was in a frenzy. Who was Susan? Was Susan my mother? Where was she? I didn't ask. Dad was on a roll and I had no intention of stopping him.

"And then Susan ended up with appendicitis and was carted off to St. John's for an operation. I prayed some time away might make her see things more clear. But when she was done and all better, she wouldn't come back. Said no, she'd seen the last of Lost Harbour and good riddance to it. There was no talking to her. Her own family was disgusted. Hard to believe, a mother just up and leaving like that."

I glanced at Melinda in her chair, her hands squeezed together against her chest. How awful for her, her own mother not wanting her, even walking out on her.

"I didn't know what I was going to do," Dad continued, his voice thin and high. "I needed help. I was running out of money and had to get back to making a living. And then…well… then Josephine here, well, God love her, she moved in to give me a hand."

Melinda sprung up. "Yeah, right. The widow bride was the one in need."

Josephine's jowls shook. "I was just fine – "

"All I knows is she was a big help to me," Dad said with a nod to Josephine. Melinda ignored Dad. "The hell you were, nothing fine about you – "

So did Josephine. "You don't know nothing – "

"I know what I heard – "

"Bah! All old gossip…"

Dad's shoulders slumped and he gave me a weary look as the shouting and finger pointing escalated. Melinda was throwing out every rumour she'd ever heard about Josephine, who was denying them all flat out, the red circles on her cheeks rounding outward till her entire face was lit up. It might have been enlightening except their voices kept growing louder so that one drowned out the other until nothing made any sense, and Dad seemed so fed up he looked ready to stop his telling of the story altogether.

I found myself on my feet. "Shut up!"

The room went silent. Josephine and Melinda both turned to stare at me, mouths agape. Neither was more shocked than I was.

"I want to hear what Dad has to say." My voice had quickly lost its power.

Dad nodded. He looked proud of me. "So…" He paused. "What was I…?"

"You were talking about her moving in to help," I prompted.

"Who?"

"Her," I said, sticking my arm out and pointing. "Josephine."

He looked befuddled for only a second. "Right. Herself."

The upshot of it all was that Josephine, who was his cousin from Little Big Harbour, had just returned from her honeymoon in St. John's where her husband had disappeared. They'd been out rowing on Quidi Vidi Lake. It was late at night. They'd been drinking. They started to fight. The boat overturned. He was never seen again.

Josephine clapped her hands to her chest. "I had the brains to wear a life jacket."

"Amazed it fit," Melinda spit out.

Josephine ignored her. "Not my fault if he was too drunk and too stupid to do the same." She pushed herself up, swaying slightly when she got there. To my surprise, there were tears in her eyes. "I needs a drink if you're going to keep this up."

"Yes, girl, I suppose you do." Dad said, looking at his own empty glass.

She reached out. A peculiar look passed between them, not the here-we-go look, but one I'd noticed before but hadn't ever thought about, as if they understood each other. "Give it here," she said, and took his glass with her to the kitchen.

With Josephine out of earshot Melinda muttered under her breath, "Fellow probably swam to shore and ran for his life. Better dead than living with that."

"Stop it, Melinda," Dad said. "You don't know what she went through."

"Hang on," I said to Dad. "You said you and her are cousins?"

He nodded.

"And you're not married?"

He shook his head.

"Oh," I said, finally understanding why they each had their own bedroom while I was stuck in a pantry. "Well, okay. Good."

"Lucky man," said Melinda. She looked like she was sobering up.

Dad gave us a warning glance as Josephine shuffled back in, two drinks in hand, one lighter coloured than the other. She gave the darker one, the one with less rum and more Coke, to Dad, then plunged herself back into the sofa.

He took a swig. "Anyways, 15 years later, who walks in the door but Susan."

"Fifteen friggin' years," Josephine said, her little lips spitting saliva. "Can you reckon that? And she had the gall to try to take over. Blabbering on about how she's the mother now, like I gave a rat's arse."

"Hardly," Melinda mumbled.

I was doing the math in my head. Had she shown up just in time to get back with Dad and have me?

But Josephine was still talking, not to Dad or me or Melinda, to the room, her head against the back of the sofa as if she had an audience on the ceiling. "Sweeping in nice as you like, acting like the cock of the walk, the Frenchman behind her, you'd swear she left the day before. Insisting Melinda call her 'Mom', and Melinda, the foolish thing, her falling for it, 'Mommy this' and 'Mommy that.'"

Frenchman? What Frenchman?

"Better than you – " Melinda threw out.

Josephine spoke over her. "It was enough to make you sick, it was…"

"Now that's something you'd know about…"

"…watching her fawning all over that woman, and her after being gone all them years, some mother-figure I tell you."

"Yeah well, you made her look pretty good," Melinda shouted.

Josephine's mouth opened. The sofa plastic squeaked as she leaned forward jabbing a finger at Melinda. "You little – "

Dad's hand sliced the air. The intensity of his frown caused his eyebrows to form one bushy line across his forehead. "Stop. You two hold your horses and let me finish."

I was impressed. Perhaps he should drink more often.

He pointed at me. "Look at Bridgina here. She's the one with the questions, she's the one who don't know nothing about all this, but is she butting in every second? No, she is not. So shut up, the two of you."

Yes, definitely, booze was good for him. "Go ahead, Dad. You were saying?" If he didn't get the whole story out in one go, he might never attempt it again. And I wanted to hear it from him. Josephine would skew it in her favour. I was beginning to suspect Melinda would too.

Dad lit a cigarette and took a long drag. "Susan wasn't alone. She had a fellow with her. Pierre," he said, tapping the ash into the ashtray, "from Quebec."

Ah, the Frenchman. Pierre – I liked the sound of that, foreign, French. Pierre.

"She called him her husband but that couldn't have been because we were still married, which the whole town knew full well so he wasn't staying with her in the house. The barn was heated so I put him in there. He didn't mind, made himself right at home there. Too much so, it turned out."

So much for Susan and Dad reuniting. Despite my confusion, I was impressed that my boring family had such intriguing skeletons.

Dad's lips puffed out in disgust. "All of a sudden women were stopping by the barn, saying he paid them to do his laundry or cut his hair, bringing him baking and jars of preserves, some for no darn good reason at all that I could tell, hanging off his every word, laughing and carrying on. Women I'd known all my life, married women, widows, old and young, like they'd never seen a good-looking fellow before. And Susan, she laughed it off, said it was just Pierre "being French," that they all acted flirty like that but it was innocent fun. He was having fun all right, I wanted to say. But I didn't. She and Melinda were hitting it off, and I didn't care about that for Susan, but Melinda was like a new person. She used to be so mopey all the time, but now she was laughing and singing around the house. And that was Susan's doing, I knew that so I couldn't begrudge her, and what did I care what Pierre was up to anyway?"

As Dad spoke, Josephine let out an occasional snort or derisive grunt. Melinda, on the other hand, had gone quiet and was sinking further into the chair, into herself it seemed. Looking at her there in her creased wedding dress I felt sorry for her, yet glad. Yes, her mother had deserted her, but she'd come back. There was a happy ending.

"…and Susan acted like she was really trying to make up for what she done," Dad was saying, "talking about Melinda visiting them in Quebec. I wasn't sure I liked the sound of that but I let it be, for Melinda's sake. She was happier than I'd ever seen her."

He took several draws on his cigarette without speaking. I waited impatiently. Josephine was beginning to nod off in the corner.

"What happened to them, to Susan and Pierre?" I spoke louder than necessary. I didn't want this confession, or whatever it was, to end, especially because I was starting to wonder if Susan and the dashing Pierre, who was obviously nothing like anybody in the room except, I dared to think, maybe me, that they might be my parents.

Dad stubbed out his cigarette. "Had to run them out of town. He was up to no good, owing money at the store, taking advantage of people's good nature. I said to get off my land and never come back. Had the shotgun in hand when I said it."

I had a moment of panic, as if I was the one with the gun to my back. "But… what did you do that for? Where did they go?"

He shook his head in that way he did when something bad was coming, with that helpless look on his face. "About a month later, I got a phone call.

RCMP. They were on their way home one night, Susan was at the wheel, on a stretch of highway near…some strange place I can never remember. Where was it again, Josephine?"

Josephine's head bobbed. "Huh? What?"

"That place where it happened, something right odd, haha or something."

Josephine snorted. She was doing a lot of snorting that night. "St. Louis du Ha Ha, up there in Quebec. Why they'd call a place that I'll never know."

"Yes, that's right. Anyhow, they were after getting T-boned by an 18-wheeler. Killed instantly, the pair of them. I felt bad for that. I never wished her any harm, not him either, not that kind anyway."

That deflated me. Was I Josephine's daughter after all? No one had said I wasn't.

I glanced at Dad. He was staring at Melinda, tears in his eyes. I assumed it was because her mother had died.

"My poor little girl, you were still a child, weren't you?"

Melinda's lips were pressed tight together.

"She didn't act like one." Josephine was awake and alert. "Besides, have you forgot how old Susan was when you married her? You didn't think she was a child. Neither was little Miss Priss here, prancing around her own stepfather, or good as."

Melinda bounded from her chair. "I told you then and I'm telling you now, it was him forcing himself on me. I had nothing to do with it – "

"Your real mother didn't believe you. Why should I? Why should – "

"Because he convinced her. She was in love with him, what could she – "

"The man had women fawning all over him, why would he come after you?"

"Maybe he liked younger girls, you ever think of that? Huh? Or did you have your fat little eyes on him too? Maybe you were jealous because he didn't want anything to do with a big old tub of lard. At least he could get his arms around me. Poor man would have smothered to death with you on top of him."

They were flinging words at each other so fast it was impossible to keep up.

"You always did like other women's men."

"Shut the hell up, Josephine." There was a warning note in Melinda's voice.

"We all knows why you came back here and it had nothing to do with you-know-who. You came back because you got caught with that married man and got chased out of the Northern Peninsula." She stood up. "I rest my case. Sweet dreams, the lot of you," she said, flicking her fingers at us and waddling off. Seconds later, we heard the dull thump and shuffle of her slippered feet as she made her way up the wooden stairway.

Was that it? Was the story over and done? "But what about…?" I stopped.

Melinda stood there, arms at her sides, silent tears trickling down her cheeks.

"Dad?" I turned to him.

Tears slid down into the creases of his face. "I wish I sent Susan away sooner." He wiped his eyes with the back of his hand. "None of this would have happened."

Melinda crumpled onto the sofa. "She ruined my life," she sobbed.

Part of me wanted to go to her, to try to comfort her, but I didn't know how. Who was she talking about? Who ruined her life? Susan? Josephine?

"I know. I'm sorry, Melinda girl, I'm some sorry." Dad did go to her. He sat down and patted her head as she sobbed against him.

I think I knew then; in my mind, I think I knew. But part of me was blocking out the truth. Part of me refused to grasp what the other part had started to see. My heart felt crushed, like an ice cold hand was squeezing it inside my chest. I closed my eyes.

"Bridge?"

I must have missed a second. Melinda was standing, looking directly at me. "What?"

Her eyes were full and heavy, but they were no longer crying. "I'm your mother."

I took a step backwards. "Melinda...no, don't say that. You're my sister, you're not...you can't be."

"I'm sorry, Bridge. It hasn't been easy for me...this, Dad telling you, or hearing it all dragged up again...or the last 18 years, for that matter."

"But..." I was afraid to ask the question, afraid of the answer. "Didn't you want me?"

"I was a kid. What did I know? I wasn't married. I had nothing. Come on, think. What was I supposed to do with a baby?"

"So...so you gave me..." I could hardly say it. "You gave me...to *her?*"

Melinda's hands came up. I thought she was going to reach out to me but she gestured towards Dad. "No, that's not how it was. I gave you to Dad so I could go away to nursing school. Herself was just part of the package."

My shoulders went slack. I wanted to slide down onto the floor, just curl into a ball and hide inside myself.

Melinda wasn't finished. "But look where I am. I came back." Her voice rang with a self-righteous anger. "I didn't have to, you know, no matter what she said. I could have gone to work in St. John's, had a regular life. But no, I came back, goddamn it."

I didn't say what came into my mind. That she should have come back. That she was my mother and the least she could do was want me. The least she could do was try to save me from the life she'd had, the small mean life that Josephine provided.

Melinda put her head in her hands. Her ribcage strained against the white sheen of her dress as she inhaled deeply and held it there. She exhaled and raised her head. Her face was streaked black from her mascara and her hair was a mess but she looked calm. "Now I need to get on with my life. I need to move on, and that's what I'm going to do."

"But what about us?"

She shrugged. "What do you mean, 'what about us?' Sure we're the same."

"You mean…that's it? That's all you got to say? All you're going to do?"

"What more can there be at this stage? Be realistic. You're all grown up now."

"But…you're leaving and…" I hurt so much that I couldn't figure out what I was thinking. "Come on, Mel," I tried. "Give me a break here. Don't I get a chance to…to talk about it and…I don't know…it's not right…" I trailed off, my voice breaking.

"Try to be mature about this. You got a new life starting in September, and I got one starting now." She spread her palms out in front of her. "I'm not dealing with this anymore tonight. It's my goddamn wedding day, for Christ's sake."

"But…"

"Listen," she hissed, "I've waited my whole life for this and you're not going to ruin it for me. That shit's in the past and I'm fucking leaving it there. And so are you."

She marched off. Seconds later, the sound of running water came from the bathroom.

Dad came over beside me. "There, there." He patted my back. "There, there."

There, there? What did that mean? Where was there?

Everything had changed. My life as I knew it was no longer mine. I was a stranger to myself. I thought I might throw up. I leaned in towards Dad – I couldn't think of him as anything but "Dad." He put his arms around me and held me, the smell of smoke and sweat and rum oddly comforting.

When Melinda returned, her face was clean. You could tell she'd been crying, but she had reapplied her lipstick and fixed her hair. She looked normal. She was no longer almost beautiful.

I took a step away from Dad and faced her. She had to say something more, something that might show that she cared, that she had some maternal instinct towards me, or a sisterly one. "Mel?" I said.

She tilted her head as if concentrating, but she was actually listening. "He's here. That was Victor's car."

Moments later, the front door opened. Victor walked in. No one spoke right away.

"Melinda?" he said.

She gestured towards me and nodded.

He looked relieved. "You told her?"

Melinda moved to stand next to him. The weight that had been in her eyes was gone. "You were right. I should have done it long ago."

Victor gave me a cautious smile. "Are you okay?"

Melinda answered for me. "We've talked it all out. She's fine. Everything's fine."

"I'm sure it's a shock, Bridgina, but it is better to know, isn't it?"

Melinda's determined eyes locked onto mine. I found myself nodding.

She took Victor's hand. "Let's go home," she said, and led him from the house.

Two days later they left Exile Cove for Toronto.

5

Our one-bedroom basement apartment was off Elizabeth Avenue, easy walking distance to the university for Sylvia and me, a little farther to the Trade School where Katie was enrolled in a secretarial program. It was a dungeon of a place, but it was ours. The whole apartment was one long skinny room with a few walls thrown up. In one corner was the kitchen. The fridge was ancient, the kind that you pulled down the handle to open, with an icebox that was exactly that – a box of ice with a slit of foul-smelling air in the middle. There was no room to put anything in there, not that you'd want to. The stove was a hot plate with two burners, and the rust-stained sink was so shallow it must have originally been part of a bathroom. A narrow table was pushed up against the wall and past that, a sofa and a coffee table with a small black and white TV on it. You could only turn around in the bathroom if the door was either fully open or fully closed, and you weren't too fat.

"Bridge, get in here," Katie called out from the bedroom.

"In a sec," I yelled back, tapping the last nail into the Desiderata poster.

Victor had given it to me the day after the wedding. "I've had it so long I know it by heart, thought you'd appreciate it," he'd said. "Melinda will be over before we head to the ferry. She's busy getting the little ones sorted out but she wants to talk to you about Christmas." He'd hugged me then and patted the poster like he was parting with an old friend. "If you need anything, anything at all, call us, okay?" His voice had been insistent. He meant it. "Yeah, thanks," I'd said. At the time the poster seemed an odd gift, but I was beginning to like Victor so I hung it on my bedroom wall. By summer's end it was imprinted on my brain. It was what I saw every day lying on my bed, trying to forget that Melinda hadn't stopped in to say goodbye, hadn't made time to call me before she drove off to Toronto. I felt like I was floundering in the universe, its orphan child, lost and alone. Abandoned. By my sister, by my mother. The poem became my mantra as I willed time to pass so I could say goodbye to Exile Cove and start my new life.

Now here I was in St. John's with my two best friends. Striving to be happy.

I tossed the hammer onto the sofa, planted a smile on my face, and took four strides to reach the bedroom where Katie, wearing a bright blue plastic shower cap, was crouched down in front of our communal six-drawer dresser stuffing her clothes into the bottom two because she'd lost the coin toss. Behind her, three single beds filled the space, each less than a foot away from the next.

"You going for another shower?"

Ten minutes after we'd moved in that afternoon, Katie was in the bathroom with the water running. She and Sylvia were both excited about having a shower. They'd been envious when Dad had one installed in our house years before. I hadn't told them the reason for it, that Josephine had gotten stuck in the tub. Admittedly, a small tub.

Katie pulled the cap off and scratched her head. "Nah, just sick of all this fucking hair. It's driving me nuts."

"This room is going to drive me nuts," Sylvia complained. "It's packed to the gills. And look at the size of that window. God help us if we ever have a fire."

"Better than no window," I said.

Katie stood up and shuffled her feet between her and Sylvia's beds. "Give over with your whingeing, Syl. There's room to spare, sure."

"Shit," Sylvia grumbled, tugging the fitted end of her sheet towards the corner of the mattress while she was lying on it.

I crawled onto Katie's bed, which was in the middle, and reached for the sheet. "Here, lift up and I'll pull."

With a series of yanks and tugs we soon had all three made. Sylvia went to the kitchen and came back with three beers. We sat on our beds and grinned at each other.

Katie hoisted her bottle high. "To us!" she said and took a drink.

Sylvia drank and raised her arm. "The three musketeers!"

"The three stooges!" Katie drank again.

"The three wise men," Sylvia sang out. "Especially Seamus for getting us beer." She took a long swig. "Let's get rip-roaring drunk."

"I can't believe we're finally here," I said.

"I can't believe I get a whole bed to myself." Katie rubbed her hands up and down her quilt luxuriously. "No friggin' Mary kicking me in the middle of the night."

"I know," said Sylvia. "Or Molly's scratchy toenails digging into my legs."

Katie and Sylvia had slept with younger sisters all their lives. In our house no one had ever shared a room or a bed. After a long lonely summer, I was looking forward to waking up with someone nearby. My hand went up. "To the three bears."

Sylvia held her bottle up to the light. "I'm empty."

"Already?" Mine was still half full.

She stood on her bed and spread her arms. "Woo-wee, I'm free. Hey, drink up you guys. I'm starved. I haven't eaten all day."

"Mom sent spaghetti for dinner," said Katie. "We'll get groceries tomorrow."

"I brought a few things too." I had taken whatever Josephine might not miss, some oatmeal, half-eaten jars of peanut butter and jam, teabags, a few cans of tuna and beans from the back of the cupboard. I'd also nicked a bottle of champagne, or something with bubbles in it. Victor had bought some for the wedding but it had gone unopened. We weren't champagne people. Josephine hated the stuff.

"Don't be so friggin' boring," said Sylvia. "We're in Town. They don't call it Sin City for nothing. Let's get Chinese food and crash a party somewhere."

"We can't go out on our first night," I said. "Let's stay in."

Sylvia rolled her eyes. "Didn't you spend enough time inside this summer? Jesus, live a little, would you."

I would have loved to splurge but the fact was I had $360 to my name, 200 of which was thanks to Maeve Mullins. I'd won the Maeve Mullins Mercantile Memorial Scholarship for the highest graduating marks in Exile Cove. Maeve, who wasn't dead, looked none too pleased handing over the cheque. Another 60 was thanks to Dad, who'd slipped me three 20s when he'd seen me off in Mr. Dollmont's truck that morning. He'd already put a hundred into my new bank account, "to get her started," he'd told Josephine when she found out. "Jesus, Andy, she's Melinda's responsibility," she'd said. "I think we done enough all these years, taking care of her, putting up with her back talk. Bad enough you said you'd pay her tuition. Time her mother did something." I hated the fact that I agreed with Josephine. I had tried to talk to Melinda about it when she'd phoned at the end of August, but she'd gone on about how she wasn't working, and how she didn't think she should spend Victor's money on something like that. Something like what? Supporting your only child? Your illegitimate bastard? I'd had a number of conversations like that with Melinda over the summer, but only in my mind. After more than a month in hibernation – me, the social butterfly of the Ashe clan – something in me had changed. I wasn't sure how to act, how to be, anymore. Whereas once I never gave much thought to what came out of my mouth when I spoke to Melinda, I no longer knew how to talk to her, not that she gave me much opportunity the two times she called. Josephine was worse. I used to love to say things to shock and provoke her. I had felt superior to her. Not anymore. She'd gotten the better of me. She'd won. I was not her responsibility and never had been. She no longer had to pretend. I had thought I was the smart Ashe. I was the one who "got it." I would be the one to make us more like other people, to bring the Ashe name up a notch. But I was barely an Ashe. If I'd figured out one thing during those long days and longer nights, it was that being a member of the Ashes-From-Away was better than nothing.

"I vote for staying in." Katie, always more sensitive than Sylvia, backed me up.

I reached into my drawer and held up the bottle of bubbly. "Besides, we need to christen our new digs. Who wants champagne?"

Sylvia's eyes lit up. "Now you're talking."

None of us had ever opened a bottle of champagne before but Sylvia said she'd seen it in a movie. She undid the foil and the wire and stuck her thumbs under the plastic cork, which gave a loud pop and whizzed past my head so close my hair moved.

"Hey, watch it!" I yelled.

"Jesus, Syl, you could've took her eye out."

"Oh chill out, the pair of you." Sylvia, who had put the bottle to her mouth when it overflowed upon opening, passed it to me. "Here, drink."

I was so relieved to be where I was that I couldn't be mad at her. I took a swig and sputtered half of it back up, lukewarm bubbles frothing from my nose. We sat on our beds and passed the bottle and talked and laughed, reminiscing about the past and planning the future. We hadn't seen each other much over the summer. Sylvia had been busy flitting from one boy to another and from one party to the next. She'd called me a couple of times but I'd made excuses why I couldn't go out, and then she didn't call anymore. I might have gone if Katie had been there but she'd been away at her grandmother's all summer. By the time she got home I had everything bottled up so tight inside me I didn't know how or where to start.

"I tell you one thing," Katie said, "it's the last summer I'm spending at Gram's."

"Yuk, hanging out with a bunch of fossils all summer. Old people give me the creeps." Sylvia shivered. "They smell bad, too."

"Well, no, Gram's pretty cool most of the time. Her friends are ancient, mind you. All they do is hook rugs and play cards and say the rosary."

Sylvia took the bottle. "You knew that. Why go?"

Katie gave me a sheepish look.

Sylvia sized her up, then looked at me. "You knows something, don't you?"

I said nothing. Katie had sworn me to secrecy.

"Okay, that's it. Let's make a deal." Sylvia plunked the bottle in the middle of Katie's bed. "Put your hand here on top of mine."

Katie and I glanced at each other, then at Sylvia. Katie reached out and put her right hand on top of Sylvia's on the bottle. I put mine on Katie's.

"Now we make a pact. Whatever we say here, stays here." Sylvia's voice rose along with her free hand. "And not just tonight. From now on, everything we say or do here is between the three of us. No telling anyone."

Katie nodded. "Right on. To the three sisters."

"Here, here!" Sylvia proclaimed. "The three sisters forever!"

My heart opened up like a flower, one second a tight bud closed against everything, the next, the petals blossoming, fanning out to the world.

"Melinda's my mother," I blurted.

Their eyes swept toward me, mouths agape, speechless.

"Dad and Josephine aren't married. They're cousins." Realizing what that implied, I added, "But they don't sleep together. No, they never did that, never."

"Fuck! I knew there was something weird there," Sylvia said with a shocked grin. "Talk about keeping secrets. How could you not tell us that all these years?" Her eyes leapt to Katie. "Did you know?"

"*I* didn't know," I said before Katie could answer. "I found out at Melinda's wedding." Tears came to my eyes. "It was awful. It still is."

Katie scooched over and put her arm around me. "Oh, Bridge, I'm so sorry."

"Here." Sylvia passed me the bottle. "Now tell us all about it."

I told them about Dad and Susan and Melinda, about Josephine and her dead husband, about Pierre, my dead father. About seeing my birth certificate and finding out that my whole family had forgotten which year I was born. It wasn't a smooth telling by any means, with me sniffling and crying and drinking champagne. I had never said any of it out loud before. I didn't know how to tell it. As Katie and Sylvia asked me questions, it struck me how much I didn't know, like Pierre's last name, and that made me cry harder because I had no one to ask. I blubbered on about how Melinda didn't care about me, how no one did except Dad, who was actually my grandfather. And maybe Victor, I added. Of all people, the one who knew me least had shown me such kindness, even offering to pay my way up to visit them. Melinda still had not seconded the offer.

By the time I finished, the champagne was gone and we had moved back to beer. The tears had stopped. My mind was clearer that it had been all summer. Yet I still felt an obligation, if only to Dad. "But it's in our pact, right? No one says anything?"

"Not a word," Katie promised.

"Absolutely, not a single – " Sylvia's arm, holding an empty bottle, shot out. "Hey, just a Jesus minute." Her j's and s's sounded the same. "This all started with Katie. What's the big secret?"

Katie grinned but didn't say anything right away.

Sylvia punched her in the arm. "Did you do it? You did it, didn't you?"

Katie shook her head vigorously.

"Well, what then?" Sylvia insisted. "Come on, tell me."

"Well, last year at Gram's there was this guy and we kind of went out together. And he was there this summer, too, but then he had to go and that was why it was so boring. Anyway, before he left we sort of got into it kind of heavy, and I let him…you know…"

Sylvia was waiting. "Yeah, what? Say it, Katie," she goaded. "Say what you let him do. Be a big girl now."

"Fine. I let him feel me up." Katie kind of grinned and grimaced, like she was pleased with herself but afraid of a lightning bolt from above at the same time.

"That's it? That's the big secret?" Sylvia leaned back against the wall and stretched out. She rubbed her hands up and down her opposite arms in a sort of odd caress that any other time might have made me uncomfortable. In my uninhibited state, it made me curious. As she talked about the boys she'd gone out with that summer, there was something about the way she named them off, giving some more emphasis than others, that left me with the impression that Sylvia had done more than let them kiss her, and quite probably more than steal a feel. We let her talk on, eager to find out the dirty details, which she readily supplied, confirming our suspicions. By the time we'd each downed a few more beers, Sylvia was going on about women's rights and why was it okay for guys to have sex but not girls, and Katie and I were nodding and agreeing and raising our eyebrows at each other when she wasn't looking. Yet as shocked as I was that Sylvia had had sex with at least two boys, and maybe more, I felt a new maturity. Here we were, three girls – no, three women – better still, three sisters – living in the big city, free to do whatever we wanted, even if I had no intention of doing "it" in the near future, and realistically, no opportunity. But most importantly, I was on my own, responsible for my own decisions, beholden to no one. For the first time since Melinda's wedding, that sounded like a good thing.

With the beer box empty, Sylvia produced a bottle of some concoction she'd collected by siphoning off an ounce here and there from her parents' liquor supply. By the time we ordered in I'd forgotten to worry about money. It was the best Chinese food I'd ever eaten, although it didn't look or taste as good at two in the morning coming back up.

My first night in St. John's was all I had ever dreamed it would be.

6

Limping along Elizabeth Avenue, I wiped my hand across my eyes, grateful the pouring rain hid my tears. I had twisted my ankle running from the library, hurrying as usual except this time on slippery steps. The stabbing pain from heel to shin was the last straw. After three classes and a lab and a four-hour shift at the library, all topped off with a sore ankle, tears of self-pity washed down my face. But that wasn't why I was crying. What hurt the most, what made me sadder than anything, was the fact that our sisterhood had been such a failure.

After our splurge on Chinese food, I had $357 left. With my skull feeling like it was too small for my head, I'd left Katie and Sylvia to nurse their hangovers and hit the streets, gathering job applications from every place with an open door. Within the week I had a part-time job at the university library. By the end of September I'd landed another at Sobeys. I also signed up to type term papers for grad students, even though I couldn't type without looking at the keys. I would learn soon enough. What it all meant was that I didn't have time to enjoy myself like Katie and Sylvia. Katie understood; Katie always did. Sylvia did not. She didn't understand and she didn't care that after paying for rent and books and food, I had almost no money, or that I couldn't phone my parents when things got tough. Sylvia had always had a mean streak, but lately she was like another person. Maybe she'd been changing all summer and with Katie away and me holed up in my room, we hadn't noticed. Unfortunately, over the last six weeks of living together, I'd become her favourite target.

By the time I got home, my ankle felt better and so did I. A walk in the rain could do that to me, which was fortunate living in St. John's. Inside, Sylvia was sitting at the table drinking beer and smoking cigarettes with her new friend, Irene.

Katie's top half poked around the bathroom doorway. "Good, you're home."

"Hey, Farrah," I waved, still surprised at the sight of her. After a week in St. John's and away from her mother, Katie had come home one day with a long shag cut.

"That's me, Charlie's Angel," she laughed, swishing her hair about. "We're just heading to Evan's party. You ready?"

I dumped my books onto the table. "No way, you guys go on."

Sylvia emptied her beer. "See, I told you. We waited for nothing."

"Come on, Bridge," Katie called out. "You never have any fun."

"I do so." She was right. I didn't. "I got an exam tomorrow."

"Of course you do, little Miss Straight As." Sylvia stubbed out her cigarette. "If I'd known how fucking boring you were going to be, I'd have found another roommate."

"Hey man, like I told you, you can crash with us." Irene looked around the cramped apartment till her eyes landed on me. "Beats this crib."

"Yeah man, you got that right."

Sylvia had taken up with a different crowd her first week of university. Irene was my least favourite of the lot. They were artsy, rebellious types, but not in a cool way. According to them, according to Sylvia, Katie and I were square. They, on the other hand, again according to Sylvia, were hip, with it, totally bad. Totally rude was more like it, rude and condescending, none more so than Sylvia, especially when she was drinking tequila, her new favourite beverage. She'd become the queen of sarcasm, constantly making belittling remarks, about me more so than Katie, in front of her friends. The night before they'd all been in the living room while I was studying in the bedroom. When I came out to get some water, they were talking about parents, how dumb they were, how old-fashioned, how stupid. As I passed by on my way back to the bedroom Sylvia's voice rose in that taunting way she used with me lately. "You know about mommy issues, don't you, Bridge?" she said. "Daddy issues, too." They'd all laughed as if they knew full well what she was talking about.

Katie came over to the table. "Knock it off, Syl."

"Sorry I'm spoiling your fun, Sylvia," I spat out.

She was at the door already. "Look, she said no, so let's go. Got to strike while the iron's hot." Sylvia had set her sights on Evan the second she saw him.

Katie glanced from me to Sylvia. "You know, I'm kind of tired, too."

"Fuck!" Sylvia threw down her coat. "We can't go if you don't. You're the one who goes to school with them." She glared at me. "It's like living with an old woman."

"Get the fuck off her back," Katie yelled. "You know what she's been through."

Sylvia gave an exaggerated sigh. "Poor baby. 'Mommy don't love me.'"

Katie rounded on her. "Some friend you are."

"Some friend she is, more like it. You've been dying to go to that party and now you're not because she's making you feel guilty."

Sylvia was right. Katie had a serious crush on Evan's roommate.

"Shut up, Sylvia," I said. "Katie, go to the party and take that one with you." When Katie hesitated, I added, "I'll study for a couple of hours and head over."

Katie looked doubtful. "You'll show up by yourself?"

"Sure, why not? You'll both be there."

"Good, now come on." Sylvia had the door open. Irene had already left. Katie shrugged at me and followed them out.

I flopped onto the sofa, knowing I would never go to the party. For one thing I did have an exam in the morning, in chemistry, which was turning out to be more work than I'd expected. I wasn't sure why I was taking it, except that somewhere along the line, I had come to the conclusion that I should study math and science, that these were serious subjects that would show that I was serious, too. I had also decided to quit thinking about boys, which was just as well. I'd had no offers. I kept purposefully busy. When I wasn't working or studying, I had more time to think, more time to look in the mirror and wonder where I came from. But I was never going to meet my father. I was never going to know if I had his sense of humour, or if that was where I got my wide face or my thick hair or my anything. Never. Deep inside, it was like a part of me, an actual physical part of me, had died.

Two days later, the phone rang.

"Hi, Bridge, it's me, Victor."

"Victor? Hi."

"I just flew in to close the deal on the house in St. Paul, in and out in one day. Can you meet me for an early supper before I catch my plane back?"

"Yeah, sure."

"We'll catch up on everything. Looking forward to seeing you."

When I went into the Pizza Delight that evening I spotted Victor at a table peering at an official-looking document, presumably something to do with the house sale. He reminded me of my favourite professor, the way his index finger tapped his greying temple, and how he looked up over the rim of his glasses to scan the entrance. When he saw me he hopped to his feet and waved, then hugged me when I reached the table. A good solid hug, with just the right reassuring amount of pressure.

He leaned back and looked at me. "Good to see you. How you doing?"

"Thanks," I said as we sat down. "I'm good. And you?"

"Good. Really good."

I had an instant where I didn't know what to say next, where I knew the next hour was going to be just plain awkward. I'd been so nervous about seeing Victor that I'd hardly eaten all day. Now I had no appetite.

Thankfully, the waitress appeared. When I ordered a small pizza, Victor told her to make mine, and his, an extra large. "Who doesn't like leftover pizza?" he said.

Something about that set me at ease, and when he started asking me questions, I found myself talking easily, about the apartment, living in St. John's, the courses I was taking. When I mentioned the second job at Sobeys, he shook his head.

"Two jobs, that's a lot." He patted my hand across the table. "You don't want to wear yourself down."

"It's not too bad." I decided not to mention the typing. I remembered reading that a good conversationalist should take an interest in the other person. "How's Toronto?"

He raised an eyebrow. "Toronto's Toronto."

"And the kids, are they liking it?"

"I think so. Charlotte sure is, too much if you ask me. And the younger ones are settling in. Your..." He hesitated. "Melinda's good with them."

This was the first time we'd mentioned Melinda. It threw me off. "Good for her." I sounded bitter. I didn't care.

There was a definite awkward pause then. Victor coughed and looked around the restaurant. He picked up his fork and put it back down. Clearly he found the subject of Melinda as uncomfortable as I did. The poor guy, tossed into a family like ours, yet here he was making such an effort, far more than Melinda had before she'd left or since, and now more than I was.

"Do you miss Newfoundland?" I asked. "I can't imagine living so far away."

"I do. I forgot how big Toronto is, so many people, all rushing all the time. I even miss the weather. How crazy is that?" he laughed, looking up as the waitress approached with our food. "Oh my God, pizza. It's been months since I've had a slice."

The smell of spicy pepperoni wafted around us. My appetite resurfaced. We tucked in, talking while we ate, about pizza and food and cooking and coursework. Not about Melinda. Her name didn't come up until we were at his rental car.

"Do you want me to drop you off?" he asked, unlocking the car door.

"Nah, that's okay, I'll walk. It's just over the way."

"If you need anything, you'll get in touch with me, won't you?"

"I will," I answered honestly. "Thanks for dinner." I held up the two boxes of leftover pizza. "And for breakfast."

"My pleasure." He looked uncertain. "Bridge, look, about Melinda…I'm sorry she doesn't call more. She's…she's really busy."

"It's okay, Victor. Say hi to her for me," I said, letting him off the hook. "See you next time."

He got in the car, backed out, and gave a little wave in the rearview mirror. At the entrance to the parking lot he stopped, waiting for an oncoming car to pass. Having sold his house, he no longer had ties to Newfoundland, except maybe me, and I wondered when, or if, I'd see him again. I started to wave back. He'd already pulled away.

The sun had set. There was no moon visible in the darkening clouded sky. A cold breeze warned of winter as it swept through the parking lot. The restaurant had been too warm and I hadn't zipped up my coat. Clutching my leftover pizza in one arm, I pulled my jacket closer and hurried home.

Christmas was rotten. In the past, while Dad was out cutting down the tree, I would make popcorn and string it to use as garland. Later, once the tree was secure in its stand, Melinda and I decorated it, although in retrospect I realized Melinda did little once the lights were on. While I carefully placed the fragile glass bulbs on the branches, spreading them out so they were equally spaced in the front of the tree, she would sit back with her book. Dad turned off the TVs without my asking for half an hour and we listened to Christmas carols on the radio. I had felt like we were a real family then. For 30 minutes.

When I walked in on Christmas Eve, the living room was the same as always. "Where's the tree?" I asked.

Dad was sitting still in his chair, staring straight ahead, an unlit cigarette in his hand. He turned his head to look at me. "Huh?"

"The tree. How come there's no tree?"

He squinted at me. "Who…?"

"Dad?" He was scaring me. "You okay?"

He rubbed his forehead and looked at the cigarette, then at me again.

Josephine trundled in. "Bridgina. You're here."

"Of course I am."

Dad's eyes brightened. Relief spread over his face. "You…Bridge…you're here. Jos…she said…you weren't coming."

"That's not what I said."

I turned to her. "What exactly did you say?"

"Said I didn't know." Her tone said the rest. She didn't care either.

"Where else would I go? It's Christmas."

Josephine sank into a chair. "Like I said, I didn't know."

I gave up. I didn't care what she thought anyway. I set my wrapped presents, slippers for Dad and a scarf for Josephine, on the coffee table and went to raid the fridge. One thing could be said for Josephine, there was never a shortage of food.

On Christmas morning Dad handed me two white envelopes. The first, from him, contained two 20s. The second, from Melinda, contained three, inserted into a family Christmas card of Victor and his four children with Melinda, looking more contented than I'd ever seen her, in the middle. Charlotte was the only one not smiling. The card was unsigned.

There were no other presents. There was no turkey either. Josephine had pre-made fish and brewis the day before and sat around drinking rum and Cokes all day. I heated a can of mushroom soup for dinner. Ordinarily I would have gone to Katie's but they were spending Christmas in Alberta. Mr. Dollmont wanted them to move to Fort McMurray.

I went to bed early and lay there, thinking how life was not turning out the way I'd hoped. Katie and Sylvia were always busy, out with boyfriends or off to a party. Our apartment wasn't the hotbed of social activity I had dreamed of in high school but it didn't matter. Between school and work, I didn't spend much time there. Still, it was better than home. Actually, it was home. It was my home, and had nothing to do with Josephine or Melinda or Exile Cove. On my worst day, I still felt I'd gone from a dark dank cellar to a place of light and air, where people laughed and loved and were happy, where those things were common, although not necessarily for me. If I sometimes felt adrift among people who all had somebody, I pushed it aside. I had begun to understand and, for the most part, to accept, that love was not a given in my life.

On Boxing Day, I caught the bus back to St. John's. Most people wanted the week off so I had signed up for extra shifts between Christmas and New Year's. I also had a grad thesis to type. On New Year's Eve, I bought myself a frozen dinner and a bag of chips and watched TV while I typed the last of the paper. I fell asleep on the sofa.

In the night, I had a dream. I had been typing something important for a man I couldn't see. He wouldn't show me his face or talk directly to me. He gave me instructions through someone else who I didn't know and who didn't care if I did it right. I needed to see the man's face because that would somehow tell me how to type the paper. But I always just missed catching that glimpse and time was passing and the paper was due but I couldn't finish it because I couldn't see him. I awoke, my heart racing as my eyes searched the room, the only light the moon's reflection off the snow outside the small window near the ceiling. The man wasn't there and I was filled with the same frustration and disappointment as in my dream. Seconds later I was doing a double check.

Not the most auspicious start to a new year but at least I was free, living on my own, in St. John's. This was my new life. My new normal.

Then along came Iggy.

7

My head was deep into a calculus textbook when Seamus, in town for a party, stopped by to drop off some figgy bread from his mother. Having broken up with her latest boyfriend, Katie was more interested in the party than the bread.

"Come on, Seamus, let me come. I'm bored out of my gourd. Please?"

"No way."

"I'll be good, I promise."

"Look, I'm not taking you to no party where you won't know anyone and I'll have to babysit you – "

"Bridge'll come too, so I won't be on my own."

I looked up to find them both staring at me. "I got my first quiz tomorrow."

Katie leaned across the table. "Come on, Bridge, you got to get out more. How else you going to find a boyfriend? When was the last time you had a date, sure?"

"Katie!" Seamus might have been the closest thing to a brother I was ever going to have, but I didn't want to discuss my lack of a love life in front of him.

Seamus patted my head. "Hard to find true love, isn't it, Bridgie?"

"Don't mind him," said Katie. "He never goes out with the same piece twice."

Maybe not, but I knew there was no shortage of willing girls. "There's more important things than boys, you know," I said with feigned superiority.

"Like what? Friggin' calculus?" Katie leaned back in her chair. "See, Seamus, you got to help me get Bridge a fellow. What do you say?"

Seamus shrugged. "Ah, what the hell, I'll be gone next week."

"You're really moving to Alberta?" I said.

He placed his palm flat on his chest. "'Go west, young man, and seek your fortune.' That's us on Monday. Not stopping till we get to Simon's in Montreal."

"How the heck is Simon?" I asked. "I haven't seen him in ages."

"Pretty darn good. He just got into med school, you know."

"Isn't that great? I knew he could do it."

"He's going to show us around, find us some action." Seamus grinned. "Want me to say hi for you? I'm sure he'd like that."

"Yeah, and tell him congratulations. How long you staying in Montreal?"

"Couple of days and we're off again, straight to McMurray. Dad got me a job on the rigs. Good money, lots of hours. Beats the friggin' docks."

"But what about your dreams of being a doctor?" I teased. "You and Simon taking over Montreal?"

"That wouldn't be fair to Simon." He gestured to his face. "I mean, seriously, how could he compete with this?"

I glanced at Katie, expecting a smart retort, but she had crossed her arms and was slumped into her chair. She'd been quiet ever since he'd mentioned Alberta.

Seamus looked at his watch. "Anyway, you two coming or what?"

"Fine." I closed the calculus book. "But I'm heading home early. Come on Katie, time to go to a party."

Katie's face brightened a little. She stood up and tucked her arm into Seamus's and squeezed him lightly. "Give us 10 minutes to get dolled up."

Ten minutes? So much for finding a boyfriend.

The party was the type Katie and I had heard about but never been to. This was the truly cool set, older, more worldly than our teenage crowd. There was no disco here, no one doing the hustle. They were a hard rock crowd, Alice Cooper and Led Zeppelin. Many had been going to MUN off and on for years and they were full of ideas and ideals. They smoked dope and laughed and argued and hugged each other for no good reason. They sat on the kitchen counters, talking heatedly about Peckford and politics, about Trudeau versus Clark, about federalism and the Constitution, about the lingering effects of the FLQ and the Vietnam War. I kept my mouth shut and nodded a lot.

I saw Iggy as soon as I walked into the living room. I knew who he was in a general sense, Simon's older brother from St. Paul, but I'd only seen him from a distance. I'd certainly never spoken to him. Now he was six feet away from me.

Iggy Connors wasn't just handsome. He was Greek-god beautiful. His thick dark wavy hair fell just below the nape of his neck, and his high cheekbones and full lips accentuated a lean face that was shadowed by a hint of stubble.

He was standing in a group of people where some girl had wrapped herself around him like a feather boa. He glanced at her occasionally, but his right hand was at his side and his left held a beer. All eyes were on him yet he didn't strike me as a show-off. When someone spoke, he would sip his beer and make a comment. Everyone listened. Someone else would speak and he'd give that person his attention. The others would follow suit, very adult, civilized.

"Bridge," Katie nudged me. "Quit staring."

I immediately looked in the opposite direction, praying that nobody else had noticed. My eyes hit on a painting, a wild mix of colours and swirls and shapes, propped up on a table and leaning against the wall. I walked to it, grateful for something to do. I moved in close then stood back, enjoying how light and distance played with the image. I turned to tell Katie to come see. She was gone but Iggy was watching me. He disentangled himself from the girl and came towards me. Desperately trying to fit in, I pretended to study the painting.

"Welcome to our Ukrainian Christmas party," he said.

I turned to him. "Christmas? Sorry…" I stuttered. "I didn't know…"

"I won't make you eat the pickled herring."

"Pickled…?"

"Or the borscht."

I must have looked confused because he draped an arm around my shoulders, not a hug, more a friendly gesture. He pressed his beer bottle into my nervous fingers and I looked into his eyes for the first time. Near black, with long lashes top and bottom, those eyes drew me in as I took the bottle from his hands.

"You okay?" he asked.

"Yeah. Thanks." I felt a pulse of intimacy as I placed my lips where his had been moments before.

He inclined his head towards the painting. "What do you think?"

Something about the way he asked, a measured nonchalance, made me wonder if it was his. I longed to say something brilliant, something artistic and insightful. "The colours, they're so…rich. The red…and the black, I love the black. It's great."

"Really? You really think so?"

I wasn't sure what I thought other than it was colourful. "Definitely. I've never seen black so…I don't know, so deep?"

Iggy nodded slowly. "Wow, that's cool, you see it."

"You didn't…" I waited a moment. "This isn't yours, is it?"

He looked at the painting then back at me. "I just finished it."

"It's really good."

"Most people don't get it, the colours, the soul. You do. Far out."

His eyes peered into mine. Was he wondering if I meant what I said, or if I had a clue about art? Maybe he just wanted his beer back. I pushed the bottle into his hands.

"I'm Iggy, by the way," he said. "What was your name again?"

"Bridge Ashe. From Exile Cove."

"That sounds familiar." He started to take a sip of beer but pulled back. "Wait a minute. Did you go to school with my brother? Simon Connors?"

"Yeah, we were in debate club together," I said, trying to sound older.

My eyes were drawn to his mouth, the soft lips, the teeth so white against the dark stubble. What would it be like to kiss those lips? And although sensual was not a word I'd ever spoken, between his eyes and his mouth, the word, the feeling, was all I could think of. I had not been kissed often, mainly in high school party games. What would it be like to feel his mouth…?

I was staring again. I blinked and moved my focus to his eyes. He was still looking at me, nodding his head as if he'd figured something out. For the life of me I couldn't imagine what that might be.

"I'll tell Simon I met you."

"Seamus said he's in Montreal. How's he's doing?"

"Up to his eyeballs in books. Our Simon," he said, his voice taking on a posh accent, "is going to save the world."

"Oh?" I laughed.

"Brainiac thinks he's going to be a friggin' doctor."

"Good for Simon. He always said he wanted to go to med school."

He studied me a moment, his face serious. "He could have been anything, you know, a lawyer, engineer, anything he wanted. But no, he picked medicine." His voice hardened. "It's almost like he did it to spite me."

I had no idea what he meant by that and didn't think I should ask. It seemed too personal. "He was some smart in high school," I said. It sounded lame.

He must have thought so, too. He ignored it. "Ashe? Your sister the nurse?"

My sister? For the first time since I'd told Katie and Sylvia, I had the urge to tell someone else, and I was sober this time. For some reason, I knew Iggy Connors would understand how I felt, even if I wasn't completely sure what that was.

"Yeah, Melinda. You know her?" I asked, immediately wishing I hadn't. Of course he knew her. Why else would he bring her up?

"Umm." He looked unsettled for a moment, then his smile returned, wide and sultry, except his eyes, which were almost closed. That's when I realized he was stoned, and although I'd never smoked dope, I wished I was stoned, too.

He reached out, his hand moving from the side of my head to the ponytail at the back. "Man, what great hair."

I swallowed, embarrassed and mesmerized at the same time.

He tugged a little at the elastic. "May I?"

I think I nodded. He put down his beer and used both hands to gently remove the elastic. His fingers spread my hair out, fanning it around my face.

"Way cool," he said. "It's black, too." He combed his fingers through the strands that fell around my shoulders. "And deep. Black and deep."

My breathing sped up, quick shallow breaths that made it impossible to respond. I was saved by a commotion as three guys charged through the front door. Iggy waved them over and they all hugged like long lost friends.

One of them elbowed Iggy. "Hey man, they finally let you back in school."

"What's your major this time, Ig?" asked another.

When Iggy told them he was studying education, they whistled and hooted.

"A teacher? Holy shit man, that's too funny. You, a teacher!"

I didn't know why that was funny, but Iggy laughed, so I did too. Then he introduced me as if it was natural for me to be standing there with him.

"Dude," said the guy he'd called Ferg. "I got some 'shrooms. You want in?"

Iggy shook his head. "No way. Never again."

"Oh, get over it. That batch must've been laced or something."

Iggy's raised his hand. "Fergus, my man, all I know is there's no magic in mushrooms."

The girl who'd had her arms around him earlier came over and whispered in his ear. As much as I'd felt included moments before, I knew I wasn't part of this. As Iggy let her lead him outside, he looked back at me and smiled.

I didn't talk to him again that night, despite trying to be in his way more than once. He was always surrounded by friends, and it was easy to see why. Wherever he was, the space felt charged. He was funny, smart, totally captivating.

Unlike anyone I had ever known.

"She's right here." Katie covered the mouthpiece. "I think it's that hunk from the party last night," she whispered. "Simon's brother."

I had been daydreaming about him when the phone rang but had not for a second thought it would be him. I grabbed the phone. "Hello?"

"Hey there, how's it going?" His voice was warm and lazy.

"Iggy, hi." I held the receiver with both hands, trying not to hyperventilate. I never thought to play coy, to ask who it was or how he'd gotten my number. I was too busy trying to think of something to say, something that wouldn't sound desperate. "Good. I'm good. How are you? What are you doing?" Why was I talking so fast?

"Just hanging. Hey, you want to catch some jazz tonight?"

"Yeah, great," I said, not quite sure what jazz was. My heart was pumping.

"Cool." That lazy voice again. "See you around nine," he said, then hung up.

I held the phone in my hand. Katie and I stared at each other, eyes wide.

"A date. I think," I said. "Tonight. Jazz." I couldn't form a sentence.

"Let's get you ready." She took the phone and hung it up and pushed me towards the bedroom.

By eight I had tried on everything I owned and settled on my blue polyester blouse with the mauve flowers, and my best pair of jeans. As I picked up my brush, I caught my reflection in the bathroom mirror, pale freckled skin surrounded by dark drab hair. I remembered Iggy's face as he removed my elastic the night before. Black and deep, he'd said. I closed my eyes. Black. And deep. I tried to recall the feel of his fingers combing through the tangles. My scalp tingled. I left my hair down.

I spent the next hour and a half sneaking peeks through the thin slit in the curtains on the basement window, afraid to lift the corner to look out in case he showed up at that exact moment. My mind was jumping. What would we talk about? Painting. Of course, yes, I would ask him about his paintings. And teaching. He was studying education. How should I act? Was this a real date? Yes, or at least it was realer than any date I had ever been on. Would he kiss me? I remembered staring at his mouth, how I had imagined that very thing. What would that feel like? I brushed my teeth again, swishing toothpaste and water inside my mouth. And then, why was he late, had he changed his mind?

At 9:40, I saw feet strolling towards the house. I ran upstairs but forced myself to wait for his knock before opening the door. He smiled, slow and easy, and took my hand. I forgot about time. He seemed oblivious to it. I could see that time was not important to him. After living with Josephine's rigid schedules, dinner at noon, supper at five, no noise after eight, this sounded like a character trait I should aim for myself, to not be so wound up by the hands of the clock. As we sauntered off down the street, I decided that Iggy Connors was going to be a good influence on me.

We made our way downtown talking about art and artists. Several times I brought up the subject of education but his interest was piqued only when it came to teaching or studying art. When he discovered that I hadn't been to any of his favourite galleries, his face lit up. "You want to go tomorrow?" Without giving me a chance to answer, he laughed and turned me to face him. "You'll be my first student. What do you think?" All I could think was that I had a second date lined up.

We arrived at a seedy bar just up from the waterfront. When he opened the door the smell of beer and cigarettes and something pungent that I later learned was marijuana filled my nostrils. Iggy took my hand and led me through the crowd to where his friends stood drinking beer and watching the band, surrounded by the din of trumpets and saxophones. Four black men on stage kept referring to us as brothers; all around me were shades of pale. I clapped along with everyone else even though the music made my head hurt.

"Here." Iggy leaned in and pressed a joint into my fingers. "Try this."

I took a small puff and blew out.

"You got to hold it." He took the joint and inhaled, holding my eye as he held his breath, then exhaled. The smoke settled around us. "Works better that way."

Then he kissed me. A small kiss, but completely different from any boy I had kissed during spin the bottle. This time I had been kissed by a man. When he pulled back he kept looking at me, his face serious. The moment stretched, lingered. I didn't try to look away. I didn't want to look away from those intense black eyes. I wanted only to kiss him again.

That night I got stoned for the first time. I never laughed so hard in all my life. Iggy was funny, his friends were funny, even I was funny. Everything was hilarious, except the jazz. The jazz was awesome. What had at first sounded like bursts of noise became something powerful and profound, unbelievably harmonious. My nerve endings felt directly connected to the rhythm of the music, to the beat, to the crowd.

And at the end of the night when he walked me home, I told Iggy about Melinda and Josephine and Dad and Susan. I told him about Pierre, the father I would never know. When I was finished, when I had told him everything, I cried for a long time, and Iggy, who I had known for barely a day, held me close all the while. Then his warm fingers wiped the tears from my cheeks, and he looked into my eyes as if he could take my sadness into himself. I felt an immense release, followed by a rush of pure joy. I reached up and put my arms around his neck. No longer shy, no longer insecure, no longer quite me, I gazed into those pools of black. Then I kissed those incredible lips for such a long time my mouth felt bruised for days.

8

Katie slammed shut her accounting book and pushed out a chair for me at the table. "Long time, no see. How the fuck are you?"

Friday's empty chicken bucket sat on the counter. "Four days?" I said. "Longer than I thought."

I stepped over a garbage bag and sank into the chair. The floor was gritty from dried on slush. Ever since we'd seen a mouse skitter across the floor, we didn't dare remove shoes or even winter boots anymore. "We really should clean this place up," I said, looking at the sink full of dirty dishes and the cheese-slice wrappers on the counter. We always had the makings for a grilled cheese sandwich.

Katie reached under an old pizza box and retrieved her hairbrush. "Who the fuck cares? Not like we're around much."

Katie had let her hair grow out after that first cut in the fall. She said it was cheaper and easier but I suspected it had something to do with her mother's claim that her father had cried when he'd seen her picture. Now it was long and shiny again, sort of like Katie herself, who was tall and slender and pretty, completely different from the short round tomboy with the frizzy orange curls who stood up for me in Grade 1. Except for her mouth.

"Fuck, sure I haven't seen Syl in a week," she added as if to prove her point.

"She still going out with that loser Darren guy?"

"He's better than the last few. At least he doesn't freeload."

I flipped open Katie's shorthand book. "You think she does it with all of them?"

"Have you heard the racket they make in that bedroom? She doesn't even care that we're out here waiting for them to finish so we can go to bed ourselves."

"How about you?" I asked. "Still holding out?"

"Yeah, might as well. Sylvia's having enough sex for all of us."

"Honestly, I think she'd sleep with anyone."

Katie eyed me as she pulled the brush through her hair. "Not everyone will sleep with her, though."

"Oh? Come on, what's the dirt? Who said no?"

"Remember that crush she had on Simon in high school? Well, apparently she tried to do something about it when he was in St. Paul last August."

"I didn't even know he'd come home until he was gone again." I'd been disappointed that I hadn't run into him, but then again, I'd been holed up in my room most of the summer. "It's been two and a half years since I saw Simon."

She leaned in. "He wouldn't touch Sylvia. She told me herself when she was drunk."

"Now that doesn't surprise me. Iggy said he's turned into a right snob."

"I thought you liked Simon." Her hand stopped in mid-stroke. "Actually, I thought it was funny when you ended up with his brother."

"Have you seen the brother?"

Katie laughed. "Fair enough."

"According to Iggy, he's after getting so full of himself, he wouldn't be caught dead with a Newfoundland girl. He likes rich girls from the mainland now." I said it with disdain, but I was still glad he hadn't slept with Sylvia.

"Not hard to do better than Syl these days, she's such a slut." Katie paused. "Hard to believe that of Simon, isn't it? I mean, think about it, he was always at the house, and he never minded the noise or the mess or the youngsters wanting him to play with them, and he always did the dishes after dinner."

"Your mother had to make lots of extra chicken if he was there."

"He was just so down to earth."

"I know. Never would have expected he'd turn out to be one of those people who goes away and thinks they're better than everyone back home. But Iggy knows him better than anyone. He's some fed up with him."

She batted her eyes at me. "How is that gorgeous hunk of yours?"

"Still friggin' gorgeous." I sounded far more offhand than I felt.

She propped her elbows on the table. "How long's it been now?"

I pushed the book away. "Few months." One month, two weeks and two days.

By some standards, not that long, yet long enough that I thought about him constantly, and woke up every day waiting to see him. Long enough that I'd come to know his ways, how he was so forgetful, how he was always late, how he was either so unaware or so genuinely sorry that I could never hold it against him. I loved how he would appear at odd times, outside one of my labs or after work at Sobeys, always smiling, laughing, ready for anything. I loved his passion for music and books and art. Especially art. If he wasn't working on a painting, he was reading about painting, or going to galleries to study other artists. He'd insist I go with him, "Come on, you got to see this guy's stuff." I usually did because even though I didn't know much about art, I loved how he loved it. Besides, he wanted me to be with him. Me, Bridge.

"Fuck!" Katie threw out her hands. "How do you keep your paws off him?"

"Who says I do?" I said in my best suggestive voice.

She practically came across the table at me. "You didn't shag him, did you?"

"Well…" I acted coy.

"Oh my God! Was it wonderful? Did it hurt?"

I laughed and waved my hand at her. "I'm kidding. Not yet anyway."

"Such a good girl. Remember what Sylvia says, older guys won't wait forever." She gathered her books and stood up.

"Aw, where you going?" I said. "I never see you anymore."

"Study date with Adam."

I folded my arms and leaned back as she put her coat on. "Study date, my arse. Bruce might fall for that, but I know you don't study."

"What Bruce don't know won't hurt him," she called over her shoulder as she headed for the door. She stopped abruptly and turned back. "Shit, I forgot, Josephine phoned. I told her you were at the library."

"Thanks." That was our code. If one of us wasn't home when family called, whoever answered said we were at the library. In my case it was irrelevant. Josephine rarely called, and she wouldn't have cared anyway. But Katie's and Sylvia's parents still checked up on them so I played along. "She say anything about Dad?"

When I'd phoned home the Sunday before, which I did every Sunday right after lunch because I knew Dad would be sitting near the telephone studying his TV Guide, Josephine had answered. "He's in the hospital since Tuesday," she said. "A checkup, nothing serious." When I asked why they'd admit him for a checkup, and for so long, she said they wanted to run a few tests, and said "nothing serious" again. I was in the middle of mid-terms and couldn't make a trip to Exile Cove so I made her promise to call me when he got home.

"She said to tell you he's out of the hospital. Everything's fine." Katie dropped her books and tucked her hair up inside her apple-green hat. With her freckled face and smooth complexion she looked downright innocent. "Some fucking saucy, that Josephine. When I said you were at the library, she goes, 'What, again? What's she studying, brain surgery?' They know about Iggy?"

"Not from me."

Knuckles rapping on old single-pane glass sounded from upstairs.

She grinned. "There's Adam. Later, 'gator."

"You back tonight?"

"No. Crashing at Bruce's." She spun around and was gone.

Like me, Katie and Sylvia often stayed at their boyfriend's. I assumed I could think of Iggy that way, considering the speed with which things had progressed, from sharing a few sips of beer the night we met to sleeping in the same bed before the week was done. Occasionally the three of us girls overlapped at our apartment for a day or two, but usually we were all off in different directions. Sylvia lived from party to party. She rarely went to class. Katie had started working at a Chinese restaurant near Bruce's so she often stayed there after a shift. Given her numerous "study dates" I sometimes wondered if that was why she kept Bruce in the picture. As for myself, with a full course load plus typing assignments and my shifts at the library and grocery store, I scarcely had time to think. I had yet to decide my major. Nursing appealed to me but I didn't want to follow in Melinda's footsteps. Besides, knowing how Iggy felt about doctors, I doubted he'd have much love for nurses.

I still found it amazing that someone like me had ended up with a guy like Iggy, never more so than when I caught a glimpse of us in a mirror or reflective glass, plain-Jane me on the arm of the most handsome man for miles. And it wasn't as if he was using me. We hadn't gone beyond second base.

Yet he was so sweet to me, always buying me treats, showing up with a couple of the cookies I liked from the bakery and, when he discovered my love for Cheezies, making a point of keeping them at his house for when I was there. My clothes were getting tight.

Iggy was smart, too, although it wasn't obvious from his grades. That being said, he managed to pass exams and finish papers without ever appearing to study. Marks were not important to him. Ideas, and discussions about those ideas, were what mattered. He was an intellectual, a deep thinker. His desk overflowed with books by people whose names I couldn't pronounce, like Nietzsche and Sartre. He could even read in French. Once, I made a comment that the book he and his friends had been discussing, *L'Étranger* by Albert Camus, sounded interesting. The next day, he had a copy for me, in English. I read it right away. That book was strange all right. I told Iggy it was great.

Besides being sweet and smart, he was also protective. He and his friends smoked some pretty strong weed and it didn't take much to get me stoned. After a couple of tokes he would say, "That's all you need, babe." Then he'd hug me and pass the joint on to the next person. He never offered me other drugs they occasionally tried, the uppers and downers, the little blots on a piece of paper. That was fine with me. Drugs, harder drugs especially, scared me. Whenever Iggy's crowd did stuff beyond weed or hash, I was extra nervous, fearful of strange reactions, or worse, potential addiction.

I mustered the courage to bring it up one day as we were walking home from Sobeys, bags laden with pizza fixings for later that night when we all got the munchies. He assured me that he never took as much as the others. "And look at them," he said. "They're fine. They're all working or going to school. Right?" That was true. None of them acted like drug addicts. "It's a bit of fun, babe," he told me. He took my hand and stopped and turned me to look at him. "Besides, I made a promise to myself a few years back, and I'll make it to you now. I'll never take what I can't handle." His voice had that tone he used when he'd given serious thought to something, the tone he used for political or philosophical conversations with his more academic friends. Firm, determined. He meant what he said.

Iggy and I saw each other often but it was always at his instigation. I didn't have the confidence to drop in on him or to call and suggest going somewhere. Once, I didn't see him for four days even though I knew through the grapevine that he was around. But then, when we got together, he treated me like the most important person in the world, as if we were a long-standing couple. It was confusing but I'd never been in a relationship before. Perhaps this was standard couple behaviour.

Usually, if I didn't hear from him for a few days, he would have a new painting to show me. He'd wait impatiently for my reaction, looking from me to the painting and back again, as if my opinion was vitally important. It was easy to be forgiving then, even if he had no idea there was anything to forgive. I admired his work. Extreme, never understated, a frenzy of colour and texture. It reminded me of him. "So? What do you see?" he would say. When I couldn't figure out what it was I liked about a painting, I would compliment specific features directly, one of the colours perhaps, or the texture, the shades and shapes and brush strokes. Or I would relate it to him. "It's so intense," I would say, or "I love the wildness," or "There's this crazy energy."

Iggy said I had artistic vision, that I was one of the few people who understood what true art was. According to him, most people were full of pretentious words but had no concept of light and colour and texture and the interaction between them. But I got it, he said. I felt so proud, and was filled with a sense of commitment, to him and to his art. I was Iggy's most loyal fan, his biggest supporter. One evening I heard a friend of one of his roommates criticize a new painting. "That's giving me a fucking headache," he said. I marched over. "This work of art was painted by a true artist. Iggy Connors," I said. "Remember the name." I pictured a life of art shows and celebrations, Iggy, the artistic genius, at the centre, and me, his muse, right beside him.

Iggy claimed that the only other person who understood his work was his mother. My heart started a marathon when he said this. No one was more important to Iggy than his mother. When he spoke of her, I could hear the pride in his voice, the open affection in his tone. I was pleased to be in any category that included Mrs. Connors.

Still, the day after I hadn't seen him for four days, I was surprised when he mentioned that his mother had already seen his newest painting.

"But how?" I asked. "Did you bring it out home?"

"Huh?" He seemed distracted. "No…no, she was here."

"What was she doing in St. John's?" Even though I didn't have a real mother, most mothers I knew, like Katie's and Sylvia's, rarely came to town. Mrs. Mercer didn't even drive.

Iggy was cleaning his paintbrushes in the kitchen sink. It was late at night and I watched his reflection in the window. His forehead was furrowed as he worked at the brushes. "Well, she tries to come when I…" He stopped. "Mom's different," he said. "She comes in to go to plays and to the art galleries."

I picked up one of the cleaned brushes to dry it off. "Does she come alone?"

"Yeah…yeah, most of the time."

"She doesn't mind the drive, all by herself?"

He took the paintbrush from me and started to clean it again. "No…well, I guess not. She's really independent."

"She sounds pretty cool. I'd like to meet her some time."

"Sure. Maybe next time." He stopped cleaning and stretched his neck.

"You look exhausted. You okay?"

He nodded, then took my hand and led me to bed. He fell asleep immediately.

Considering the amount of time I spent at Iggy's, we were lucky his mother hadn't shown up when I was there. I cringed at the thought that she might have caught us in bed, even if we weren't doing anything. When we spent the night together, it was always at his place, a big old house he shared with a group of friends, although it was hard to tell who paid rent and who was crashing. Some were couples, others not. There were no rules in that house, no expectations, no limits. They shared everything: the cooking and cleaning, the dope and the beer. And at times, apparently, each other.

I pulled Iggy's door to as quietly as possible. It was 7:40 on a Saturday morning. I was due at work in 20 minutes.

"Hey, Bridge." Bobby Watson's hushed voice came from down the hall.

I looked up to say good morning and got an eyeful of his bare bum as he shut Marion's bedroom door. Then he turned around. I pushed Iggy's door open, went back inside and shut it with a bang. Iggy didn't stir.

I waited until I was certain that Bobby was in his own room, the room he shared with his girlfriend, Anne, who was away for the weekend. I peeked out, then crept down the hall, pulling on my coat as I hurried from the house.

Bobby was the first naked man I had ever seen, even though I'd spent many nights in Iggy's bed, with Iggy, both of us fully clothed. Iggy never pushed me to have sex, although it was obvious from the way he pressed against me that he wanted to. Sometimes I'd awaken to him rustling about on the far side of the bed. I would lie absolutely still, terrified that he'd discover me listening, knowing he would fall fast asleep when he was done. I longed to touch him, to lay my hand on his arm, his shoulder, his chest. But I had grown up under Josephine's puritanical eye, constantly scolded for things I hadn't done but might someday think about doing. Her warnings of dire consequences were always at the back of my mind.

When I returned to Iggy's that evening, I mentioned what I'd seen. "Bobby came out of Marion's room," I whispered, glancing about to make sure no one else could hear, although that would have been impossible. Iggy had Led Zeppelin blasting from the stereo. "He had nothing on."

Iggy didn't look up from the joint he was rolling. He was already high, having finished a toke just as I arrived. I watched him tamp the weed into the paper.

"I think they were sleeping together," I said.

He rolled the joint between his fingers until it formed a tight cylinder. His eyes closed as the music reached a climax. His face was covered with a two-day growth and I imagined how rough it would feel against my cheek.

"I mean…like, having sex, you know?" I said, getting the nerve to say the words out loud even though I was whispering in his ear.

His eyes, those gorgeous eyes that were now lazy stoned slits, met mine. He touched the tip of his tongue to the side of the paper and licked along the edge. When he finished, he placed it with the small pile he'd already made and reached for me. His hands caressed my back, then moved up past my neck, his fingers spreading into my hair. I was helpless as he pulled me in and kissed me.

"I guess he missed Anne," he said eventually, his voice hoarse. I neither knew nor cared what he was talking about as I leaned back in. He drew me on top of him and lay back on the old leather sofa. His hands slid down the sides of my breasts to hold my hips tight against his, then moved up across my bum and into the little vacant space in the back of my jeans. His fingers pressed into my skin, drawing me closer, releasing me, closer again. I heard breathing, his and mine, breathless breathing, tiny groans that I thought were from him, then realised had come from my open mouth.

Voices, then footsteps, passed through the living room. I sat up. Iggy followed. He looked uncomfortable and adjusted his jeans.

"What did you mean before, about Anne and Bobby?" I asked.

Iggy's eyes were intense as he reached out and traced a finger down the opening of my blouse. His hand slowed, then stopped at the edge of my breast.

"Bobby missed Anne," he said, leaning back and taking his hand with him. "That's why he went to see Marion."

I felt a chill where his finger had been. "But…what about Anne?"

"They have an understanding. We all do. It's cool, babe."

I pulled my hair into a ponytail as I thought about that. "You mean…you all…like…do it together?"

Iggy laughed lightly. "Not all together. But no one owns anyone. We're all free."

"So…Anne won't mind?"

"She wouldn't want him to be lonely."

"And…everyone… agrees with this?" I often fantasized about having sex with Iggy. Having sex with anyone else, or with several people, was more than I could fathom.

He took my hands in his. "It's a big bad world out there. Extra love is a good thing. You can't get too much love. None of us can."

I looked away, afraid to ask the questions that ran through my head. Was he free? Did he love freely? Did he and Marion visit each other on lonely nights?

He tilted my chin to look at him. "You okay, my sweet?"

The endearment caught me off guard. Tears sprang to my eyes.

"Oh, my poor little Bridge," he said. "What's wrong?"

"It's…do you…you know…do that, too?"

He eyed me seriously for a moment. "But I have you now, don't I?"

What did he mean by "now?" Did he or didn't he have free and easy sex with his roommates, before or now? "But we don't…you know…" I couldn't say it out loud.

"Hey, that's okay."

"But what about everybody else? Would they think…I don't know…"

"Shhh, when you're ready." He took me in his arms. "Don't worry about them."

He pulled me snug against him, our bodies so close I imagined our hearts touched.

That night, we all sat listening to music, drinking beer and toking up. As Procol Harum broke into "Whiter Shade of Pale," Iggy took a long drag of the joint and moved towards me. He pressed his lips to mine and blew the marijuana smoke into my mouth. I inhaled and held it as long as I could. He passed me the joint and I did the same to him. He smiled at me, into me. A soothing mellowness settled over my body. Head to toe, my nerves and muscles relaxed like I was immersed in a warm bath. A bath of love. Iggy was my warm bath, his smile, his deep dark eyes, his thick waves of hair, I wanted to sink into them, get lost in them forever. In a crowd of people, we were the only two in the room. I reached for the Cheezies.

Later, alone in his bedroom, when he started to undress me, I simply let him. I never thought to stop him, or help him. My body, my mind, felt no resistance, only a longing to be with him, to please him. Nothing else existed beyond the moment and my conviction that I was the woman who would keep him from ever being lonely again. This man, this beautiful man, with that soft full mouth that I wanted to kiss all night long, was mine. With a March storm lashing against the window pane, I stood silent, unable to move as he unwound my hair from its elastic, as his fingers unbuttoned my blouse, slipped the bra from my shoulder, undid the zipper on my jeans, piece after piece of clothing until I stood naked in front of him. He gazed at my body then traced a path along my thighs on up to my breasts. My skin felt hot and cold at the same time, burning as it shivered from his touch.

Only when he started to remove his own clothes did I look away, embarrassed. Not enough to stop him, but enough to stop staring at his hands as he unzipped his jeans.

Spellbound. Sleepwalking in a dream. Yet the clearest reality I had ever known.

I had finally found a place to belong.

9

As I swished the lettuce around in the ice-cold water, my newly awakened artistic side noticed how the leaves crinkled at the edges, and how the shades of green changed within each leaf and from leaf to leaf, from almost white to shamrock. Iggy would love that. He'd probably want to paint it. I sorted through the leaves and picked out the curliest, most interesting and colourful one and set it aside.

I warmed my fingers in my armpits and turned back to the recipe. What was a garlic press? How much was a clove? The only garlic I had ever seen was a bottle of beige powder at Katie's house. I picked off a segment of the round lumpy thing I'd bought from Sobeys and smacked it with the bottom of a pot a few times, then measured oil and mayonnaise and vinegar. Shaking the Parmesan cheese from the green plastic container, I felt about as sophisticated, and as far removed from Josephine, as I could be. The only salad she ever made was a bowl of iceberg lettuce drowning in bottled French dressing, and some-times, if she was feeling generous, a cold wedge of tomato on top.

Josephine. Just thinking about her made me angry. I had spent the night be-fore in Exile Cove. I tried to go out more often since Dad had been in the hospital. He said he was fine but I worried about him. I always picked Friday because Josephine had developed a Friday night bingo habit and would have left by the time I arrived. I would make a pizza, the kind that came in a box with the tin of sauce and the packages of herbs and cheese and dough mix. Dad and I didn't talk much, but from the persistent smile on his face and the way he kept patting my hand, I knew he enjoyed my company. He would pour us both a beer and we'd sit on the sofa watching TV, the plastic squeaking every time we moved. He ate the pizza even though he would have had his supper already. Maybe he wasn't fond of fish and brewis either. I'd be in bed when Josephine got home so I didn't see her until breakfast on Saturday mornings. Dad would make awkward small talk. For his sake I'd try to pitch in. Josephine would watch television, but at least she showed up and cooked us a pot of porridge. But when I had come down that morn-ing, Dad was standing at the stove, looking helpless as smoke rose from a pot. The kitchen smelled of burnt oatmeal. I took the pot and dropped it in the sink. "Where is she?" I asked, turning off the burner. "Gone out," he said, "antiquing or something." He turned on the tap. Cold water hit the hot pot in a sizzle of steam and smoke. "Her and Maureen left an hour ago." It shouldn't have bothered me. I didn't like Josephine. She didn't like me. Yet it still hurt. She was the nearest thing to a mother I had ever known and she hadn't even looked into my room to say hello. She hadn't cared enough to pretend to care.

To hell with her. I had our dingy little apartment all to myself. Any minute Iggy would come bounding through the door and down the stairs. I was preparing a romantic supper – Caesar Salad and Pasta Alfredo, neither of which I'd made before. Iggy joked that pasta tasted better than spaghetti.

The anticipation of sleeping in my own bed with Iggy beside me gave me goosebumps. When I was with Iggy I couldn't wait for him to touch me, to reach for me with that look of longing, his eyes that extra bit hazy. My mind still registered a moment of shock when I remembered that I was no longer a virgin, and that I was rather proud of it. That first time, waking up naked with Iggy next to me, I was wracked with worry. Would I get pregnant? Did I do it right? Was I as good as other girls he'd been with? How fat had I looked? Iggy didn't have a single roll of fat anywhere. Where I was soft and round in too many places, he was tight and muscular all over. I hoped the lights hadn't been too bright. Just as I had begun to wonder if I should cover up and slip my clothes back on, Iggy had stretched, rolled, and snuggled into me, pulling my naked body into his, his chest pressing against my breasts, his hands like fire on my skin. I forgot everything then, even my morning breath. But when he tried to enter me, I cried out in pain. He stopped immediately. The blood on the sheets terrified me. Iggy explained that a little blood was expected for a girl's first time, which was also why we hadn't needed to use birth control because I couldn't get pregnant. "We'll be more careful from now on," he said, holding me close. After that he tried to pull out before he came.

With the sauce simmering on the stove, I tidied the apartment and set the table. It looked drab for such a special night. Maybe Iggy would buy me flowers. He'd said he would bring wine. How cool was that, the two of us sharing a home-cooked meal, sipping wine, doing the dishes together after? I found Sylvia's green goblets under her bed, red stains crusted on. I set them to soak and moved the Chianti bottle with the candle in it from the windowsill to the table. I stuck the plastic flowers that Katie had worn in her hair for the toga party the week before into an empty beer bottle, washed and dried the glasses and placed them next to the napkins from the cafeteria. I stood back and thought a moment, then went to the hall closet and found Katie's Mexican shawl. I took everything off the table, spread out the shawl then set everything out again. I tossed the salad in our fake wooden bowl and placed it in the centre. There, now that was a table.

Eight-thirty. Iggy should have been here by now. Then again, Iggy still paid little attention to time. He said people were too caught up in watching the clock. And after all, we had the whole night.

I called his house. The line was busy.

By the time I cooked the noodles and mixed them with the sauce, it was after nine. Where the hell was he? Had he forgotten? Had he started smoking dope and lost track, sitting with Bobby and Marion and the gang, eating pizza? He wouldn't deliberately stand me up. He wouldn't deliberately hurt me. He was too sensitive for that.

Ten o'clock ticked by. I went to the stove and looked at the pasta. The long thin noodles had soaked up all the sauce and sat like a dead lump of intestines on the bottom of the pot. I found a lid and placed it on top. It didn't fit right. Tears stinging my eyes, I took it off and slammed it back on. I did that a few more times.

I called his house again. The line was still busy. I kept calling, over and over, until my finger was sore from the rotary dial. I gave up and took the pot of pasta to the sofa. If they'd settled into some good dope, they might have taken the phone off the hook. It could be hours before someone hung it back up.

Why would Iggy do this to me? After all the trouble I'd gone to, how could he? Didn't anybody give a shit about me? First Josephine, now Iggy. I hadn't heard from Melinda in ages. My eye landed on the Desiderata poster on the wall. If this was how my universe was supposed to unfold, it was just one broken dream after another.

My fork scraped metal. I looked down. Except for a couple of noodles clinging to the side, the pot was empty. I felt sick. Sick and fat and ugly and stupid. But mostly fat. I tugged off my jeans, pulled on my flannel pyjamas and flopped onto the sofa.

I didn't understand it. Iggy was not a mean person. Even tired or hungover, he was still thoughtful and considerate. And he generally had a reason if he was late or needed to cancel. Maybe something was seriously wrong. I ran upstairs to look out the small window in the porch door, checking the snow-covered steps for new footprints, then further down the street for signs of life, or worse, someone face-down in the snow. Nothing.

I went back down and sat at the table. The crisp salad greens had slumped into a soggy mess in the bowl. I threw them in the garbage. I tried to distract myself with television but the best thing on was a rerun of *Front Page Challenge*. My mind kept filing through an endless array of possibilities, from Iggy lying dead in a ditch to Iggy lying in bed with some other girl, some woman more likely, maybe Marion, someone who was prettier and thinner and smarter than me, someone who was more than happy to keep him from being lonely.

Midnight rolled around. I turned the TV off and curled up on the sofa. Twice I drifted off. Both times I bolted upright thinking someone was at the door.

Two in the morning, the phone rang.

"Bridge?" he said before I had a chance to speak. "Bridge, is that you?"

My heart did that leap it did when I hadn't heard his voice in a while, except this time it wasn't so little. "Iggy, where are you?"

"I started this painting and I fell asleep on the floor and I just woke up."

"Iggy!" I tried to sound scolding but was too relieved to pull it off.

"I know, Bridge, I'm sorry, I really am, honest..." His voice shot from remorseful to excited in an instant, "...oh, but you should see it, you got to see it, man, it's so cool..."

I'd spent the whole night torturing myself, and now here he was, alive and well, with an honest-to-God excuse that made up for everything. I couldn't be mad at him. Besides, I hadn't truly suspected him of being with someone else, even though I knew he had plenty of opportunities. A guy like Iggy always had opportunities. This was a fact I would have to accept if I was going to be Iggy Connors' girlfriend. "Iggy Connors' girlfriend." God, I loved the sound of that.

"Come over," he insisted. "Come on, right now."

"Iggy, it's two in the morning."

"Two? In the morning?"

"Yes. Didn't you notice the time?"

He took a second. "Well…sure…but you got to see this, babe. It's exactly like his music, full of black sound – "

"Whose music?"

"Cash."

"Johnny Cash? When did you start listening to him?"

"I love his stuff. You know that."

I did not remember Iggy ever talking about Johnny Cash. That didn't mean he hadn't. Some days it was hard to keep up with him.

"Get over here." His voice was so insistent that my resolve, such as it was where Iggy was concerned, started to dissolve. "I really want you to see it first. The sound is incredible –"

"The sound of what?"

"Of the painting. You'll understand when you see it."

"Maybe tomorrow – "

"No, now, right away. It'll be worth it, I promise. Please, Bridge, please?"

"But it's late and it's so dark and – "

"I'll be right over." The line went dead.

It usually took me 20 minutes to walk to his house. I'd barely had a chance to stash the pots and pans and wash my face before Iggy was at the door, panting, breathless, with that amazing grin on his face. He grabbed me up in a hug so fierce I coughed my breath out, then he wrapped my coat around me while planting kisses on my cheeks and my eyes and telling me how sorry he was and how great I was and wasn't life incredible. I shoved my feet into my boots and let him pull me outside, slowing only to shut the door. The night was overcast with a moody wind blowing from all directions, but Iggy's hold on my hand erased the prickle of unease that crept over me.

With Iggy leading, we ran and jumped and skipped along, meandering down Elizabeth Avenue, dancing around Churchill Square and the university campus, past the turnoff to Iggy's street and onto an empty parking lot, venturing further and further, up one unfamiliar street and down another, me in my winter coat and boots and pyjamas. I lost track of where we were as Iggy kept moving, nonstop, singing all the while. I would have sung with him but I didn't recognize the lyrics. We hugged and kissed as he lifted me high off the ground in the middle of a street, swinging me around until we both fell into a snowbank on the side of the road. Iggy jumped up and pulled me onto a path in the woods where we came to a bridge over a stream. He climbed up onto the railing and twirled and bounced from one foot to the other.

"Come down," I called up to him. "Come on, before you fall."

He laughed at me, big whoops of joy. "I can't fall," he shouted, his arms flailing as he fought for balance. "Don't you know that? They won't let me fall. Ever."

"Who?" My laughter faded. What did he mean? Who wouldn't let him fall? "Who's 'they'?"

"God. Life. Everyone," he yelled. "The universe." He jumped down, safely, and took my head in his hands and turned it sharply so I was looking downwards. "Look at that water. That's manna from heaven, man. It can't hurt me." A light snow had started to fall. His arms spread out and he turned in a slow, complete circle. "Do you see it, Bridge? Have you ever seen anything so beautiful?"

I looked around me. Cold clear water gushed over the pebbles on the bottom of the stream, tiny wavelets of silvery black rippling with the current. A nearby snowbank reflected the light of an almost full moon that had escaped its earlier cloud cover. The air shimmered with ice crystals. We were in a world of silver and white, clean and clear and sparkling. I looked up into Iggy's face and, for a moment, my breath held. His mouth was open to catch the drifting snowflakes and some had settled on his long, curled lashes and his thick, black hair. His eyes gleamed from the moon's reflection off the white snow and the night sky. I inhaled sharply. He was right. I had never seen anything more beautiful.

I saw the city through Iggy's eyes that night. It was magical. The criss-crossed streets were ours to explore, one leading to stone arches, another lit by neon signs, a wooded trail darker than the blackest night sky, each ripe with beauty and wonder. You just had to open your mind and it was there, in front of you, surrounding you, everywhere you turned. I marvelled that I hadn't seen it before. I was in love with life. And with Iggy.

We arrived at his house at five in the morning. Usually we made love quickly and quietly, sometimes twice. That night, Iggy put one finger to his lips and pushed me gently onto the bed. "You're so beautiful," he whispered as he removed my flannel pyjamas. "Don't move. Stay there and let me touch you, really touch you." His fingertips trailed down the sides of my legs, tracing a path along my hips to that sensitive spot he'd discovered behind my knees, down my calves to my ankles. He massaged the tops of my feet with his thumbs, pushing the skin in tiny circles, then nibbled at the tips of my toes, his eyes meeting mine across the length of my body. Slowly, ever so slowly, he walked his fingers upwards until he reached my arms, then my neck and shoulders, my face and my head, all the while teasing, stroking, kissing. When I tried to rise, to join in, he shook his head. "Shhh," he said. "Relax." I lay back and closed my eyes, feeling faint as he neared my breasts, waiting for him to touch me there. He circled the outside with his fingers, and then, like an electric shock, I felt his tongue on my nipple.

I heard myself moaning, my hands pulling at his hair, pulling him closer as my hips rose off the bed. His tongue slid down my breast, along to my belly button, then lower, and lower still. Iggy and I had never done that before. It had seemed wrong to me, and I'd always pulled him back. But that night, that night it was the most natural thing in the world, to be loved completely, brought to life by his touch, an artist's stroke on a blank canvas, rendering me real and beautiful, almost as beautiful as him. If Iggy could make me feel like that, nothing else mattered. I was his forever.

10

The Moody Blues album dropped from Iggy's hand and did a hula-hoop on the hardwood before settling onto the floor. "You're what?" he said.

I shivered, feeling extra vulnerable sitting alone on the edge of the unmade bed in a room crammed with easels and half-finished paintings and used brushes. "I'm pregnant," I said. My voice sounded thin, like I was in a cave.

His face had a stunned look to it, like the word was one he'd never heard before, an unknown concept. "Pregnant?"

I nodded. I'd done the test twice, yesterday afternoon and again this morning, spending scarce money on the hope that the new home pregnancy tests weren't as dependable as the box claimed.

"You mean…like…you're knocked up?"

"Yes." The single syllable belied the pounding fear and the unending questions that had racked me the last two days. What the hell was I going to do? What would Iggy want to do? Would we get married? Had this ever happened to him before? He was older than me. If so, what had they done, him and her, this nameless pregnant woman, all belly, who popped into my head? Would Iggy want a baby? Our baby? Or would he want to get rid of it? I'd heard about abortions at the Health Sciences Centre but I didn't know anyone who'd had one. Maybe Sylvia? I couldn't talk to her, though.

Trying to ignore the prickling behind my eyelids, I glanced up at Iggy. He had such a look of disbelief, of non-comprehension, that I didn't quite recognize him. He was looking at me as if he didn't know who I was, either. For a moment I was afraid he might ask if the baby was his. How did he feel about me? Did he love me? Good God, I was pregnant; he had to love me, didn't he? But he'd never said it.

"You got to be kidding?" he said. "You're knocked up?"

I focused on the black shiny vinyl circle on the floor. "Yes." My hand went to my stomach. My legs closed tighter. That's when I realized, although I wasn't sure how or why, that I could never have an abortion. I could never let anyone do that to me. But what about Iggy? Would he expect me to? And if I said no, what then? Would he leave?

His hand, the long fingers twitching, worked at buttoning the red plaid shirt he'd pulled on over his faded MUN T-shirt. He gave up after the middle two buttons. "Are you sure? Are you absolutely certain?"

I nodded, looking away to the pile of dirty laundry on the side of the bed.

"Christ!" From the corner of my eye I saw his hand fly up to whip shut the cover of the stereo on his dresser. "What the hell have I done? What am I going to tell Mom? And Simon, Jesus, what's he going to think? It was just supposed to be a bit of fun."

Nausea hit me. I stood up. My knees felt wobbly. I went into the bathroom, closed the door, turned on the taps full blast, and threw up as quietly as I could. Rinsing my mouth, I studied my reflection in the mirror. What did he mean, it was just supposed to be fun? Sex? Me? What? And who cared what Simon thought? Why the hell would that matter? The face in the mirror was no help at all.

When I got back to the room Iggy was sitting on the bed, leaning forward with his head bent and one hand covering each ear, which made me hopeful that he might not have heard what I was doing in the bathroom.

"God, I am so fucking stupid," he muttered, to himself it seemed, then he sort of flopped back, his body collapsing into the mattress like a dead weight.

I perched on the end of the bed. He turned to look at me. His face was gaunt. His eyes seemed smaller, deflated, the skin around them wrinkled and pale as he peered at me through the thick hair that fell over his forehead. He looked up at the ceiling. He stayed that way for so long I thought he might have fallen asleep with his eyes open.

I sucked in a mouthful of air. "Iggy? I'm sorry, really, I am…I didn't know… how, you know, to be more careful…" My voice shook as I stammered along. "… you were the first and I…I don't know what to do…oh God…what am I going to do…oh Jesus…" I was blathering senselessly now as I pulled my sweater sleeves down over my hands and hugged my arms to my chest. I felt Iggy looking over at me. I bunched my lips together and dared to look back, trying so hard not to burst out crying.

He sat up, blinked, and blinked again, several more times, shaking his head a little as if he was trying to clear fuzz from his brain. Finally, finally, he reached for me. He looked more like my Iggy then, the Iggy who made me laugh even when I was sad. My Iggy, wilder and crazier and smarter than anyone I had ever imagined being with.

"It's okay, Bridge. Everything's going to be all right." He stroked my cheek. "We'll figure this out. We will, I promise, okay."

Tears started pumping out of me in great gasps. He drew me closer. I crumpled into him, certain that as long as I had Iggy, everything would be okay. As my cheek pressed against his shirt, stale marijuana fumes hit my nose. Hand clamped to my mouth, I jumped up and ran to the bathroom.

I was in there a long time, sick with relief as well as everything else. I also wanted my face to return to its usual plain roundness rather than the blotched skin and swollen eyes that looked at me from the mirror. When I came out, Iggy was in the living room, his face so pale he looked like he might throw up himself.

"Mom called," he said. "She's on her way in. So I guess…maybe you should head home for tonight?"

I hadn't heard the phone. Then again, I'd been busy. "Should I meet her, I mean, considering?" I said, not that I wanted to, at least not right then. I was too shaky for that.

He rubbed his hands over his face. "It's not the best time," he said, adding, "It's...it's about Dad...yeah...that's why she's coming. You see, right?"

Iggy didn't talk about his father but it was common knowledge there was something wrong with him. "Yeah, sure." I tried not to sound too relieved. "Okay, I'll head out."

"I'll call you tomorrow," he said, leading me toward the door and passing me my coat, his twitchy hands finding my scarf and tying it around my neck, his hand on the small of my back, his raspy voice calling goodbye as the door shut behind me.

I walked home, alone in the fading light of a wet wintry day. I tugged at the scarf. Iggy had tied it too tight. As I turned the corner at the end of his street, I pulled it loose and breathed easier.

"No!" Katie's eyes and mouth made three distinct circles on her face.

"Yes." I drew my housecoat tighter.

Katie had arrived home 10 minutes earlier and immediately changed into her pyjamas and curled up next to me on the sofa. I'd been there all evening, by myself, pretending to study. I couldn't focus. I hadn't heard from Iggy since I'd told him.

"But...when? I mean, how long?"

"I only missed the last period. So, a month maybe?"

"Holy shit. Does Iggy know yet? What about your folks? Christ I can just see the look on Josephine's face? That fat-arse – " She must have seen the look on mine. "Oh, Bridge, I'm sorry. But what are you going to do?"

"I don't know. I still can't believe it. We weren't even having sex that long." I doodled a stick-man family on the side of my notebook. "Iggy says we'll figure it out."

"Oh, so he knows. Good. What else did he say?"

"Just...that it'll all be okay."

"What about...have you thought about having...you know, an abortion?"

I shook my head, then rubbed my forehead to try not to cry. It didn't work.

"Ah, Bridge." Katie put her arms around me. "Iggy's right. It'll all work out."

I nodded against her shoulder but couldn't stop crying. Tears had been leaking out of me off and on for two days – two long, petrifying days that I'd spent worrying and throwing up. I was about to tell her that, to tell her how afraid I was that he hadn't meant any of it, when the door opened upstairs and someone stumbled in, followed by Sylvia's brittle laughter and, "Fuck, watch it man, don't wake the nuns."

I pulled back from Katie and whispered, "Don't say anything to her, okay?"

"Of course not." She pushed me towards the bedroom. "I'll keep her out of there for a bit."

I curled up under my blankets, shivering even though I wasn't cold. Eventually Sylvia stumbled in, followed by Katie who shushed her to be quiet. I lay on my side feigning sleep until long after Sylvia's drunken snores had stopped for the night.

The next afternoon, I called Iggy. The clock on the wall ticked along as I waited for someone to answer, then for Iggy to come to the phone. My gut was in knots after three days of wondering if he'd changed his mind, whatever that had been, growing more terrified with each passing minute that I would end up alone, except with a baby.

As soon as he heard my voice, he wanted to know why I hadn't called sooner, how was I, did I feel okay, question after question, one running into the next in that high, fast voice he got when he was excited. Before I could answer, the gist of which would have been to ask why he hadn't called me, he said never mind, that it was okay now, and that I should get a taxi and come right over. "It's cold out, Bridge, and slippery. You don't want to fall, not now. Get a cab and I'll pay for it when you get here."

He was waiting at the door, cash in hand, when the taxi pulled up.

Inside, he tossed my coat onto the stair rail and led me to the sofa, where he laid an old afghan over my lap and pushed aside some empty beer bottles on the table so I could put my feet up. He disappeared for half a minute then returned, mug in hand, steam wafting from the top.

"Here you go now, it's some kind of ginger thing, Mom said that's good for the stomach. So, you doing okay? Everything all right?" He had a beer in his other hand and was pacing in front of the large picture window in the living room. "Are you warm enough? You don't want to catch cold. I can get my quilt? You're okay? Okay, so I've been thinking. We better tell your folks. Huh, what do you think? This weekend?"

"Already?" My immediate instinct said, what's the hurry. "But – "

"Yeah, yeah, I was thinking, yeah, you go out on Friday, and I'll come over for dinner on Saturday. Yeah, we'll tell them together."

My eyes followed him as he paced. "I don't want to spend two days with her."

"I know, but think of your father. You're always saying how much he likes it when you go home." He took a long swig of beer.

"Yes, but…"

"Now babe, we got to be mature about this." He put down the beer and took a last drag of the joint he had going in the ashtray. The paper burned down to his skin but he didn't seem to feel it. He stubbed out the roach, sat on the floor and leaned his head back against my legs with a great exhale of marijuana smoke. "After all, we're going to be parents," he added, turning to look at me. He moved the blanket and reached up to rub my belly. He stared at it for a few moments as if he expected it to do something, then leaned up and kissed it. He nodded slowly and laid his head in my lap. "I think it's time I break bread with the in-laws."

His voice slurred slightly. I ran my hand down the back of his head. His hair was greasy.

He stood up and marched off to the kitchen, leaving me wondering what he'd meant by in-laws. Was he planning to ask for my hand? That didn't sound like Iggy.

I followed him in. He had turned on the tap in the sink where a load of dishes was soaking. Gusts of steam rose up from the hot water but he plunged his hands right in as if it was lukewarm.

"Now, you got to get lots of rest from here on in. And eat better, too. And take vitamins. Yeah, and no more dope." He dropped the bowl he was washing and scooted off into the living room then hurried back with a dishtowel in his beet-red hand. "What else? You might need to back off on work hours. Yeah, you don't want to get sick. And I suppose you better see a doctor. Get some advice, what to do and not do and all that, yeah, yeah, there's a doctor on campus – " He stopped a half a second. "Simon's coming home next week. Mom said him, but no way. He's such an arse these days. Never calls, misses birthdays. Goddamn mainlander, Newfoundland's not good enough for him. No, find your own doctor. He's not one yet, anyway." He was talking nonstop as he scrubbed at the dishes in the sink.

"Hey, I'm five minutes' pregnant."

He rinsed a cup and put it in the rack. "You can't be too careful."

"I know, I know." All the talk about pregnancy was making me nauseous. "So anyway, what have you been doing the last few days?"

"Oh, you know, this and that, working on some new stuff," he said, swishing plates and bowls together. "Grab us a couple of beers, will you."

I looked into the living room. His half full bottle sat on the table. I went and brought it to him along with the tea he'd made me.

"You have a new painting? Where is it?"

"Yeah…but no, no…" He frowned as if trying to remember. "Mom took it… yeah, she took it to get framed," he said.

"She must have really liked it."

"Huh?" He yanked the plug from the sink, sending water spitting in all directions.

"Your mother, she must have liked the painting."

"She wanted Simon to see it when he's home. Prick…you're just a stupid teacher…that's what he thinks…fuck…med school so fucking hard…"

"I'm sure he doesn't think that. Sure your mother's a teacher."

He wasn't listening. "…not like being a teacher…can you believe that…" He was drying the dishes now, rubbing the dishcloth in hard arcs against the plates. "…I knows that's what he thinks…teacher and an artist I'd tell them…"

"Hey," I interrupted, "maybe I can meet her this weekend, too."

"What? Who? Simon? You know Simon already – "

"Not Simon. Your mother."

Iggy wiped his hands and drained his beer. "Oh. Right, sure. That's what she said too. Sure, that'll be good." He rubbed his index and middle fingers against his temple, pressing hard, his eyes squinting. His face was pallid and the whites of his eyes were etched with red streaks. The neckline of his T-shirt was dirty and a dark stain ran down the front of his red plaid shirt, the buttons of which were undone, except the middle two.

"You okay there, Ig?"

He raised his arms and wrapped them around the back of his head. "I got such a headache. You mind if I lie down?"

Trying to ignore the gust of stale sweat that had hit me when he'd raised his arms, I put my hand to his back and nudged him into the bedroom. The same pile of dirty clothes was lumped off to one side of his unmade bed. I pushed them over the edge.

Iggy curled up on his side on the bed, head bent, arms and legs drawn inward. His eyes were closed. I pulled the quilt up off the floor and snuggled it around him.

"You take it easy, stop fretting about me." I kissed his cheek. "It's all going to work out."

His eyelids fluttered then closed again. "That's what she said, too," he mumbled. "Going to work out...be okay..." His right arm came up and pulled his head lower.

I sat and watched him, my hand resting on the quilt over his shoulder. Within a minute the rise and fall of his body under my palm told me he was sleeping. I moved his hair back from where it had tumbled over his eyes. Would our baby have Iggy's thick, rich hair? The thought made her, or him, almost real.

11

Josephine twisted herself around from stirring the pot of porridge on the stove. Small piggy eyes squinted at me, her deteriorating eyesight trying to bring me into focus.

"Why in God's name would we want to have someone stopping in to eat with us?" she said in that exasperated tone she reserved especially for me, fixing me with that look, the one that said why was I messing with the status quo, why couldn't I leave things be, and maybe, why was I in her kitchen? "And why you staying an extra night? You never does that."

I didn't care that it was a fair question. "I just want to invite someone to dinner."

"You mean supper?" She turned back to the pot.

The fleshy bags on her swaggy arms swayed as she stirred. Maybe it was the pregnancy but I couldn't stand to be near her. Couldn't stand the sight of her fat everywhere. That was all I saw when I looked at her.

I crossed my arms. "Some people call it dinner."

"Dinner's in the middle of the day. Supper's at night."

"Fine." I leaned back against the counter. "I want to invite someone to supper."

"Go away with your nonsense."

"For God's sake, it's just a meal."

"Yes, and when was the last time you and me had a meal together?" she bellowed over her shoulder. "Christmas? Not even then. So don't go telling me it's just a meal."

"There's no need to yell."

"What are you talking about?" She turned and looked at me like I was crazy. "Sure I'm not yelling."

"God help us if you start," I muttered under my breath.

Dad shuffled in and sat at the table. He reached over to turn on the TV, then lit a cigarette. The first puff sent him into a fit of coughing.

I dropped into the seat across from him. "Would you talk to her?"

"Bridge," he said with one of those huge smiles he gave me lately, as if he hadn't seen me in a while and had missed me. "When did you get here?"

I studied him for a second. "What's wrong with you? I got here yesterday."

He rubbed his forehead. "Right, sorry." His hand waved at the smoke rising from the ashtray. "It's these darn cigarettes."

Josephine frowned. "Old fool can't remember to put his socks on half the time."

I touched his arm. "You okay, Dad?"

"Yes girl, I'm fine. Just tired." He seemed to think a minute. "When is it… right, Wednesday. How about coming to the airport with me Wednesday to get Melinda?"

"I might be working," I lied, "and I got so much homework."

"No, see, I can pick you up soon as I gets to St. John's and we'll head to Torbay then I'll drop you off at your apartment after, before I heads back out to here. Please? I knows Melinda would love to see you."

Not likely. "I don't know, Dad, I'm so busy."

"I'll come early and take you out for your supper." When I hesitated, he added, "We'll go to that Chinese place on Kenmount Road, just the two of us, have that cod au gratin you loves. What do you say?"

I was surprised he remembered. We hadn't been there in years. "Okay, sure." I gestured toward Josephine. "I want to have someone in for supper. Can you talk to her?"

He made a helpless face, as if such a notion was beyond his, or perhaps anyone's, capability.

"Yeah, some stranger," Josephine called out.

Not for long.

"…messing with dinner," she grumbled. "Friggin' nuisance."

"It's only half an hour," I said. Please God, let them all eat fast.

"Hmphh," Josephine grunted.

No wonder I'd been hesitant. Iggy would be running for the hills once he met the pair of them. I should have followed my first instinct.

Josephine jabbed at the chicken on the counter. "That's not going to feed us all."

"He won't eat much."

"How do you know? You can't tell him not to eat when he's here for his supper."

I jumped up from the table. "I won't eat much." So far, neither of them had thought to ask who this stranger was or why it was so important to me to have him in to disrupt their lives. "One meal. Is that too much to ask?" I was yelling now. "Christ, make no wonder Mel took so long to get a husband."

Josephine stopped stirring. She spun around, surprisingly nimble considering how much there was to spin. "Get your coat on, Andy. Go buy another chicken."

I spent the afternoon trying to study but that was impossible. Not only did I have to make the big announcement at supper, I was on edge about everything, about Iggy meeting Dad and Josephine, about the four of us sitting down to eat, about whether his parents would be around when I picked him up. I was especially nervous about meeting his father. I'd heard the gossip, that Bernie Connors had joined the army one man and left it another, that he was occasionally found wandering the streets in a white nightshirt and stocking cap, a ghostly spectacle that would either make you smile in sympathy or flee in fear. Shell-shocked, they called it, or nuts or cracked up, depending on who was doing the calling. Was he dangerous? What if he had a fit in front of me, or went all crazy or whatever it was people like that did? I'd never met a mental person before. I had no idea how to act around one. Hopefully Iggy's mother would be there. From all accounts, she was the exact opposite, a teacher at the elementary school, educated and refined. Some questioned why she chose to stick with such an obvious disappointment as Bernie Connors. Others admired her loyalty.

Did anyone think that about Dad, about why he stayed with Josephine, the mean miserable woman who no one knew wasn't his wife or my mother? I no longer considered Josephine part of my family, the definition of which, I realized with a swell of excitement, was about to change. How strange, to automatically be connected to a whole new set of people. It had never crossed my mind in high school that the Connors family, the smartest boy in school and his deranged father and sophisticated mother, would become part of my life.

"...stranger for supper...pain in the arse...better be worth it..." Josephine's grousing carried from the kitchen. "...should have waited till Melinda was here..."

Outside the living room window, thick, wet snowflakes fell relentlessly. I would have to leave early to scrape the windshield.

"...let her handle it, least she can do, gone the year...hoity doctor's wife now..."

Josephine was still complaining about Melinda when I shut the door behind me.

The fresh layer of snow made the road slippery. I slowed as I approached the bottom of the hill near the gas station. Jed Power was pumping gas into Maureen McCarthy's station wagon, the back of which was alive with tiny dog heads scurrying about and bopping up and down. Hose in hand, Jed was smiling at Maureen who, although at least 30 years older, stood close to him with her hand on the back of his neck. Every time I saw Maureen I thought of the red lacy garter I'd spied when her legs had gotten stuck to the plastic sofa cover at Melinda's wedding.

Melinda. This would be her first trip home since she'd moved to Toronto. Except for those few unprecedented moments the night she got married, moments that were given at once more and less importance by her subsequent admission that she was my mother, we had never been close. Her wedding night confession had done nothing to change that. We'd spoken on the phone a few times since, short obligatory calls where she talked about her new life, her committees and charities, her luncheons with other doctor's wives. As always when she called I could hear Victor speaking nearby. She would pause for a few seconds then come back on the line and say he said hi and when was I coming to visit or was school going okay or he hoped I wasn't living on leftover pizza, this with a little laugh from him in the background. She would sign off, her voice falsely cheery. Each time I said little, partly because she gave me no opportunity, partly because I didn't know what to say. I seemed to be waiting for something. Whatever it was, I was not getting it.

Our last conversation had been after I discovered I was pregnant. I didn't tell her. Melinda had gone on in that new voice of hers, an uppity tone that had little room for a Newfoundland accent. She'd talked about Victor's children, about their schooling and sports and piano, about how much they looked up to her. Except for a note of frustration when she mentioned Charlotte, she'd sounded like a proud mother, or what I supposed a proud mother might sound like. Listening to her boast about her younger stepchildren, I wondered what kind of mother she'd have been to me if she'd had the chance. Would she have been proud of me?

And what about me? Would I be a good mother? What was a good mother?

One single word came to mind, one word that filled my consciousness, so that I knew as well as I knew anything that love was the answer. As I drove through the slushy streets of St. Paul, I thought about love, about how it might feel to be well and truly loved, to be immersed in love like the foggiest Newfoundland day so it was all you felt whichever way you turned. What would it be like to be sure of love, where being loved was expected from the moment you were born?

Out of the blue, it hit me. I would soon have my own baby to love and to cherish as mothers supposedly do. I would be part of my own real family, with two people to love who would love me back. And I knew that I wanted this baby more than anything I had ever wanted or could ever want, and that the most important thing I could ever do for my child was to make her feel so loved and so wanted that she never doubted it for one second. Keeping one hand on the steering wheel, I placed the other on my stomach and made soothing circles around and around. "I love you, baby." My voice sounded small, embarrassed. I had never said those words out loud before. I decided right then that every day of her life I would tell my child that I loved her.

By the time I reached Iggy's street, I was almost looking forward to supper.

I counted off six houses to find a blue two-and-a-half-storey set back from the road. It was situated on a rise so that the whole front was visible even though the wood fence surrounding the property was at least six feet tall. On the top floor, two small windows looked down onto the street. There were three more in the middle, and two large ones on the main level, all framed with lacy curtains.

I parked next to a late-model red Datsun covered in a thin layer of fresh snow. An older model blue sedan with a thick crust of snowpack was parked in the corner. Simon had driven me home from debate meetings in that car in Grade 9. Sylvia had been sorely peeved at that. Iggy didn't have his licence. He'd never needed one, he said, living the life of a student in St. John's.

There was a tap on the driver-side window. "Hello? Are you Bridge?"

Through the steamed glass I saw a thin, pale face and shoulder-length silvery hair.

"I'm Grace, Iggy's mother," she said. "I thought I'd come get you."

I opened the door and got out. "Sorry, I'm early." I noticed her eyes, a distinct blue, Paul Newman eyes, I thought, Simon's eyes, except Grace's eyes were surrounded by an abundance of tiny wrinkles. They were the eyes of a woman who worried.

"No, no, you're right on time." She tucked her arm into mine. "Let's get in out of this snow."

She moved us toward the house, all the while talking about the weather, wishing winter away, hoping for an early spring, wasn't I cold in that short coat, did I hate the snow as much as she did, insisting I call her Grace, all in a fast, breathy voice. I could feel her bones, thin and sharp. Iggy had never described his mother but I had pictured her as strong and self-assured. I suppose it might have been the way he talked about her, how she was confident enough to drive to town any time she wanted, by herself, how she liked theatre and art, how she wasn't like other mothers. His tone had a touch of pride that I wasn't used to hearing when someone my age, or his, talked about their parents. I had expected her to be intimidating. She seemed more nervous than I was.

When we passed through the open gate she turned to secure the latch, tying a cord around it several times, then hurried us up the hill to the front door, which she opened with a key. Most people in Exile Cove didn't lock their doors, except us, of course. Josephine was adamant that no nosy neighbour was going to pop in on her any old time. Sure, like they're beating down the rafters to get in, I was tempted to say.

Before opening the door fully, she slid her hand in and grabbed what turned out to be a bell, presumably to prevent it from ringing. Once inside, she closed and locked the door. Meanwhile, she'd moved on to the subject of tea, and did I like tea, and wasn't it the ticket on a cold winter's day? We went through another locked door into a dimly lit hallway. Grace opened the door on the right and led me into the dining room. She pulled out a chair at a scarred wooden table. There was a bowl of fruit in the middle with a tube of glue plopped in the middle of it.

"Sit, sit." She sat, too, for a moment, then hopped to her feet and looked out the window, straining her neck in all directions. "Ignatius'll be here in a minute." She sat back down, twisting one hand within the other. "I'll put the kettle on." She jumped up and left the room.

As I waited, I was drawn to a black-and-white wedding photo in a large, antique frame on the opposite wood-panelled wall. I recognized Grace immediately. Her hair was dark and her face fuller, but otherwise she was a younger version of the woman in the kitchen making tea. Dressed in an elegant white gown with nothing on her head, she was tall and slender, though not as thin as now. The man next to her could only have been Bernie; I could see Iggy in his face, the full mouth, the high cheekbones. He was very handsome in his uniform, with a confident smile and pitch-dark eyes that stared straight at the camera as if they saw beyond the lens. There was a sense that here was a couple whose children would undoubtedly be just as photogenic, their futures just as promising.

Below that were two baby pictures, one with dark hair, the other light, obviously Iggy and Simon, both with dimpled chins. On the far side of the panelling was a trio of saints, Jude, Christopher and Patrick. There were two windows, each with a cluster of decorative bells at the midway point between the upper and lower panes, situated so that they would sound if the windows were raised. The other walls were covered with faded flowery wallpaper, the edges curling back from the Krazy Glue that failed to hold them in place.

Grace came in and placed a teapot on the table. She pointed at the wedding picture as if she knew I'd been looking at it. "Ignatius was born a year later."

"You made a lovely couple."

"My father didn't think so." She wagged a finger in the air. "Said I'd rue the day."

"Oh?"

She lowered her voice. "He didn't like Americans. 'Damn Yanks,' he called them. And he thought Bernie was beneath me, that I should have married a professional man, a doctor like himself."

"Your father was a doctor?"

Grace nodded again. "Wanted me to be one, too. I almost did it."

"Really?" I said, unable to hide my surprise.

"I guess you could say it runs in the family, now, you know with Simon." She moved to look out the window again. "Iggy says you're right smart yourself. An A-student, he said."

"I do okay, I guess," I said, embarrassed but pleased that Iggy had bragged about me. "You must be some proud of Simon, getting into med school so early." I didn't mention that Iggy wasn't proud, that he was more annoyed at Simon than anything. Apparently, I didn't need to.

"I wish Ignatius could see what an accomplishment it is. But yes, indeed I am proud. I figure he took up where I left off all those years ago. I was just after getting accepted myself when I met Bernie at a dance on the base in Argentia. A friend of mine was from Placentia and I'd gone out with her for the weekend. We fell head over heels, the pair of us." Her mouth tightened. "My father was furious. He never forgave me, even after I graduated from Teacher's College. Cut me out of the will. His only child and he never mentioned me when he died. Mom made up for it when she passed on, God love her, left me the works. She promised him she wouldn't. She was still mad at him, even if he was dead – "

Iggy barged through the door in his shirtsleeves, his head sprinkled with snow.

Grace's relief was obvious. "Ignatius, where were you?"

I stood up, happy to see him after two days apart.

"Walking out back," he answered his mother, though he was staring at me. "What are you doing here?"

"You're coming for supper, remember?" I said.

His eyes shifted. He glanced at his mother.

Grace latched onto his arm. "Don't mind our Ignatius. He gets his head in the clouds when he goes wandering off in the woods, don't you dear?"

He looked disoriented. "Is that today?"

I nodded uncomfortably. For lack of anything better to say, I gestured toward the baby pictures. "Is that you on the left, Iggy?"

When he didn't answer, Grace squeezed his arm. "Wasn't he the cutest little boy? And there's Simon too." She sighed. "Montreal is too far away. I was so glad when he called last week to say he was coming home for a few days. What a grand birthday present. I can't wait to see him."

"Oh, so he did call." I smiled at Iggy. "See, he remembered."

Iggy did not smile back. "Long live King Simon."

"Nice wedding picture," I said to change the subject.

Grace reached out to trace her finger along the edge. "It is a nice picture, isn't it?"

"It really is, Mrs. Connors. He was some good-looking."

"Like I said, call me Grace. 'Mrs. Connors' makes me feel old. And yes, indeed he was." Her voice, which had been wistful and soft, turned hard. "Goddamn army."

Iggy was staring at the picture, his index finger digging at the skin above his nose. "Goddamn doctors, you mean."

There was a fumbling sound at the door. Grace turned, and the smile covered her mouth again. "Here's our Bernie," she said.

The rumpled old man who shuffled into the room shared no likeness with the image captured on the wall, but it wasn't just because he was older. The vitality in the eyes of the man in the photograph was gone. Bernie's eyes were washed out, the colour no longer discernible. He looked innocent and harmless, and a little bit sad.

"Gracie? We got any dinner? I'm hungry." His voice was thin and reedy, the American accent barely discernible. "Gracie?"

Grace rubbed his arm affectionately. "We have company, Bernie. See? This here is Bridge Ashe from Exile Cove." For just a second she looked at my belly. Her eyes lifted to meet mine. "Bridge is a friend of Iggy's, a very good friend."

"I'm hungry, Gracie," he whined. "When is…?" He noticed my presence. "What's that?" he asked, looking at me as if he'd never seen anyone like me before.

"Christ," Iggy muttered. He sighed and turned to his father. "It's Bridge," he said, his voice gentle now. "Her name is Bridge, Dad."

Bernie looked confused. "Bridge? What bridge is he talking about, Gracie?"

Iggy glared at his mother. "He's worse than last week. What the hell did they give him this time? Christ, I wish you'd listen to me."

I was startled by the anger in his voice, especially directed at his mother. "It's okay, Iggy," I said. "Calm down."

His eyes, a glossy black now, shot from Grace to me. "What the fuck would you know about it?" His right hand held tight to the back of a chair.

I could feel my face redden. I bit my lip to stop it from trembling.

"Now, Ignatius," Grace started. "Don't be like that."

"Oh, fuck it." He shoved the chair into the table and walked out.

Grace turned to me. "I'm sorry, Bridgina. He worries so much about his father."

"It's okay, Mrs. Con…Grace."

The front door slammed. Iggy had left the house. When I moved to follow him, Bernie reached toward me with a smile so wide it brought some light back into his eyes. "Pretty girly. Who is she, Gracie?"

"Bye, Mr. Connors," I said, trying to inch past his outstretched arm.

"You want dinner?" He put me in mind of a child, naïve and trusting. He did not look dangerous.

"No, no thank you. I better catch up to Iggy."

He pointed to the untouched teapot on the table. "You'll come back later? And have some tea? And play cards?" he asked, each question rising slightly in tone.

Behind him, Grace nodded her head silently at me.

"Sure, later on, okay?" I said.

He took my right hand and brought it to his face, squeezing and holding it there, still smiling. I smiled back and patted his hand with my left, then eased free and away.

"Okay, bye. Gracie, I'm hungry."

I hurried outside. Iggy was leaning against my car, arms crossed, hands fisted.

"Right," he said, staring off down the road. "See you later."

"What about supper?"

"I'm not going." He took a pack of cigarettes from his pants pocket and lit one, his face scrunched into the flame. I had never seen him smoke anything other than weed. His bedroom had often smelled of cigarettes but I'd put that down to all the smokers who lived in the house.

"But she made two chickens."

"Not a good idea. Not today." The hard voice held a warning. "I'm heading back to town, soon, tonight. I just got to go."

I wasn't sure how to respond, but I sensed it would not be wise to remind him that the dinner had been his idea. "I'm sorry." What had I done wrong?

He closed his eyes for a moment, opened them and reached out to graze my cheek. "Oh God, no Bridge, it's not your fault." His voice was tender now. "But I can't do it after all. It's got nothing to do with you, I just can't do it."

"Iggy, did I do something?"

"No." He looked at the ground, then up at me. His eyes were misty, near tears. "Go home, babe, okay. Please? We'll do it next weekend. Next Saturday, okay? Tell them I'm sorry, something came up, and...tell them thanks."

I touched his arm. "But Iggy..."

His hands clenched. "Fuck, just go, okay!" He actually shuddered.

I yanked my hand away and turned to hide the tears that sprung to my eyes. When I turned back, Iggy was walking away, fast, heading not to the house but towards the woods. As I stood there, he broke into a run.

12

There was a pay phone outside the drugstore across from Mary Brown's Restaurant. For the first time in memory, the smell of spicy fried chicken did not make me hungry. Josephine answered after eight rings, an abrupt angry "What?" I made an excuse about old plumbing and burst pipes, said I was staying to help out. Could we reschedule for next weekend? Because really, she, Josephine, was right, I added in a rush. We should wait for Melinda.

Josephine was not giving in without a good gripe. She ranted on about the price of one chicken, never mind two, about Melinda not bothering to come home earlier, about Dad losing his marbles, until, after mouthing off about wasting food, she hung up.

I drove away from the drugstore and stopped at the intersection. Which way? Where was I going? I took a right, away from Exile Cove. Straight ahead was the hospital. I turned left and kept driving, past the church and the priest's house, the convent and the baseball diamond. Past the Ship's Pub where a group of young people, many underage just as I had been the few times I had snuck in, had started to gather on foot and in cars.

Tears streamed down my face. I took the next turn into the high school parking lot and turned off the ignition. I pulled my coat close and tried to figure out what had just happened. Never before had Iggy raised his voice or sworn at me. Why would he act like that, especially now? And what had he meant when he said, "I just can't do it?" What couldn't he do? Supper? Me? The baby? Jesus, what the hell did he mean?

I stared out at the field, empty now, where Katie and Sylvia and I had spent countless hours talking about leaving Exile Cove for St. John's. I'd been more excited than either of them. Going to university had been my dream since Grade 9. My English teacher, Sister Alphonse, a short, stocky, tough old nun who rarely had anything good to say about anyone, had convinced me to join the debate club. According to her, my brain needed more exercise. Being inclined to gain weight, I'd felt insulted at first. When I mentioned it at supper, Josephine snickered, "What brain?" and laughed out loud at her own joke. I realized that Sister Alphonse had meant it as a compliment, backhanded though it was. So I joined up. And it was there that I started to think that maybe I wasn't as stupid as Josephine said. I had no problem keeping up with everyone else, mostly people like myself who didn't fit in easily, and a few others, like Simon, who fit in everywhere and always would, even though they didn't try or seem to care. I came first in class that year, and Sister Alphonse's scowl disappeared for a second when she called out my name at the year-end assembly. "You're on your way now," she whispered. "Don't mess it up." That taste of success gave my confidence a boost, which was fortunate because Sister Alphonse died that summer, as did the debate club along with her.

I pounded the dash with my fist. What had I done? I wiped the sleeve of my coat against my eyes, felt the rough wool scratch my skin. Across the street, the waves rippled on their way to the breakwater, caught in the perpetual rise and swell of that enormous ocean. Infinite. Titanic. Dear God, help me. I pressed my forehead onto the cold steering wheel.

After all the trouble I had gone to just to get him invited, why would Iggy back out at the last minute? How could he…? I lifted my head. Iggy didn't know. He didn't realize that Josephine hadn't wanted him to come. I'd been ashamed to tell him, embarrassed that my own family couldn't be bothered to put themselves out to meet one of my friends, and that, in the end, it was only the possibility that he might take me off her hands that had prompted Josephine to give in to such an unreasonable request as to share her chicken supper with a stranger.

Still, it was rude of him. Wasn't it? Was it really such a big deal? Josephine had to cook anyway. Maybe I was overreacting. Iggy and I had a long life ahead of us. Did I want to start out like this, worrying about every little thing? Let it go, Bridge, I told myself. Focus on what's important. Focus on Iggy, sweet considerate Iggy, so gentle and kind, the type of man who would make a great father. His face filled my mind, with that brilliant smile. Then I remembered him standing by the car, that same face so haggard, hands shaking as he lit a cigarette, swearing and telling me to go. I pushed the image away.

I thought of his father. Iggy had been okay until Bernie came into the room. Was that it? Was he embarrassed too? Who knew what impact Bernie would have on a child's life, especially someone as sensitive as Iggy?

Iggy wasn't like other guys. I'd known that all along. That was part of what I loved about him, for heaven's sake. From now on I would be more understanding. So he missed dinner. Not the end of the world. He was having a bad day. Give the guy a break.

I was starting to feel better. There was a good reason after all. Well, not so much a good reason, but an explanation, sort of. Besides, the day hadn't been a total waste. I'd gotten to meet his parents. Bernie was harmless, someone who made me feel protective more than anything. I liked Grace, too, and thought she liked me. I remembered her looking at my stomach. Considering how close Iggy was to his mother, it made sense that he'd told her. And she obviously wasn't too upset about it given that she'd been so friendly. So I was pregnant. Life would go on.

I looked at my watch. Dad and Josephine would have long finished supper and she would be a little drunk from her third or fourth rum and Coke. With any luck she'd be snoring in her chair. Seamus was flying back to Alberta the next day and I was catching an early-morning ride to town with him. I had a good excuse to head straight to bed myself. I would be gone before Josephine got up the next morning.

As soon as I arrived back in St. John's, I called Iggy to confirm dinner on Saturday night. He wasn't there so I left him a message. When I hadn't heard from him by Monday night, I called again.

"He's not here, Bridge," Marion told me. "Haven't seen him since last week."

"Do you know where he is?"

"Bobby said something about him and Gord heading out of town."

"Gord?"

"Gord MacDonald. He's just back from Vancouver, some old friend of Iggy's." Her tone implied that he was no friend of hers. "If I see him I'll tell him to call you."

Iggy didn't phone and he wasn't there when I called him the next day, or the day after that. I tried to stay busy with work and study but it was hard to concentrate, alone, pregnant and scared, with no one to talk to. Katie had taken the week off school to go to a cousin's wedding in Nova Scotia. Sylvia was rarely around, but that was a relief.

I tried to carry on as normal even if I didn't see the point. What did Sister Alphonse's opinion matter now? The only math I cared about was the number of months left in my pregnancy, the only biology, reproduction. But final exams were on and it was too late to withdraw. At least I'd have a year of university to my credit. And I was already registered for spring session.

By Saturday morning, I was beside myself. I dreaded the thought of telling them, especially Josephine, by myself. I would be fulfilling every expectation she'd ever had of me. And poor Dad. He would be the subject of her relentless "I told you so's." And just how was I going to tell them? What was I going to say? I needed a plan. I needed Iggy.

And then, there he was, coming out of the library. He lifted me up into a hug as if he couldn't believe his luck running into me and said how glad he was to see me and how he'd missed me so much, before launching into a description of his latest painting and how I had to see it. "Oh, and guess what?" He nodded his head like he was ever so proud of himself. "I got us a ride home today."

"Great." Finally, I got a word in. "With who?"

"This friend of mine, he's got to make a delivery out there." He was backing away and waving goodbye. "We'll pick you up later."

Weak with relief, I went straight home. I didn't know what time he was coming and I did not want to miss him. Four hours later, an old hand-painted, two-door Beetle pulled up. I was waiting at the door.

I crawled into the back seat hoping Iggy would follow so we could have a chance to talk during the drive, but he let the seat flop back and sat up front. Before the door had shut the car was off in an angry burst of speed, the gears grinding from first to second to third within seconds.

"I'm Bridge," I shouted to the driver's head in the rearview mirror.

There was little face to be seen. The bottom half was covered by a black bushy beard, while on the top, tangled mounds of hair sprouted from his large head and fell over his eyes. Those eyes caught mine in the mirror. Growing up in Exile Cove I had often felt excluded but even then I knew there was nothing personal about it. You were an outsider because you fit certain criteria. You weren't from the area and that was that. It did not mean they didn't like you. I was pretty sure this man disliked me before he laid eyes on me.

Iggy turned to me. "He's Gord."

"Hi, Gord. Thanks for the ride."

Gord's eyes found mine again. Cold eyes, eyes that told me to shut up.

I burrowed into my coat in the drafty car and stared out the window. Fog had settled in like a grey blanket; only the dim outline of the trees was visible. The misty landscape, combined with a week of restless nights, soon had me dozing off.

I woke up coughing in a car filled with marijuana smoke. Despite my numb toes I leaned forward and asked Iggy to roll down the window.

"Hey, shut that," Gord ordered.

So he wasn't mute. "The smoke," I said. "It's – "

"It's fucking freezing. Roll it up."

Iggy turned to look at me. I pointed to my belly and mimed a baby.

Iggy smiled lazily, his eyes heavy.

"It's my fucking car," Gord shouted. "If she wants a ride, tell her the goddamn window's up or she's out on the road."

Iggy gave me a helpless shrug, too out of it to stand up for me.

"I get car sick," I lied. "Can we leave it down a bit?"

Gord gave Iggy an indignant glare. "Fucking women."

"Please," I added. "So I don't throw up."

"Fuck. Fine, don't fucking puke in my car." He yanked the sound to full volume.

Aqualung belted out of the tape deck. I turned my face to the stream of cold air from Iggy's window and said nothing for the rest of the ride.

"It's the next right," I yelled as we roared down the main street of Exile Cove.

Gord hit the brakes. My stomach lurched. He made a swift sharp turn up our hill, accelerating as hard as the old Beetle would allow past the ice-cream shop on the left.

"Stop! You passed it, the brown house on the right."

He slammed on the brake and pulled over three houses down. If I could have willed it I'd have vomited over the back of his seat right there.

Iggy pulled the seat forward to let me out, then jumped back in and shut the door.

"She's holding dinner for us, Ig," I said through the crack in the window.

He rolled it down. "Sure, babe. Yeah, no problem."

"Six o'clock, okay? Don't forget, Melinda will be there too."

"Melinda?"

"She got home a few days ago, remember? I told you she was coming."

He nibbled at his lower lip. "Yeah…yeah, sure you did."

"You want me to come get you?"

Iggy started to roll up the window.

"Iggy?"

He stopped and looked at me with a glazed expression.

"I said, you want a ride?"

"Where?"

"Here. For supper. Should I come get you?"

He thought a second. "No, that's right, Simon's home." His voice was mellow. "He'll give me a lift."

I started to lean into the car to kiss Iggy but Gord sped off, leaving me standing in dirty tire tracks of snow and slush. I braced myself and walked back to the house.

Inside, Melinda sat in her chair, her face behind a book. Josephine and Dad were watching television. Dad held a cigarette, Josephine a drink. Except for a new floor lamp between Josephine and Melinda and the unusual aroma of turkey wafting through the house on a Saturday that wasn't Christmas, it felt as though little had changed.

Dad looked up with the usual puzzled expression he greeted me with lately. Josephine gave me a vacant uninterested once-over and turned back to the TV.

"Welcome home, Mel," I said, moving further into the room.

She lowered her book. Her mouth cracked into a thin smile. "Hello, Bridgina."

The light from the lamp illuminated her from head to toe. Pink lipstick outlined a mouth that looked wider than I remembered. She was wearing mascara and eye shadow, and her manicured nails matched the shade of her lipstick. A navy skirt and light blue blouse were accented by a cream-coloured, fine-meshed shawl draped over one shoulder. Her legs were crossed, the top calf shining from the light reflecting off her expensive hose. She was wearing heels.

"Sorry I wasn't at the airport." After convincing me to go with him to meet Melinda, Dad hadn't shown up. When I phoned him later that night to ask what had happened, he'd mumbled something about slippery roads and needing to get on the highway before it got too late. I was fairly sure he'd forgotten.

Melinda shrugged. The shawl shifted. "I hadn't expected it." She spoke clearly, enunciating each syllable.

"How's Toronto?"

"Very well, thank you. How is school?"

"Good. How's Victor?"

"Victor is fine, thank you." Her tone was curt, as if it was presumptuous of me to ask. "Busy with work, of course, and with the children, as am I."

"It was nice of him to take me out for pizza when he was in St. John's."

Melinda flicked her hand. "He regretted it the next day. We don't eat that sort of food." She raised her book back up to her face, not a romance novel as I'd assumed, but a self-help book on raising teenagers. Not me, apparently.

There was a silence that only I appeared to find awkward. No one objected when I headed to my room. I lay down, planning to rest for five minutes only. I opened my eyes, sat up and looked at my watch – 10 minutes to six. I rushed out to the kitchen. Melinda was taking the turkey out of the oven.

At 6:30, with Josephine fuming in the background and Dad lighting one cigarette off the butt of the last, I called Iggy's house in St. Paul.

"Hello," answered a male voice that wasn't Iggy's.

"Can I speak to Iggy?" As much as I had liked Simon in high school, I was in no mood to talk to him.

"He's not here at the moment. Who's this?"

Shit. "It's Bridge Ashe."

"Bridge! How the heck are you? This is Simon."

"Simon?" I tried to sound surprised.

"Why are you looking for Iggy?"

"He's coming for supper."

"He is?"

I did not want to discuss Iggy with Simon. With all the negative things Iggy said about him, I wasn't sure how I felt about Simon anymore. Besides, I was in no mood to chat. "Sorry, I'm in a hurry." I tried not to sound irritated. "Do you know where he is?"

"Well…yeah, I think. Are you sure he was coming for dinner tonight?"

"Yes," I said, exasperated, for a moment understanding why he got on Iggy's nerves. "Where is he?"

"Sorry, Bridge, but you know Iggy. He's so forgetful, I'm sure he didn't mean – "

"Simon!" I gritted my teeth. "Tell me where he is."

"He's gone back to St. John's."

"What? Why?"

"I'm not sure. He dropped off his bag and said he was going to town and left."

"Why would he drop off his bag if he was going back to town?"

"That's what I thought. You know, I must have misheard. I bet he's coming back. He must be if he's supposed to be going to your place. That makes – "

"With Gord?" I cut in. "Did he go with Gord MacDonald?"

"Yeah, unfortunately." His tone said more.

"Oh. Okay. Thanks." I wondered if I sounded as small and insignificant to Simon as I did to myself.

"I haven't seen you in ages, Bridge. What are you up to?"

"I'm at MUN. Just home for the night."

"I'm heading to town in the morning if you need a ride."

"I'm not sure what time I'm going back."

"Call if you want me to pick you up."

"Sure, yeah. Okay."

"Listen, about you and Iggy – "

My mouth tasted sour. "That's Dad calling, I got to go. See you, Simon."

I pushed past Josephine and ran to the bathroom, slamming the door behind me.

After I splashed cold water on my face, I sat on the toilet, trying to think.

"Bridgina!" Josephine's voice screeched up the stairs. "Get down here."

I took several breaths, opened the door and went downstairs. Josephine stood in the kitchen doorway, cheeks bulging. Behind her stood Melinda, lips set in a taut bunch. Dad sat at the table fiddling with the TV dials.

"What the hell is going on?" Josephine barked.

"Give me a minute, would you? I got to make a call."

I dialled Iggy's number in town then moved as far from them as the phone cord would allow, and away from the turkey on the counter, the skin wrinkled, lifting from the carcass.

"What are you doing there?" I hissed when I heard Iggy's voice.

"You're not going to believe this – "

"You were supposed to be here an hour ago."

"I know, but listen, Gord needed – "

"But everybody's here, waiting for you."

"I know. Next time, I promise. But I had to do this for Gord – "

"To hell with Gord. What am I going to say?"

"Say I'll be there next week. Honest, I will."

"We were going to tell them." There was silence. "Iggy!"

"You tell them. And tell them we're getting married. And we will. This summer, after spring session. What do you say, Bridge? You want to get married?"

I held the phone in my sweating hand as an uneasy relief spread through me. This was not a proposal I'd have ever dreamed of, but at that moment, with Josephine's poison breath at the back of my neck, it was a dream come true.

13

I placed the receiver back into its cradle and turned around. They were waiting. "He couldn't get a ride out from town." They hadn't asked how I'd gotten home. They wouldn't know we'd come together.

Melinda folded her arms across her chest. "Who is this boy anyway?"

I didn't like the way she said "boy," but at least she had asked about him.

"Iggy Connors," I said almost proudly.

Melinda's arms unfolded and dropped to her sides.

Josephine pulled out a chair and heaved her bulk into it. "Where's he from?"

"Did you say Iggy Connors?" said Melinda.

Dad switched channels again. "That them Connors from St. Paul?"

"You mean up by the Bartletts?" said Josephine. "Near Mary Condon's?"

Dad nodded. "Saw Mary the other day." He looked under the TV guide. "Where's my smokes?"

"Christ's sake." Josephine reached over and smacked at the rectangular bulge in his shirt pocket. "Mary's dead this two year."

Melinda's eyes were intent on mine. I looked away.

"So, is that the Connors he's from?" said Dad, lighting a cigarette. He exhaled and went purple in a fit of coughing.

"Yeah," I nodded.

"How long have you been seeing him?" Melinda asked.

I shifted my weight to my other foot and sucked in my belly. "Oh, ages now. Since last year."

Josephine went and took a knife from the drawer and sized up the turkey, her face creasing in such concentration that her lips disappeared into her mouth. "Connors? What was it I heard about that name?" She cut off a flap of skin and chomped down on it. I felt the nausea rise up. "I knows what it was," she said. "Isn't the old man nuts?"

Melinda's left eyebrow rose and she stared hard at me.

"Yeah, but that's from the war." I tossed it off as if I had inside knowledge. "Everybody knows that."

"Everybody assumes," Melinda said with added emphasis on the last syllable.

Josephine waved a turkey wing about. "Yeah, there was something about that. You remember, Andy? What was it he done?"

Dad gave her a blank look. "Who?"

She stopped chewing and glared at him. "Talk about nuts. Who do you think? Bernie Connors, who they found at the church in his underwear."

"Right…sure." Dad, not looking at all sure, stood up.

Melinda looked from Dad to me. "What's up with him?"

"Nothing, going senile or something."

"In the middle of winter," Josephine said, then gestured towards Dad who had come to stand beside her. "Your father is starving, waiting this long to eat."

"What odds about Bernie," I cut in. "I'm not going out with him."

"Maybe it runs in the family," said Josephine. "Them things do, you know. Remember the Elliots? They were all simple. Right nuts, they were. And the Greens from Boyd's Cove…"

God help me.

"…The whole lot of them was *mental*." She said the word with utter disgust. "And then there was – "

"For heaven's sake," Melinda interrupted Josephine's trip down Crazy Lane. "Let it go. After all, she's not marrying him. It's just a date." Melinda turned to me, her face a question mark.

"Okay, enough." Josephine said. "Supper's on. Sit. Now."

I took a short breath. "It's not just a date…"

Melinda pointed her finger at me. "Now listen to me, Bridgina – "

"Jesus, it's not a big deal, Mel."

"Don't be stupid, you hardly know the man."

So now he was a man. "How would you know?" I said to Melinda.

"Because you never mentioned him before."

"Turkey's getting cold. Come on, Andy, get to the table." Josephine gave him a light push to get him started. "Doctor said to watch your blood sugar."

"Why would I?" I crossed my arms and planted my feet apart. "Not like anyone ever asks. All you can talk about is your fancy life in Toronto."

She paused. "Okay. Why now?"

Josephine took Melinda's elbow. "Never mind that. Time to eat."

"Why what now?"

Melinda brushed off Josephine's hand. "Why's he coming to dinner now?"

"What? Don't you want to meet him?"

"Oh, I have already. So has Victor," she said pointedly.

My throat seemed to close up. My breath felt shallow.

"You're only 17," she pushed.

"Eighteen, actually," I said, leaning towards her and wagging my head. "Although you'd think you'd know that."

"Yeah, yeah, so what? The point is, you're too young to get serious…"

"Oh, and who says?"

"…and he sure as hell isn't the pick of the crop."

Josephine, who had given up trying to get us to the table, was going at the turkey with a knife and fork. "How do you know about him?" she asked through a mouthful of food. "And how does Victor know him?" She brought Dad a piece of meat, popped some in his mouth and some in his hand, then went back to the turkey.

"He was brought in one night." Melinda nodded with certainty. "I don't know if he was on something or what but he was right off his head."

Fear wrapped around me like a straitjacket, fear that if she said anything else, if she kept on talking about Iggy, I would end up alone, unloved, again. Life with a baby without Iggy – the thought knocked the wind out of me. I was suffocating. She was suffocating me. Life was going from bad to worse, and the only person I could blame in the moment was Melinda.

I struck out the only way I knew how, the one way that would hurt her and maybe shut her up. "Don't mind her," I said, presumably to Dad and Josephine even though Dad was staring with wonder at the turkey in his hand and Josephine was head first into the bird. "She's jealous."

Melinda looked incredulous. "Jealous of what?"

We faced each other in the middle of the kitchen. "Of me and Iggy."

"My husband is a doctor. What in God's name would I be jealous for?"

"Because I didn't have to settle for an old man."

Melinda gave a mean little laugh. "I wouldn't push that one too far."

"Yeah? Well…" I sputtered. "You're just mad 'cause I've had a bit of romance."

"You have, have you?" Her voice dripped with condescension.

"More than you and Victor, making eyes over a dying woman. Never had a date, for Christ's sake, let alone a bit of fun. Not that he wanted any."

"What the hell's that supposed to mean?" Her Toronto accent was gone.

"Means he wasn't after you. He just wanted someone to take care of his brood."

"That's a rotten thing to say. Why don't you shut up?"

Now I had her. "Yeah, well it's true, isn't it? You got four of his to mind, and you don't even get to have one of your own. At least this one's ours."

Silence. Deafening. Silence. I tried to swallow but my throat was dry as chalk.

"Fuck!" This was from Josephine, followed by the sight and sound of her fork bouncing off the floor and skittering across the linoleum. Her face was a red blotch.

I moved closer to Dad.

Melinda slapped the counter. "I can't believe you're that stupid."

Dad took in a wheezy breath. He glanced at the clock on the wall, at the fork on the floor, at me standing next to him. "What's going on?" he said.

Melinda groaned. "Jesus, what the frig is wrong with him?"

"For Christ's sake, Andy." Josephine squinted at him across the room. "She's pregnant. Bridge is. The stupid thing got herself knocked up by that Connors fellow."

"Aw, Bridge." He looked at me sadly. "Aw, girl, that's too bad now."

Having sacrificed her fork, Josephine yanked off the second turkey wing and chomped at the meatiest part. "Like mother, like daughter," she muttered, wiping the grease from her mouth with her palm.

Dad took my hand and rubbed the back of it. "It's all right, we'll manage – "

"Manage? My arse we will!" Josephine flung the wing bone at the table.

He dropped my hand as the wing bounced in front of him, then took momentary flight before landing on the floor.

"I'm the back end of 60, Andy. I'll not be managing nobody's youngsters, not again. And look at you, you don't know your arse from a hole in the ground half the time. No, you're on your own, my dear…" She was walking towards me, her greasy finger jabbing the air above her grey head.

I jabbed back at her. "I'm not your 'dear.' And did I ask for anything from you? Huh? Did I, you big fat slob?"

Josephine's hand formed a pudgy fist. "No shame at all, I swear to God. And this is the thanks I get. You see that?" she said to Melinda.

"She reminds me of Charlotte before I took a firm hand with her. God knows where that girl would be now if it wasn't for my intervention." Melinda gave an upward eye-roll. "Young women certainly have changed since my day."

I stared at her, flabbergasted. "And I thought Dad was the forgetful one. Jesus." I put my hands on my hips. "Accidents happen, as you should well know."

"There's no need to get defensive," said Melinda.

"Defensive? You make out like you're some saint and then you tell me I'm stupid and you don't think I should get defensive?"

"Now, Bridge – " Dad tried to intervene.

I kept my eyes on Melinda. "Who are you to be giving advice anyway?"

"Well, I am raising four children."

"Yes, that you are. And like I said, we all know why."

Melinda's eyes narrowed. "When did you get to be such a mean little bastard?"

I narrowed my eyes back at her. "When I found out I was one."

"Shut up, Bridge."

"No, you shut up."

"How dare you. Show some respect."

I laughed out loud. "Respect? Why? I thought Herself was a bad mother but you take the cake, you do. You don't know the first thing about being a mother."

"And you do, I suppose?"

"Anybody would be a better mother than you, Miss High and Mighty from Toronto with your fancy clothes and your uppity accent. Well, you don't fool me. You're still just a bay-wop who never had a real date in her life." I was in over my head but I couldn't stop myself. "At least my child will be born out of love, not like you, throwing yourself at your own mother's boyfriend."

"You're a nasty little fucker." Her hand came up as if to smack me.

I stood my ground. "Hit me, will you? Go ahead. Try it. See, that's the difference between you and me. I'll love my child. I won't pretend she doesn't exist. I won't find someone else's children to love because I couldn't love my own."

She looked me over from bottom to top, then stared me in the eye. "Look in the mirror. You're not easy to love."

I couldn't speak. I felt like I'd been punched.

She wasn't finished. "I'm so fucking sick of you." Her Newfoundland brogue was back in full force. "Always mouthing off, ever since you were a youngster. Full of piss and vinegar and sauce. A bitchy goddamn bitch if there ever was one."

"Takes one to know one," I managed to squeak out.

"You're going to be a terrible mother."

"Not if I do the opposite of you two."

"Seventeen years putting up with this shit. Well, that's it. I got a new life now, even if it does come with Charlotte. I'm free of this hell-hole at last and everything in it." She grabbed her coat and glowered at me. "Especially you."

"Like I said, 18. And anyway, who cares? I got a new life, too."

"That makes it official. We're done, me and you. You got that?" She stabbed one finger at me. "And don't think you'll be getting any sympathy from Victor. He's my husband. He's not your father. He might have took pity on you but when I tells him about what you said here today, he'll be shed of you, too."

"Fine. We don't need you or anybody else. Me and Iggy are getting married."

She shoved her arms into her coat. "He can have you, the poor stupid nut. Good fucking riddance." She walked out and slammed the door.

Josephine watched her leave, then turned to me. "Now look what you done. And you thinks that fellow will marry you? Is that what he said?"

I felt weak at the knees, like I might faint if I didn't concentrate on staying upright. I fought back another stirring of nausea and waved at the smoke drifting from the ashtray. "Yes. He'll do his last course in the summer and when he's done he can get a job teaching. See? So we'll be fine."

"Married?" Dad looked shocked. "Bridge, are you sure…?"

"Andy!" Josephine snapped.

"The girl is talking about getting married."

"Goddamn right she is."

"Now, Josephine – "

She glared at him. "First Melinda, now her. Dragging my name through the mud. I don't know what I did to deserve this, I really don't."

"But she's so young," Dad protested.

"Well, that's the pot calling the kettle black." She set her sights on me. "As for you, I've had it up to here. I done my best, God knows I did. But now I wash my hands of it all. If you're set on getting married, you go right ahead."

"Fine. Just watch me," I yelled, then stormed into the bathroom and threw up.

14

Set on getting married? Was I? The way Iggy was behaving lately, I wasn't sure of anything. I would have listened to alternatives, suggestions, solutions, anything that might drag me out of the pit I was sliding into. After holding the secret in for weeks, I had thought I'd feel better once I'd told them about the baby, especially since I could also say I was getting married. Instead, there was a new queasiness that I could not put down to being pregnant. The pit had deepened. Walls were rising, swallowing me up. I would never get out.

When Simon called to see if I wanted that ride to town, I jumped at the offer. By nine o'clock I was in bed. When I heard Melinda come home, I closed my eyes, feigning sleep in case she came into my room. It wasn't necessary.

Everything we'd said kept replaying in my mind, except louder and uglier in the slow chokehold of darkness. I rose with the sun. The light of day brought little relief. I wrote a note for Dad and stuck it in his cigarette pack. I was waiting on the step when Simon's rental car pulled up.

He got out and came towards me, arms out, smiling. Still thin, but no longer skinny, his features, the long nose, the slightly pointed dimpled chin, now fit his face.

"Hey, Bridge. Great to see you." He gave me a short hug. "Here, I'll get that." He picked up my bag and put it into the back seat, then opened the passenger door for me.

"Thanks. Good to see you, too." I meant it. "Thanks for the ride."

"I was some glad when you said yes. Give us a chance to catch up."

As he pulled away from the curb, I tried to stare straight ahead but my eyes kept straying to the side view mirror. No one came out to wave goodbye. Feeling like a five year old again, I pressed my hands against my cheeks.

Within minutes we were on the highway, leaving most of Exile Cove sleeping or sitting down to their morning tea and toast. We talked without saying much, commenting on the fog, the sorry state of the roads, people we knew in high school. Simon was as easy to be around as ever, a straightforward guy who made me feel better about myself. As the tension I'd felt since arriving home drained away, I began to wonder why Iggy was so critical of him.

"So where do you live in town?" he asked.

"We got an apartment near the university, Sylvia and Katie and me."

"Right, Seamus said you were living with Katie. I didn't know Sylvia was there, too. God, but she was loud at basketball games."

"Sylvia likes to be noticed, especially around jocks."

He rolled his eyes. "She must've dated half the team. I could never figure out what the guys saw in her."

"Hazard a guess?"

Simon laughed and lifted his hands defensively from the wheel for a moment. "I'm not saying anything. No way. But if you really want to know, ask Seamus."

"Get on with you? Seamus?"

"Oh yeah. He and Sylvia ended up together on a few nights."

"You and Seamus, you're still good friends, aren't you?"

He looked surprised by the question. "Sure. Why wouldn't we be?"

"I don't know." There were plenty of reasons. Seamus struggled through high school; Simon was the top student. Seamus went through girls like wildfire; I'd never known Simon to have a girlfriend. Mainly it came down to how Iggy talked about him, how Simon thought he was far too superior – Iggy always said that with a haughty tone – to hang out with riff-raff from home. "You're so different from each other."

"You'll never meet a better guy than Seamus. Give you the shirt off his back."

"All the Dollmonts are like that. When I was little I wished I lived there." I had never said that out loud before.

He turned and smiled at me, a sympathetic smile but not a pitying one. Given his father, perhaps he'd felt the same way at times.

I changed the subject. "Katie would have a fit if she knew about Seamus and Sylvia. She's right fed up with the way Sylvia's been acting."

"Listen, I think the world of Seamus, but the man is something else when it comes to women. So I wouldn't be too critical of Sylvia."

"I know, but it's not the same, is it?"

"You tell me. You're a girl. Why is it okay for him and not for her?"

I remembered my own situation. "It isn't," I said, my voice flat.

We were quiet then. Simon kept his eyes on the road and his hands tight on the wheel. Tension started to build inside me again.

"Look, I'm sorry. I'm not sure if anyone's supposed to know but Mom told me last night."

I focused on the intermittent yellow line. "Oh? What did she say?"

"She filled me in about you and Iggy. And about…you know…"

The yellow blips turned into a solid stripe. "Yeah…I know."

"I told her about you calling, and Iggy going back to town."

There was that churning in my stomach again, the one from the night before, the one that wasn't just morning sickness. I put my arm across my belly and stared out the side window.

"Iggy didn't tell me about you two." He paused a moment. "Anyway, congratulations. A baby, wow, that's big stuff." He sounded sincere. "There are excellent prenatal vitamins these days. I'll send you some."

"Thanks." I felt like crying.

I sensed Simon's eyes on me, checking the road and coming back to me again.

"You know he doesn't mean anything by it, right? Last night, I mean."

I sighed. "Sometimes I don't know what to think when it comes to Iggy."

"How long have you been going out?"

"Since January."

"So not that long."

I blushed. "I'm not that type, you know – "

He extended his arm. "No, I mean…" He paused. "Just that it's no wonder you don't know what to make of Iggy. I've known him all my life and he still surprises me."

I said nothing. I was starting to feel disloyal.

"He was a really good big brother, that's for sure. You know about Dad, right?"

"You mean, about him getting hurt in the war?"

"Sort of. He was working on the base. There was an explosion or something, he ended up with a brain injury. That's all Mom would ever say. She hates talking about it."

Close enough. Showed what Melinda knew. "I met him last week. He was really sweet."

He looked pleased. "I'm glad you liked him. Most people don't know whether to run away or give him a hug. You know, Mom said Dad was one of the smartest men she ever met. A real career man, loved the Forces." His voice became subdued. "It all changed overnight."

I didn't try to make small talk. Exhausted from the night before, I let my eyes close and listened to the radio. The Beatles. Elvis. Paul Anka. I opened my eyes.

"Iggy's going to be a good father, Bridge," Simon said after a while, then added, "I never knew Dad as a father. Iggy was the man of the house, trying to take care of everyone. I remember all of a sudden Mom and Dad would be 'gone to town' again. I was probably seven or eight before I figured out that 'gone to town' meant the Waterford. Sometimes it was just me and Ig for weeks at a time."

I turned to face him. "How old was he?"

"He'd have been a teenager by then but I don't know when it started. It's been that way as long as I remember. Him and Mom trying to protect Dad, and me, too, I guess. I suppose that's why she and Ig are so close, they counted on each other to keep the family together. They did a pretty good job of it too."

"How about you? Are you close to your mother?"

"Me? Yeah, but it's different. The two of them are like a closed shop, hard to penetrate, you know? Not that I mind. It's just the way it is." He glanced over. "Sorry. I'm going on, aren't I?"

"No, it's great. Explains a lot, actually. I kind of wondered about his relationship with your mother. It's different from other guys'." A few seconds passed. "How about you and Iggy? You close?"

He nodded. "I can't imagine growing up with a better brother than Iggy. I was kind of a sickly kid, scrawny, not much meat on me." He gave a little shudder. "Iggy would pump the cod liver oil into me, and pour more milk than tea in my cup in the morning, and he'd never let me leave the house without breakfast. He never ate it himself." He paused, frowning into the windshield as if trying to figure something out. "That being said, we're not anymore. Close I mean. Most of the last 10 years either he's been gone or I have, so it's been hard to keep up with each other. I miss him, actually."

"I suppose the neighbours watched out for you when your folks were gone?"

He looked shocked. "They never knew a thing. I remember one time someone came to the door asking for Mom. Iggy said she was gone to Mass. She'd been in town for a week. He told me it was no one's business, to just say she was at church and people would leave us alone."

I shifted to face him. "What did you do for food? Iggy doesn't cook."

"Tomato soup and ham sandwiches, sometimes TV dinners. We didn't have them too often. Mrs. Greene at the store might have got suspicious. Iggy would write up a list like Mom did, even copy her handwriting, then pretend she sent him for groceries. She kept a stash of cash hidden in the house so if she had to take off, we'd never go hungry."

"That must have been hard on you guys, being alone so much."

He leaned his head back against the headrest. "Iggy always made an adventure out of it. Two-brothers-surviving-alone-in-the-wild sort of thing. It was tougher for him, I suppose, knowing what was actually going on, but he never complained."

"He doesn't talk about your father much." I looked out the window, off into the distance. "I wish he would."

"I know. It really gets to him. When he got older, he hated when Mom took Dad to the hospital. 'Goddamn quacks,' he'd say. Thing is, they never proved him wrong."

I looked over at him. "What do you mean?"

"Nothing they did made a difference. Dad never got better and Mom kept having to bring him in. Iggy said every time he came back home he was worse than the last."

"That's why Iggy hates doctors. And now you're going to be one."

"He was some pissed when I told him. 'What's with this doctor bullshit?' he said, 'shoving pills at people all your life?' He's still mad at me."

I took a moment. A question was forming but I wasn't sure how to put it, or if I was ready for the answer. "Can I ask you something?"

He looked over, his forehead creased. "Of course, Bridge. Ask me anything."

Who better to ask? Simon knew Iggy better than anyone except Grace. "Is Iggy…I mean…he doesn't have anything wrong…does he?"

He glanced sharply at me. "What are you getting at?"

"I mean…" I hesitated. "I mean like your father."

"That's crazy. Dad had a brain injury."

"So there's nothing wrong with Iggy?"

He looked offended. "Hell no, no way, he's fine," he said. "The doctors said so."

"Doctors?" Little alarm bells rang. "Why did he go to the doctor?"

Simon stared straight ahead. I had the impression he'd said more than he wanted to. "Actually, I wasn't supposed to know about it but I kind of eavesdropped," he said. "It was a few years back. Iggy…he went sort of haywire. They thought it might have been from a bad batch of magic mushrooms."

I remembered the night we met and Iggy's friend offered him mushrooms, how adamant Iggy had been when he said no. Relief flooded through me.

Simon looked over. "Iggy's just…he's wired different."

"You mean, like as in artistic?"

"Yeah…right. He's high strung and goes a bit off the rails sometimes but that's what we love about him, right?"

I had been breathing in short shallow breaths. I inhaled, long and deep, followed by a controlled exhale. Simon was almost a doctor. Surely he would know.

"Right?" he said again. "That's what makes him Iggy."

"Absolutely," I said. "That's what makes him Iggy."

15

Katie sat on her suitcase at the foot of the bed. "Come on, pull harder."

I tugged on the tiny zipper pull-tab. It didn't budge. "See, that's a sign. You can't go to Fort McMurray if your suitcase won't close."

"I have to. Aunt Louise got me a job, a real job, in an office, making real money," she said, rubbing her fingers together. "Besides, it'd be a shame to waste all that time in school, even if I'd be happy to never see another Jesus typewriter."

"But you love working at the restaurant. Think of all the free food."

"Confucius say, 'girl cannot live on chop suey alone.'"

I laughed, then slumped onto the bed. "Everybody's leaving, one person after another. What's so great about Alberta anyway?"

"Jobs. People want to work, Bridge. Simple as that." She eyed the clock. "Okay, pull that sucker. Taxi's on the way."

I looked around the bedroom, crammed wall-to-wall with three beds, a dresser, a nightstand and mirror. There was almost no visible floor. "I'm going to miss this dump."

Katie nodded, her face downcast. "I know. Me too." She picked up my hair-brush and grinned at me. "Maybe you can work in the ice cream shop."

"Don't be talking. I offered to spell Josephine off, give her more time to make her foolish dolls. She looked right at my stomach and said no way was I going to be on display for innocent children to gawk at."

"As if she gave a flying fuck about children."

"Anyway, there's no youngsters out there. All that's left are old people. Old people and me." I took the brush from her and pulled it through her long red hair. "And now you're leaving, too."

She reached up and grabbed my hand. "I know. I'm sorry, Bridge. But with Mom and Dad and all the kids there now, I want to be there, too. I miss them."

So did I. Whenever Mrs. Dollmont had sent in food or some sort of treat for Katie, there was always something for me, too. Not for Sylvia, just for me. And if they came to town they would take me out for supper with them, like I was part of the family. I forced a smile. "You think they'll stay all the way out there?"

"Yes, girl. Sure half the family's there. Mom's sisters, a couple of Dad's cousins. And everybody got jobs. Mom's talking about building a house. Seriously, can you see us, the Dollmonts, in a brand-spanking-new house? Jesus Mary!"

Katie lifted herself up and dropped back down on the suitcase. I pulled. The zipper zipped.

I sat on the bed. "You're going to have so much fun. Seamus'll be bringing home all his buddies from the rigs. I hear they make piles of money."

"Should be good for a few suppers." Katie hugged my arm. "I can't believe you're getting married. It's so grown up."

I leaned my head on her shoulder. "Who's going to stand up for me?"

"You could ask Sylvia – if you can find her."

We hadn't heard from Sylvia in weeks. We'd seen little of her all winter. She'd dropped out of university and spent most of her time at Darren's, so much so that she thought she shouldn't have to pay rent. We couldn't make her understand that until she gave us notice, she'd have to keep paying because we couldn't afford the apartment by ourselves. She knew better, or should have. But she'd been doing a lot of drugs, not just marijuana, harder stuff. She didn't tell us that. She didn't need to. The last time she'd come home to get some clothes, Katie and I had tried to talk to her about it, but Sylvia had told us both to mind our own goddamn business. And when she found out that I was pregnant and Iggy and I were getting married, she laughed out loud. "Glass houses, Bridge," she said. "Glass houses." "What does that mean?" I asked. She laughed again. "That's what you'll be living in with Iggy Connors. He's a fucking head, man, a righteous fuck-up if ever there was one." "You're a fucking head!" I yelled back, a not unfamiliar sense of disquiet amplifying my anger. "Nothing but a strung-out whore, you big – " Katie put herself between us and got Sylvia out of the house. The next day there was an envelope on our door with the last month's rent, "CONSIDER THIS MY FUCKING NOTICE!!!" written across it in red marker. We hadn't seen her since. I knew Katie was worried about her. I wasn't. My worry plate was full up.

"Sylvia can go fuck herself," I said now.

"Tut tut tut, Bridgina, watch the language."

"You're one to talk. I think you're worse than ever."

"Fuck!" Ever since her aunt had called with news of the job, Katie had been trying to cut down on her swearing. "I'm some sick of it, watching what I say all the time. Fuck, fuck, fuck!" she screamed. "So there."

I laughed but immediately felt sadder. "I wish you weren't going." Katie was more like family than my own mother. I would certainly miss her more.

"We'll write all the time, and you can tell me about the wedding and how fat you're getting. Iggy's such a hunk, you're going to have the most adorable baby. I can just see it, a little bit Iggy and a little bit you…"

As Katie talked, I tried to envision it, this baby, this little human who would be part me and part Iggy. I couldn't picture a person, more a plasticized doll, faceless, not male or female, not human.

There was a knock on the upstairs door.

We hugged each other so tight it hurt. "Have fun in Alberta," I said. "Say hi to everyone for me."

She got halfway up the stairs then turned back to hug me again. "Send me a picture, okay? And don't worry so much. It's all going to work out. You'll see."

Then she was gone.

The rent was paid till the end of the month. I couldn't afford the apartment by myself, and Dad had said that if I could fix up his mother's old place over the ice-cream shop, Iggy and I could live there rent-free. I tried to savour every day of freedom I had left, but it was no fun without Katie. Our life in St. John's was over. On the last day of June, with spring session behind me, I closed the door to our tiny home and returned to Exile Cove, alone and pregnant.

After two nights of sleeping under Josephine's roof, two mornings trying to ignore her scowling face at the breakfast table, listening to her slurp her tea and watching her eat with her mouth open, I decided to get to work on the apartment.

"I'll get more done if I sleep there," I said to Dad when he asked where I was going with the bag of clothes.

"Aw, but you just got home." He was holding my hand and patting the back of it.

"I know, but I'll be right upstairs over your office."

"Ha, some office," Josephine said.

I ignored her. "I'll bring you cups of tea."

Dad looked confused.

"Your insurance office. You know, under the apartment."

"No one to keep an eye on her there." Josephine smirked. "Not that it matters anymore."

Dad looked even more confused at that. "What does she mean?"

I leaned into him and shook my head. "I haven't the foggiest idea," I lied.

He giggled. "I don't know what she's talking about half the time," he whispered.

"Consider yourself lucky," I whispered back. I picked up my bag. "Don't miss me too much, Josephine."

"I'm sure I won't get the chance. Doubt you'll be buying your own grub."

I almost told her to stuff her food, but I had so little money and so many things to spend it on that I had decided I'd try to eat when she was out or asleep. As it was, I already had a stash of groceries packed away in my bag of clothes, along with three big bottles of prenatal vitamins from Simon that had been waiting for me when I arrived home. "Welcome to the family," the note had read. "Can't wait to meet 'Little Bridge.'"

"Lots of food here," Dad said.

I kissed him on the cheek. "Thanks, Dad."

He took my hand and pressed it to the spot where I'd kissed him. I was reminded of Bernie.

As I walked the 50 yards down the street towards my new home, I thought how wonderful it was, after all these years, that Dad and I had slipped so naturally into giving affection. We touched each other now, on the arm or the back or the head, a quick pat, a brief moment of contact, for no reason at all. And we hugged each other. The first few times when Dad had hugged me I'd barely hugged him back, and had wondered what was wrong with him. But then I thought, what the hell? He was sweet and gentle and kind and fatherly, what could be wrong with that? I was more than happy to reciprocate. Had he always wanted to be more loving? Why had we wasted so much time?

The apartment was small and dank and dirty, with an odd chemical smell that I could not identify but that wasn't from the refrigerator. When Dad had replaced the ancient ice-box with their old harvest gold fridge he'd had the sense to leave the door open. I shut it and plugged it in, grateful for the rattle of the motor kicking in to accompany the intermittent hiss of the toilet. I tried the stove. Two of the four electric burners didn't come on and a third flicked sparks at me. I would have to master the art of one-pot cooking. The tiny windows let in limited light and no air at all because, except for the bedroom window, they were painted shut. Looking at the walls, I wondered why anyone in their right mind would paint such a small space brown. Then I remembered the walls of the funeral home. There must have been leftover paint. Josephine hated waste.

I mixed a big bucket of bleach and water and started with the bedroom, scrubbing everything from top to bottom, then did the same with the bathroom. The rings of rust in the toilet bowl looked to be permanent. I poured the bleach in full strength and hoped for the best. By the time I made up the foamy into a makeshift bed, the room smelled far better than I did.

I woke up, disoriented, to the sound of my stomach growling and the plop, drip, plop, drip of the kitchen and bathroom faucets leaking in concert with each other. I sat up and opened my eyes. I remembered where I was.

And where was Iggy? Iggy was in St. John's, living like he always had, except now Gord MacDonald was there, too. Gord. The last time I had seen him was when he'd dropped Iggy off at the apartment two weeks earlier. As I'd opened the door, Gord had caught my eye. "Have fun with the old ball-and-chain," he yelled out to Iggy. Iggy had laughed, then blushed when he'd turned and seen me standing there.

I flopped back down to the floor. A few months ago I was wild and free, happy and in love. Everything, the world, was open to me. Now, here I was in Exile Cove. I would get married, have a baby, settle down, just like countless girls before me.

Yes, I would have a baby, someone to love and to cherish and to hug every day. By the end of the summer Iggy would have his teaching degree, even a job. Martin Foley, one of Grace's fellow teachers, was in the hospital. He'd had a stroke right at the end of the school year. Jim Johnson, the principal, had told Grace that the temporary position was Iggy's if he wanted it – one of the perks of small-town life. So Iggy would have a respectable job and we would be a family. Plenty of people had done it before me, and under far worse circumstances. Their lives had turned out fine. So would mine. I just needed to accept what had happened and make the most of it.

Over the next week I worked on the tiny kitchen and small living room, cleaning everything, fixing what I could. I had a phone installed. Dad got the toilet running more smoothly, and he fixed one of the stove burners. I began to feel hopeful.

I saw little of Iggy. He had to stay in town and study, he said, the job depended on it. When he did come out from St. John's we were busy planning the wedding, such as it would be, although in truth, Iggy did more nodding than planning. And that was starting to get on my nerves.

Iggy had just finished rolling a couple of joints while I kept a nervous eye on the door. There was no television at the apartment so I had watched out the kitchen window until Dad and Josephine left the house. Every Saturday afternoon they ran errands. Why they waited until Saturday was anybody's guess. As Dad got behind the wheel I wondered if he should still be driving. But he backed out of the yard and changed gears and drove off in the right direction. Within seconds, the car had disappeared from view and Iggy and I headed over.

"Like I said," he shouted over the blare of the sports announcer. "Whatever you want is fine with me."

I put down the slip of paper where I'd been keeping track of the wedding plans. "For God's sake, Iggy, put the friggin' dope away," I said, no longer pretending I didn't mind. "Look, it's your wedding, too. Should we have fruitcake or chocolate cake?"

Someone scored on the television. He bounded off the sofa. "Goddamn it!" The plastic covering squeaked as he threw himself back down onto it.

I didn't care who was playing or what kind of cake we had. I just wanted him to be involved. He had no opinion on the rest of the food either, whether we should do a roast beef or a turkey or a pot of spaghetti. His pat response was to drink a beer and nod.

Other than his parents and Simon, he hadn't asked a single person to the wedding. Neither had I. Katie was too far away, and I hadn't seen Sylvia since she'd moved out. Anyone else I'd associated with in St. John's had been more their friends than mine. Iggy's friends weren't mine either. If he didn't want to invite them, I couldn't. I hadn't heard from Melinda since she'd returned to Toronto. Except for the few neighbours and relatives that Josephine felt obliged to have in for the big day, there was no one to invite.

"So?" I said impatiently.

He drummed his index finger on the coffee table. "Fine. Fruitcake."

"That's what Katie said in her letter, but you told me you hate fruitcake."

"I do." He picked up a joint and sniffed it.

"Then why have it?"

"Because you wanted me to pick."

"But why pick something you don't like?"

"Christ! Who cares? It's friggin' cake. It doesn't matter."

I could feel my eyes filling up. "It should matter."

Iggy sighed. "Don't, okay? You're always bawling lately."

"I am not." It was true though.

"Fine. You're not." He took out a book of matches. "By the way, Simon's not coming."

"Yeah, right." After our conversation in the car, I was pretty sure Simon wouldn't miss his brother's wedding.

"It's true. The man is going to be an important doctor, you know, he can't just drop everything to fly to the colonies." His tone was sarcastic, his face serious.

"You're kidding?" I'd been counting on Simon. Even if he was there as Iggy's brother, he was also my friend, regardless of what Iggy had to say. "Why?"

"Hospital bullshit, rotation or something. Well, he can rotate himself, he can."

"You don't believe him?"

"Nope." He rolled the joint between his fingers.

"Why not?"

"Because it's a load of bullshit. He's doing it to spite me."

"What are you talking about?"

He shook his head. "Nothing, never mind."

"Come on, Ig."

"Forget about it, will you." His voice had gone from angry to resigned.

"What's the big deal? Tell me."

He leaned back. "Fine. I think he's jealous."

"About what?"

"Mom. It's always bugged him that we're so close."

"I don't think so, Ig." Simon had been pretty clear about that.

"And now I'm beginning to wonder," he said, looking at me with a curious expression. "Maybe you, too."

"What? Now you're being ridiculous."

"No, think about it. He knew you first. You were friends in high school."

"Exactly. We were friends."

"Maybe he wanted more." He nodded. "Yeah, I bet he did. And now he's poking his nose in, trying to take control, sending vitamins, for Christ's sake."

"Don't be silly. He was just being nice."

"I'm not silly. I know him, remember. Simon doesn't get what he wants, he pouts. Or runs to Mom." He jumped up off the sofa. "Momma's boy, that's what he is. Prick can stay in Montreal. I don't give a shit. I told him that too. You know what he said? He said fine, have a nice life. What a prick."

"That doesn't sound like him at all."

"Oh that's Simon. Mr. Doctor. Wants it all, doesn't care about anyone else."

"Funny, I never thought of Simon like that." I glanced at my list. "I wouldn't worry about it. He'll show up."

"Oh? And why do you think that?"

"He's your brother. He loves you."

"How would you know? You haven't seen him in years."

"He drove me to town a couple months ago."

"Wow, a whole hour, maybe two." He stopped moving. "Don't be picking up for him. That's the last thing I need." He flipped open the matches.

I stood up. "Are you nuts? You can't light that here."

He looked defiant for a second, then closed the matches. "I better go. Pick whichever cake you want. I'll be fine either way."

He already had the door open and was putting on his coat.

I followed him out to the step. "But we still got stuff to figure out." My voice was louder than I had intended. The curtain moved at the Smiths' across the street – old Gladys, watching and waiting for something to report to her two crazy sisters.

"Right. I'll be back later on. I got a few things to do."

"For Christ's sake, Iggy," I said, reaching out to grab his arm, "do it later."

But he was walking down the path, more like running, waving and weaving, oblivious to the cold and the wet. I watched him go, knowing he was gone for the day.

To hell with it. Fruitcake it would be.

16

Random sounds – a cough, a door opening, a whisper – echoed through the nearly empty church. Josephine was parked in the front pew on the right, Grace sat in the one on the left, Bernie dozing next to her. Simon had not shown up. In the second row a few neighbours and relatives waited, occasionally glancing at their watches as if they had somewhere to be, or twisting to peer down the aisle to where I sat in the last pew.

Grace turned and gave me a little wave. Even across the length of the church, she looked tense. She usually did, although I still didn't know her well enough to read her moods. She had no time to play doting mother-in-law-to-be. She was a full-time teacher and when she wasn't at the school she was with Bernie. He had a caregiver during the day and for times when Grace had to be away, but otherwise Grace took care of him. During the summer she was with him full time. While Iggy had been away at university, I hadn't felt comfortable going to their house. Grace hadn't pushed me to visit, but she did stop in to the apartment, hurrying in and out in that nervous way she had, each time for just a few minutes, less if Bernie was with her because he'd often be asleep in the car. Perhaps she drove around so he would nod off and give her a few minutes' peace. When he did come up to the apartment he did the same thing as the day I'd met him, take my hand and hold it to his face and smile at me. I kept his favourite treat, Oh Henry! bars, in the fridge for him, which earned me another childlike smile. Grace always had an excuse for coming by – bringing over some of Iggy's things, showing up with a lamp she no longer needed or some perfectly good pots and pans when she bought herself a new set, and the week before, their old television. And there was always something for the baby, some clothes she'd found on sale, a stroller she'd picked up at a yard sale, a new car seat Simon had asked her to buy for us – Iggy called that a guilt gift. Occasionally Grace had something for me – a pretty maternity top, the raisin scones I loved from the bakery in St. Paul, a new hair buckle. "You're exactly what Iggy needs," she told me. "A sensible girl to straighten him up." Shortly before the wedding, I over-heard Iggy asking her which shirt he should wear to the ceremony, to which Grace replied, "You have Bridgina now. Discuss it with her." The blue stripe, I decided. He never asked.

I had hoped that Melinda would soften her stance and call to say she would be home for the wedding, if only for Dad's sake. That didn't happen. When the phone did ring, it was Katie and her family calling from McMurray, all of them taking turns to send best wishes, Katie, her parents, her younger brothers and sister singing "Here comes the bride...," Seamus making wisecracks about the honeymoon. I didn't tell him there wouldn't be one, or what Josephine had said to Dad when he'd asked about it. "Honeymoon?" she yelled. "They already had that. Besides, how do you afford a honeymoon when you don't got a can to crap in?" Dad had slipped me two 50s when she wasn't looking. "If you wants to go away for the night," he said. I'd stuffed it in my purse. Josephine was right.

Josephine must have felt me staring at her because just then she turned and glared in my direction, her cheeks abloom with the same red angry patches that had appeared the night they found out I was pregnant. I had thought she would pretend to be happy, if only so that those in attendance, the invited guests and the nosy old biddies who had nothing better to do on a cold rainy July day, might think that all was well, that this was a joyous occasion. But Josephine was too bitter to fake it. We both knew she wasn't my mother. No one else did. To the neighbours, I was her pregnant unwed daughter. So no, she felt no joy over my marriage and my growing belly. She felt anger. Anger and shame, plain shameful shame. Shame on all our heads.

Now she had another reason to fume. Iggy was late.

Dad waited, stone cold sober, in the vestibule. For Melinda's and Victor's wedding the year before, he'd abandoned his usual sobriety and been half-crocked before the mass started, singing the hymns like he'd been saved by God Himself. Which is how he probably felt when he passed his 34 year-old daughter into the hands of the local doctor, even if four children came with him. Now it was my turn. Why did he look so worried? Did he, somewhere within his sporadic consciousness, sense that something was not quite right? Or was he simply trying extra hard not to forget anything? I'd gone over the procedure with him a couple of times and had written down what he had to do and put the piece of paper in his pocket. Was he out there reading it and wondering why it was taking so long to get going?

I heard Marion trying to make small talk with him. All she got in return was an occasional mumble. I felt bad for her. I knew she didn't want to be here. She and Bobby, who had broken up with Anne shortly after I'd seen him coming out of Marion's bedroom, were a couple now. Bobby was Iggy's best man and had convinced Marion to be my maid-of-honour.

As the wet wind battered the stained glass windows, I tried to ignore the fusty smell of old damp wood combined with yesterday's incense. I knelt on the riser in my white Woolworth's summer dress and closed my eyes. I might not have wanted to get married, but more than that, I didn't want to not get married. What if Iggy had taken off? What if Gord MacDonald had shown up? Iggy could be in St. John's by now, counting his lucky stars that he'd escaped.

I shoved my hands together, the fingers so tightly entwined that the underside of my nails flooded with blood. "Jesus Mary, help me," I prayed. "Don't let him do this to me. Don't let him leave me at the altar. Please, God, please, please, please, help me."

I felt a presence beside me. I opened my eyes to find Grace kneeling in the aisle next to my pew. "He'll be here, Bridge," she whispered, her anxious eyes darting first to the rear of the church then to Bernie at the front. "He will. I know he's coming."

I couldn't look at her. I didn't believe her.

She pressed my hand. "He gets so nervous when something important is happening, and when he goes walking in the woods he loses track." She leaned in closer. "You know Iggy, he doesn't pay attention to time. He's a good man, Bridge. He wouldn't do this to you. I know he wouldn't."

I studied her face. She meant every word. Could it be possible?

"It'll be good for him to settle down, get away from all that stuff he does in town. That's all he needs, stability. You. And a baby. He won't need the other stuff then."

There was a noise from outside, a car door slamming, a man shouting. The church door opened. A cool breeze hit my legs. Grace gave me an overly bright smile and hurried to her seat. I slid over to the end of the pew out of view. We had enough bad luck.

I heard laughter. Someone stumbling. Others trying to help. In the front pews, heads turned, straining to see through the back wall. They couldn't so they looked at me. Soon Iggy and Bobby sauntered, arm in arm up the aisle, the shoulders of their suit jackets damp, their hair soaked. They looked like they had all the time in the world.

I went out and took Dad's arm. The music started. Marion stepped forward and proceeded down the aisle. Dad and I followed, his eyes focused straight ahead, his face stern. As we neared the altar, his arm pulled me closer to him. He stopped and hugged me and kissed my forehead. He looked into my eyes and I nodded. "Thanks, Dad," I said and stepped away. Still he stood there. I took his arm and led him to sit next to a rigid Josephine, then went to stand in front of Father Murphy.

I looked at Iggy. He smiled back, a gentle tranquil smile that lasted throughout the entire ceremony. His eyes were glazed, his movements clumsy, his voice slurred. I'd never seen him so wasted. It was our wedding day and my husband-to-be was zonked out on something, not just a few joints, something far more powerful. Yet no one said anything. Not the priest, not Dad, not his mother.

And not me. I stood there and married him, prompted him when he couldn't remember his lines. I promised to spend the rest of my life with him, a man who, if I was honest, I did not know all that well. As I said my vows, I felt I had to force the words out of my mouth and into the air. Quick, onto the paper to become fact. Hurry, before I looked at him again. Because whenever I looked at him I knew that whatever the future held, I had no one to blame but myself.

Iggy spent the next two days between the bed and the bathroom. When he wasn't throwing up or sleeping, he was moaning about how he was no good for me. "I'm sorry, babe," he'd add, teary-eyed. "You deserve better. You do, Bridge, you really do." Seeing him so sick and sad and apologetic made me feel better, at least. Then he went back to school. A week later we consummated the marriage.

With Iggy away, I spent my time trying to transform our small, cramped apartment into a home. While I scrubbed the glue off the walls and hammered nails into the floor to keep the lino in place, I had time to think. Too much time. What did I know about raising a baby? All the love in the world wouldn't help if she got sick and died of a fever or drank poison because I hadn't put a lock on the cupboard or fell over the stairs or the apartment caught fire and we couldn't escape. The possibilities were endless.

I practically memorized the pamphlet the nurse at the doctor's office gave me. Everything at the library in St. Paul was old and outdated. I read it all, from infants through to teenagers: what to do, what not to do, and how to do it or not.

One day a heavy package arrived from Simon. Inside were two hardcover books, along with some nutrition pamphlets, more vitamins, and a note saying he was sorry he missed the wedding. He'd signed off with, "Take good care of our little Bridgie-Bee, Your favourite brother-in-law, Simon." That made me smile.

I read the book on raising a healthy baby from cover to cover, twice, and started to feel more confident. But first I had to get her out. I turned to the second book. It made childrearing sound easy compared to childbirth. I remembered the blood after the first time with Iggy. What happened when you were dealing with a head and shoulders?

I had to stop thinking about it. I had to keep busy. I used some of Dad's honeymoon money to buy a gallon of bright yellow paint and started in on the kitchen. Halfway through, the fumes were getting to me so I tackled the windows, chipping away at the layers of dried paint, trying to coax the wood apart. It was futile so I opened all the doors, upper and lower, and set up a fan to increase circulation. I spent the next few days painting the kitchen and living room. Iggy said it was like living inside a giant lemon. I had to admit it was bright, too bright, but I couldn't afford to change it.

I bought some thick rope and made a homemade ladder that could be secured to the leg of the bed and almost reached the ground when it was thrown out the bedroom window. I borrowed some of Dad's tools and an old manual on home repairs and puttied the holes in the door where the latch had been and screwed the latch back. It was still loose but at least the door shut.

Even though Iggy had officially moved in, I felt like I lived alone. He had class one night a week but spent most of his time in St. John's. There was always something on the go – graduation parties, a friend wanting help moving, a concert he couldn't miss, a new art exhibition. When I complained, he said he needed to keep busy, something to take his mind off the possibility of failing that last and final course, his ticket to freedom, he called it. Waiting was not good for Iggy.

He couldn't sit still, not even to eat. After a minute in his chair, he'd jump up, sandwich in hand. He would trace a figure eight pattern between the two rooms. By the third lap, I'd be dizzy. The sandwich would end up crusting on the counter.

Then he would run to his mother, literally. "I got my own room there," he explained one day. "I can't paint here, it's too crowded. Besides, Mom needs help with Dad. He's not doing so well lately." Grace had said as much herself, so I didn't argue. And although I felt he should have been more interested in fixing up our apartment, after his first few attempts, I'd come to think it would be more productive to do it myself. He had become so frustrated with the loose latch that he'd ripped it off altogether. Now the door didn't shut. After that, he decided to paint the bathroom, which seemed like the ideal job for him. He wouldn't let me see it until it was finished. For two days I couldn't take a bath and had to use the toilet downstairs in Dad's office. All Iggy would say was that it was brilliant and I would love it. Fortunately, he made such a mess at the kitchen sink cleaning his brushes that I had some idea what was coming. Three walls were covered in black with broad swaths of red overlapping, the black seeping through the red. Glowing with pride, he stood and waited for my reaction.

"It's amazing," I told him. I didn't ask why he hadn't painted the fourth wall.

"It's like what I'm working on. Abstract. Totally abstract. God, I love that word. It's perfect." He squeezed me too hard and ran out the door, paintbrush in hand, presumably to the easel in his childhood bedroom.

Between the uneaten sandwiches and jogging back and forth to his parents' house in St. Paul, he was beginning to lose the softness he'd developed over a summer of late night parties and junk food. Yet he was still full of spastic energy that needed burning, and I had bare bedroom walls that needed paint. I figured as long as I stayed on the job with him, I could avoid a repeat of the bathroom.

"Now that your course is over, maybe I'll put you to work," I said one morning.

He was staring out the window, drinking cup after cup of coffee while he tore strips from the weekend paper and twisted them between his fingers into tightly wound paper corkscrews. His fingers were black from the ink.

"You think you can paint a straight line?" I said, kidding.

His coffee mug slammed onto the table. "What the fuck does that mean?"

I jumped. My hand instinctively went to my belly. "Iggy!"

The anger in his eyes blew away in an instant. He rushed over and put his hand over mine. "Oh Bridge, I'm sorry. Did I frighten you?"

"No, of course not, but what's wrong?"

He hugged me to him. His body was trembling. "It's the goddamn taps. They won't stop. I never get any sleep. Drip, drip, drip all night long." His voice rose. "All fucking night long."

His grip on my shoulder was starting to hurt. I tried to twist out of his grasp. He let go and stepped back. "I'm sorry. Oh God, I'm sorry."

I rubbed my shoulder. "It's okay, Ig. But why are you so tense?"

"I told you, it's the taps. It's like Chinese water torture, for Christ's sake."

"Is that what that is?"

"What?"

"I always wondered what people meant by that. Is it just drippy taps?"

He looked bewildered and dropped into a chair.

I went behind him to rub his neck and shoulders. "We got to loosen you up."

"That's nice," he said. "That's really nice. Yeah…yeah, sure, that…that's good." His voice was jerky and his skin seemed to be tightening, his muscles growing more taut under my fingers. I patted his shoulder and stopped.

"I'll put the kettle on." I rummaged in the cupboard for the teabags and cups. "I bought those chocolate cookies you like," I said over my shoulder. "You want a few with your tea?" He didn't answer. I turned around.

He was sitting at the table, his face drenched with tears. "Iggy!" I rushed over and knelt in front of him. "What is it? What's wrong?"

He looked down at me. His mouth was closed tight and tears streamed past his nose and over his lips.

"Please Iggy, tell me."

"I…I don't know."

"Are you worried about your marks?

His head sort of wavered. I took it as a yes.

"But you said you thought it went okay?"

His eyes seemed to be begging for something but I didn't know what. He put me in mind of the saddest dog in the world. Helpless. Wounded.

"You know what, Ig? It's all going to be okay. It really is. Even if you didn't pass, which I'm sure you did, but even if you didn't, we'll be okay. We got each other now. We're a family. Right? And the other stuff, it's just school, it's not the end of the world." I rubbed his arm, trying to press my confidence, my sureness, into him. "Okay?"

Those sorrowful eyes searched mine. "You're so good to me. I don't know what I'd do without you." A note of panic came into his voice. "Don't ever leave me, Bridge. Please, don't leave me okay?"

"What are you talking about? I'm not going anywhere."

"You promise? You'll never leave me, no matter what?"

"Iggy, I love you. You're my husband. We're having a baby." I leaned in to hug him. "This is all just crazy talk, you know that."

He stood up so fast I staggered backward.

"I need some air." His breathing was ragged, uneven.

"Sure. You want to go for a walk?"

"No…no I can't…later…yeah later." He was already at the door. "I got to run home for a bit." He waved and ran down the stairs.

Home? He was home. Wasn't he?

Reality hit me. As hard as I'd worked and as determined as I was to call it home, it wasn't Iggy's home. And who could blame him? Not only was the apartment small and cramped and too damn yellow, it smelled bad. Impossible to air out now, I couldn't bear to think what it would be like in winter. Who knew the smell of stale vanilla wafting up through the floorboards could be so disgusting? There was that odour too, the one I couldn't pinpoint but that put me in mind of the funeral home. The linoleum curled in the corners and dirt collected in the cracks. I had spent the better part of two months trying to make it a decent liveable space for a new baby, yet it was still like something from a Depression-era movie. I knew it bothered me more than Iggy but at least I called it home. Iggy hadn't changed his address.

Which was why Grace called a few days later.

I hurried to wake him. "Your mother's on her way over."

He groaned and rolled further away. He'd been out till all hours and had collapsed into bed with his clothes on. The previous night's boozy perspiration seeped through his pores. I hated that smell but it no longer made me throw up.

"She got mail for you." He didn't stir. "From MUN," I added.

His body stiffened. He sat up and took the instant coffee I held out to him. Despite the heat of the cup he held it tight between both hands. He took a swallow then shoved it towards me and dashed to the bathroom.

I lit some incense and stood at the window, praying Grace wouldn't arrive until he was finished. Finally, the toilet flushed followed by the rush of the bathtub faucet.

Just as he emerged from the bedroom, Grace's Datsun pulled up below. She got out of the car and looked up and waved with her free arm. The other held a bag of groceries. Grace never arrived empty-handed. She shut the car door softly so as not to wake Bernie, whose cheek was pressed against the side window.

"He any better?" I asked when she came in.

She made a helpless gesture and passed me the bag and Iggy the envelope.

I put down the groceries and turned to Iggy. Were all potential university graduates so nervous when the final moment was upon them? Did they all have that look of dread, that feverish twitch to their eyes, the unsteady fingers as they opened the envelope?

Iggy licked his lips and unfolded the paper. His eyes scanned the sheet. He glanced at his mother, then up and down the sheet again and back to Grace. "I did it."

Grace exhaled slowly. She and Iggy smiled at each other, their eyes saying more than words could. I thought of Simon and knew what he meant about being on the outside. Like Simon, I didn't mind. I was too relieved. Iggy had passed. He had his degree. Our real life could start. He could stop drinking and staying out late with his unemployed buddies and settle down. We would have a baby, become a family. He'd be a teacher. We'd probably be better off than most people in Exile Cove or St. Paul. Everything really would be all right.

"Congratulations." Grace held up the car keys. "These are yours now."

"He can't drive," I said without thinking. Luckily, Iggy was fixated on the mail.

"You can." She passed me the keys. "I already bought a new one."

"Grace, thank you. This is so generous." My first thought was that I wouldn't have to go to Mullins' store anymore. Every time I went in there, Maeve made a point of looking at my midsection. I kept expecting her to ask for her $200 back.

"And now that the baby's coming you'll be needing to get around, especially when Iggy starts working."

Iggy put the sheet of paper on the table and hugged Grace so hard her feet left the floor. "We'll be teaching together, Mom, me and you. Oh my God!"

I hadn't seen him so happy since before I got pregnant. I didn't stop to consider whether or not he could do the job. He didn't either, I suppose. How hard could it be? Go in at nine, teach a bunch of kids for six hours, come home. Except for Sister Alphonse and a few others, most of the teachers I'd had over the years were old and cranky and uninspiring, putting in time until the day was through and retirement that much closer. Iggy was new and young and energetic. This was the ideal job for him.

From day one, all he did was complain. There was always something wrong, always someone or something that ticked him off. The kids didn't listen. They all answered back. He had no time to prepare. He didn't know the material. The other teachers thought they knew everything. They wouldn't help him. In fact, he blamed them for all his troubles.

Fearing he might quit, or worse, get fired, I called his mother, who reassured me that all new teachers needed help getting organized. She arrived that Saturday morning loaded with books and binders and charts and rulers. I sat at the table and listened as Grace talked about lesson plans which, despite his degree, Iggy appeared to know nothing about. Grace was a good teacher and made the process seem straightforward, to me, anyway. Iggy grumbled throughout, saying how silly it was, that he didn't need a plan to teach a bunch of kids. Late in the afternoon, Grace said she had to get back to Bernie, finished up a week of lessons and left them with him.

I had paid close attention to what she did and how she did it. Iggy had not. On day six he had nothing. Worried that it was all going to come crashing down, I started doing the lesson plans for him. Not only did it keep my mind busy, I enjoyed it. Each night I would brief him on what the students were supposed to know, pointing out areas in the textbooks that were to be covered. Each morning Grace would check it over before school. Within a few weeks we developed a rhythm. I started to breathe easier again.

17

In mid-November, Bernie went off the deep end altogether.

"Iggy?" Grace's voice called up the stairs one Saturday afternoon. "Bridge?"

I was scrubbing the counter. Iggy had left a paintbrush on it overnight and there was a purple splotch that wouldn't come off. I hurried to the bedroom where he'd just gone for a nap. He'd been sleeping a lot lately.

"Your mother's here," I whispered in his ear.

He rolled over and looked at me. His eyes were bloodshot, his skin blotchy. The air around him smelled sour. I heard Grace's footsteps coming up the stairs. I hurried out and shut the bedroom door.

"Hi Grace. Iggy's changing. Cup of tea?"

"No thanks." Her face was thin, her skin too white. She was unusually quiet.

"Something wrong?"

"Just the flu. I'm on the mend."

I glanced out the window at the car below. "Where's Bernie?"

She sighed. "He's in jail."

"Oh my God, poor Bernie. What happened?"

She was about to answer when Iggy appeared. He went straight to the fridge, opened a Coke and took a long drink.

"Something's happened, Iggy," I said gently. "Your mother needs to talk to you."

"Yeah? What?" He leaned against the fridge and took another swallow.

Grace turned to me. She looked tired and helpless.

"It's your father," I said.

"Where is he? In the car?" He sounded hoarse and tired.

Grace sunk into a chair and put her head in her hands. Her shoulders shook.

Iggy immediately went and knelt in front of her. "Mom, it's okay. Tell me."

"Oh, Iggy," she cried. "He's at the police station."

Iggy stood and slammed the Coke can onto the counter. "Fuck!"

Grace pressed her forehead into her hands. "Ignatius, please – "

"God, there's always something with him."

"You know he can't help it."

"Oh, so that makes it all right? What did he do this time?"

"They found him at the ball diamond. He was watching a game." Grace closed her eyes for a second. "He …he had no clothes on."

"Again? Jesus! Where the hell were you? How did he get loose?"

I shivered. "He must have been freezing."

"I was in the bathroom," said Grace. "I haven't been feeling well – "

"So that's why you weren't at school yesterday. I was worried. You should let me know when you're not going to be there. What is it? What's wrong?"

"Never mind me. He's at the station, probably curled up in a ball on the floor."

"The poor guy," I said, trying not to picture Bernie naked in the fetal position.

Grace nodded. "He'll be frightened, Iggy. We have to go to him."

"And do what, Mom? Huh? What the fuck can we do?"

"We have to bring him in again."

Iggy put up his hands. "No way."

"I called Simon. He said we should."

"Simon? What the fuck does he know?"

"He's going to call you."

"I don't care if he's almost a fucking doctor. He still doesn't know shit."

"What place?" I asked, though I thought I knew already.

Iggy slammed a cupboard door. "The fucking Mental, where all the nutcases go to get more nuts."

"He'll be safe there, Iggy." Grace sighed. "It's that or jail. We can't let that happen again."

"When was he in jail?" I asked.

Iggy gave me an exasperated look. "What difference does it make?"

Grace reached out to him. "We've got to go take care of him."

Iggy pushed her hand away. "No, I'm not going there again."

"Iggy, she needs –" I started.

He spun around and pointed at me. "You stay out of this. You hear me?"

I was shocked into momentary silence staring at his finger.

He turned back to Grace. "You do this, you're on your own."

Grace looked at Iggy for a moment. "I'm sorry, Ignatius." She stood up. "I'll be in St. John's for a while. I already talked to Jim about finding a replacement."

"You're leaving the school? Jesus, Mom, you can't do that."

"I will not leave Bernie in there alone. I can't abandon him."

Iggy was twisting his hands together. "But what about me?"

"You have Bridgina now. You'll be fine."

"You can't leave me, not now." He looked terrified.

"Your father needs her, Iggy." I touched his arm. "I'll still be here, I'll do the lesson plans. It'll be okay."

He pulled away and grabbed Grace's hand. "Don't leave me alone here, not again, you said you wouldn't. Okay?"

"I have to, Iggy."

"If you go, that...that's it. I can't...I'm warning you." He slumped into a chair at the table. "Don't do it," he begged, his voice raspy.

Grace leaned down and squeezed his arm. She hesitated then stood up straight. "Pull yourself together, Ignatius. You need to quit drinking and whatever else it is you're doing and be a man. You're going to be a father. It's time to take charge of your life and act like an adult. Do you hear me?"

Iggy stared at the wall, mouth closed tight, eyes narrowed.

"What can we do? What do you need?" I asked.

"Can you take care of the house, make sure it's okay? Iggy knows where the chequebook is to pay the bills. Oh, and I just bought groceries so could you clean out the fridge, take it all home? I could be gone for a bit this time."

"Yes, of course, don't worry about a thing."

She took my hand and brought it to her face. "For Bernie," she said, then added, "You're in good hands, Iggy. Bridge is good for you."

"Thanks, Grace," I said, grateful for her faith in me.

She nodded towards my huge belly. "Take care of my grandchild."

"I will. You go take care of Bernie."

She did not look at Iggy as she walked out. He didn't look at her either.

He sat staring at the wall for several minutes.

"Cup of tea?" I asked, more to break the silence than for want of tea.

He stood up. "I'm going to the house to paint. I'll see you tomorrow." A statement. No response required.

The next afternoon, I drove to the house in St. Paul. Iggy didn't answer when I called out to him but the rear door was unlatched so I assumed he was out back walking in the woods. I went upstairs to where he kept his easel. There was nothing on it.

I set to work cleaning out the fridge. I did the same with the cupboards, putting the bread and buns into another bag, along with some potatoes that were growing eyes. I threw an open bag of Cheezies in the garbage – the smell made me gag these days – and left everything else. Hopefully, Grace and Bernie would not be gone long.

I was just considering whether to go and look for Iggy when the phone rang.

"Bridge, how the heck are you, girl?"

"Simon, hi. I'm pretty good. How about you?"

"Great. Nice to hear your voice." He sounded like he was smiling.

"Yeah, you too. Sorry about your father. Grace was by yesterday."

"Poor Dad. Poor Mom, too."

"Hey, thanks for those books. I sure needed them."

"Glad they helped. You need more information let me know, okay?"

"Yeah, sure. Iggy's not here right now. He's…gone for a walk."

"That's okay. I'm happy to talk to you first."

"How's med school? You mostly in classes or at the hospital?"

"Like I was telling Iggy the other day, I pretty much live on the wards."

"Oh," I paused. "That's odd." I had thought Iggy wasn't talking to Simon.

"Not really. Plenty of times I don't make it home at all. I swear to God I don't have time to turn around some days."

"Wow," I said, glad he'd misunderstood, "it's hard to believe you're going to be a doctor soon. That's so cool."

"Thanks, Bridge. Too bad not everyone agrees with you, hey?"

I laughed even though I knew it might be at Iggy's expense.

"How's that baby coming along? I can see her now, a tiny little Bridge."

Her? I smiled. That sounded right. "She might be tiny but I'm the size of a house."

"Well, that's okay, you're eating for two."

More like three. As Iggy's appetite – for everything – diminished, mine grew exponentially. I had to settle for food. "You should see me. I got a belly out to St. Paul."

"You're in St. Paul so it can't be too big."

"Not if you're from Exile Cove." When had I last had such a lighthearted conversation? "And she's always kicking, like she can't wait to get out."

"Sounds feisty, like her mother."

"That's debatable these days."

"Ooh, funny. Good one, Bridge."

"If it is, then you win."

"Not likely, if I'm up against you. Remember that time you took on old Alphonse herself? What was it, against the death penalty?"

"Yeah, that was fun, but you know, Simon, I don't think she was ever as proud as when I beat her. She was like a mother hen, she was. Poor old Alphonse."

"She was a character all right…"

I was having such fun talking to Simon that I hadn't noticed Iggy in the doorway. When I turned and saw him there, I lowered the receiver. I immediately felt guilty, and, just as quickly, defensive. I was not doing anything wrong.

Simon's voice drifted up from the earpiece. "Bridge, you there?"

Iggy walked toward me, his hand out. I didn't even say goodbye.

He held the receiver for several seconds before raising it to his ear. "Hello, Simon." He stretched the phone cord into the living room and shut the door.

With Grace and Bernie gone, I had two less people in my life. But it wasn't until the first snowstorm in late November that I realised how lonely I was. I felt frozen in time, stuck in a world where grey was the predominant colour, where people disappeared indoors and pulled their curtains.

I didn't have Dad downstairs anymore either. He was no longer capable of running the business. "Sure who'd buy insurance from him?" Josephine said. "He don't know an underwrite from an overbite." I missed having him so close but he still dropped in every day for tea and Jam Jams. He would hug me and ask how I was feeling. He'd pat my belly shyly and reminisce about Melinda, about when she was born and what a lovely baby she'd been. A couple of times he called me Melinda. Not wanting to talk about her, I let it go. She still hadn't phoned or written, but Dad would not have known that. He probably didn't remember the fight we'd had.

One afternoon he came in and hugged me and patted my belly and asked for a cup of tea. I made the tea but I could have cried. He had left me 10 minutes before.

Katie wrote every few weeks, short dashed-off letters about her life in Mc-Murray, the people she was meeting, her job at a lawyer's office, how her boss was an old letch. She had a new boyfriend, an engineer this time. They went out to fancy steakhouses, and he brought her flowers and took her to movies. It was the type of life we used to daydream about in high school. When I answered her I would pretend my life was happy, telling her how excited we were about the baby, how much fun it was setting up a nursery, how I was getting so fat but that was okay because Iggy thought it was sexy. Writing her was exhausting. Sometimes I forgot to do it.

I was disappointed that we didn't hear from Grace or Simon. Grace had her hands full with Bernie, and Simon had told me how busy he was, but it made me feel even lonelier to think they couldn't take a minute to make contact, just to keep in touch. Then I saw Grace's phone bill in a pile of papers on the counter at her house, the Montreal and St. John's phone numbers. Iggy had been in contact with Simon and Grace all along but hadn't told me. When I asked him about it he said he talked to them because he had to, about the bills and the house and to check on his father. And he was not calling long distance on our phone. His mother had more money than we did. "It's their fault Dad's stuck in there, Bridge. I'm fed up with the pair of them." When I tried to defend them his hand shot up. "I don't interfere with your family's problems, do I? And God knows you got your share, more than most, I'd say. So do me a favour and butt out of ours."

I tried watching soap operas but they made me feel more isolated, with their impeccable houses and handsome, attentive husbands who kissed their wives with such passion. Iggy hadn't touched me like that in a long while, not since St. John's probably. We hadn't made love in ages. I couldn't blame him. When I looked in the mirror, a budding version of Josephine stared back. I had gained over 30 pounds with nearly a month to go; my face was bloated, with fat puffy cheeks and eyes half sunk into my lids. I would have settled for just Iggy's company, but when he finished copying the lesson plans I would prepare for him each evening, which he did in case the principal noticed they weren't in his handwriting, he would curl up in bed and sleep till morning, or go on a painting frenzy on the easel at his mother's house, or say he needed to unwind and have a few beers with the guys. From his recent phone conversations, I knew "the guys" included Gord MacDonald. Fortunately, it also included going to the bar to play pool. Gord was the last person I wanted to see, or to see me.

Each morning I drove Iggy to school. If it wasn't too cold out I took a walk along the breakwater. There was something freeing about watching the gulls circle and squawk, the wind blowing and whipping the waves up. Looking onto the ocean cleared my head of the claustrophobia I sometimes felt when I thought about our dingy apartment. Or about my life. In the afternoon I would run errands, getting the mail in Exile Cove, grocery shopping in St. Paul, stopping at the library to see if there was anything new, before picking Iggy up. He still hadn't gotten his licence. This had never bothered me before. It was one of his quirks, like his forgetfulness, or his habit of rushing to answer the phone, or the way he'd sometimes be surprised to the point of panic when someone came upon him out of the blue, or how he would hole himself up in the bathroom for an hour or more, the toilet flushing occasionally, the steam from the tub seeping out under the door. He wouldn't answer if I called out to him, and I couldn't get in because he locked the door. He always said he hadn't heard me. He must have had his head under the water, he said. For how long, I'd wanted to ask. And why? Why on earth would he stay underwater for that long?

When he continued to ignore my increasingly less subtle hints that he learn to drive, I confronted him and said that when the baby was born I didn't want to be dragging an infant back and forth to St. Paul to pick him up. He needed to get his licence.

That was when he told me that he didn't drive because of his condition.

He was standing at the kitchen sink. Every evening, as soon as the last bite was taken, he'd do the dishes. The sooner they were done, the sooner he could head to the bar or to his mother's house or to bed. He didn't do a great job but it was the one thing he did around the apartment so I wasn't about to complain.

"What condition?" I asked.

"It's nothing…" he stalled, rattling dishes together. We had the latest pattern of Corningware, my china pattern, we called it, unbreakable, meant to last a lifetime.

"Nothing?" I snapped. "It can't be nothing if you can't drive."

"So I can't drive, so what?" he shouted, raising a wet plate in the air and sending water droplets flying. "Quit harping on it."

"No. I will not," I shouted back. Although I had learned to be careful about what I said around Iggy, I'd never thought to be afraid, had never had any reason to fear him or any other man. The possibility didn't enter my mind. "What's this condition you're on about? What the hell is wrong with you?"

The wet plate slammed onto the linoleum and shattered. He stood perfectly still and stared at the wall. His eyes seemed darker. A vein pulsed on the upper left side of his face. I had never noticed it before. My gut tightened.

"Iggy?" I said. He didn't respond.

The door opened at the bottom of the stairs. "Melinda?" Dad's voice called out. "You up there?"

Iggy swallowed and blinked. He turned to look at me. "Sorry," he said, and reached for the broom. He started to sweep the plate shards together. "So much for the good china, eh." The light was back in his eyes but his voice was rough.

It took me a second to answer. "Yeah, right. Ha-ha. Good china indeed."

Then Dad was in the room and life returned to normal. Except that I had, for just a second, felt a sense of uneasiness, perhaps even fear, not just for myself but for Iggy, too. What was this condition he talked about? How worried should I be?

I was trying to figure out how to bring it up without upsetting him when, a few days later, he mentioned in an offhand voice that he sometimes had seizures.

"Seizures?"

"Yeah, or blackouts or something."

"How?" I folded the tea towel I'd taken down from the small clothesline above the stove. "I mean, what is it? What's wrong?"

"Well, we ... I'm not sure, but I probably shouldn't drive."

"That's sounds serious, Ig. How long..."

"Look, it's no big deal. I take medication for it, so it's okay."

I had noticed him taking pills a few times but he claimed it was something the doctor had given him for headaches. When I'd questioned him further, where and when had he seen a doctor, it turned out he'd gone before the wedding, in St. John's.

"So it's like epilepsy?"

"No...not really..."

"What then? Did you ever talk to Simon about it?"

"Fuck Simon."

"But you have to find out more. How long's it been going on? You need to – "

"Jesus! What is this, the third degree?"

"No, I was just – "

"'I was just'..." he mimicked in a high-pitched voice. "Look, I told you, so now leave it alone, would you?" His chapped lips clamped shut. He wouldn't look at me.

"Iggy." I pulled at his arm. "Talk to me. What else did the doctor say?"

His eyes squinted and he put his hand on the top of his head, let it lay there for a second, then reached out and yanked the clothesline from the wall.

"What did you do that for?"

"'What did you do that for?'" Again with the mimicking.

"Jesus, I'm only asking a question. You should call Simon – "

"Christ!" He slapped at the dangling line. "When are you going to shut up about it? Just shut the fuck up. Shut up, shut up, shut up, shut up."

I dropped the clothes I'd been folding and took a step back. There was that vein again, a throbbing blood-engorged blip. I said nothing, knowing that whatever came from my mouth would be the wrong thing.

As Iggy stared at me, his mouth opened and a sound, like an anguished cry, came out. His hand came up and pushed against his temple. Then he slammed his fist into the fridge with such force that it jarred and he stormed down the stairs and out the door. A crimson smear stood stark against the dull gold of the refrigerator.

He came home hours later and went straight to bed. In the morning he nailed the clothesline back up, but otherwise it was as if the incident had never happened.

I didn't ask about his condition again.

18

"Iggy! Wake up!" It was six in the morning, the week before Christmas.

He rolled in towards me and pulled the blankets up to his chin. His eyes shot open. The covers flew off. "What the fuck is that?" He leapt off the bed.

"It's my water. It broke."

"What?" His face was a mix of disbelief and disgust. "Did you piss the bed?"

I had to laugh. He was standing there naked, handsome as ever, almost, his thick head of hair sticking out in all directions, thinking his wife was a bed-wetter.

"It's not funny, Bridge." His voice was scolding and sulky at the same time.

"The baby's coming. That's why my water broke."

He looked sceptical. "What do you mean?"

"The water protects the baby," I said, no longer amused, trying to keep the exasperation out of my voice. This wasn't the moment to remind him that I'd told him already, and more than once. Between him and Dad, I felt like a broken record half the time. "When it breaks, it's time for the baby to be born."

"Oh…yeah, right. Sorry." He sized up the wet bed. "So what should we do?"

I was trying to get myself into a sitting position. "We go to the hospital."

He looked from the bed to me and to the bed again.

I stuck out my hand. "Fuck the bed. Help me up."

We wasted time searching the apartment for my overnight bag before remembering that Iggy had, in a rare moment of foresight, put it in the trunk so we'd always be ready. I drove, although it had nothing to do with Iggy not having a licence. He'd been driving whenever he felt like it lately, except to school because they knew he wasn't licensed. But I could smell the booze off him from the night before and wasn't sure how sober he was. He hadn't objected when I'd gotten into the driver's seat. Although the hospital was 10 minutes away the trip felt much longer as I drove through the early morning streets through three contractions. Iggy was dead silent, staring straight ahead. He looked scared to pieces. So was I.

Several hours later, the doctor was checking to see how dilated I was when Iggy poked his head in the door.

"Is everything okay in here?" He came over to the bed and took my hand, his forehead creased with worry. "I can hear you in the hall. Are you okay, Bridge?"

I nodded. "Yeah, just…you know, having a baby."

"I forgot to put your hot water bottle in the bag when I packed it. Should I run home and get it?"

Another contraction hit me. I cried out, and felt an urge to push.

The doctor held up his hand. "Not yet."

Before I could think to stop him, Iggy went to stand by the doctor. His face went ghostly and he clutched the side of the bed. He started to moan. I took rhythmic breaths as instructed by the nurse. Iggy kept moaning.

The doctor looked to the nurse. "Get him out of here. We don't need him passing out on us." He gestured to Iggy and pointed at the door. "Go home and get some sleep."

Iggy didn't protest as the nurse took his arm and led him from the room.

Not long after, Maggie was born. She was Maggie from the minute I saw her, with her waves of soft dark hair, and her tiny lips that puckered at the centre. She had warm, pink skin and long, slender fingers and a dimple in her chin that I wanted to kiss each time I looked at her.

I had always loved "Margaret" and how it could be shortened to Maggie or Peggy, both of which were lovely all on their own. Whenever I had tried to discuss names with Iggy, he'd always looked overwhelmed, like he couldn't possibly choose one name from all the names in the world, especially for a baby who, I came to realize, was not real to him. Dad had chosen my name. I was supposed to have been Bridgita, after his grandmother, but somebody messed up on the birth certificate.

By the time Iggy returned that afternoon I was sitting up in a chair with the baby in my arms. "I thought we'd call her Maggie," I said.

Iggy stared at her for the longest time, his body so still he seemed not to be breathing. "Maggie." He knelt in front of us and touched her chin, then drew in a sharp breath and looked up at me, his eyes filled with wonder. "Yes. Maggie."

"Do you want to hold her?" I asked.

"Should I?"

"Of course. She's your daughter."

He looked stunned. I sensed that, until he held her, he would not fully comprehend that this baby, this live human being, was on this earth because of him.

We stood up. "See how her head is nice and snug in my arm here. You have to hold her like this because she can't hold her head up yet."

I started to pass him the baby.

He took half a step back. "Are you sure, Bridge?"

"Yes, of course." I was not the least bit sure.

He cupped his arms like mine and stood stiffly while I transferred Maggie over. My body was already missing her.

"Relax. Drop your shoulders a little. She's not heavy." I kept my voice calm and low, my hands under his. "You want to sit down?"

He lowered himself onto the seat and eased backward in the chair. He smiled nervously at me, then looked down at Maggie, transfixed.

I took the opportunity to eat the stale toast and hardboiled egg on the bedside table. It all tasted delicious, even the cold milky tea that I gulped back. By the time I finished, Iggy's face was awash with tears. He was still staring at Maggie. I wondered if he'd looked away at all.

"Iggy? You okay?"

A tear slid into his mouth. "She's so…she's so amazing…so perfect."

I eased myself off the bed and knelt in front of them. "She is, isn't she?" I said, wiping his face with my napkin.

"I can't believe she's mine." He brought Maggie close to his face, touched his nose to hers, smelled her hair. He closed his eyes, his cheek against her forehead. They both looked perfect, together.

For the first time in months, I felt hope. Maybe it wasn't all one giant mistake.

When we got home from the hospital, Iggy was great. He only went out to get groceries or to check on his mother's house. Sometimes he stayed there for quite a while but I didn't mind. Having Iggy around too much was exhausting. He'd fuss and fidget and was constantly checking on Maggie, placing his hand on her back or tummy if she was sleeping to make sure she was breathing, often waking her up in the process.

Christmas was quiet. Dad came over with a teddy bear for Maggie and two plates of turkey dinner. There was a cut on his ear but he couldn't remember how it had gotten there. What little hair he had was neat and trim and his head had been shaved up the back but he swore he hadn't had a haircut in months. He fell asleep in the chair watching TV then woke up and went home. Iggy followed him to make sure he didn't stray.

Grace came out from St. John's a few days after Christmas. She made several trips up and down the stairs from the car, arms laden with presents: clothes and a tiny bassinet for Maggie; new paints and brushes for Iggy; slippers and a velour tracksuit for me. There were gifts from Simon, too: a musical mobile for Maggie; a sweater for Iggy; and for me, a Mordecai Richler novel. I had rewrapped the gloves Iggy had given me and gave them to Grace, along with a bag of Oh Henry! bars for Bernie. Iggy hadn't told me she was coming until the day before. She brought lunch, too, enough for a small army, a huge ham which just needed heating through in a pot on the stove, two large casseroles, one scalloped potatoes, the other Brussels sprouts cooked with eggs and bacon and cheese. I had never heard of Brussels sprouts. They were interesting. For dessert there was gingerbread and sugar cookies, and a big box of chocolates from Simon. No fruitcake.

The star of the day was Maggie. Grace could not get enough of her, carrying her around and around the apartment while we heated everything up. She only let her go to have a quick bite while I breastfed. After lunch she insisted on taking Maggie for a walk around Exile Cove with Iggy. I dozed off as soon as the door shut behind them.

When they came back, the mood was tense. Iggy sat, arms crossed, at the table. He said nothing as Grace gathered her purse and gloves and got ready to go. Coat on, she took Maggie from me and cradled her in both arms, peering down at her for a long while. It was the stillest she'd been since she'd arrived, as if she was concentrating on filling herself up with the moment and the memory of her only grandchild.

She gave Maggie to Iggy. "You have a beautiful daughter, Ignatius."

"I know that." His voice was petulant.

"Why not stay the night?" I said to Grace. "Or a couple of days."

"Bernie will be upset if I'm not there in the morning." She sounded resigned, yet not resentful. I wondered if Grace needed Bernie, too, if perhaps she wouldn't know what to do or how to be if she didn't have him. Was this their version of love?

"Thanks for the presents, Grace, and all the food. I won't have to cook for days. And thank Simon for us, too. Right, Iggy?"

Iggy held Maggie and stared out the window.

"Goodbye, Ignatius." Grace paused, hand out towards him. "I'll call you."

He looked at her, his mouth set in a stern line. "Unless you're calling to tell me you're both coming home, don't bother."

"Iggy!" I said. "That's not – "

His eyes glinted as they zeroed in on me. "Not your business, remember?"

I glared back at him then turned to Grace. "I'll see you off."

We went down the stairs together.

"I don't know why he's so angry. Sorry, Grace."

"It's because I'm taking Bernie to New York. There's a facility there." She didn't sound hopeful. "I doubt it will do any good but if there's a chance, well…"

"New York? That seems so far."

"Not really, not these days. And Bernie's from there. Guess you could say he's come full circle."

"I'll cross my fingers for him, for both of you."

Grace got into her car and started the ignition. "Don't be too hard on him, Bridge. He doesn't mean it."

I thought he meant every word. "Drive safe. Give Bernie a hug for me."

I walked ever so slowly back up the stairs, trying to figure out what to say to Iggy. When I entered the apartment, he passed Maggie to me and went into the bedroom and shut the door. He slept till morning.

Iggy went to his parents' house each day for the next three, spending hours there alone. He had taken the paints and brushes his mother had given him for Christmas so I hoped he might be painting again. I didn't mind that he wasn't around much. The time he spent there calmed him. One evening when he came back he brought up the subject of his father. "He should be home. I tried to tell that to Mom the other day when we went for a walk but the doctors got her brainwashed. I can't talk any sense to her at all. Goddamn Simon's not helping."

I was relieved he was talking about it. I didn't necessarily agree with him but thought better of arguing. After all, what did I know?

On New Year's Eve he went out with Gord and some other guys I didn't know. He called in the middle of the night to say he was in St. John's, then mumbled something about me not worrying and that he'd be home soon. He showed up two days later.

Iggy was completely in love with Maggie. Every day he sang to her and rocked her and changed her diaper. But he was still Iggy. He hated his job. He hated the apartment. He hated Exile Cove. His dissatisfaction grew on a daily basis. It didn't help that winter had set in with a vengeance.

"It's fucking Siberia out there." He had just come in from scraping the windshield and was stamping his feet on the small hooked rug I'd picked up at a yard sale. Snow scattered across the floor. He slapped his hands together. "No better in here, this place is freezing." He reached over to scrape at the frost on the inside of the window.

I was packing his lunch at the counter where Maggie slept in her bassinet. "At least the sun is shining," I said, trying to counteract his negativity. "And it's supposed to warm up soon. Apple?"

"To what? Minus 50? And it's still fucking January." He stood inside the door waiting for me, his hands curled under his chin.

"It's almost February." I dropped an apple in the bag, then took Maggie's snowsuit from above the heat register where I'd left it to warm up. "Can you put the milk and butter in the fridge? If we don't hurry you're going to be late for work again."

"Who cares?" He headed to the table, tramping snow across the floor.

"Iggy, your boots."

"You asked me to do it."

"It's easier for you to take them off than for me to clean the floor."

He walked backwards to stand on the mat. "Fine. You do it."

"I'm just saying – "

"It's friggin' water. Should be used to that in this hell-hole."

"What odds – "

"What odds? What the fuck does that mean anyway? 'What odds,' what odds are you talking about..." He ranted on. I stopped listening.

Maggie started to fuss. I picked her up and cuddled her. "Shhh, that's my girl," I whispered into her soft curls. "Mommy loves you, Maggie." Her warm close baby smell made me want to curl up with her forever.

"You're the one in a hurry," he said. "So come on."

"Just a minute – "

"Oh for Christ's sake." He marched over to us and took Maggie from me and pushed her arm into her sleeve.

"Careful," I yelled as she started to cry. "You'll hurt her."

He stopped abruptly. He looked shocked, then ashamed as he placed Maggie in my arms. "I'll walk to work." He backed away and rushed out the door.

After that, he found his own way to work, walking or hitchhiking. When I offered to drive, he said no, it was too cold to take Maggie out so early in the day. I didn't push the issue but still picked him up after school if he couldn't get a ride. I was relieved he was so concerned. Maybe it took time to grow into fatherhood.

Motherhood, on the other hand, was instant – it had to be. Maggie was here, now, a constant presence in my life and she needed me. And I was happy to be needed. Her very existence shone a new light on Exile Cove. People stopped me in the street to peer into the stroller, offering compliments and advice in equal measure. I couldn't pass the Smiths' house without at least one of the spinsters coming out to see her. Maeve Mullins made such a fuss when I went to the store that I no longer did all my shopping in St. Paul. And Mrs. Mercer, who I'd never been close to when I hung around with Sylvia in high school, stopped by the apartment with two velour sleepers and a rattle. "What a beautiful baby you have, Bridgina," she said, nestling the tip of her pinkie in Maggie's dimple. "You're so lucky. If only our Sylvia would settle down like you." Looking ready to cry, she hugged me and left.

Exile Cove was growing on me.

The February sky hung like a dull grey cloud, a low ceiling to the dirty grey snow on the road, creating the perfect sandwich to keep my grey mood intact. Sleep-deprived, I was almost as gloomy as Iggy. Maggie had woken up at least half a dozen times through the night, unable to calm down until I held her in front of the open bedroom window to let her breathing clear enough so I could nurse her back to sleep.

I dozed off and on till nine but still only managed to get a few hours in total. There was a note from Iggy saying he had driven himself to work and would park at his mother's house and walk from there.

I dragged myself through the morning. Around noon, Maggie fell asleep and I crawled back into bed. I'd barely drifted off when she woke up crying. I tried not to hear her but that was impossible. I got up and repeated the process from the previous night until she drifted off. I lay down but my mind would not shut down. Through my bleary head all I could hear was her coughing and crying even though she wasn't. I knew I would never hear anything else for the rest of my life.

Eventually, exhaustion won out. Then Maggie woke up.

I hauled myself out of bed. The afternoon stretched before me, three hours to go before Iggy got home. I had some cold toast and a couple of oatmeal cookies, stuffing them in my mouth and chewing and swallowing even though they were dry and didn't taste like much. I ate the last two and tossed the bag. I turned on the TV and lay on the sofa with Maggie by my side. The drone of the television made my eyes droop and I dozed until she started to fuss. When I opened my eyes I saw that I was crushing her. Alarmed, I twisted away, too fast as it turned out. A sharp spasm hit my neck. Maggie was crying full out by now. I picked her up and held her, trying not to put more pressure on my neck as I found some aspirin and downed a couple with a glass of water. Even that hurt.

I walked with her until she fell asleep. As I placed her onto her mattress another spasm jolted me. I jerked sideways, waking her up. Afraid to try to pick her up, I rocked the bassinet until she settled. Thinking she was sleeping, I stopped rocking and tried to stretch my neck. She let out a screech and I jerked again. Pain shot through me. I cried out, which seemed to quiet her. Not for long though. Within seconds she was at it again. I stared at her, willing her to stop. "Shut up," I begged, too tired and too sore to yell. "Please, just shut up." She did not shut up.

Rage hit me like a smack in the face. My teeth clenched against the scream that rose from my throat. I dug my hands into my scalp and rushed out the door and down the stairs. The sound of her cries through the bedroom window decreased as I walked further and further away. When I could almost not hear her, when that moment of panic was almost upon me, I reversed direction. Walk. Listen. Turn. Repeat.

The cold fresh winter air was beginning to work. So was the aspirin. I no longer wanted to kill her.

On the third time back Josephine came out of the house. I slipped inside the building. After all the terrible things I'd said about her and Melinda, the last thing I needed was to get caught playing hooky, leaving Maggie alone and crying. Even though I still believed most of what I'd said that night, I was beginning to comprehend how little I knew about parenting, how much I needed to learn. How mean I'd been to both of them. Being a mother was harder than I'd ever imagined. I hurried upstairs and picked Maggie up. She was red faced and snotty-nosed, but otherwise fine. I had never felt such guilt.

Winter was never-ending. The shortest month of the year was one interminable day after another. Cold. Dull. Foggy. A closed triangle of gloom. Thank God it was not a leap year.

Thursday afternoon, desperate for company, I picked Iggy up after school. As usual, we were quiet on the drive home. If I let him sit back and relax for those few minutes, by the time he lifted Maggie from her car seat and brought her into the apartment, he was able to smile, at her at least.

Once inside, I put a tuna casserole into the oven and took out the small one that was already cooked through. "Can you stay with Maggie for a bit?"

"Why?" He did not look pleased. "Where you going?"

"Josephine's still at that doll thing – you know, the craft fair in St. John's. Dad's probably living on tobacco and toast. I'll take this over and be right back."

"Don't be long. I thought I might go out later on."

Might? Why would today be any different, I felt like saying as I headed for the door. He'd gone out every night that week.

Josephine had been away two days. The house stunk of leftover fish and burnt toast and stale cigarette smoke. The ashtrays were overflowing and the sink was clogged with used tea bags. On top of the garbage pile lay one of the frozen dinners Josephine had left him, thawed and uncovered, but otherwise untouched. The sandwich I'd dropped off the day before was still in its wrapper on the counter. There was dried blood on Dad's ear and a razor-rash on the back of his neck. Somebody had to do something about Lizzie at the salon.

I tidied up then sat with Dad while he ate, partly for his quiet company, partly to make sure he did eat. Bit by bit he was losing the ability to care for himself. Bit by bit I was losing him.

As soon as he was finished and settled for the night, I went home.

When I opened the downstairs door, I heard Iggy's voice. "…found the chequebook in the drawer and I needed money so I wrote one… I didn't think you'd mind, I'll pay you back…no I will…what…I don't care what Simon says… pisses me off…" He went silent, obviously listening to the person on the other end of the phone. "Fuck, I told you, Mom…stupid doctors, they don't know everything…" A pause, then he was weeping, "Come home, Mom, please… you're always leaving me alone…ever since I was little…" Another pause. "… fine, I don't care, do what you want, you always do anyway." The phone banged into its cradle. The bathroom door slammed.

I waited half a minute before noisily making my way up the stairs. I went straight for Maggie who had started to cry with the slam of the door.

Iggy came out of the bathroom. His eyes were overly bright, like he had a fever. "What took you so long?"

"I know, sorry about that," I apologized, not because I'd been gone long, but because it was best to placate him. "You should have seen the mess. Poor fellow is helpless on his own." I passed Maggie to him. "Did I miss anything here? Anyone call?"

"Right, like anything ever happens in this godforsaken dump."

Having given him an opportunity to tell me about it, I couldn't ask about his conversation with Grace now, or why he'd needed money. "Smells like dinner's ready."

The edges of the casserole were a little burnt, which I liked but Iggy didn't so I cut him a portion from the middle. He poked at it for a couple of minutes and ate a few bites. We followed the same procedure every evening. Iggy would pick at his food; I'd have seconds. We'd eat without talking, the only sounds from Maggie in her bassinet on the counter. I was starting to envy Dad and Josephine the TV at the end of their table.

"I think we need to get a crib or playpen or something." I gestured towards Maggie. "She's pretty much outgrown that. Shouldn't be too expensive."

"Sure."

I waited but there was nothing else coming. "I wonder how your mother's making out," I said as if out of nowhere. "Hope everything's okay."

"Not friggin' likely, considering what she's doing." He looked at his watch. "Shit, I better get going. Don't want to be out too late."

I put down my fork. "Can't you stay in for one night?"

"Come off it, Bridge. I'm just going out for a beer."

"I got beer here." I tried not to sound broody. "Let's hang out like we used to."

"Get off my back, will you? You know I need to unwind after being stuck in there all day with those friggin' kids. It's enough to drive you nuts, I'm telling you."

"I know." I didn't, though. I did not understand what could be so hard about teaching, why he hated it so much. And I was sick of hearing it. "But I'm here all day with Maggie."

He looked puzzled. "What's wrong with that?"

"Nothing. Sometimes I need a break, that's all."

"Did you want to go out?"

"Maybe." I definitely did not want to go out. I just wanted to have an adult conversation, maybe share a beer and a few laughs and crawl into bed. Maybe have sex if we could remember how.

"Go." He crossed his arms. "Never mind I got to work all day, teaching them brats the difference between a plus and a minus. Go. Don't let me stop you."

"How about we both stay home and watch TV?"

His face brightened. "We will, we will. I'll be half an hour. We can both relax later on." He was putting on his coat as he spoke, lacing his boots, pulling his hat down over his ears. "I promise, just a beer with the boys. I'll be back in no time."

In the middle of the night he stumbled in, banging into the dresser before landing in the bed. Maggie had just fallen asleep after a feeding. I said nothing, fearing more noise would wake her up. When I awoke in the morning, I found him lying next to me, fully clothed. He was snoring, mouth open, dried spittle on his cheek.

When had I thought he was handsome?

"God I hate this town. Nothing but a fog hole… freezing cold… covered in pea soup…"

It was a Saturday morning in March. A storm had come up overnight and a thick blanket of snow covered everything. The roads hadn't been graded and there was no way our little car could go anywhere until they were cleared. Iggy wanted to go check on his parents' house. Sometimes he stayed there overnight. Once he didn't come home for two days. I suspected if Maggie hadn't been here he might have stayed longer.

"…ugliest town in God's creation…rats on the beach in summer, icebergs in the spring, don't know why anybody ever settled here in the first place…"

As Iggy ranted, I leaned in closer to Maggie and tickled her cheek, bringing an instant smile to her face. I sang the spider song as I walked my fingers up her chest. I tried to tune Iggy out but lately, when he spoke of Exile Cove or St. Paul, there was a resentment in his voice that was hard to ignore. And although I didn't always listen to what he said, I always heard the tone. Anger coated his words, giving them more meaning than the words themselves. On the other hand, I didn't have the opportunity to listen to him that often. After a quick supper, he would head out to the bar or to his mother's house to paint, or maybe just to sleep. His fingernails were clean. And it had been months since he'd talked about one of his paintings.

Every time he came home he went straight for Maggie. He would hold her, smell her, sing a lullaby. She would fall asleep in his arms. He would watch her, his face soft and tender. He always looked as if he didn't want to leave her, but he always left.

Once, when he came home stoned, I found him leaning over Maggie while she slept, his fingers tracing the soft curves of her face. He was smiling. I felt happy then.

At other times his love for Maggie spooked me, like the day I found him sitting on a chair staring at her, tears running down his face. He looked frightened. I asked him what was wrong. "I don't know if I can do this. I don't know if I can be a good father." He got up and walked out, still crying.

Sometimes, when he wouldn't stop staring, when he didn't hear me calling his name, then yelling at him to get his attention, my voice would run hollow and my gut would tense up like it had when he'd broken the plate.

I didn't ask myself if we were happy. I knew the answer. The man I'd fallen in love with, who had loved to make love to me, now had no interest at all. I was stuck in a marriage where both partners merely existed, side by side, miles apart.

19

Then came the day in mid-March when he arrived home, smiling. That morning I'd had to force him out of bed. There were days when he hardly left the bedroom, which didn't matter on a weekend. I couldn't let him do that on a weekday, not again. He'd used all his sick time and his pay would be docked. So I'd fixed him an extra strong cup of coffee, packed him and Maggie into the car and drove him to work. And now here he was, seven hours later, smiling a smile the likes of which I hadn't seen in months. Were things improving at school? Had something good happened? Dear Lord, don't tell me he was fired.

After a brief snuggle with Maggie, he placed her in her new playpen and turned to me with a self-satisfied air. "We're moving," he said.

I was heating a bottle of milk in a pot on the stove. My nipples were too sore to breastfeed. I'd been up half the night with Maggie, who had croup, or something, I wasn't sure what, just that when her tiny little body was wracked with the cough, it put the fear of God into me. I'd spent the wee hours sitting on the edge of the tub holding her as the hot water enveloped us in a cocoon of steam.

"Did you hear what I said? We're moving."

"We could use more room, I suppose. But this place is free at least."

"No. You don't get it. We're moving away."

"I'm sorry, what?" I asked, testing my wrist with a spray of milk.

He took hold of my arm. "Jesus, would you listen. We're moving to Calgary."

I had never set foot outside Newfoundland. The furthest I'd been was St. John's. I had assumed I'd return there when things got back to normal, whatever that was. I would do it right then, not screw it up like I had the first time, having to quit school, coming home with nothing to show for my time away but a big belly.

Tears welled up. How could I think like that about Maggie?

"Iggy, what are you talking about?"

"Martin Foley's all better. He's coming back to work. Isn't that great?"

I'd forgotten all about Martin Foley.

"I'm free, Bridge. At the end of the month, I'm a free man!"

Behind him was Maggie's playpen. She'd been crying off and on since Iggy had put her there. He spun around and picked her up, too roughly, although he held her carefully once she was in his arms.

"Give her to me," I said, reaching.

"She's fine, leave her be."

It was difficult to concentrate on what he was saying. My eyes were on Maggie, who was swaying to and fro in his arms as he bounced her up and down. "Pass her over," I said, my arms out. "The bottle's ready."

He stood defiantly. "No. You're always saying you need a break. I'll feed her." He grabbed the bottle and slid it between Maggie's tiny lips. "We'll take off at the end of the month. That gets us there in plenty of time for the construction season."

"Construction? But you're a teacher."

"It's near the end of the school year. Maybe in September…yeah, September. Sure, sure, I'll teach in the fall. So, what do you say? Huh? What do you think?"

"I don't know. What did your mother say about this?"

"Fuck! Not that it fucking matters but she thinks it's a great idea."

"She does? But why?"

"Because the climate will be better for me."

"Let's call Simon, see what he says."

"Jesus, would you listen to yourself. 'What about Mom? What about Simon?' The fact is they're both too busy to care. Mom spends all her time making sure Dad stays put, and Simon got his head up his arse being the big doctor. Besides, who the fuck cares what they think? This is about us, not them."

"Well sure, I know, but – "

"No, listen to me. There's new research, I've been reading about it. It's the higher elevation, the mountain air. It clears the head."

"Really? How can…" I stopped as Maggie started to cry. Iggy pushed the bottle against her lips. "Don't force her," I begged, my hands reaching for her.

He twisted away. "Never mind that for a minute. What about Calgary?"

Maggie's face was growing redder as she coughed and sputtered on the milk in her mouth. My breasts tingled and surged.

"Sure, sure. We'll move to Calgary." As I spoke I moved closer until I had the bottle in one hand and the other under Maggie's head. "Sure we will." Iggy still held her in his arms, but I could feel him relaxing, could feel him begin to release his hold.

"It's going to be good for us, just wait and see."

"Uh-huh…sounds great." I kept my voice calm, quiet. Iggy let Maggie slip into my arms. I put her to my breast as we stood there in the kitchen. Iggy kissed us both on our foreheads and squeezed us to him. Tears in my eyes, I cooed into Maggie's face, soothing sounds that were as much for me as for her.

Iggy set to work getting ready for the move. I suggested we wait until we saved more money. He insisted we'd be fine. When I pushed the issue, he raided his mother's freezer and cupboards so we didn't have to buy groceries except for things we needed for Maggie. We lived the rest of the month on rice and freezer-burnt meat. He rarely went out to the bar. He even had the phone disconnected, saying we could use Dad's or his mother's if we needed to make a call.

Within days, the whole town knew we were moving. Everyone was giving us advice – at the store, at the post office, on the street, where to go, how to get work, the best route to take. Too much advice. Yet not enough. Nobody said, don't go, don't leave your home, don't take that new baby all the way across the country. Not Dad, who thought Maggie was Melinda and who kept wondering where he'd put her stroller. No one. Least of all Josephine, who barely acknowledged Maggie's existence and would doubtless be glad to see both our backs.

Never one to hold her tongue though, Josephine did manage to get her two cents in. She caught me at my weakest. I'd had another sleepless night, with Maggie fussing and Iggy snoring and me worrying, about Maggie's endless cough, about Iggy's increasingly odd behaviour, about living in a city where I didn't know a soul. I had just returned from driving Iggy to school. Maggie was crying so hard that I'd had to pull over to settle her down. The front wheel slipped into the ditch. The car wouldn't budge. Before long I had joined Maggie, both of us crying our eyes out until some guy came along and pushed us out. The rest of the way home, all I could think about was that if that happened in Alberta, no one would stop. Or if someone did, he would rape me or steal Maggie. Imagining all the horrible things that would happen to us, I cried all the way. Josephine was unlocking the door to the ice-cream shop as I pulled up. When she saw my face, she asked what was wrong. I admitted that I didn't want to go to Alberta.

Her lips tightened. "Don't be ridiculous, Bridgina."

I shifted Maggie from one arm to the other. "But what if…?"

"What if nothing!" Josephine cut in. "Do you ever think about anyone but yourself? Huh? Do you?"

"But I think something's wrong with him." I spoke the words fast before she could interrupt, or before I could think through the meaning of them.

What looked to be a moment of recognition in her eyes disappeared in a flash. "Ignatius told me himself this is what he needs. Least you can do is give it a try. He's your husband. You got a youngster together," she said with a rare nod to Maggie.

"But – "

"'For better or for worse.' Remember that." She went inside and shut the door.

In sickness and in health – the words imprinted themselves onto my brain – *till death do us part.* My life stretched before me, in all its wild uncertainty, in all its unending fear. Dear God, what had I done? And dear God, what was I going to do all the way out in Alberta?

On April 1st we boarded the ferry to North Sydney. I had $461 in my purse, 212 of which Dad had slipped me the day before, emptying his pockets when he'd seen me packing the car. I was grateful he was a man who had never used a credit card and carried a lot of cash. I'd heard Iggy thank Grace over the phone for money, but when I asked him how much, he said it was just a few bucks for the road.

As we pulled out of Port aux Basques, Iggy made his way to the bar. With Maggie in my arms, I stood on the deck and watched the land fall away.

Generally, I hated it when Iggy got into one of his hyper moods. This time I was grateful for his nonstop energy. I was also grateful that he didn't get us killed as he careened along the highway with Jethro Tull blaring on the eight track, and that by some miracle we didn't get stopped by the cops. The last thing we needed was a speeding ticket, or for the police to find out that Iggy didn't have a licence, or, God forbid, for them to find the bag of dope he'd stashed under the driver's seat.

He was like a man possessed, like he himself was driven, to get us to Alberta and as far away from everything we knew as fast as he could. We drove off the ferry and kept going, straight through the Maritimes and into Quebec. When I saw a sign for St. Louis de Ha Ha I thought about asking Iggy to stop, but what was the point? I had assumed that we'd at least stop at Simon's in Montreal and spend the night and have a shower and a hot meal. Iggy was on the line for only a minute before he hopped back into the car. "He's out of town. Gone the rest of the week." Knowing I would see Simon had been the one thing keeping my spirits up – a familiar face, a friend, someone who cared about us. "No? Really?" I said. "Yeah, really," Iggy shot back. "But did you tell him we were coming?" I asked. "Of course. Son of a bitch got better things to do obviously." That did not sound like the Simon I knew, but there was no sense arguing. Iggy pulled out of the parking lot and back onto the Trans Canada. On we drove, through Northern Ontario and onto the prairies, that flat land an endless horizon taking us farther and farther away.

Even though Iggy did most of the driving, with me spelling him off for a few hours here and there, I was exhausted. It was impossible to get any decent sleep in the car because the seat didn't recline. My head kept whipping forward. Every part of my body was stiff and sore. Whenever I bent my head a stabbing sensation shot from the base of my neck to the top of my skull.

Somewhere after a sign that said "Chestermere," Calgary came into view. Under a sun-filled April sky, the city stretched in all directions, construction cranes scattered here and there, then clustered together in what must have been the downtown core. Beyond that, the backdrop, the mountains, so white and flawless and picture-perfect on a cold clear day they looked like someone had painted a mural and propped it at the far edge of the city.

Within the space of a few miles and minutes, the sun disappeared. By the time we stopped at a pay phone in Calgary, sleet pellets the size of beach pebbles battered the windshield so hard I could barely see Iggy in the phone booth.

I leaned back in the seat and stretched as best I could. When I raised my arms the pong of sour sweat hit my nostrils. Washing with paper towels in gas station bathrooms was not doing the trick. I hadn't had a bath in five days, or slept in a bed, or eaten a decent meal. We'd been living in the car and subsisting on sandwiches, trying to save whatever we could for when we arrived in Calgary. Our biggest expense besides gas was disposable diapers. Confined to such a small space, it was impossible to ignore a dirty diaper. I had less than $200 left. I doubted Iggy had much in his pocket either.

He hung up the phone and sprinted towards us. When he opened the door, a damp chill shot through the car. Maggie woke with a start.

"Any luck?" I lifted Maggie up from her car seat and pulled up my T-shirt, thankful that I hadn't stopped breastfeeding even though I was one of those unlucky women who did not lose weight while doing it. I was constantly hungry and always eating, but it was still cheaper than formula. Once we were settled, I would switch, and then hopefully fit into something other than sweatpants. Maggie sucked for a few seconds then pulled away. She grabbed at my thumb and held on to it, her bright curious eyes looking left and right till they landed on Iggy.

"Yeah." Iggy brushed the ice pellets off his head. "Got us a place."

"Oh my God!" I was so shocked I leaned over and hugged him, squishing Maggie between us, which didn't bother her at all. "That's great. Where is it? What's it like?"

Iggy looked pleased. "Near downtown. Place called Victoria Park." He tugged on Maggie's foot. "Doesn't that sound pretty, Maggie? You want to live in Victoria Park?"

For the first time in weeks I felt like smiling. We had pulled over into an empty lot on 16th Avenue, the skinny stretch of the Trans-Canada Highway that runs east to west through the heart of Calgary, blocks of gas stations and fast-food outlets, shopfronts and motels, a continual line of asphalt and cars and streetlights and sirens. Victoria Park had a nice ring to it, evoking TV images of lovely homes surrounded by white picket fences, with mown grass and big trees and well-tended flowerbeds.

"I can't believe you found us a place." I paused. "But how much is it? We don't have much money left."

Iggy let go of Maggie's foot and rummaged through the clothes and garbage on the floor of the back seat until he found a can of Coke. He'd been living on the stuff lately. "It's a house, I think. And they'll spot us till I get a job."

"Wow! That's awful nice." I was too relieved to question it.

"See? I told you Alberta was going to work out."

He steered the car back onto the street and took a left turn. Ahead of us was the jagged cityscape of downtown with the red top of the Calgary Tower spiking above it all.

I put Maggie back in her car seat. "What do you mean, 'you think' it's a house?"

"Well, no, it is a house." He drank some Coke, then offered it to me. "He said 'house,' so it must be."

I took the can, along with one of the sandwiches I'd made when we stopped for gas outside Swift Current that morning. "A whole house?"

"No. No, we have to share."

I chewed the stale bread and ham, the process cheese sticking to my teeth, then swished some Coke around my mouth. Hopefully we wouldn't be in the basement, but I wasn't going to be picky. A basement apartment would be fine, better than our cramped little place above the ice-cream shop, at least for a while. "I can't wait to see it."

Maggie started to fuss. Iggy made funny faces at her in the rearview mirror and reached back to tickle her feet. Within a minute, she was cooing and smiling.

"I'm so glad we can get settled into our own apartment right off." I ate the last of the sandwich and drained the Coke. "But what about furniture?"

"Actually, we don't get an apartment all to ourselves."

"Oh." Share with strangers? With a baby? That was less appealing, but I told myself to snap out of it. So we didn't get our own house, or our own apartment.

"But it is partly furnished already," he added.

"Well…that's good. Anyway, I'm glad you found it." Feeling a burst of energy I started reaching around and cleaning up the car. "By the way, how did you?"

He was peering through the front windshield, his face covered with a week's worth of beard that hadn't grown in evenly, his hair stringy from need of a wash. "Oh…you know, friends," he said.

"Really?" He hadn't mentioned having friends in Calgary. "Who?"

"Some guys…fellows from home." His tone was evasive.

I stuffed the last of the garbage into a bag. "Anyone I know?" I smiled uneasily.

He knew enough to hesitate. "Gord MacDonald."

20

Victoria Park. Smack in the middle of the hooker and drug trades on the eastern edge of downtown Calgary. Renamed after Queen Victoria, it was originally known as East Ward, which was more appropriate. With its pawn and porn shops, its seedy bars and broken windows, a warden would have come in handy. So much for white picket fences.

Gord and his brother Dave, who looked a lot like Gord but with dirty red hair and meaner eyes, and who spoke in a shrill voice that seemed at odds with his brawny frame, had bought a big dilapidated two-storey and rented out rooms to whoever was passing through. The smell of wet dog and stale urine didn't bother Iggy. Nothing did. He was out of Exile Cove.

Lucky for us, a few days before we arrived the cops had come by looking for the basement tenant. He wasn't there at the time, or welcome back later. The MacDonalds did not appreciate being on police radar. The room was ours.

The basement had obviously been an afterthought because someone had dug it out after the house was built. They must have run out of drywall because one wall was just painted concrete. The ceiling felt too low but that might have been because there were no windows. My first purchase in Calgary was a pair of night-lights so I could see through the pitch black when Maggie woke up. The air was musty and cold, which didn't help Maggie's cough, and the thin carpet didn't reach to all corners. On the plus side, there was a small area outside the bedroom that some previous tenant had furnished with an ancient brown sofa smelling only slightly of smoke and sweat. And there was a coffee table with a fake plant and an old TV on it. Maggie and I spent most of our time down there, trying to avoid the MacDonald brothers and Satan, a huge German shepherd that looked so longingly at Maggie every time we were in the same room that I made Iggy promise never to leave her alone with the thing. But the best thing about the basement was that no one else went down there. We had the space, such as it was, to ourselves. Once I taped up Victor's Desiderata poster, it felt a little like home.

As much as I hated being left on my own in that house, I was relieved when Iggy found a job. Unfortunately, he was unskilled labour. His teaching degree meant little with a hammer in his hand. After he paid off his debts from the previous week, the hits of dope and his portion of the beer kitty that kept the fridge stocked, there was little left. We'd spent the last of Dad's money to pay for second-hand bedroom furniture. When the car broke down we couldn't afford to get it fixed and had to sell it. I was stuck in Vic Park.

I hesitated to go outside. It was nothing to come across drunks in the middle of the day, or underdressed women in thigh-high boots hanging around street corners, waiting for a car to stop, a transaction to take place, a short ride down the road before being dumped back on their corner shifting their clothing into place. I couldn't stay indoors forever, though. One day I pushed Maggie's stroller as far as the Stampede Grounds. Looking through the gates, I pictured us there come July, me and Iggy and Maggie, riding the Ferris wheel, eating mini-doughnuts, looking at the horses and wandering through the tipis. Head filled with images of cowboys and Indians, I started for home. Across the street, a black dog the size of a small horse rummaged among the garbage that littered the sidewalks. His tail was wagging but I couldn't remember if that was a good sign or bad. He looked mean and he looked hungry, like Maureen McCarthy's Chihuahuas would make a nice lunch. There was no sign of an owner. I walked faster, as quietly as possible, trying to go unnoticed. I never thought I'd be glad to see the MacDonald house.

At one point, I counted 14 people living there, although it was hard to say who belonged and who didn't. I doubted they knew my name. I didn't know most of theirs either. I gave the regulars nicknames – "Big Hair" looked like she'd spent time on the street corner, "Boy" had "MOMMA" tattooed across the back of his right hand, and then there was "Cow-Boy" who wore a Stetson and an oversized belt buckle that he always had his hand on, like it was a talisman. The place reminded me of Iggy's house in St. John's, except everyone there had been friendly. Dave's crowd were a hard lot who, if they bothered to notice me, didn't appear to particularly care for me or have any interest in a five-month old baby. Not that I wanted them anywhere near Maggie. They were always getting high or coming down, and the air had a permanent reek of spilled booze mixed with hash and marijuana fumes. Used needles in the garbage were common. There was an ominous atmosphere of something ready to pop, not a party exactly, more the vibe that comes from a drugged-out crowd ready to either start a fight or fall down. It was hard to predict which way it might go. Once, when Iggy was at work, I thought I heard a gunshot, followed by the dog barking and Dave yelling and tossing someone out through the back entrance at the top of the basement stairs. By that time I'd pushed the dresser against the bedroom door and was curled up in the corner with the lights off, holding Maggie tight. We survived the day but Satan wasn't so lucky. He'd run after the guy and got hit by a car. Iggy said Dave was heartbroken, crying and moaning and threatening to kill the driver who killed his poor dog. Two days later he brought home another German shepherd who looked almost identical to Satan, which is what they called him.

Some of the tenants worked, but most, including Gord and Dave, didn't appear to. Yet they drove expensive trucks and had the latest stereo equipment. Music blared at all hours, hard rock with monotonous drum rolls and electric guitar solos. The MacDonald brothers travelled to Vancouver on a regular basis, trips that had an air of mystery about them, one-sided phone conversations that made me think of speaking in code, hushed voices that often went silent when I entered the room. I knew what was going on. When they were home, there was a revolving door of burly men in black leather and tough looking women covered in tattoos, picking up or dropping off packages. Exchanges, sometimes discreet, sometimes not, were made. The doorbell, a harsh triple clang, sounded day and night.

Time was sluggish, the days dragged on. I read whatever I could get my hands on, cheap paperbacks from the drugstore, the day-old *Herald* that Iggy would have brought home the evening before. Iggy liked to read the newspaper. In fact he placed an inordinate amount of trust in what he read there, as if being in print in a daily paper made a thing gospel, which was interesting given that he was so unconventional otherwise. I came to realize that reading the *Herald*, and quoting from it, made him feel superior to others who were less educated or not as well read. He still considered himself an intellectual, but a rebel to the system at the same time. He let others think that was why he worked construction, that he was following his conviction that it was more worthwhile to do honest labour with his bare hands than to lower himself to work for "the Man."

Maggie liked it when we read to her, regardless of what it was. She would sit in Iggy's lap before he headed upstairs in the evenings and he would quote snippets from the paper. During the day, I read to her from whatever book I had on the go, changing my inflection for the different characters, like in the plays I had put on in my room before I had a friend, before Katie. Now I had Maggie.

I left the basement to shower, and then only when Iggy was home so Maggie wouldn't be alone, and to cook our meals. I tried to use the kitchen when fewer people were around but it wasn't always possible. I would lug the playpen up and set it up next to the fridge. Gord hated that. "Hurry on and get that fucking thing out of here," he'd say. Or if Maggie was crying, I would hear mutters of "… shut that goddamn kid up." Shut up yourself, I'd mutter under my breath.

Our meals were simple. The corner store, which had bars on all the windows and was run by surly men who looked through me if they looked at me at all, was three blocks away. They didn't carry much meat or fresh vegetables, and what they did have was more expensive, but I wasn't going too far unless Iggy was with me. When Maggie and I took our daily walk it was usually in circles around those same few blocks. I only bought what I could carry while pushing Maggie's stroller, which was just as well because I didn't trust the other tenants not to eat anything I left in the fridge. We could hardly afford to feed ourselves, or, more specifically, me. Maggie still breastfed most of the time. Iggy didn't eat much.

I always took Maggie with me, ever since the Saturday morning I'd left her sleeping while Iggy dozed on the bed. "I'm just running to the store," I'd whispered in his ear. "Stay here with Mags till I get back, okay?" He'd nodded and I went off, enjoying a rare taste of freedom. I walked farther west to a bigger store with a better selection, taking my time to enjoy the spring sunshine. When I got back an hour later, Iggy was in the kitchen with Gord. Maggie was down for a nap, Iggy told me.

"Jesus! I told you to never leave her by herself in this house."

"What the fuck's wrong with this place?" Gord actually sounded surprised.

I was already heading for the stairs but took two seconds to turn and glare at him. "It's a fucking drug den and I got a kid, that's what's fucking wrong with it."

Iggy looked nervous. "Now, Bridge, don't – "

"Oh fuck off, the pair of you," I called out over my shoulder before hitting the stairs two at a time. On the bottom step I stopped cold. Satan-Number-Two was lying on the floor, his nose pointing at the partially open bedroom door. I walked past him, so close he could have bitten my ankle. When I reached the bedroom I scurried inside and shut the door. I checked on Maggie, who was fine, then peeked out. Satan looked at me, one ear rising slightly, then got up and left. After that, I wasn't afraid of him.

Sometimes when I woke up in the night Iggy wasn't beside me even though Maggie was sound asleep in her playpen. I'd find him sitting on the brown sofa drawing on a pad of paper, the end-of-night snow hissing on the TV. The first time it happened I asked him what he was drawing. He tried to explain, but it was a muddle of words that made no sense. The next day he didn't remember any of it. He shrugged it off and said he'd been a sleepwalker since he was a kid. Great. Something new to worry about.

I longed for home. In my mind, Exile Cove took on a welcoming aura, free of fog and bathed in sunshine, where Josephine was less mean and Dad was his old self. I tried to call collect, but when the operator couldn't make Dad understand about accepting the charges, I told her to forget about it and hung up. The second time I called, Josephine answered after six rings. "What?" she yelled into the line. I put down the receiver before the operator asked. Both times, I had waited until Gord and Dave were out. Dave had made it clear that the phone was off limits. It was a business phone, he'd said looking straight at me, not a gossip line to Newfoundland. If we needed to make a call, he'd added, there were plenty of pay phones in Calgary. I hadn't had the opportunity since.

I had written Katie as soon as I knew about the move, hoping Fort McMurrary wasn't too far from Calgary, and I'd sent her our address the day after we arrived. I still hadn't heard from her.

One afternoon in mid-May, I happened to be upstairs when the mail came and saw a letter from Grace. I grabbed it and put it in my pocket, then waited impatiently for Iggy to get home from work. I was cooking supper when he came in. I gave him the letter and forced myself to wash dishes and be quiet until he'd reached the end. His face remained expressionless, but as soon as he finished he stuffed the letter and the envelope into his pocket and marched from the room.

"Iggy!" Before I could pick Maggie up to follow, the bathroom door slammed.

He trudged back in 15 minutes later, holding a tissue to his nose. He'd been having a lot of nosebleeds. I held Maggie in one arm and stirred a pot of tomato sauce with the other hand. He tossed the tissue and took Maggie from me, swinging her up high and making her giggle.

When I asked if I could read the letter, he took a pile of shredded paper from his pocket. I stared at the scraps in his hand like someone had torn up my last meal ticket. "What did you do that for?" I was too upset to yell.

"We're having nothing to do with her," he said, throwing them in the garbage.

"Iggy, she's your mother."

"She's his wife and she's killing him."

"What do you mean?" I picked a couple of pieces out of the garbage.

"He's back at the Waterford." He grabbed the paper from my hands and flung it back into the plastic bag. "New York was a waste of time. I told her that the last time."

"The last time? You heard from your mother before this?"

Maggie was starting to fuss. Iggy bounced her up and down in his arms.

"When did you hear from her? Why didn't you tell me?" I'd been feeling cut off, and angry too. I hadn't expected to hear from my family. Melinda was still mad at me, Josephine didn't care one way or the other, Dad probably didn't remember I'd left. But Grace or Simon should have made an effort.

"It doesn't matter."

"It does so. I haven't heard a thing since I got here. They can't call if anything's wrong."

"So what? Sure there's nothing wrong."

"I miss home, Ig." Didn't he know how much I needed to hear from someone? "Has she seen Dad? Did she mention him? Tell me what she said. How is everyone?"

"Who cares, for Christ's sake? He shouldn't still be in there."

I didn't need to ask who he was talking about. "Maybe he needs to be in there."

"No. No way. If she'd take him home, he'd be okay."

"How do you know?"

"Because! Fuck, would you listen to me for once. I know that's what he needs. She knows it, too." He was bouncing Maggie faster. "But no, she's tired of it. It's her fault he's there in the first place, and she won't do a goddamn thing to help him."

"But Iggy, why?" I was so frustrated I didn't stop to watch my tone or how I phrased it. "Why is it her fault? What the hell is she doing that's so goddamn wrong?"

Maggie was crying now, her arms out to me. I took her from him.

"Fuck! I already fucking told you." He picked up the dishtowel and started twisting it into a tight coil. Sweat was popping out on his forehead and that vein near his left eye was pulsing again. I hated that vein.

I tried to backtrack. "Sorry, I'm just lonely." Maggie was rubbing her nose in my cheek. I took the towel from him and wiped both our faces. "Hey Mags, you're a drippy girl," I said in an extra light voice, pressing our noses together, which brought a small smile to her face. "That's my girl. Such a good little Maggie."

But Iggy wasn't done. "I wish you'd listen to me. Fuck!"

Maggie's arms tightened around my neck. "Yeah okay, you're right, sorry – "

He was in no mood to be pacified. "It's all bad enough, you think you'd be on my side, not sticking up for her…"

"Iggy, what are you talking about?" I tried the light and airy voice again. It had worked on Maggie. "I am on your side. You know that."

"How the fuck would I know that?"

"Because I'm your wife, whatever you need – "

"Leave it, okay? Just fucking *leave* it."

"I'm sorry. I didn't – "

"See, there you go. You can't stop. You can't shut up."

Gord walked in. He glared at Maggie, who was screeching by this point, snot trailing down her nose and into her open mouth.

"Fuck," he muttered. "Listen here, lovebirds, keep it down to a dull roar."

Iggy gave me a reproachful look. "Sorry about that. A little misunderstanding."

"Hey, if you need a break from the old lady, you can do a run to Vancouver."

I tensed. Not Vancouver.

"I don't know…" Iggy started to say.

"Easy money, man."

I moved closer to Iggy. "No, no need for that. We're great, sure we are."

Iggy eyes met mine. "Thanks, Gord, but I kind of need to be here, you know? The baby's so little and all."

"Marriage, it's your goddamn funeral." He moved closer to Iggy, but I heard him. "Especially to fatso there." He pulled a joint from his pocket and left the room.

Iggy made an odd noise, somewhere between a half-hearted laugh and a cough. "Don't mind him, okay, Bridge? But leave Mom out of it, understand?"

I nodded. If I tried to speak, I would cry.

Iggy rubbed his hand up and down my back. "We'll be fine on our own." He squeezed the top of my shoulders, then followed Gord into the living room.

I turned and stared out the kitchen window. My reflection stared back, the fat face, the dishevelled hair, the crying baby in my arms. What the hell was I going to do?

21

"Hey!" Dave's voice shouted down into the basement.

I was eating my standard lunch of a peanut butter and jam sandwich. PBJs were cheap and I could keep the fixings in our room. Maggie had just gone for a nap.

"Someone's here for you."

"For me?" I put down the jobs section of the paper, which I'd been searching in hopes of finding some sort of work I could do from home. "Who is it?"

"I don't fucking know, do I?" he yelled in his weird falsetto.

I glanced at the bedroom door and decided that this one time Maggie would be safe for two minutes. I ran upstairs. Just inside the front door, wide eyes peering into the living room where Dave and his cronies were drinking beer, stood Katie.

She turned. "Bridge, thank God." She looked back into the living room. "I wasn't sure I had the right place."

My eyes followed hers – discarded food containers, dirty ashtrays, overflowing garbage, empty bottles littering the floor. "Yep, you do." And then we were hugging and shrieking, none of which aroused much curiosity from Dave's druggie friends.

"Come on." I grabbed her hand and pulled her towards the basement stairs.

"Where's the baby?" Katie said at the bottom. "I'm dying to see her."

I put my finger to my lips and opened the bedroom door. Maggie was lying on her back, eyes closed, one hand peeking out above her pink fleece blanket.

"Oh my God," Katie whispered, "she's gorgeous. And look at all that hair, and the teeny tiny little fingers." She touched Maggie's chin. "She's got Simon's dimple."

I thought of it as Iggy's dimple but I let it go. "And her eyes are after getting right dark, just like Iggy's."

She brushed her finger across Maggie's cheek. Maggie's mouth pursed but she didn't wake up. "I knew you guys would have the perfect baby. How's Iggy with her?"

"He's great. You should see the two of them together." Despite his shortcomings, Iggy was a loving father. The nights that Maggie woke him up coughing, he would walk the floor with her, more patient with his daughter than he'd ever been with me, or with his students, or with his drug buddies. "She just went down so she'll sleep for a bit yet."

We tiptoed out and pulled the door almost shut behind us.

"I can't believe you're here," I said when we sat down. "When I didn't hear from you I thought something might be wrong."

"You didn't hear from me because you gave me the wrong address and my letter came back. And when I got your last one, which was only yesterday, by the way, because Mom didn't want to forward it because she keeps saying I should move back up there – "

"What? You're living here?"

She nodded. "I keep tormenting Mom, telling her I'm a big city girl now."

"Oh my God, that's great."

"I love it here. Anyway, when I got the letter I figured out that it was supposed to say SE instead of SW. Seamus tried to hunt down a phone number but he couldn't find one. So I decided I'd just show up on your doorstep and here I am." She spread her arms and looked around.

I might have been embarrassed if it had been anyone but Katie. "Yeah, we're not supposed to use the phone. But never mind. How long can you stay?"

She looked at her watch. "I'm on lunch so I only got half an hour left."

"Lunch? You want a sandwich? I got bread and peanut butter."

"No, I had something at my desk earlier. I'm filling in at a small oil company, secretary's sick or something. Just temp but it'll tide me over for now."

I grabbed her arm with both hands and squealed quietly. "Oh my God it's really you. Why did you leave McMurray?"

"A fucking man, what else?" She rolled her eyes. "Brian, that guy I was dating, he got transferred to here so I thought I'd come in and stay with Seamus, check Calgary out. Son of a bitch dumped me two weeks after we got here. Turns out he already had a girlfriend. And me after quitting my job." She grinned. "I hated that fucking job, mind you. There is nothing worse, and I mean nothing, than sitting on your arse all day every day typing shit you don't care about or understand. And I was fed up with McMurray. I was fed up with Brian too. But he's still a prick."

I laughed. "Listen to you. You sound just like your old self, potty-mouth and all."

"I know. Fuck, as long as I watch the swearing at work, who gives a shit?"

"And look at you, you look like a million bucks." She was dressed in a stylish skirt and blouse that fit her to a tee, showing off her tiny waist and long, slim legs. And the blouse was a forest green that made her eyes pop, even in the dim basement lighting. I looked down at my clothes – Iggy's old blue sweats and a baggy plaid shirt that was permanently stained with baby vomit. No wonder Iggy never wanted to have sex. "Not like lump-o-lard here."

"Go on, you'd never know you just had a baby."

I ignored that. "You're definitely staying in Calgary, right?" I'd only just found her again. Already I couldn't imagine Calgary without her.

"Well, I got to go back to help Mom – " She stopped abruptly. "Shit, that's right, you don't know. Mom got pregnant again. Can you fathom that, at their age? With twins, no less. She didn't know it till she was well along. Thought she was in menopause, poor thing. Anyway, she had them yesterday, two boys, God help us, two months early, and there's all kinds of complications."

"That's awful. Your poor mother."

"She had to have a C-section and ended up losing a lot of blood for some reason I still can't figure out. Dad wasn't making much sense on the phone. Then she and the babies ended up with some kind of infection and they're all hooked up to IVs. I'm not sure of all the details but me and Seamus are driving up right after work. I'll be back soon as I can, though."

"Good." I breathed a selfish sigh of relief. "So Seamus is living here, too?"

"Sort of. He shares a place with a bunch of other roughnecks, spends his time off between here and McMurray and St. John's. Got a girl in every port, he does."

"Does he ever hear from Simon?"

"Yeah, sure. He dropped in on him in Montreal last time he went home."

"How's he doing?"

"He's great." She looked puzzled. "Why? Don't you guys hear from him?"

"No, Iggy's still mad at him for not coming to the wedding." Changing the subject, I squeezed her hand. "It's some good to see you. You promise you'll be back?"

"Hell, yeah. I love this city. There's so much to do, and lots of jobs." She grinned. "And the men! Holy Shit! Don't you just love it?"

"I haven't seen much of it, having a new baby and all." I turned as if to check the bedroom door and wiped the tears that had appeared out of nowhere.

"Bridge?" Katie grabbed my hand, which was busy plucking at the stuffing coming out of the arm of the sofa. "What's wrong? Tell me." She dropped my hand and slapped herself upside the head. "Shit, of course, your father. And here I am going on and on about me. Christ, I'm so sorry."

"What are you talking about? What…what's wrong with Dad?"

"Wrong? Well…sure he's…Jesus, you don't know, do you?"

I felt sick. And scared. "Katie, what…?"

"Oh, Bridge, don't tell me no one told you." She looked away for a second, then turned back and took both my hands in hers. "Your father, he died three weeks ago."

I could feel my face go all wobbly, like I had no control over it. I tried to pull my hands away but she held on tighter, then moved over and put her arms around me.

"But…no, it can't be. Dad's…dead? What…what happened?"

There were tears in her eyes. "It was a stroke. He died right away."

"Oh my God."

"No one got in touch with you?"

"No." I sobbed into her silky shirt. "Nobody told me anything."

"Oh, Bridge, that's so rotten. I can't believe Melinda didn't call."

"She didn't have the number. I only sent it to Dad in case of emergency."

"She could have done something. Didn't she write or anything?"

"No – " A thought hit me. "Can you stay with Maggie a minute?"

"Yeah, sure."

I ran up the stairs. Ignoring everyone, I headed for the cardboard box near the front door where I'd seen mail piled up for previous tenants. I rifled through it. There, in the middle of a bunch of envelopes, was one addressed to 'B. Ashe'.

Back in the basement I opened it. One small page in Melinda's handwriting.

"Bridgina, Dad died yesterday. Josephine gave me your address when she called. She's not doing well. Very upset. I'm going home tomorrow to arrange the funeral. I don't suppose you'll get this in time to make it. You should get a phone. Melinda."

I sat looking at the sheet of paper. I wanted to blame someone. Melinda. The MacDonalds. Iggy. There was no one to blame. Melinda did write. The MacDonalds probably thought B. Ashe was an ex-boarder. It wasn't Iggy's fault, or Josephine's, or anyone's. Maybe Dad's for dying, for not giving the phone number to Josephine. It didn't matter. Dad was dead.

"Bridge? You okay?"

"He was the only one who ever cared about me."

"Come on, that's not true."

"Yeah it is. Josephine didn't. Melinda didn't."

"You got us. You're like part of our family."

"I feel like everything's falling apart. And I don't know what to do." My breath sped up, short and quick and uneven. "I don't know if I can do this anymore."

"What do you mean?"

"I'm just…Oh God…"

"Bridge!" Katie's voice was sharp. "Tell me."

I opened my mouth and everything I was worried about came rushing out. Except Iggy. I couldn't bring myself to talk about him, or about us. But all the rest of it poured out of me – how lonely I was, how I worried about Maggie living in a damp and dingy basement, how I had no money to make things better. How I never laughed anymore, but only felt like crying. How awful it was living in Gord MacDonald's house. "One morning I came home from a walk with Maggie, and some guy I'd never seen before was passed out in our bed. There was a used needle next to him." I lowered my voice as all the fear I'd been pushing down foamed to the surface. "I know they're dealing drugs. What if they piss somebody off, or somebody shows up with a gun to steal drugs, or – "

"Bridge, stop." Katie moved over and gave me a hug. "We'll sort it out. What about Iggy? What does he think?"

"Oh, you know." I blew my nose with the tissue she'd stuffed into my hand. "He couldn't get a teaching job so he's doing construction. He works all day and sometimes late but the money's not very good and it's so expensive here. You know what it's like."

"Frig, do I ever. I wish I had some money, I'd give it to you."

"I'm sorry, Katie. I haven't seen you in so long and all I can do is tell you all my problems."

"What are friends for, girl. Now let me think on this. I'd ask Seamus if you could stay at his place but it's no better than a cheap motel half the time." She glanced at her watch. "Shit, I'm going to be late. And I don't want to piss them off because I only just started and already I got a family emergency and needing time off. So look, I got to go but I'll call you as soon as I'm back from McMurrray."

"No phone, remember. Give me your number and I'll call you."

"Okay, but in the meantime, you got to try to figure out where you can get some money. Josephine, Mel, somebody, anybody. Fuck the pride nonsense, okay?" She wrote down Seamus's address and phone number and her parents' number and pressed it into my hand. "You got to get out of this dump."

I turned as Maggie started to cough in the bedroom.

Katie jumped up. "I was hoping she'd wake up before I left. Let me get her."

I followed along so Maggie could see me. Her breathing was a little raspy as she stared at Katie, then, lower lip quivering, reached out to me. I scooped her from Katie's arms, grateful that she needed me so much. Me, fat old me, in my baggy sweats and stained shirt, with my runny nose and my eyes all red-rimmed and swollen. I took my soggy tissue from my sleeve and wiped her nose.

Katie tickled Maggie's chin and made clucking noises. "I wouldn't worry about the cough, by the way. Babies cough and cry and puke. It's what they do."

Safe in my arms, Maggie was soon smiling, yet keeping a firm grip on my ear.

Katie looked at her watch again. "Shit. Call me, okay?" With a quick hug to the both of us, she turned and ran up the stairs.

Something changed in me that afternoon. I could sense it happening as the minutes ticked by, never more strongly than when I looked at Maggie. What if anything happened to me? As much as Iggy loved her, could he take proper care of her, especially in this place? I was the adult. I was her protector, her everything, at least for now. Seeing Katie, then finding out that Dad had died, triggered something inside me – anger, pride, rebellion, who knows what. I could no longer just wait for something to happen, I had to make it happen. I pushed aside my sadness over Dad's death. That would have to wait for another time. I spent the rest of the afternoon thinking and stewing, weighing the possibilities, until I came up with a plan. At four o'clock I bundled Maggie into her stroller and headed down to the pay phone near the corner store. By the time Iggy got home, I had it sorted out. I just had to find the right moment to tell him.

22

Our apartment was on the second floor, one-bedroom, partly furnished. After we moved in our bed and dresser, there was still room for Maggie's playpen in the corner, and though the closet was small it had a row of shelves so we'd have more than enough room to store our clothes. The dining area consisted of a metal table with one leg shorter than the others so that the table tilted when we leaned on it. Some tape and a scrap of wood fixed that. There were three chairs, which would leave more space for Maggie to roll around. The living room had a sofa with a chair that almost matched, and although the coffee table was old and water-stained, it had rounded corners so I wouldn't need to worry about Maggie falling on a sharp edge and bashing her head open. There were a few dishes and pots, and toilet paper and soap in the bathroom. Best of all, there was no Gord. No Dave. No drugged-out strangers. Just me and Iggy and Maggie in our own safe place.

The first morning I awoke to a soft breeze tickling my cheek and the lovely caw-caw-caw chatter of magpies. I opened my eyes. Sun streamed through the sheers that covered the open window. I didn't need to remind myself where I was. I had woken up several times in the night, hugging myself with joy at the sight of moonlight in the bedroom. Later, cooking peas in my own kitchen without rushing in case someone else wanted the stove, then sitting at the table, mushing the peas and feeding them to Maggie in her thrift-store highchair, the sound of birds chirping as warm air breezed through the open patio doors, I almost cried with happiness. We were above ground again.

When I'd phoned Melinda I'd been desperate, ready to lie and beg, whatever it took. Victor answered the phone, fortunately, as it turned out. After commiserating about Dad, he started asking questions about Calgary, how I'd gotten there, who I'd gone with, where I was living. It wasn't long before we both discovered that he knew nothing about my marriage to Iggy or about Maggie. Everything – my determination, my energy, my hopes – deflated as the realization dawned on me. How could I ask for Melinda's help knowing she cared so little that she hadn't even told him?

Victor must have heard it in my tone. "Bridgina, you okay?"

"Yeah, sure," I said, trying to keep the wobble out of my voice.

He took a moment then spoke firmly. "I'm not sure what Melinda's up to but that's neither here nor there at this moment. Right now, I want to know what's going on with you."

Poor Victor. Had he known what he was getting into when he married Melinda, that he'd end up having to help me out of a bind? "I'm sorry, Victor. This isn't your problem."

His tone softened. "We're family, Bridge, and I'm making it my problem, okay? Now let's start at the beginning and go from there." When I didn't say anything, he added, "Remember, I am your stepfather."

My stepfather? Melinda wanted no part of being my mother, yet here he was stepping so readily into the parental role. The man did not deserve this.

"Think about Maggie," he said.

That did it, of course. Victor would have known that.

So I told him everything, starting with the fight with Melinda and the awful things I'd said, "even about you," I admitted. I told him about the MacDonald house, the drugs and the prostitutes, Maggie's cough which, despite Katie's assurances, I still worried about. Everything except Iggy. He didn't mention him either.

When I was done, he asked for the pay phone number then told me to stay put and he'd call me back as soon as he could. Fifteen minutes later, I rushed to answer the phone. As soon as Victor started to speak, I could feel a weight begin to lift. His brother in Calgary knew someone who owned a small building up in the northwest part of the city. Victor would send him enough money to pay the deposit and first month's rent. When he suggested we keep it between the two of us, I was happy to agree.

The next thing I had to tackle was Iggy.

I had given serious thought to how best to approach him about moving. I'd learned over the course of our marriage that he was in his best mood with about two beers in him. Less than that and he could be grumpy, more and he was likely to forget half of what was said or disappear upstairs for the night. I was also counting on the leftover sympathy he'd have from hearing that Dad was dead, which I'd told him on beer number one. I had held my sadness in check all afternoon, trying to figure out how to get us the hell out of Victoria Park, and it came out in a rush of sorrow once I started. Iggy had been sweet, asking was I okay, and saying how sorry he was and how it was good Katie had been there when I found out. He held me in his arms as I cried myself dry.

"There's something else I need to talk to you about," I said afterward.

"Sure, babe," He gave my hand a sympathetic squeeze. "What's up?"

"I'm concerned about Maggie's cough. It won't go away." Maggie had woken me at least once every night of her short life, and since we'd moved to Calgary it had gotten worse. "And I was reading in the paper how cigarette smoke is bad for babies."

Iggy nodded. "Sure, yeah okay. I won't smoke around her anymore."

I smiled appreciatively. "I knew you'd say that. Problem is, it's not you so much as everybody else here. They all smoke like chimneys. I don't think they understand that we got Maggie to take care of. And I suppose it's not their fault. It's not till you become a parent that you know how important that is." I let that hang for a minute. "Anyway, I thought we could get our own place."

"How?" He dragged his eyes away from the game on TV. "From what I read there's not many vacancies. We're lucky we got this."

"Yeah, so lucky. But here's the good news." I went into my spiel then, the one I'd been rehearsing since talking to Victor, how Melinda had found my number in Dad's wallet, how she'd felt the need to touch base now that he was dead, how Victor's brother was thrilled to have a dependable young couple to move into one of his apartments, how it was the same price as we were already paying, which was almost true. The MacDonalds had been charging us a pretty penny.

"But what about a security deposit and furniture?" Iggy asked. "We don't have anything saved for that stuff."

"Melinda told him that might be a problem, that she didn't know if we were set up for that because we just moved here." I was starting to get the hang of this lying thing. "He told her we're family," I said, my voice upbeat, "that we shouldn't worry about it, just to go and give him a call."

Iggy raised his eyebrows. "Awful generous for not knowing us."

"Yeah, but that's what Dave and Gord did for us when we first got here." I could have choked on that one. "Anyway, that's what families do, according to him." Maggie began to cough in the bedroom. "So, what do you think? Should I give him a call?"

"Suppose it couldn't hurt. Sure, why not?" He held up the empty bottle. "Hey, grab me a beer while you're up, will you?"

I was so relieved I got him the beer before I went to see to Maggie.

Our building was one in a group of four in a middle-class area of town, well-kept family homes with children's toys scattered about on lush green lawns. There was a mall with a grocery store not too far away, and the nearby corner shop, R&B's, was owned by a friendly middle-aged couple named Ruth and Bill whose children took turns working there, and who made a fuss over Maggie every time we stopped in. There were no bars on the shop windows, no one hanging around the street looked like a prostitute or a drug dealer. Who knew a place named "Brentwood" would outshine Victoria Park?

Feeling safe again, I began taking Maggie for long walks in the neighbourhood, venturing out in a different direction each day, keeping my eye out for that white picket fence. The late June sun felt good on my face and the prairie wind lifted my hair as I pushed the stroller farther and faster, sometimes breaking into a run. I hadn't had so much energy in ages. My jeans were getting looser. The fresh air was good for Maggie, too. She rarely coughed anymore. Within a week of moving in, she slept through the night.

One of the best features of the apartment was the south-facing balcony. Maggie and I would sit outside on warm summer days and watch the world go by, enjoying the rabbits and squirrels and chipmunks. She'd point at everything that caught her attention. I would name it – a bird, a baby, a boy. She'd try to imitate me, her lips coming together to sound out a "b." I was so proud of her, six months old and trying to talk. I couldn't wait for that time to come. With Iggy either sleeping or working, I didn't have anyone but Maggie to talk to most days, except Vivian, my neighbour in the next apartment. She was working at the university while finishing her master's and came and went at odd hours, rushing in and out, always so busy but still taking a minute to chat. When she discovered that I'd done some typing back at MUN, she offered me $10 and her typewriter to finish up a short paper that was overdue. That was a very good day.

The other two tenants on my floor were an older couple who were downright unfriendly, and a middle-aged woman who, on the few occasions I'd seen her, had such a miserable look on her face that, even though she wasn't heavy, she'd put me in mind of Josephine. Victor phoned every few weeks from his office, asking did I have enough money, how was Maggie, how was I, wanting details, not letting me off the hook with "fine." He was less forthcoming with me when I asked about his children and Melinda. Still, I had the impression that all was not well. I didn't push. After all his help I felt compelled to tell him about my life but I did not feel I had the right to pry into his.

Katie had decided to stay in Fort McMurray for the time being. Her family needed her, her mother especially, she said. Seamus was staying close by as well. I missed her. I had often pictured us sitting outside, the sun shining, drinks in hand, laughing and playing with Maggie. There was a rose bush underneath the balcony and when a breeze blew the perfume would waft up. I had never smelled anything so pretty. Katie would love it, too.

My first July in Calgary meant my first Stampede. Going to the fairgrounds alone with Maggie did not appeal, but the free breakfasts did. Four mornings out of ten I packed up the stroller and we hit the pavement, each time ending up in a crowd of happy chatty people, young mothers and children like us, lining up for pancakes and sausages and juice. There were western bands and country singers, and the stores and businesses were decorated with bales of hay and cowboy paraphernalia. One day we went downtown for a free lunch where everyone in white-collar Calgary was outfitted in jeans and cowboy hats, not a suit to be seen. People were so open and welcoming I felt as if we'd been personally invited to join the party. It was the most fun I'd had since we'd arrived.

After the noise and the smoke and the rush of people at Gord's, life was calm in our new apartment. Every day I would cook supper – beef stew or spaghetti or chilli – something easy and cheap and that could be packed into Iggy's lunch the next day. He didn't have much appetite in the evenings, which concerned me considering how hard he worked, so I sent him off with extra food in the mornings. I assumed he ate it because he'd gotten a little pudgy. Most days, unless he dropped by Vic Park after work, he would arrive home about six or seven, spend a few minutes with Maggie then take a nap. I figured he must have been exhausted from the long hours of physical labour until I realized he was taking pills. He said he'd been feeling run down and had started to worry that if he didn't get more sleep he'd get sick and then where would we be. A doctor had prescribed sleeping pills. I managed to get a look at the bottle, but couldn't pronounce the name on the label. Imagine him being so sensible! Maybe if he felt better, he'd start taking care of himself again. He rarely shaved and sometimes wore the same clothes for days, which I found odd but he said they'd get dirty on site anyway so why make for more laundry. He did shower though, at least once a day, long showers that steamed up the bathroom and hallway and used up every ounce of hot water.

After his nap, Iggy would have a beer and play peek-a-boo with Maggie, or sometimes, hide-the-rattle, both favourites of hers. And mine. There was no sound more joyful than her laughter, especially when it was punctuated with Iggy's.

Once we put Maggie to bed Iggy would have another beer while he picked at his food and we watched the second-hand television we'd splurged on. Occasionally I would have a beer to keep him company, but beer was expensive. And heavy. Carrying it under one arm while pushing Maggie's stroller with the other was a pain. I could have told him to lug his own damn beer from the liquor store but I didn't. I had to have something for him to come home to, something to keep him from stopping off at Gord's.

He usually fell asleep on the couch. On the few occasions when I attempted to get close physically, it was obvious by his body language, by the way he removed himself from the situation, from me, that I should not pursue it. He wasn't rude or mean. He simply had no interest, no desire. While it made me feel sad and lonely for the both of us, my libido wasn't in overdrive either.

Despite working long days and most weekends, Iggy seemed to be making less money than ever. There was so little left after paying the bills that twice I'd had to ask Victor for money to make the rent. When I asked Iggy about it, he mumbled something about expenses and taxes and union dues. I hadn't known he was in a union.

I was disappointed that Grace hadn't written to Iggy again. I would have expected her to be more persistent. And Simon, how could he just ignore us, especially after how he'd gone on in the car about what a great brother Iggy was? He had seemed so sincere that I'd questioned Iggy's comments about him. But Iggy had been right. Simon did not have time for us. As for Iggy, he refused to discuss his mother or his brother. It was like he had wiped them from his life, and consequently, from mine.

When Katie's letter arrived in September, I sat right down on the stairs and ripped it open. Except for hers and an occasional letter from Victor, which always included money even if I hadn't asked for it, the only items in our mailbox were junk and bills. I gave Maggie the envelope to keep her busy while I settled in to read the single page.

"Mom's in a right state," she wrote. "She's still not her old self and the twins are in and out of the hospital all the time. I can't leave, not yet. I'd feel too guilty having fun down there with you knowing she needed me up here." After filling me in on the latest news, she added, "I got to run now but I'm still planning to get back to Calgary, soon as I can. Seamus gave up his share in the apartment for a couple of months so I might need to crash on your sofa for a night or two. Hope Iggy won't mind. I promise not to cramp your style, ha ha. It'll be like the old days, well, almost."

I slumped into the stairwell, dejected and lonely. No one knew me here, and I knew no one. I needed conversation. I longed to look someone in the eye and talk about something interesting. I wanted to laugh again and have fun like I did during Stampede, but that had been an anomaly. What I wanted more than anything, however, was for someone to tell me that everything was okay, that everything would be okay.

Life was good, I told myself over and over, along with the usual litany of catchphrases – we had our own place, we were safe, Maggie was healthy, I was healthy, … and there I would stop, at Iggy. What was Iggy? I didn't know how to read him anymore, if I ever had. He wasn't home much, and when he was he slept most of the time. He had no hunger for food, or for me. We talked little. When we did have a conversation, I had to watch what I said. I felt trapped inside my head, stuck with thoughts and fears I couldn't voice, and it was becoming harder to talk my way, my self, out of that desperate, sinking feeling I had about him. Knowing Katie would be back soon had kept me going.

I read the letter again. I closed my eyes for a moment and thought about Mr. and Mrs. Dollmont, about how good they'd been to me when I was growing up, how I'd wished they had been my parents, how difficult this must be for them.

I looked at Maggie drooling on Katie's envelope. "Give me that, silly." I picked up my healthy happy baby and buried my nose in her soft curls and breathed.

23

I stood at the stove, trying to figure out why the stew wouldn't thicken. I turned the heat up and poured in another paste of cornstarch and water and watched as it started to boil.

Maggie was at my feet trying to haul herself up by my sweatpants, but only succeeded in pulling them down.

"Maggie, stop it."

She kept dragging on my sweats. I kept stirring the stew, which was still too thin, and hauling them up.

"What the hell is wrong with this?" I reached for the cornstarch with one hand and gave my pants a good yank up with the other, the force of which sent Maggie reeling.

"For Christ's sake." My voice was loud. Angry.

I looked down at Maggie. Her mouth was open. She looked frightened. Frightened of me. Jesus, what was I doing? Maggie let go of my sweats and staggered for a second. Before I could reach down to grab her, she fell backwards and bumped her head on the edge of the cupboard. She went rigid for several seconds then started to shriek. I dropped the spoon into the pot and picked her up to check the back of her head. There was no blood, no dent, no bump. She was more tired than hurt. She'd gotten up way too early that morning, thanks to those same magpies that had awoken me my first morning in the apartment and still did almost every single day. As she rubbed her face into my sweater, I cooed into her ear, holding her close and walking around the living room. We stopped at the sliding glass doors where a blue jay pecked at a scrap of bread on the balcony. Maggie was easily distracted.

I smelled something burning. Shit. The stew. I set Maggie on the floor where she could still see the bird then rushed to the stove to find a wild bubbling mess spitting gravy up and out all over the stove. I pulled the pot off the heat and reached in for the metal spoon. With a loud "ow" and a "fuck" I let it go and brought my hand to my mouth. Maggie started crying again and fell sideways as she tried to shuffle in my direction. By the time I picked her up she was screeching.

I dropped into a kitchen chair and looked at the red line on my palm, a superficial mark that would be gone in a day. "Mommy's fine, Mags. Shhh, it's all right, that's my girl." I put my hand to her mouth. "Can you kiss it better for Mommy?" Maggie leaned forward and put her little pink lips on my palm. I did feel better.

Careful not to scrape up the burnt bits on the bottom, I spooned the top part of the stew into another pot. I noticed the clock on the stove, 7:30 already. Iggy had been working late most nights so they could finish the current job before it started snowing. He didn't seem to mind the long days. I think he liked working construction. Earlier in the fall I had brought up the possibility of teaching. He'd said that his Newfoundland certificate wasn't valid in Alberta. The answer had rolled off his tongue with such relief in his voice that I wondered for a moment if it was true. I didn't challenge him. What was the point? He'd be miserable in a classroom.

By eight o'clock the turnips and carrots had dissolved into unrecognizable lumps in the gravy. I mashed up some for Maggie, which she loved, her eyes brightening with each spoonful as I plane-dived the food to her mouth, her giggles causing some of the food to spit back out. I forgot about Iggy for a while.

At 9:30, after I'd put Maggie to bed, I called Gord's house.

"Yeah?" answered a voice I thought might be Gord's.

"Is Iggy Connors there?"

"No."

"Are you sure?"

"Haven't seen him since he came for his mail."

"What mail?"

"Fucked if I know."

I could sense he was about to hang up. "Wait, wait. Are you sure it was Iggy?"

An exasperated sigh came over the line. "What am I – stupid?"

"Yeah, yeah okay. Sorry. Look, if he shows up tell him to call home, okay?"

"And you tell him we're not a charity. And we're not the fucking post office." The sound of the receiver hitting the cradle reverberated in my ear.

I held the phone in my hand. There was nowhere else to call. That feeling of doom I'd been pushing aside for days, for weeks, crept back.

I watched TV for a while, but there was nothing good on. Tried to read, but the words had no meaning. Sometime after midnight, I went to bed, but even though I'd spent many nights on my own in our apartment in Exile Cove, and even a few in St. John's, I had never slept alone in such a big city. Strange noises kept me alert as the building settled into night, doors opening and closing, creaks and groans, vibrations, sounds I'd never noticed before when Iggy was home. Did Calgary always have so many sirens sounding in the middle of the night?

Each time I closed my eyes, I'd imagine someone at the door trying to break in, or the police on the other side, bearers of bad news. All my concerns about Iggy played themselves out in worst case scenarios as I lay there, trying to tell myself that things always seem worse in the night's black hours. Morning would make things clearer, better, more manageable. Not believing a word of it.

Around three, Maggie woke up. I fed her a bottle, grateful to have another human being awake with me. I was sorry when she drifted off in my arms. Instead of putting her back in her playpen, I cuddled her warm body beside me in bed. Eventually I dozed off but the magpies woke me up with the sun. I was starting to hate those goddamn birds.

I was trying to get back to sleep when I heard a thumping, rolling noise in the hall. Careful not to disturb Maggie, I put pillows around her and rushed to open the door.

"Sorry," Vivian whispered when she saw me standing there in my night-gown. She was bending down to pick up a thermos. "My briefcase fell open when I was locking the door. Hope I didn't wake you."

"Oh…Vivian, it's you," I said, trying to keep the disappointment from my voice. I scanned the small hallway and craned my neck to see down the stairs.

"I'm just heading out, trying to get a few hours in the lab before everyone shows up for work." She looked me over for a second. "Anything wrong?"

I shook my head and turned to go back inside.

She must have sensed something. "Wait. Are you okay?"

"Iggy…he didn't come home last night," I whispered.

She came over to me. "Did he call?" She put her arm around my shoulder and led me into my apartment.

"No, and I don't know what to do."

As she walked me to the sofa and sat me down, she murmured, "It's okay, Bridge, everything will be okay."

Something in me snapped. There was that simple word, "okay," but I knew with absolute certainty that everything would not be okay. I also knew I'd have been happy with "okay," that "okay" was a word I would have gladly used to describe my life, if I only could. And knowing that, I burst out crying.

"I'm sorry," I finally said. "I don't know why I can't stop bawling."

"You probably didn't sleep much." She patted my back. "Is there anyone we can phone where he might be? Some friends, family?"

"It's just me and him. We don't have any family here."

"Anywhere else he might have gone?"

"Where we used to live, but he wasn't there last night. What if something happened to him? I don't know what I'd do then. I don't know anybody else." I was babbling now. "We don't have any money, it's just whatever he brings home, that's all we got. What if he's hurt? Or…I don't know…something worse…oh my God…"

"Has he ever done this before?"

"No." I hesitated. "Not since we moved to Calgary. Should I phone the police?"

"I don't think you need to do that yet, but maybe we should start with the hospitals, you know, to make sure he wasn't in an accident or something."

"Oh God! Do you think –?"

"No, no, no, I don't think anything. Really, I don't."

The shrill peal of the phone cut the air. Even though I'd been waiting for it to ring for 12 hours, the sound terrified me.

"Should I get that?" Vivian asked on the third ring.

I grabbed the receiver. "Hello?"

At the sound of Iggy's voice, a wave of relief hit me and, briefly, a rush of love. He was alive. He was well enough to talk. Maggie and I would not be left stranded in a strange city where no one cared if we lived or died.

"Iggy? Are you okay? Where are you? Are you all right?" The words tumbled out, the long night temporarily forgotten.

"Yeah…I'm…I'm fine." He sounded weary, yet uncertain. "Sorry…but look, I… I got caught up in something last night. I'll be home later."

"But where were you? I was so worried – "

"Look, Bridge, I'm sorry…but I got to go…my ride's going. I'll see you this evening. I really am sorry, okay?"

It was posed as a question but the line went dead. I sat looking at the phone for a moment, then remembered Vivian sitting next to me. I was about to make up some excuse, some lie, when I heard Maggie waking up.

"That was Iggy," I said over my shoulder as I headed down the hall. "Something important came up and he couldn't get home. But he's fine."

"Why didn't he call?"

I was in the bedroom by now. "That's just Iggy," I called out. "He gets all excited and forgets. It's nothing." I forced a smile and walked into the living room and towards the door to the apartment with Maggie in my arms. "Thanks, Vivian. I don't know why I was so worked up. It's silly. But we're all fine now, just fine…" I blathered on, wanting to get her out of the apartment without having to answer more questions.

She met me at the door. "Okay, but if you need me, I'll be home later, okay?"

"Right. Thanks. I appreciate it. I really do. See you later…" I shut the door.

I was filled with energy. Not the energy that comes from the excitement of good news, more the kind that's running from the opposite. I set to work, fixing Maggie's breakfast, singing her a song, turning on the radio then switching to the television. I needed noise. I started a batch of chocolate chip cookies. Between moving trays in and out of the oven, I gave Maggie a bath then played with her on the floor, the television blaring behind us. I emptied out the fridge and cleaned the shelves, then started on the cupboards. For three hours I kept busy, too busy to stop and think about the night before. Every time it came to the front of my brain, I shoved it back with a song, or a cookie, or shaking the rattles on Maggie's kiddie-gym.

And still it was only 10 o'clock in the morning.

The clock on the stove stared back at me as I wished the time away. How was I going to get through another nine hours until Iggy came home? I cleaned the apartment. From beginning to end, I scoured it, taking time out only to tend to Maggie, and to gulp back a cup of tea and some toast when she was sleeping. I could bake something, a cake, or more cookies. Banana bread, yes, without the nuts so Maggie could try it. I didn't remember I had no bananas until the batter was almost ready so I used a couple of jars of Maggie's applesauce. Waste of baby food.

Around three in the afternoon I thought about going out, perhaps to the corner store where I knew I would get a kind word from Ruth and Bill, or to the park. Maybe I would meet someone there, someone I could talk to, not about Iggy, no, just regular talk, about the weather, or where we were from, what we wanted to do with our lives.

And what would I say? What did I want? To be me again, to see the positive no matter what, to be able to look forward instead of back. To laugh. I so much wanted to laugh at life again. But life wasn't funny anymore. I was stuck in the present, stuck with a kid in a strange city where I knew no one. Never mind the next nine hours. How was I going to get through the next nine weeks, or months, or years?

I didn't go out.

When Iggy came home that night, he looked terrible. His right hand was swollen and there were scrapes on his left cheek that looked like a bad rash. When I asked what had happened he looked at me as if to say, "Why bother?" or maybe, "I don't know." He muttered something about an accident at work. I knew it was a lie. I didn't care. I was too tired for the truth. I didn't even mind his falling straight to sleep on the sofa. He had no good answers, nothing that would make it better. I had no answers either.

I did have a moment of surprise, not at Iggy, at myself, for not being indignant, for not being angry with him for leaving me to worry and then ignoring me. And then I realized that I actually was angry. At myself. I was to blame. I had let it all happen.

When I had Maggie down for the night, I wrapped some cookies in foil and, leaving my apartment door open, went across the hall and knocked on Vivian's door.

"Bridge, how are you?" She squeezed my arm. "I've been thinking about you."

"Hi, Vivian. I'm fine. Embarrassed but otherwise just tired. I'm sorry about this morning, for getting you involved and for rushing you out, especially after you were so nice." I passed her the cookies. "Do you like chocolate?"

"Love it. Thank you." She opened the package and sniffed. "Smells yummy." She looked back at me. "Maybe we can help each other out. How would you like to do some more typing for me? Between work and school I'm swamped."

"Sure."

"There's 30 bucks in it if you can do it by Friday. Interested?"

Thirty dollars! "Can I use your typewriter again?"

She nodded. "I use the one at the university anyway."

"This is great." I was so happy I hugged her. "Thank you."

Minutes later, loaded down with a typewriter and blank paper and the written transcript, I practically danced back to the apartment.

Iggy's absences became a regular thing. It was as if something inside him had stopped functioning as it should. At least once a week, sometimes more often, he would go back to Vic Park, or to some other place with his friends, or whoever. At times, he seemed unaware that Maggie and I existed; at others, he doted on us, or more precisely, on Maggie. When I tried to talk to him, to tell him how worried I was about him and about us, he would look so sorry, and tell me he forgot to call, or forgot to go to work, or forgot to come home, or plain forgot. My biggest fear was that he would forget about Maggie and me altogether. I had no money, no nest egg for a rainy day. We barely eked by on the sunny ones. We lived paycheque to paycheque, each one less than the last, counting pennies, stretching every nickel. I don't know what I would have done if not for Victor and the typing jobs for Vivian and her friends.

When Iggy was home, he slept on the sofa. This evolved naturally and we never discussed it. We were more like sister and brother than husband and wife, people who cared about each other at a fundamental level, who innately belonged in each other's lives.

One Friday in November, a payday, Iggy didn't come home. I had to do something before all the money, little though it was, was gone. I phoned and found him at Gord's. After a bus change and a 20-minute walk pushing Maggie's stroller along the dark slushy streets of Victoria Park, we arrived at the house. I didn't knock, just walked in, past Big-Hair and Cow-Boy who were passed out together on the loveseat, past the dog who gave me an inquisitive glance before putting his head down again. I parked Maggie in a corner where I could see her, then approached Iggy where he sat on the sofa. Through glazed eyes he smiled at me, as if I was a friend he hadn't seen in a while and he was trying to place. I reached into his pocket and removed his wallet, left him two 10s, and took the rest.

After that, I would meet him after work on paydays. Iggy never resisted, just looked at me guiltily as I shoved a 20 back in his pocket. I didn't resent him. I don't think he resented me. This was simply how it had to be. And the funny thing was, once we had that established, once I accepted that this was our normal, that normal for us was not normal, and that "we" meant me and Maggie and, only sometimes, Iggy, I didn't feel quite so lonely.

In December I heard from Katie. Her mother and the twins were all doing well. She'd be back in Calgary in January. Things were looking up.

I pulled the towel tighter around my wet body and hurried to answer the phone. I didn't want to miss a call. At Vivian's suggestion I had put my name on a list at the university to type term papers. Given Iggy's dwindling paycheque, I was desperate for work and took every typing job that came my way. And if the call wasn't about that it might be Katie. I was expecting to hear from her any day now that Christmas was over.

"Hello?" I answered hopefully.

"Iggy Connors there?" There was a distinct Newfoundland accent.

"No. Is this Gord?"

"Dave. Who's this?"

"Bridge."

Silence on the other end, then, "Who?"

I had lived in this man's house for two months. "Iggy's wife."

"Oh. Yeah, I remember you." His pitchy voice, which had lightened from a snarl to a sneer, went nasty again. "Where's that goddamn husband of yours?"

Iggy hadn't been home for three nights. I'd assumed he was at the MacDonald house. "He's not at your place?"

"Why the fuck would he be here? He don't pay no rent to me."

"He's got nowhere else to go." I pictured him on a park bench or under a tree, no blankets, no pillow. "Where's he staying? Does he have a place to sleep?"

"I'm not his fucking mother. And I'm sick of getting his mail here. Fuck's sake, never mind. Where is he?"

I pulled the towel closer. "He's probably at work."

"They haven't seen him all week. When's the prick get home?"

"Six or seven, if he comes home."

"Where do you live?" The tone was harsh, demanding.

My gut clenched. What had Iggy done? Did he owe him money? If he did, would Dave think that I owed him, too? Dave MacDonald was not a man to provoke. He was used to dealing with drug dealers, prostitutes and pimps, people with knives and guns.

I hung up. The phone rang again almost immediately. It sounded louder, angry. After a minute, it stopped. I ran to the bedroom and threw on some clothes. When we'd had the phone installed, Iggy had insisted on an unlisted number. At the time it had seemed odd, but he'd said it was a big city, we couldn't be too careful.

Ten minutes later the phone rang. I picked it up but said nothing.

"Tell that bastard if he doesn't pay – "

I slammed it down, afraid the caller could trace my location. I didn't know if that was possible, just that I had seen it on television.

It was 3:30 in the afternoon. Iggy might or might not be home soon. In the meantime, what if Dave MacDonald showed up, demanding...what? Money, most likely. I had six dollars to my name.

Grabbing my coat, and my six dollars, I stuffed Maggie into her snowsuit and stroller and headed to the small, snow-covered green space nearby. I took a blanket from the bottom of the stroller and tucked it around Maggie and held her close, trying to cover any exposed skin. It was minus 30. Calgary was in the middle of one of its infamous cold snaps. The day before it had been minus 38 with the wind chill. I had not known that air could be so cold.

Angling myself next to a tree where I could keep an eye out but not easily be seen, I watched the road for signs of Dave MacDonald. With his reddish hair and beard, he would be easy to spot. My own hair was damp from the shower and starting to freeze. I took my hand out from under the blanket and pulled the hood of my parka closer, grateful for the fake fur trim. I shoved my hand back in, squeezing my fingers together. In my rush to get out of the apartment I'd forgotten the mitts Iggy had given me for Christmas. I had been touched that he'd remembered to buy me a gift, and relieved that he'd pulled himself together enough to be home for the entire Christmas season, especially Maggie's first birthday. We had some nice quiet days together, the three of us. Iggy slept 20 hours a day but that was okay. If he was asleep on the sofa, he was safe. By New Year's, he was gone.

After half an hour my face and fingers and feet were numb and Maggie was starting to fuss. I couldn't stay out all night. I circled the building then decided to go in and lock the doors and windows. I would stick a chair under the doorknob. Maybe move the sofa over to the door. What else could I move there, what more could I do to prevent someone from breaking in? What about the balcony? Would they break the glass to get in? Should I phone the police, or would that get Iggy into more trouble?

I climbed the stairs, struggling to lift a now sleeping Maggie in her stroller. As I reached the top, the downstairs door opened. There was a pause, followed by sure footsteps. Frantic, I rummaged through my pockets, cursing myself for not having my keys out already. How could I be so stupid? I pushed the stroller towards the door. My fingers found the keys. I fumbled to get the key in the lock.

The footsteps were at the top of the stairs now. Fear rose in my chest. Jesus help me, why wouldn't the key go in?

"Hey, Bridge."

I turned. There was Katie, hair piled up under her old green hat, cheeks scarlet from the cold. She had a suitcase in her hand, a knapsack slung over her shoulder, and that wonderful saucy grin all over her face.

24

Katie took the keys and opened the door. "What the heck is wrong with you? You're shaking like a leaf." She pushed the stroller inside with one hand, me with the other, then went back out and returned with her suitcase.

"Shut the door," I said. "Lock it. Lock the door."

She pushed in the doorknob and turned back to me. "Why?"

I heard the main entrance open downstairs. I looked at Katie and put my finger to my lips. After a prolonged peek through the security hole into the empty hallway, I turned and leaned my back against the door.

Katie was eyeing me with alarm. "What's going on?" she whispered.

"It's…it's…" I couldn't seem to fill my lungs.

Katie clasped both of my arms and looked me in the eyes. "Bridge, calm down." She led me to a chair, then went to plug in the kettle. "You okay?"

"I'm sorry, I just don't know what to do. What if he comes after me?"

"Who? Are you talking about Iggy?"

"No, no, not Iggy. Dave MacDonald."

"Okay, now you lost me. Why would Dave MacDonald come after you?"

Trying to keep my voice steady, I told her about the phone call.

She turned on the tap, letting the water grow cold over her fingers, then filled a glass with water. "What's he got against Iggy?"

"I don't know. Just…well, Iggy used to stay there sometimes, I think."

"You think?" She put the glass into my hands. "What do you mean? Doesn't he come home every night?"

I shook my head, took a sip of water.

"Do you know where he is now?"

I looked away and shook my head again.

She crossed her arms. "Do you mean to tell me the son of a bitch left you to deal with that scum MacDonald all on your own?"

"No, it's not like that. Iggy's…"

She stood there, hands on her hips now. "Iggy's what? Come on, out with it."

"He's sick, Katie." There, I'd said it. I almost felt better. I actually might have, except it didn't change anything. He was still sick.

"Sick? How?" The kettle whistled. Katie went to turn it off then came back to me. "What do you mean by 'sick' exactly?"

I hesitated, unsure if I could say it aloud.

"Are you saying…," Katie paused now too, "…that…that he's *mental?*"

She said the last word like it tasted bad in her mouth, much the same as

Josephine had said it, how I'd thought of it until Iggy's father came into my life. Did Bernie actually have a brain injury or had his mental decline started out like Iggy's? What had Grace and Simon, and Iggy, of course, been through all these years, watching him?

The time had come to admit what I'd been trying to ignore for months, to face up to my worst fears. I told her everything, my concerns about Iggy, about my inability to take care of Maggie all on my own, about money, about how desperate I felt sometimes, how lonely I was all the time.

Katie sat next to me. "I knew things weren't great living with the MacDonalds and all, but I thought you and Iggy were okay at least." She put her arms around me and gave me a hug. "Oh, Bridgie-Bee, I'm so sorry."

I managed a small laugh. "Your father used to call me that. It always made me feel special." I took a breath. "I'm after making such a mess of my life. I wish – "

Someone was coming up the stairs. I gestured to Katie to follow as I wheeled Maggie's stroller into the bedroom. I shut the door and leaned down over Maggie, worried that she would wake up and cry. We heard someone at the door, a knock, hesitant at first, then louder. Someone was fumbling with the doorknob. Gord would know how to get in, he'd have a master key or use a credit card or something to break through. The door opened and closed. Katie eyes met mine. She looked as terrified as I felt. What could we do? How could we defend ourselves? And Maggie, what about Maggie? Surely to God even the MacDonalds wouldn't hurt a baby.

Whoever it was seemed to be in the kitchen. I remembered the recently boiled kettle. Would they notice and know we were here? We heard a few small noises, footsteps walking away from us, the door opening and closing again. I listened, not moving a muscle or making a sound, even though instinctively I knew, no one was there.

We tiptoed to the bedroom window and peeked through the crack in the curtains. A man, stooped over and scruffy looking, in a coat that was too big, trudged through the snowy parking lot and away from the building.

"Who's that?' Katie whispered over my shoulder.

I could have called to him then. Perhaps I should have. "Iggy," I said.

"You're kidding? That's Iggy?"

I nodded.

"He looks like shit."

The wind came up. His bare hand pushed his hair away from his face. As he hoisted himself over the rail that separated the parking lot from the play area, I saw the envelope in his other hand – the letter that had arrived from Grace the day before, the first since we'd moved to the apartment. I had so wanted to open it but Iggy would be as angry with me as he already was with her. He still refused to talk about his mother or Simon except to say that he didn't want anything to do with them, that they were out of our lives. Another topic off limits. I didn't even try anymore. As he moved further away from the building, I regretted not opening the letter. Then I had to wonder, why had he shown up today, and why hadn't he stayed?

"Bridge?" Katie's voice interrupted my thoughts.

"Huh? Yeah?"

"I said, are you afraid of him?" Katie asked.

"Lord no, I'm not afraid of Iggy. He loves Maggie, and me, too, in his own way probably. He just has trouble sometimes, you know?"

"Yeah, right. And you get stuck with the consequences." Katie crossed the room and opened the bedroom door. "Enough with this bullshit. Nobody's coming to get you, okay? Come on. I'll make us a cup of tea."

I wheeled Maggie out to the living room, trying not to disturb her even if it was too late for a nap. Peering through the keyhole I locked the door even though I agreed with Katie. If the MacDonalds knew where we lived they'd have been here already.

"What are you going to do?" Katie got the cups down.

I sat at the table. "I don't know. I can't go home. I can't afford it. Besides, Josephine would have a fit if I landed on her doorstep with a baby, and rightfully so."

"Have you thought about getting a job?"

"All the time, but what about Maggie? And what would I do? I'm not trained for anything useful."

Katie placed a mug of tea in front of me. "Listen to yourself. You, who had three jobs in university and still got A's in math and chemistry and God knows what. I've never known anyone who worked so hard and complained so little."

"Go on, don't be so foolish – "

"No, give yourself some credit. Calgary is dying for workers like you." She sat and stared at me, as if trying to figure something out.

"What? Why are you looking at me like that?"

"What's after happening to you?"

"What do you mean?"

"I mean, you had plans, you had dreams, and, I don't know, you were never like this," she said, pointing at me, "cowering, frightened of your own shadow."

"It's not like that – "

"It isn't? Then what is it like? Seriously, stop for one friggin' second and think about it. You're a bundle of nerves, afraid to answer the door, only thinking about what's wrong, what you can't do, not what you can. That's not the Bridge I knew."

She was starting to irritate me. "Yeah, well what do you know about it? Life changes you sometimes. Having a kid changes you."

"So does having a fucking mental case for a husband."

"It's not Iggy's fault he's sick. I can't blame him for all this." As soon as I said it, it hit me. If not him, then who? "Jesus, is this who I am? A big coward?"

She leaned forward. "Horseshit! You, who stood up to Josephine, the biggest bully that ever was. That took balls. The woman scared the bejesus out of me."

"Really?" I'd never known Katie to be afraid of anyone.

"Why do you think we always hung out at my house? So I could spend more time taking care of all them youngsters? Huh! Not likely."

I rubbed my forehead. I was getting a headache.

"Why do you do it? Why do you put up with him?"

"No choice I suppose, he's my husband, my family. I need money to pay the rent, although I can't count on that anymore. And he's Maggie's father. She loves him, and he loves her even more. I guess having Iggy is better than having no one."

"Is it? Is he really better than nothing? And like I told you before, you have us."

"Katie, I love your family. You don't know how often growing up I wished they were mine. But I'm here, now, in Calgary, just me and Maggie, and sometimes Iggy. I have to face that." I stood and walked to the window. "I thought when we moved here to this apartment, things would get better. I was so proud of myself, figured I had it under control. I almost felt like my old self again." I looked out at the snow on the balcony, the graceful drifts curving up the sides, pure and white and flawless. "But it was just the beginning, I know that now." I sat back down across from Katie. "You're awful quiet."

She grinned. "Letting you talk it out. I can't do all the work, you know."

I grinned back. "Saucy brat. I'm some glad you're here." I sat up straight. "Okay, let's say you're right and I can get a job. What about Maggie?"

"Day care, day home, there's lots of choices. Women do it all the time, Bridge."

True as I knew that was, it didn't make the thought of leaving Maggie with a stranger any easier. "But what will I work at? I don't have training like you do."

"Right," Katie smirked. "The world's greatest secretary." She gave me the once-over. "You got over a year university. That's more than lots of people who are working downtown, or how about the hospitals? That's where my aunt works up in McMurray and she only did Grade 10. There's cleaning jobs and clerical stuff and working in the cafeteria." Katie slapped the table with her palm. "What about the university? It's just over the way. You could walk from here as long as the weather's not bad."

Maggie's eyes had shot open with the slap to the table. She started to cry. I picked her up and snuggled her. "Who's going to look after you if Mommy gets a job, huh Mags? Who's going to take care of you?" I looked over at Katie. "I know, I know, women do it all the time. But she's 13 months old and I'm all she has." Katie looked about to interrupt but I put my hand up. "I'm not being melodramatic. Iggy loves her but he's incapable of taking care of her. I'm it, Katie. If anything happens to me she's got no one." I leaned back and squeezed my eyes shut for a second. "God, I never thought I'd be raising a kid alone. And yes, to be honest, it scares the hell out of me but that's the way it is. So if I'm not chomping at the bit to leave her, that's why, okay?"

"I'm sorry, Bridge. I didn't know how bad it was." She glanced around. "What if I stay here for a while, seeing as Iggy's not around much? I'll even watch the swearing."

"Are you kidding? I would love that."

She got up and went over to her suitcase and came back with a half empty bottle of Newman's Port, along with two glasses from the cupboard. She opened the port and sniffed the contents. "Mom gave me this before I left. Said it was in the cabinet for ages and she was afraid it might go bad." She poured two glasses and handed one to me. "Calls for a celebration, what?" Her eyes were serious. "It's going to be okay, Bridge."

I didn't care if it was premature, or that I didn't know if I liked port. I toasted her back. "Yeah, I think it is, too." The port tasted like thick, sweet red wine. Not bad, I thought, as the liquid warmed my tongue. I took another sip, a bigger one this time, and the warmth spread to my head. A happy glow settled over me, a halo of hope and optimism that I hadn't felt in ages.

25

My job at the university library was entry-level, sorting and shelving books, filing index cards, cleaning up the stacks. Given how frugally we lived, it paid more than enough to cover basic needs for Maggie and me, and it came with benefits like a drug plan and sick leave. Most importantly, it was steady money, something I didn't get from Iggy anymore. Knowing how easy it was to fall behind, I kept up the typing jobs at night.

In April, the miserable old couple down the hall moved out of their three-bedroom apartment. We grabbed it. With Katie sharing expenses, I could afford a proper crib for Maggie, who finally had her own bedroom. I also installed a deadbolt and an interior latch on our apartment door, then splurged on some work clothes so that I didn't have to borrow the few pieces of Katie's that fit me. Not that she needed office clothes anymore. Having decided she was done with typing, Katie had found a waitressing job at a nearby steak house, which was great because she could look after Maggie during the day when I first started working. The university job had come up quickly and I thought I'd have to turn it down but Katie said we'd figure it out, which we did. It was an unfamiliar feeling to have someone around who was happy and willing and able to share the responsibility. After a week I found a day home right in our neighbourhood.

Maggie and "Auntie Katie" were a perfect fit. Katie was lively and fun and goofy, full of energy and used to being with kids. Maggie was fascinated with Katie's hair, constantly fingering the long red strands, and Katie would make crazy faces at her as she tried to disentangle Maggie's fist. Then she'd swish her hair in Maggie's face, tickling her nose and cheeks and sending Maggie into fits of giggles.

Iggy came and went. He didn't question Katie's presence, nor she his absences. What had started out as a night away had turned into a few days then a week or two, then longer. Maggie was the pull that drew Iggy back home. I was okay with that. When he showed up, I tried to feed him, to get something good into him. He looked so unhealthy, at times bloated and thick-tongued and zombie-like, at others gaunt-faced and fidgety. At one point, I was so worried I decided to phone Grace in St. Paul even though Iggy would be furious. She'd begun writing to him again and while he wouldn't let me read the letters, I was relieved to know that she was trying even if he wasn't. When there was no answer at Grace's I called Josephine, who said Bernie had been in St. John's for ages and Grace was with him. "No, I don't know how to reach her in there," she said when I asked. "What am I? The phone book?"

Occasionally I pushed Iggy, asking questions he hated – what he'd been up to, where he'd been staying, what was he living on. He was always evasive. I sometimes saw him taking what appeared to be prescription medication but he refused to discuss it with me and kept the pills in his pocket. Other than that he didn't drink or take street drugs when he was home. Who knows what he did when he was away?

He never stayed long. After a few days he would put some money on the counter, usually a $20 bill. I didn't know where he got it but was glad he made the effort. He would leave as casually as if he was going to the corner store for a loaf of bread. I came to know the signs, the tears in his eyes when he held Maggie, the increased agitation, the extended showers, hot and cold. There were times I looked forward to them.

With fall came the call I least expected. Melinda. Josephine was dead.

She'd had a heart attack on the toilet. Maureen had stopped by to pick her up for Mass like she had every Sunday since Dad died. Apparently Josephine had found religion but could not abide the 10-minute walk to church. When Josephine didn't answer the door, Maureen tried the knob. It was locked. She called out a few times then went around the house tapping on windows. The Smith spinsters across the street, one of whom was always on sentry duty, soon appeared with the crowbar they kept on hand for protection. It didn't take long to jimmy the lock, although it took longer to get into the bathroom. Josephine had toppled head first onto the floor, her underwear around her ankles, her bum lodged against the door. The smell hit them first. The weather had been exceptionally warm that September and the sun had been beating through the sealed bathroom window. They figured she'd been dead three, maybe four days. She was 71 years old.

"Victor insisted I call you. He found a number for you somewhere."

There were no pleasantries, no mention of the past.

"Tell him thanks. I appreciate it."

"I'm leaving today to get things organized. When can you get home?"

"I can't come home. I don't have the money." I did, though. By scrimping and saving and not spending a dime on anything I could do without, I had over $300 in the bank. Not only that, I had paid Victor back even though he insisted he didn't want it. All in all, I was starting to feel like my feet were on firm ground, that Maggie and I had some stability.

"Bridgina, the woman's dead." Her tone was scolding. "The least you can do is come for her funeral, especially after missing Dad's."

"What! Sure I didn't know he was dead." I would have made it to Dad's funeral. I'd have gotten the money somewhere, even if I'd had to ask Melinda.

"And who's fault was that? Huh? Like I told Victor, don't blame me."

"I don't. Really, I know it was my own fault but there's nothing I can do about that now."

"I'll lend you the money, okay?"

"I can't, Mel. I'm sorry Josephine is dead but I can't afford it."

Her tone softened a tiny bit. "Look, I know we all had our differences. But I've come to realize something. Josephine wasn't all bad."

"Yeah, I know." As miserable as Josephine had been, distance had given me some perspective. The fact was, she hadn't had much of a life. "It must have been hard, her husband dying so young and all."

"And remember, she took us on when Dad needed help."

Wasn't this something, Mel and I having a real conversation? And who to thank but Josephine? "Yeah, I guess she did at that."

Mel's voice notched back up to strident. "I know how that feels. I know what it's like. You don't know how hard it is being a stepmother, taking on that responsibility…"

"Well, I kind of do…"

"…it's ungrateful work, let me tell you. Charlotte's out till all hours and she lies like crazy and Victor falls for it. And I have to try to make him see sense and to understand why I'm so hard on her. You have no idea what it's like, what it takes to be a good mother…"

I could not believe my ears. I wasn't sure how Melinda ranked as a step-mother, but as a mother, she was right up there with Josephine.

"…we need to pay her respect. You especially, you need to do what's right and stop thinking of yourself for once." She stopped for a breath. "After all, it's only money."

Easy enough when you're married to a doctor, I thought. I didn't say it. It seemed an insult to Victor. "Well, it's only money I don't have. Besides, there's no one to take care of Maggie for me."

"What about Iggy? After all, he is her father." Melinda paused. "Isn't he?"

I almost slammed down the phone. The bitch, the rotten miserable bitch. My voice went cold. "Iggy is not available." Melinda started to interrupt but I cut her off. "I have to go. Say hi to Victor for me." I hung up.

Once I calmed down and could think straight again, I thought about the reason for Melinda's call. Poor old Josephine. Her death was as sad and lonely as her life. She had died as she lived, alone, with no one who cared enough about her to check in on her.

Later that day, Victor called. "I can send you the money, Bridge, if you want to go home, for you and for Maggie. You know that, right?"

"Thanks Victor. But Josephine and I had nothing to do with each other the last couple of years. Hell, she didn't even like me."

"You don't want to go for a visit?"

"No, I don't. Since Dad died, there's no reason to go back."

Victor had the sense not to argue. "I guess I understand that. Take care, Bridge. Talk to you soon."

"You, too. Thanks, Victor."

Melinda was one lucky woman.

We had a nice life going, me and Maggie and Katie. We weren't the most typical of families, but I was used to that. My job was boring but it paid the bills, giving me a security I'd never had in Calgary. One payday I was making a deposit at the bank when it occurred to me that I was doing okay, that life was okay, finally. I was making it on my own, me, Bridge Ashe from Exile Cove. And then I realized that the description was incorrect. I had been in Calgary a year and a half. I had no ties to Exile Cove. I was no longer an Ashe, if indeed I'd ever been one. My life was different now, with Maggie at the centre. Maggie Connors. I decided from then on I was Bridge Connors from Calgary.

I was still lonely. Watching Katie going out on the town with friends, or out on dates, and not always making it home, I sometimes felt a solitary hunger, especially lying alone in bed, fearing I would stay that way forever. Recurring dreams didn't help. In one, I had no one in my life, not Maggie, not Katie, no friends or family, no one, except that, occasionally, the dream changed and there was a man on the fringe, someone I knew but could not identify. In another, I longed to be kissed. I needed to imprint the feeling into my memory because I hadn't known the last kiss I'd had was going to be my last one forever. It took all the next morning before I could shake off the funk after that dream.

Maggie was a beauty, almost two, toddling around on her short stout legs, mixing gibberish and words as if they had equal meaning. Everything was normal to her, Katie coming and going between boyfriends and trips to McMurray, Iggy showing up for short sporadic visits. She loved us all, loved when we were all together, loved Iggy to pieces.

Poor Iggy. All I felt for him anymore was pity. While I had been forced to evolve from being a misplaced Newfoundlander afraid to turn around into a working woman and single mother, even if a lonely one, I'd witnessed Iggy transform from a decent guy trying to make sense of it all, to a disoriented shell of the man I'd fallen for. Yet, when he and Maggie were in the same room, I could still see the old Iggy, gentle, sweet, loving. Most of the time.

One Saturday in late October we were sitting together at the kitchen table. He'd been home since Thursday afternoon. Katie had left the day before for McMurray because one of the twins was in hospital and her mother needed help. Maggie had been so excited to have Iggy back that she'd stayed up late for two nights and, exhausted, fell asleep on the sofa right after lunch. As we watched her sleep, grateful for the healthy glow to her pink cheeks, I felt, for a moment, the blink of an eye, like an ordinary family. Then I looked at Iggy. His hair had no colour or shine. His lips were as dry and cracked as his fingernails. And his eyes, those soulful eyes that I'd lost my heart to, were the saddest, weariest eyes imaginable. He reminded me of his father, just not as happy.

He glanced up and caught me watching him. He looked away.

"Iggy?"

I waited.

"Yeah?" he said.

"You need help."

"Bridge don't, not now…"

I wasn't going to give up that easily. "Think of Maggie, Iggy."

He shot me an angry look. "That's not fair."

"None of this is fair. But you can't keep on – "

His hand hit the table. "And what do you propose I do? Huh?"

"There are pills that can help – "

"Fuck!" He was on his feet. "You think I haven't tried? Fucking doctors, they're all the same, even here. Every time they pump you full of drugs. Every time they promise it'll be better this time, 'just take this one, no take that one, how about this one?' They haven't got a fucking clue."

Except for the sleeping pills when we'd first moved into the apartment, this was the first time he'd admitted to taking medication. For a moment I was hopeful we might have a real conversation. "Iggy, that's great. You're trying. I didn't know you were seeing a doctor. Why didn't you tell me?"

He smirked. "Seeing a doctor? Is that what you call it?"

"Well…yeah, I guess. Why? What do you mean?"

"When they stick you inside, you don't get a choice, do you? Every time my father went to 'see a doctor,' all just bullshit…" He was pacing, his fists squeezing and straightening. "…know what he saw…in for weeks, longer even…"

I wasn't certain who he was talking about, himself or Bernie.

"…make you a guinea pig, sticking needles in you, tying you down…" His hands twitched at his side now, the fingers flicking.

"Iggy, let me help you."

He turned his back to me and screamed, a cry of frustration or helplessness or anger. Maybe all three. I glanced at Maggie who was sleeping through it.

"Please, let – "

"Shut up!" He spun around and glared at me. "Leave me the fuck alone."

"Iggy, I'm just trying – "

He took a step toward me; his eyes narrowed to slits. Then he stopped, turned and bolted from the apartment.

The incident played over and over in my mind until I was fed up with thinking about it. The situation was ridiculous. I didn't care what Iggy thought: I needed to talk to his mother or Simon. After numerous attempts to catch Grace in St. Paul, I phoned directory assistance in Newfoundland and in Montreal, looking for a listing for Grace or Bernard or Simon Connors. I found one for B. Connors in St. John's, but no one ever answered the phone. If only I had written the numbers down from Grace's phone bills back when Iggy was paying the bills for her. I considered writing to Grace in hopes that it would be forwarded to an address in town, but something stopped me. Putting it in words and on paper would be proof that I'd gone behind Iggy's back.

"Never mind his back, you got to watch out for your own," Katie scolded from McMurray during our weekly phone call. "You didn't sign up to be Iggy's mother."

"I know, I know. Can you just ask Seamus if he's got a number for Simon?"

"Now that's the Connors brother you should have ended up with."

"No thank you." I was more annoyed with Simon than Iggy was. I still could not believe that he hadn't been in touch. So many times over the last couple of years, times when I'd been discouraged, feeling hopeless, I'd imagined opening my door to find Simon on the other side, ready with an irreproachable excuse as to why we hadn't heard from him – he'd been on another continent saving dying children or something equally farfetched. Why else would he have ignored the brother he professed to care so much about? But it just never made sense to my sensible self.

"Will you get me the number from your brother?"

"Yeah, yeah, soon as he's back from Ireland." She paused. "There's something I have to tell you. It's about Sylvia."

In that moment of silence, I knew. Sylvia wasn't in jail; she wasn't ill; she wasn't anything. I knew it because, without realizing it, I'd long feared it might happen to Iggy.

I felt sick. "What happened?"

"She overdosed. It happened back in October but I only found out yesterday. Dad heard it from her brother. He just started working on the rig with him."

"Shit," I said. "It's…it's hard to take in. I mean, God! That's so rotten."

"Yeah, I know."

We were quiet then. I felt sad and guilty, sad that I would never see her again, even if that hadn't sunk in yet. Guilty because I'd been so angry the last time I had seen her. "Strung-out whore," I'd called her. I could never take that back now, or make up for it. An image popped into my brain, Sylvia, dead, with a needle in her arm. I shivered and felt nauseous.

Katie broke the silence. "We'll talk about it more when I'm back there."

"Yeah, okay. When are you coming back?"

"I promised Dad I'd stay until Christmas and New Year's were over, same as last year, so some time early January. But I'll send the rent cheque next week."

"Hardly fair if you're not here."

"Of course it's fair. We both know that. Besides, Dad's so glad to have me here he's throwing dough at me left and right."

"Okay, thanks. What about your job? Will they hold it?"

"Yeah, I talked to Chris. He said not to worry, it'll be there when I need it."

"He's got a crush on you."

"Don't I know it? He's kind of cute, mind you. Maybe, when I get back. Another notch in my belt?"

That stopped us both. Sylvia had gone through a lot of guys.

"Guess you can add him to the list." I tried to sound light but it didn't work.

"Actually, I kind of got my eye on someone." Katie's voice was serious. "Seamus's buddy, really good guy. I'll keep you posted."

"Sounds good. How's your mother? And little Jason and Jack? They any better?"

"The babies are coming along, I hope so, anyway. Mom goes to church a lot. Seems to help her."

"Tell her I said hi and one of these days me and Maggie will be up to see her."

"I will."

"Anyway, I better go. I got a paper to type."

"Okay. See you in a few weeks. Take care of yourself."

"I will." Neither of us was in a rush to sign off. "You too," I added.

"Merry Christmas to everyone."

"Yeah, same here."

"Give Mags a hug for me. See you soon, Bridge. I promise."

I hung up and sat on the sofa. I thought about Sylvia, about Mr. and Mrs. Mercer having to bury her. I thought about "the three sisters" who never really were, and about Iggy, whose dreams were gone, along with mine for a normal family. I thought about Dad and Josephine, alone and cold in the ground. I let myself grieve for a short while, then got up and went into Maggie's room where she slept, safe and sound, in her crib.

I was expecting Iggy back soon. He wouldn't miss Christmas with Maggie, or her second birthday. Besides, he'd been gone a while. I had begun to detect a pattern to his visits. He would turn up about once a month, stay a few days, then leave. Usually – maybe always, although I couldn't be sure before I started to watch for it – a letter from Grace would either be waiting for him on the counter or would arrive in the mail before he left.

When he showed up mid-December, he slept most of the first week. Maybe because of that he stayed longer, which made Maggie happy. He hung around, more often than not dozing on the sofa, leaving the apartment only to check the mailbox on the main floor of the building. He insisted he was fine, just tired, that he'd be okay if he could get some sleep. Sure enough, he did improve. By Christmas Day he was able to sit at the table for dinner and drink pretend tea from Maggie's tiny china cups without his hand shaking and sloshing "tea" all over himself.

A few days later the letter arrived. I knew because of the bulge in his back pocket. Since I'd quit asking to read them, he didn't try to hide the letters anymore. As usual he took it into the bathroom. He came out a few minutes later, the letter stuffed into a ball in his front pocket. His fist kept going there, pushing the letter down, his hand coming out and twisting for a few seconds before going into the pocket again, all while he paced between the balcony doors and the opposite wall.

"You okay?" I said from the kitchen sink where I was scrubbing the pan he'd used to burn a grilled cheese for Maggie.

He kept pacing as if he didn't hear me. And when Maggie reached up to him he walked right past her. She started to whine.

"Iggy?" I picked her up and went to where he'd stopped to look outside. When I touched his elbow he gave my arm a rough shove. "Hey!" I said too loudly.

That really set Maggie off, which was just as well because the sound of her cries brought Iggy back into the room. He reached out and I let him take her. He hugged her hard, too hard if the increase in her crying was any indication. He put her back in my arms, kissed me on the side of my head and walked out the door, his fist back in the front pocket of his jeans.

At the beginning of January another letter arrived from Grace. Was there some emergency for her to write again so soon? Perhaps something to do with Bernie? I had no way of reaching Iggy. So I asked myself – should I open the letter? Did I have a right to? On the one hand, I felt I did, on the other, Iggy would be very upset if he found out. He was paranoid enough about the rest of the world. He did not need to lose trust in me.

The envelope sat on the counter for two days before I gave in. I steamed it over the kettle till the glue melted, then laid it flat under a book to iron out the waffles in the paper that the steam had caused. I waited 10 minutes before removing the contents. There was one sheet of paper folded in three, with a note jotted on the outside of the fold.

"My Dear Ignatius, I just found your money in the cookie jar and realized I hadn't sent it in my last letter. I make sure I put it in the envelope right away so I don't forget, but your father's got me so addled these days I don't know what I was thinking. If we weren't so old I swear I'd move him to Alberta to see if it would help him as much as it does you. Thank the Lord you're all doing so well out there. Like I said before, I know it's hard starting out and I'm happy to help you and Bridgina. God Bless. Love, Mom."

I unfolded the paper. Inside were five crisp $100 bills.

26

I had never held $500 in my hand before. I examined the notes on each side, unsure what I was looking for. Did I expect them to be fake? I read the letter several times, dissecting the words and the messages behind them. How much had Grace sent him over the course of our time in Calgary? And how sweet of Iggy to leave a little something on the counter each time before he left. Twenty bucks, my arse!

I thought of all the things I could do with an extra $500 – pay the rent, buy a decent sofa, take Maggie to Banff. We hadn't been to the mountains yet. Maybe we could go to Fort McMurray. How great would it be to see all the Dollmonts, especially the new babies, and for them all to meet Maggie?

I tore up the envelope and sheet of paper, stuffed them in the garbage and put the trash out in the bin. If anyone asked, it had never arrived. Blame the post office.

Iggy phoned a few days later to ask about the mail. Nope, sorry, nothing for him.

A week later, Grace called. "Hello? Is this Bridgina?"

I knew her voice right away, hurried, slightly breathless. "Grace? Oh my God, I'm so glad to hear from you. How are you?"

"Good, fine. I'm sorry to bother you." Her voice did sound apologetic, too much so. "I hope I didn't wake the baby. Is this a bad time?"

"Not at all. I've been trying to call you but there's never any answer."

"No, I'm in town all the time now."

"I heard you were back from New York."

"Yes, it was costing so much money, and not helping. Anyway, we're back. Bernie's been committed, probably for good. Which is just as well after the heart attack."

"Heart attack? Oh poor Bernie, Iggy never said. How is he?"

"He's okay now. He was in the hospital when it happened so the doctors got to him right away." Was there a hint of disappointment? "I don't know why Iggy didn't say anything. I always tell him to say hi for us."

There was that word again, "always." "When did you talk to Iggy last?"

"Just the other day. He hadn't got my letter yet. Is he home?"

"No, he's…not here right now." I hesitated. Now was my chance to tell her, to explain that I knew as much as she did about when Iggy might grace us with his presence. Something held me back, some instinct to let her do the talking.

"I wish he'd let me call him sometimes. He only gave me this number for emergencies, because of the heart attack. I know Maggie's sleeping is still a problem, but if I called at suppertime, that would be okay, wouldn't it? He says you're a stickler for keeping the place quiet but sometimes a little noise is good." She tsked on the other end. "Listen to me, will you? Iggy said you don't like interfering busy-bodies and here I go telling you what to be doing."

"No, please, I could use some advice."

"Really? And you wouldn't mind me calling?" Her voice was cautious.

"Sure. I haven't got anybody out here to help." I dug my fist into my opposite armpit. "So anyway," I tried to keep my voice light, "what else has Iggy been saying?"

Plenty, apparently, complaints mainly, how expensive it was in Calgary, how he tried so hard to find a teaching job but couldn't so was stuck working long days and weekends at construction, how I wanted new clothes and a nicer apartment.

"You've moved a few times, haven't you?"

"Well, we left Gord's after a couple months. I never felt safe – "

"Was that the house near downtown?"

"Yeah, really bad neighbourhood, I couldn't wait to get out of there."

"But I was mailing Iggy there way longer than that, probably a year or more."

Gord's comment came back to me, that he wasn't the "fucking post office." The puzzle pieces were coming together. "And sending him money, too?" I used that light tone again, just slightly inquisitive.

"Yes, although it's too bad he doesn't have a bank account. I hate sending cash in the mail. Look what happened this time, it never showed up at all. Don't get me wrong, I'm happy to help, especially the deposit for the new car – "

I almost dropped the phone. "New what?"

There were several moments of silence. "What kind of car did you buy again?"

"Oh, Grace, we don't have any car." I thought twice about paying bus fare if I could walk it. "How much money did you send?"

"A thousand. But if you don't have a car what happened to it? And all the other money, every month some new expense, clothes for you and the baby…"

I slumped down into a chair. I'd always known that Iggy did drugs but I'd been reassured by the fact that he didn't have much money. I knew little about the cost of street drugs, but I didn't think they were cheap.

"…my God, what have I done? What's he been doing with that money, Bridge?"

I felt old. Part of me wanted to hang up the phone and go to bed, to haul the covers up and sleep for days. "Iggy's not doing good, Grace. Can we be honest with each other? Because he needs help."

Her voice, when it came through, was sad, resigned, the voice of a mother about to hear bad news. "I think we better be."

And finally the truth came out, or what we knew of it, the truth about the lies, the money, Iggy's problems. And for the first time from Grace, the words, "mental illness." "Did he ever see anyone or have things checked out?" I asked.

"Once, a few years back, I talked him into it. The doctor gave him medication and said he'd be okay as long as he took it. But Iggy said the drugs made him feel like a robot, so he went off them and he still seemed all right. But he was drinking a lot and smoking marijuana, and I wondered if he was taking harder drugs but he said no, just a little something to keep him stable. Then you came along and then Maggie, and I think that's when he decided he was just going to be better, that he wouldn't need any drugs anymore. He made me swear not to tell you." She paused but I didn't say anything, just waited for her to continue. "He told me he had it under control, that he'd done his research and he knew what he was doing. And now I have to wonder was he lying the whole time. Maybe even to himself, after watching his father, and I don't know what that did to him, seeing Bernie carted off in a straitjacket."

Listening to Grace talk about Bernie I felt a flash of panic, Would that be me in 40 years? And what about Maggie? Was she destined to end up like Iggy and Bernie?

"Is he doing a lot of drugs? Is he…" Grace's tone hardened. "Is he a drug addict?"

The question brought me back. "All I know is that he never does drugs when he's here. So, part of me thinks he's not, that he's just sick. The thing is, he hates to talk about it, and when he does, I don't know what's real and what's not."

Long-distance static was the only sound for half a minute. "When did he get to be such a good liar?" Her voice was earnest, as if she actually hoped for an answer. "We were so close, I didn't think he'd lie to me. He said he didn't mind moving to Calgary, even if he didn't know anyone, because he talked to Simon and he was all for it, he said it was a great idea…"

"Simon? Simon told him that?"

"Yes, and the mountain air would be good for him…"

I had trusted Simon. We were friends, good friends, family. Yet I had asked him outright and he had lied to me. Iggy had been right about his brother all along.

The phone weighed like lead. The receiver slid to my shoulder. I could hear Grace's voice but I could no longer make out the words. Then she started to cry, big sobs that made me bring the phone back to my ear long enough for her to say that she needed to call Simon, that she'd be in touch, that she was sorry but she couldn't talk anymore.

I hung up the phone, placing it gently back in its cradle. Too stunned to be angry, too hurt to slam it down, too numb.

Two days after my conversation with Grace, two nights of restless sleep knowing that Simon had lied to my face about something so serious, going over and over it in my head until disappointment took a back seat to anger, Friday evening arrived. The work week was over. I was almost home.

My lungs ached. The minus 30 wind chill made the air so sharp that it seized my breath as I rushed to beat the pending storm, forcing the stroller through the snow-packed sidewalks, thinking only of curling up on the sofa with Maggie, both of us snug in our warm flannel pyjamas. A quiet night in, a quiet weekend. If the weather improved, maybe we'd go sledding on the plastic toboggan Iggy had given her for Christmas, a cup of hot cocoa after.

With Maggie chattering beside me, I carried the stroller up the stairs to our landing. Leaning against the wall by my door was a tall thin man in blue jeans and a black jacket. He had a plastic bag in his hand. Maggie and I both stopped. She quieted and wrapped an arm around my leg. My hand went instinctively to her head, pulling her closer. The incident with Dave MacDonald had stayed with me.

"Hi Bridge."

My knight in shining armour had arrived. It was all I could do to keep a civil tongue. "Simon. What are you doing here?"

"Mom phoned. I flew out right away. She's worried to death about Iggy."

I walked toward him. "She should be." My voice was flat.

He didn't notice. He was looking at Maggie. "So, here she is."

I unlocked the door and pushed the stroller inside. "Yep, this is our Maggie."

Simon's eyes followed Maggie as she rushed past us, kicking off her boots and dropping her coat on the floor.

I switched on the lights. "Careful there, missy."

"Iggy said she was beautiful." He looked awestruck. "She's so much like him. But I see you too. Little Bridgie-Bee."

Maggie grabbed her teddy bear and hugged it, murmuring hello in her little girl voice before dropping it on its head to pick up her baby seal and kissing its nose, repeating the ritual with all five of her stuffed animals. She did it every day when we came through the door. Except if Iggy was there. Then she would run to him, her buddies forgotten in the joy of seeing her father. I could not imagine coming between them, for Maggie's sake and for Iggy's. But also for my own. That was the only time Iggy seemed real to me, the only time I could begin to understand why I had married him.

She ran to me and I scooped her up. "Maggie, this is your Uncle Simon."

Simon waved his fingers. "Hi there, I'm your daddy's brother."

Her brown eyes lit up and searched left and right. "Daddy?"

"No, honey, Daddy's not here."

Maggie went from happy to sad in an instant.

Simon moved closer to stand inches away, near enough for me to smell a hint of aftershave. He still looked like the Simon I knew, the guy who picked me for a debate partner, the guy who unknowingly helped me feel as if I belonged in my first year of high school, the guy who, instead of a Christmas card that year, gave me a postcard of a fat nun smoking a cigarette with a caption about giving up bad habits. I would never have thought he'd betray me, but that's what it was, a complete betrayal of our friendship, as in "here, take this guy and fix him for me, I don't have time, I've got more important things to do now that I'm all grown up and heading for doctorhood." At least that was the conclusion my monkey brain had come to on those sleepless nights when I lay awake wondering what had happened to my life, and why I was such a lousy judge of character, or men, or maybe just Connors men.

Reaching inside the plastic bag, Simon pulled out a stuffed panda bear and held it up to Maggie. "Could this guy play with your friends there?"

Maggie's eyes fixed on the small black and white bear. She wasn't smiling yet but she wasn't crying either.

Simon read the tag on the bear's ear. "It says here his name is Bamboo."

Maggie reached out and touched it. "Bamboo." She took the bear and brought it to her nose. "Bamboo." Obviously liking the sound, she said it a few more times. Simon laughed and said it with her.

"What do you say to your Uncle Simon?"

She held out the panda. "Thank you."

"You're very welcome." Simon turned to me, his blue eyes glistening. He'd grown into a handsome man. "You've got a lovely daughter, Bridge. I've been dying to meet her, and to see you again, too."

A handsome liar. I turned my attention back to Maggie.

Content to be home and happy with her new bear, Maggie settled into the beanbag chair Katie had given her and paid no more attention to the man in the middle of the room with his coat on, a leather bomber jacket unfit for a Calgary winter.

I took off my parka and reached out my hand. "Cool coat."

He took it off and passed it to me. "Thanks. It's not nearly this cold in Montreal." He glanced around. "So, this is your apartment." It sounded like a question.

I looked around the living room. The arms of the sofa were threadbare. The back was equally bad but it was hidden under a colourful afghan that Katie had bought at a second-hand store. The coffee table didn't match the end table, and the TV stand consisted of two red plastic milk crates positioned sideways so they could store Maggie's toys. Most of it belonged to Victor's brother.

"Yep, modern eclectic." I hesitated. "Sorry, I can't offer you a place to stay."

"I already checked into a motel. Got in early and rented a car. Mom said you were working so I drove around Calgary for a bit. This is a nice area you live in."

"It's no Vic Park, but it'll do."

He looked confused. I didn't explain. I put the coats away and went into the kitchen. Filled the kettle. Plugged it in. Took down mugs. Got the tea bags. With each movement, a nugget of anger grew, festering inside me.

"Bridge, listen."

I turned around. There he was.

His hands moved in a helpless gesture. "I don't know what to say except I'm sorry about all of this. All the lies, it's all just crazy – "

"That's a good word for it."

"Mom tried to fill me in when she called. What's Iggy been telling you?"

"Iggy? I guess we can start there. Iggy's a pretty good liar all right." The kettle whistled. I nodded towards the sofa. "Have a seat." I made the tea and brought it into the living room. "Let's see. Mainly that he never talked to you and your mother. I had no idea he was in contact. To be honest, I've been pretty disappointed with the pair of you, so caught up in your own stuff you didn't give a care about us."

Simon leaned forward and looked up at me. "But why would you think that?"

"Because that's what your brother told me and there was nothing to indicate otherwise." My voice had an edge that I didn't try to soften. "Iggy said you were too busy, too busy to come to the wedding, to come see your only brother, your niece."

"He did, did he? Did he tell you he gave me the wrong date for the wedding and by the time I found out I couldn't change my rotation? Or about the times we planned for me to come out here and he cancelled them?"

I'd been standing and holding the mugs of tea. I put them down on the coffee table. "Goddamn it." I closed my eyes and gritted my teeth, still furious but no longer sure with whom.

"Bridge, you know how much I care about Iggy. And you, right?"

"There's things you know and things you think you know. Frankly, at this stage of the game, I don't know what I know anymore." I sat at the far end of the sofa.

"Do you know where he goes when he's not here?" Simon picked up his cup so Maggie wouldn't knock it over as she scrambled up between us.

"Early on, he used to go to Gord's, but they gave him the boot ages ago. I've asked Iggy lots of times but he won't say, so I figured a drop-in centre or something."

"Didn't you ever go look for him?"

"Yeah, once." I held my mug between my palms until the heat penetrated and began to hurt. "But that was when he was at Gord's."

"And that was it? What about after?"

Maggie slid down and crawled under the coffee table to come out the other side.

"How the hell was I going to go look? Me and Maggie casing the back alleys off Electric Avenue?" I plunked my tea onto the table. "Calgary's huge, spread out in all directions, so tell me how I'm going to find a man who doesn't want to be found, who refuses to tell me anything about what he does and where he does it?"

"But he's your husband. You knew he was sick." Simon's face reddened.

"Now there's a smutty pot. I thought there was something wrong with him all right, but I had no idea how bad it was till your mother filled in the blanks." We were shooting from the hip now, our voices angry and defensive, flinging words at each other.

"Still, to not do anything – "

"And what did you ever do? You never called once since we've been here – "

"But you didn't want us calling – "

"Oh, for Christ's sake, why wouldn't I?"

"You didn't want us waking Maggie and – "

"What? All day? How long do you think a kid sleeps?"

"I was just doing what Iggy asked. Why else wouldn't I phone?"

"I don't friggin' know, do I? He just said you were too busy for us which was fine with him."

"Bridge, you should have known better – "

"How? Tell me how I'm supposed to know anything about any of this. I've been busy trying to stay afloat. You never called so I figured Iggy was telling the truth."

"Why didn't you call me?"

"Sure I didn't have your number. I didn't have Grace's in town either. Neither one of you bothered to call me up and give it to me. In fact, I was waiting for Seamus to get back so I could get it from him. How pathetic is that?"

"Like I said, Iggy told me you didn't want me calling the apartment."

I crossed my arms and glared at him. "Did you ever try to think that through? Why would I say that?"

He took a second. "Christ, I don't know. I'm not sure what to think anymore." He rubbed his forehead. "Anyway...he would call me, always collect."

"What did he want?"

"Sometimes just to talk, sometimes to wire him money. It was for Maggie and you, he said, things you needed, new furniture, stuff for the apartment."

"Everything we needed I supplied." My voice was cold. "It wasn't easy in a place where I knew no one, when my own family didn't give a shit and neither did his, but I did it. So let's set the record straight here. I'm a single parent with a deadbeat husband who shows up when the cheque's in the mail and then leaves 20 bucks on the counter."

"But Iggy said – "

"'Iggy said.' Iggy might be crazy but he's sure not stupid."

"Still, he didn't have anyone. Couldn't you have done something?"

"Jesus! You are seriously pissing me off. What did you do? Huh? Nothing."

"Come on, that's not fair."

"Fair? I haven't got time to worry about what's fair. Your brother dragged us clear across the country and left us to fend for ourselves with barely a pot to piss in. And you're telling me I should have gone out combing the streets for him?"

"No, what I meant – "

"I don't give a good goddamn what you meant." I remembered Maggie and lowered my voice. "I've been working my arse off to give Maggie some kind of life, trying to keep our heads above water, with no one to turn to."

"Look, I'm sorry. But you're all Iggy has here, too, you know."

I stared at him, dumbfounded. "You don't get it, do you? I'm 21 years old with the sole responsibility of a two-year-old child. I can't take on a grown man, so don't be thinking you're laying your brother on me. You're so concerned all of a sudden, you go find him."

"All of a sudden? Bridge, listen – "

I stood up so abruptly I bumped the table, sloshing my still full mug of tea. "No, you listen. I've had a rotten week and I'm not up to this right now."

He stood up too. "I'm sorry."

"Goddamn it, Simon, it's too late to apologize." I felt tears behind my eyes and wanted him out of there. I went to the closet and got his coat. "Just go."

He glanced at Maggie, then at me where I stood with the door open. He took his coat and stepped into the hall. "Can I call you tomorrow?"

I shrugged and shut the door. I locked the locks and switched off all the lights except the table lamp. I made Maggie a peanut butter and jam sandwich and we snuggled on the sofa watching television until she fell asleep curled up beside me in the glow from the screen. I carried her to her crib and settled her in, then changed out of my work clothes, went back out, poured myself a full glass of wine and turned off the TV. When I sat down on the couch I felt a bulge under my left leg. I fished it out – the panda bear – and flung it across the room. Too tired to fight it, too fed up with my life and just about everyone in it, I surrendered to a good long cry.

I had just refilled my glass when there was a knock on the door. Praying it might be Katie and desperate for a friendly face, I rushed to look through the keyhole. Simon stood there holding a brown paper bag in his arms, a sprinkle of snow on top of his head.

I opened the door. "What?"

"Bridge, I had to come back. I couldn't leave it like that."

"Simon, no. I can't do this tonight."

"Please, can I start over?" His eyes must have adjusted to the low light. He put the bag down inside the door and took hold of my arms. "You've been crying."

I twisted free and walked away, over to the table where I'd set down my glass. I raised it to my mouth then put it back down. It tasted salty.

The door shut. Simon came up behind me and put his hands on my shoulders. "Oh Bridge, what have we done?"

I pushed his hands away and spun to face him. "You know damn well what you did, Simon Connors. Nothing. Absolutely nothing."

He studied me for a second. "If I didn't do anything, why do I feel like this is my fault?"

"Because you lied to me. You looked me in the face and you lied to me."

"What?" He sounded shocked. "When?"

"That day in the car, going to St. John's."

He looked mystified. "I don't know what you're talking about."

I swallowed and took a breath. "You told me he was fine. I asked you…I came right out and asked you was there anything wrong with him and you said no, you said 'he's wired different.'" My tone was mocking. "Yeah, and 'that's what makes him Iggy, that's why we love him,' or some shit like that. Do you remember that?"

"I do. It was the last time I saw you."

"Why did you tell me that?" I raised my hands in frustration and anger. "I trusted you, Simon, more than anyone else, I trusted you."

"Jesus, that's why you're so mad. Bridge, listen to me. I didn't know anything more than I told you that day. Honest to God, I had no idea until Mom called two days ago. Iggy made her promise not to tell me, or you when you started going out. You got to know I would never, never, do that to you."

"But Grace said you talked to him about moving out here, about new doctors and medicine and…all of that."

"Yeah, that. Oh she told me all right. But that's Iggy putting words in my mouth. I said no such thing. I can't believe she never checked with me herself. The fact is I did talk to Iggy about moving to Calgary but it was to try to change his mind, not because he was sick. I didn't know that. I was thinking of you, alone out here with a new baby in a strange city. That's when he told me it was your idea, because Katie was there and…" He stopped and rubbed his face, pushing at the skin around his eyes. "Oh hell, what odds about it. It was all bullshit anyway."

I leaned back against the counter and looked out at the snow whipping against the patio doors. After two days of thinking that Simon was a lying jerk, and feeling hit harder by that than anything in a long while, I wanted to believe him. But I'd fallen for so many lies the past few years that trust did not come easy.

"But you're his brother. You're a doctor. Didn't you notice?"

"I haven't seen Iggy more than a few days at a time in over 10 years. One or the other of us was always away. I had no reason to think there was anything wrong with him."

I looked at him, studied his face as he looked back at me, his eyes, as honest and open as daylight. "Oh God, I'm sorry, Simon."

His hands came up to my arms and he stared into my eyes. "Bridge, I would never hurt you, and certainly not on purpose. You got to know that."

I was so tired. My head throbbed. When he put his arms around me, I lay my head against him and cried against his cold leather coat.

He reached for the roll of paper towel, tore one off and dabbed my eyes.

"Thanks," I said, taking it from him. "I'll be back in a minute." In the bathroom I washed my face, letting the cold water run as I splashed my cheeks. I felt giddy, partly from relief, partly from crying so much on top of a big glass of wine.

That's it, I told myself, forcing a smile at my reflection, enough with this sob story. I thought about Simon waiting in the living room. The smile became real. I went back out.

He was standing by the sliding glass doors. "Feeling better?"

"Better than I look, that's for sure." I held out my hand. "Pass over your coat."

He smiled and gave me his jacket. "You look fine to me."

I hung up the coat and went back to him. "And you said you'd never lie to me."

He laughed lightly. "And I never have."

"I know." We stood watching the snow swirl and fly off in the wind. "I'm sorry, I think I needed someone to blame. You're the last person I should have."

"Don't apologize. You've been through so much, Bridge, more than you ever bargained for. I'm sorry for that."

I thought a moment. "Thanks but, you know, the fact is I'm here because of choices I made. It's no one's fault, not even Iggy's. Certainly not yours."

His lips parted, took that preliminary breath that signals something is coming. But then he closed his mouth and glanced toward the kitchen. "I could use a glass of wine."

"Me too." He followed me the few steps to the counter where I found my full glass and poured one for him. "Cheers," we said in unison.

"It's so good to see you," he said, "to know you're okay. All Mom talked about on the phone was Iggy. You are okay, right?"

"Hell, compared to Iggy, I'm friggin' dandy."

"Would you mind...I mean, can you tell me about it, what's been going on the past few years. How bad is he?"

I sat and propped my elbows on the table. "Iggy's sick. He can't work. He shows up to see us when it suits him, usually a weekend morning now that I'm working because he knows Maggie will be home. I doubt he'd call this home if she wasn't here."

Simon set his glass onto the table and sat down. "You think he'll be back soon?"

"He's due, could be any time."

"I thought I'd go look for him but I don't know where to start. Any ideas?"

"Drop-in centre, Vic Park, 11th Ave., who knows? He could be anywhere."

"Has he been using a lot of drugs?"

I'd thought about that question since talking to Grace, about Iggy being here, about how, if he was some crazed drug addict, surely he wouldn't be able to just stop whenever he felt like it. "I'm pretty sure he does some stuff but I don't think that's the real issue. I think the main problem is he's sick and can't do anything about it, or he won't, or maybe it's the doctors, maybe they don't know what to do. Maybe it's both, he's sick and does drugs."

"What about you and him? Are you...you know, do you get along?"

"Yeah, I suppose." I leaned back in the chair. "We don't fight. I avoid certain topics, makes life easier. But I don't think of us as married anymore."

"I'm sorry to hear that. I guess in all of this, I figured at least he had you."

"Don't get me wrong, I'm here for him. But not that way, not that he'd want me to be. Basically, Iggy's too sick to function properly."

"You mean, as in…?" He looked embarrassed.

"Yeah, I mean, 'as in.' At least not with me, but I doubt with anyone else either."

"Poor Iggy."

Poor me, I almost said.

"What about you?" He turned his wine glass. "What kind of life do you have?"

"Oh, you know, I work and I take care of Maggie. Iggy comes and goes."

"Sounds pretty lonely."

"I got Katie, too. She lives here with us."

"Well, that's good, I guess." He didn't sound convinced.

"Maggie loves her to bits. And Iggy doesn't mind at all. If anything he's relieved she's here." I paused. "It makes sense."

He inclined his head. "I guess it does. Where is Katie?"

"On her way down from McMurray, hopefully. She's been helping her mother."

"Right. Seamus told me about the twins."

My stomach let out a growl. I hadn't eaten since lunch. "Excuse me."

He looked at his watch. "You haven't had supper, have you?"

"You either, probably." I started to get up.

He pressed his hand to my shoulder. "Sit, take it easy. I got everything we need."

I didn't resist, just sat back with my wine while he emptied the grocery bag, displaying items with panache, wrinkling his nose at the blue cheese, swooning over another. I was reminded of the Simon of high school, funny, easy to be with. As the display continued – brown-paper-wrapped packages with names like prosciutto and capicolli, which he pronounced with Italian flair, and tubs filled with fancy things like roasted artichokes and stuffed olives, items I'd never seen in the grocery store – I realized how much I had missed him.

He pulled a bottle from an ALCB bag. "Do you know you can buy wine in the grocery store in Montreal?"

"Don't they have liquor stores?"

"Yeah, but they sell wine at both. It's trés français," he said with a jaunty wink as he swished grapes under the tap before placing them on paper towels to dry. Several tried to roll away but he made a show of catching them. He glanced over at me where I sat at the table laughing at him. "I like the sound of that," he said. "Now open wide."

I tilted my head and he popped two grapes into my mouth then one in his own. They were sweet and firm and juicy, not spongy like typical January grapes.

He held up his index finger. "Hang on, it gets better." He opened one of the brown paper packages, cut off a piece of cheese, and speared it and a grape onto a toothpick. He signalled for me to open up. I watched his mouth open as he placed the food on my tongue, then close as he slid the toothpick from between my lips.

I chewed and swallowed then washed it down with wine. "My God, that's good."

"Aged provolone, what my friend calls Italian cheddar. Ready for the next one?"

"I like this game."

"Okay, so open your mouth and close your eyes and see what God will send you."

I held up my hand. "That game I'm not so sure about."

"Oh?" He looked up from opening a package. "Your family played it a lot?"

"Lord, no, not my bunch. Don't you remember, the Dollmonts were always at it. You never knew what you'd end up with, especially with Seamus. I can still taste cod lips."

"Sounds like Seamus," he laughed. "All right, come on, eyes shut."

"Fine, but no fish." I closed my eyes and opened my mouth.

I sensed him moving closer, smelled his aftershave. I had an urge to swallow but took a breath instead. Something cool was placed on my tongue. His warm fingers brought my lips together. I started to chew and opened my eyes.

He was standing to the side of my chair. "Do you like it?"

I nodded. I was finding it hard to concentrate.

"Pear and parmesan together." He smiled down at me. "Isn't that delicious?"

I felt peculiar, as if under a spell. I stood and went to the counter and picked up the cheese he'd just cut from. "The only parmesan I ever had was out of a green shaker."

He topped us up. "And cheddar that's not orange? What's with that?"

"Mutant cows? And how come you know so much about Italian food?"

"I don't have a clue, really. A friend of mine in Montreal grew up in Bridge-land, and she said I had to go to this Italian store there. The woman who owns it picked it all out for me. Had the bag in the car when you kicked me out."

"Good thing I let you back in." I put down the cheese. "So, this 'she.'" I tried to sound teasing. "She your girlfriend?"

"Nope, no time for that." He sliced into a baguette, scattering crumbs across the counter. He held up the end. "Best part," he said. "You a crust girl?"

"Maggie gets the crust in this house."

He spread pâté on the bread and held it out to me. "Your turn tonight."

"I'll share it with you."

He took a bite then passed it to me. I pointed to his mouth where there was a leftover smudge of pâté. Keeping his eyes on mine, he wiped his bottom lip.

"Over, on the other side," I said, my voice a sudden baritone. His thumb moved to the right. "Now up a bit." I felt that spell again as he found the pâté and licked it off his finger. I looked away and focused on my wine.

He cleared his throat and gestured towards the living room. "I'll bring it all over."

I filled our glasses to finish the bottle then cleared away Maggie's storybooks to make room for the food. Tired but more relaxed than I'd been in days, I sat and watched him work, opening the other bottle of wine, finding plates, arranging the food on my two plastic platters. His movements were sure, confident. He would be a good doctor, I thought. And then, a good father, a good husband. I remembered his hand on my back, his fingers on my lips. He would make a woman very happy one day.

He laid everything out on the coffee table and sat next to me. "Dig in."

The little bites in the kitchen had only made me hungrier. We were quiet as we ate and drank until, the initial hunger pangs satisfied, we slowed down.

He refilled our glasses. "You ever think about debate club?"

"That was fun. Too bad Alphonse had that heart attack."

"That's what happens when you're 50 pounds overweight."

"Ain't that the truth – look at Josephine?"

"Bridge!" He sounded scandalized. "She was your mother."

"No she wasn't. She was nothing to me. My sister Melinda, she's my mother. Dad was my grandfather." I was surprised how easy it was to tell him all that.

"You're kidding?"

"Nope, it's true." As I told him the rest of the story, I realized that the last person I'd confided in had been his brother.

"All that, and then for everything to go so off track with Iggy."

I set my empty glass on the table and turned to him. "I'd say it was worth it. I got Maggie." I was feeling better. I was also a little drunk.

"I thought you were the smartest girl in debate," he said, holding my gaze.

"Really?"

"Yeah. Obstinate, too. Once you got going there was no stopping you."

"That's because I was on your team. We worked well together."

We were still looking at each other. I took in his features, the bluest blue eyes, the gentle half-smile, the beginnings of stubble above his lip.

My eyes closed as our heads moved to bridge the short space between us. I heard a small gasp as he pulled back. I opened my eyes.

"Bridge, I'm sorry." He covered his face with his hands. "Christ!"

I rested my head against the sofa. "Yeah. Me, too." Not for the same reason.

"I can't believe I did that. Jesus, I don't know what got into me."

"It wasn't just you, you know." I didn't bother to hide my annoyance.

"No, you're vulnerable, I know that, and still..." His hand went to his forehead. "You're married to my brother, for God's sake. What's wrong with me?"

"Happy ever after, that's me and Iggy." I stared at the ceiling, more frustrated than embarrassed. "I'm not vulnerable, Simon, I'm lonely. A kiss would have been nice."

He took hold of my hand and focused his attention there. "I would love to kiss you. I've always wanted to do that. But what about – "

"I know." I cut him off. I didn't want to hear his name. "It's just that…you see, I haven't been kissed, I haven't been anything, in over two years."

His forehead creased. "That long?"

I nodded. I did feel vulnerable now, and a little pathetic.

He moved towards me. My eyes closed as he leaned in and kissed me, a light tender kiss where his mouth touched down and held a second before pressing slightly, his hand touching my cheek. I felt him back away.

I kept my eyes closed, enjoying the warmth that stayed on my lips. "I've been having this strange dream, that no one will ever kiss me again." My eyelids closed tighter. "And I can't remember what it feels like to be kissed. And I'm sad because I would have paid more attention if I'd known it was never going to happen again."

I heard his sharp intake of breath. He pulled me to him, his arms holding me tighter than was actually comfortable. I heard him whisper, not to me, more to himself, "Oh, Jesus." I opened my eyes. He drew back to stare at me, his eyes, a tiny bit angry, holding mine as his hands slid up my arms to my face, kneading my jaw with his lean fingers, then up my neck to the back of my head, tangling in my coarse hair as his mouth covered mine, his lips pressing hard as he gave a sharp little tug that didn't hurt at all. I concentrated on the kiss, his lips on mine, the pressure of his mouth as it opened, my own lips parting, the sweet pressure of his lips and his open mouth, of tongues touching.

It was the tongue that did it. It was the tongue that set my hands and my arms in motion. They'd been slack at my sides as I'd tried to put all my energy into memorizing the kiss. But that all changed with the tip of his tongue. I heard myself moan as my arms wrapped around him and my body moved tight to his. All I could think was, dear God, don't stop, then I was tugging his T-shirt from inside his jeans and over his head and trying to get his belt loose and his hands were up inside my sweater pushing it over my head and my bra was undone and he was kissing me as he took off his jeans and pulled mine down and we were lying on my ratty old sofa and he was inside me and I'd never felt so whole and so full in my life.

It was over in minutes but it was no less good for that. We lay together, spooning, quiet except for our breathing, which began to calm after a minute or so. But then, maybe accidentally, maybe not, his fingers brushed against my nipple and there was that moan again, the one I had no control over. I felt him tense. His hand came up and closed around my breast and we started in again, slower this time, his fingers kneading my breasts and brushing down over my ribs and down to my thighs, my hand reaching behind to pull him closer to me, his lips on my neck, his tongue tracing along my shoulder, then gently pushing me flat on the sofa so he could lie above me, moving in to kiss me, and kissing me so long and so hard that my lips would never forget, caught up with the feel of his lips and his mouth on mine, and him pulling away and leaning back a little, enough to see me and watch me as he entered me, my body arching forward to meet him, both of us moaning, our mouths open just that much, our breath gasping.

Afterwards, we curled into each other, the old worn afghan soft against our skin.

"Hey," he whispered. "You all right?"

I nodded against his bare chest. "Yeah. How about you, you going to be okay?"

He pulled me closer. "If God doesn't smite me down."

I hugged him back. I wanted to thank him but thought that might be odd.

A door slammed nearby. Simon bolted upright, almost knocking the pair of us to the floor, his eyes frantic as he scrambled, naked, to try to pull the afghan over us.

"It's okay," I said, laughing, knowing it was the door to our old apartment down the hall. "He'd never show up this late."

Still, we cleaned up quickly. Clothes on, we leaned back against the sofa in much the same position we'd been in earlier, except this time our bodies were touching and he held my hand in his, his thumb every once in a while moving up or down in a little caress.

I felt his head turn toward me and I smiled at him. "Thank you," I said then.

"You're welcome." He held my hand tighter. "I should go. I want to get an early start looking for him."

I waited a few breaths. "You think we're awful, don't you?"

He didn't look away. "You're certainly not. Although I might be."

I returned the hand pressure. "I'm not awful and neither are you. You know that, right?"

He reached up and touched my cheek, brushed my lips with his fingers. "All I know is that I wouldn't change what we did. I couldn't." He paused. "Would you?"

"No." I didn't hesitate, didn't need to think about it. I didn't care if it was selfish, and I didn't feel it was immoral. Yes, he was Iggy's brother. Somehow, in some weird universe, that was more appropriate than doing it with a stranger. I no longer thought of myself as Iggy's wife, and couldn't remember when I last had, in the true sense of the word. "Not for a second."

27

Two days later, on a cold and cloudy Sunday morning, Iggy appeared.

Simon and Maggie and I were sitting at the kitchen table, all of us laughing as he tried to teach her how to suck in a noodle from the leftover Chinese food. Saturday night had been perfect. The whole day had been perfect, the stuff my dreams used to be made of. Simon had shown up at noon after having spent the morning in a futile search for Iggy. Seeing him standing in the doorway, looking guilty and shy and self-conscious with a bag of donuts in his hand, I'd felt a burst of energy and hugged him hard. "Where's Maggie?" he said into my ear. "In the bedroom playing dress-up." He pulled away and took my hand. "We should talk about last night." I shook my head. "Iggy and I have been over for a long time." "I get that, but I'm his brother. We can never be over." "I know but...please, can you just let me have this?" He seemed about to speak, to protest most likely, but I kissed him, soft and slow, a kiss that lasted until I felt him kiss me back. "Okay?" I said, and he nodded and kissed me again. We spent the afternoon at the zoo. Maggie and I had never been there and she was beyond excited to see animals she'd only heard about from books. She fell asleep in her stroller before we left the grounds and didn't wake up until we were back in the apartment. We were all starving and decided to head out for dinner at a nearby restaurant. Maggie wore her best dress, I, my best pair of jeans and favourite blouse. We had egg rolls and Kung Pao chicken and chow mein. Simon was the only one who knew how to use chopsticks but we all tried. Maggie ended up eating with her hands. We drank jasmine tea out of small white cups. The owners made a fuss over Maggie, saying what a lovely dress she was wearing, what a pretty little girl we had, how her dimple was just like her father's, bringing her fried bananas for dessert without asking and an extra fortune cookie with the bill. We took a long way home. A Chinook wind had blown in that afternoon and taken the chill off the January night. We walked slowly, letting the food digest. After a while Maggie grew tired and reached up to Simon. He passed me the bag of leftovers and picked her up, his smile unsteady as her short pudgy arms wound around his neck. Once home, we tucked her in, then had our own night together, a sleeping child in the next room, wine by candlelight, Jim Croce on the radio singing "Time in a Bottle," wanting to make the day last forever. I wanted that, too. And I wanted Simon Connors in more ways and for more reasons than I'd ever wanted his brother. The moments rolled on, one into another, the air soft and warm surrounding us. And I knew without consciously thinking it that before it was too late, before our moments ran out, that I needed to feel those lips again, those lips that were unlike any I'd ever kissed. I moved toward him, my mouth meeting his. Me. Not him. He let out the smallest moan. Acquiescing. Giving in. Him, giving. Me, taking.

Sunday morning coming down, a low slow knock on the door, bringing the memory to a close. Simon looked over, his face a question mark. I nodded. We held each other's eyes for several seconds as our smiles faded. When Maggie hopped down off her chair and headed for the door, I did, too.

Iggy looked worse than I had ever seen him, unshaven with red scrapes like cat scratches on his face. There was a blister on his earlobe that might have been frostbite, and his hair was stringy and dirty. His clothes were filthy and he smelled of stale sweat.

"My God, Iggy." I didn't have time to hide the shock on my face.

His appearance didn't bother Maggie. "Daddy," she squealed, clapping and jumping up and down, almost tripping over herself to cover the last few feet to reach him. As he lifted her up and held her close, I cringed, wondering when he had last had a shower or washed his hair, the same hair that Maggie's face was burrowed into. His puffy eyes closed shut against everything else as he inhaled and exhaled deeply several times. I knew what he was doing. The father in him was trying to bring Maggie inside himself, to breathe her in and keep her close, to never have to let her go. I had done the same thing the first few days when I'd left her at the day home, and still did when I was lonely or tired or sad. I knew that need, knew how my own body reacted to Maggie's breath on my cheek. Who was to say that Maggie didn't need Iggy just as much?

She touched Iggy's face. "Daddy got a boo-boo."

Iggy kissed her fingers. "It's all better now, my Maggie."

Simon came out from the kitchen. His eyes met mine for a nervous glance before moving onto Iggy. Simon's face went white.

Iggy's eyes opened wide. He passed Maggie to me. "What the...?"

They met in the middle of the living room, their arms wrapping around each other, squeezing tight for a good minute. Even when they pulled back, they still held on.

"Jesus, Ig." Simon's voice was next to tears.

"Simon." Iggy was looking at him as if trying to take him all in. "It's been so long, I didn't know if I'd ever see you."

I watched the two of them staring at each other, afraid to let go even with their eyes. I was pretty sure they had forgotten I was in the room.

"But what are you doing here?"

Simon swallowed and took a breath. "Mom."

Iggy tightened his hold on Simon's arm. "What's wrong with her?"

"Nothing. She's worried about you."

Iggy let go. He stepped back. "No, no...I don't want her worrying."

"Where've you been, Iggy?" I said. "Simon went out looking for you."

"I was away."

"Oh? Where?" I asked.

"Just... the coast."

"Iggy, no, not for Gord? You didn't?"

He wouldn't look at me. "Don't worry, I'm always careful."

"You mean you've done this before?"

"I don't have much choice. I owe him." His hand flew to his mouth and he rushed to the bathroom.

I distracted Maggie with a noisy game of "itsy-bitsy spider," then passed her to Simon while I found a kids' show on TV. I plopped Maggie into her beanbag in front of the television, put a juice pop in her hand and went back to the kitchen.

Simon was standing at the counter rubbing his forehead. He turned to me. "I wouldn't have recognized him. Is he always like this?"

"No, I've never seen him this bad."

"And what was that about going to the coast for Gord? Was that about drugs?"

I nodded. "Things must be worse than I thought."

"So he's dealing?" His hands bunched into fists. "Jesus, we got to stop this."

We heard the toilet flush, the bathroom door open. Iggy appeared. His face was pale beneath the scratches, the bloodshot eyes.

"Anybody phone here, Bridge? For me, I mean?"

"No, not for ages."

He went still and looked about to vomit again but choked it back down.

"You're not looking good there, Ig," said Simon. "Sit down, catch your breath."

"Sorry...I just got to get myself together." Iggy pulled a chair away from the table, out of sight of Maggie. He sat, bent over at the waist, his head between his knees.

Simon knelt in front of him. "What can I do for you? How can I help?"

Iggy eased himself back up into a sitting position and leaned his forehead against Simon's. His eyes had welled up. So had Simon's. I felt like an intruder watching them.

Simon put an arm around him. "Tell me what to do, let me help."

"I don't know...so sorry, " Iggy was muttering now, and crying outright so that I couldn't make out everything he was whispering. "...been so good to me... good brother...sorry about everything...forgive me someday..."

"Iggy, stop." Simon's guilty face looked at me. His eyes closed briefly. "I have nothing to forgive you for."

"You, too, Bridge, I'm sorry...so sorry..."

I moved his hair out of his eyes. "You look so tired. You want to lie down?"

He nodded and moved as if to head for the sofa.

I took his arm and led him to my room. He was asleep before I shut the door.

I came out to find Simon pacing up and down the small kitchen. "This is so much worse than I imagined. I got to help him. I got to stop this before it gets further out of control." His face and his voice were pleading. "What can I do?"

"Oh Simon, I wish I knew. Nothing I've ever said made much difference."

"Maybe he'll listen to both of us together. When he gets up we'll talk to him, tell him we know everything, and that he can't keep on this way. Yeah, we'll make him see sense." Simon was nodding as if he had it figured out. "Yeah? Right?"

Before I could answer Maggie came over. "I'm hungry, Mama."

I picked her up and hugged her, breathing her in like Iggy had. "You want a PBJ to go with those noodles?"

"And a pickle," she added.

"Coming right up. PBJs and pickles it is. Good for you, Simon?"

He was staring at us but I could tell he wasn't seeing us. Then he blinked and tried to smile at Maggie. "Pickles, yeah, sounds great."

After lunch, I took Maggie to the playground. Simon stayed behind to be there when Iggy woke up.

I arrived back an hour later, carrying a sleeping Maggie.

Simon's voice carried down the stairwell. "Come on, Iggy, don't."

The apartment door was open. Iggy had his coat on and was smoking a cigarette.

He glared at me. "Finally. You're back."

I put my finger to my lips and got Maggie into her crib, then hurried back out. "What's all the racket about?"

"Nothing." Iggy's voice was brusque. "Where's the mail?"

"There's no mail for you."

"Nothing? At all?"

"Unless you want the phone bill." His name was on it.

He went to the counter where I kept the mail and rummaged among bills and flyers. "Fuck!" he yelled, shoving it all up against the backsplash.

"Watch the language," I said. "Sit. We want to talk to you."

"You do, do you? What are you two, a tag team, ganging up on me?" He looked at me then narrowed his eyes at Simon. "How long you been here?"

"I just got here," Simon said, some instinct kicking in. "I only have a couple of days. So come on, sit down."

Iggy glanced at his wrist. There was no watch on it. "I got to get out of here. I got to go, go now...don't know why there's no mail...should be a letter...goddamn post office..." He rambled on, glancing at his naked wrist. He zeroed in on me. "You're sure, you're absolutely certain, no one called? No one?"

I shook my head. He was making me nervous.

Simon tried to steer him into a chair. "We need to discuss what's been going on."

Iggy spun away but still managed to grip one of Simon's wrists. "We?" Iggy yelled. "Who the fuck is 'we?'"

Simon winced. "Let go." He pulled his hand away. "We're worried about you."

"Why? What the fuck's been going on? Why all this 'we' bullshit?" Iggy turned to me, squinting, sizing me up. "You sure there's no mail?"

I stared him in the eye. "No, nothing."

"Goddamn it." His mouth hardened. He started towards the door.

Simon cut him off and stood in front of it.

Iggy's arm shot up. "Move."

"No. You're not going anywhere."

"You," his index finger stabbed the air, "you get the fuck…now… get out of my way." His head twisted to look at the clock on the wall.

Simon didn't budge.

Iggy moved closer. "You don't get away from that door, I'll put you through it."

Simon held his ground. "You're in no shape to go anywhere."

Iggy lunged. With a look of shock on his face, Simon's hands came up in self-defence. I knew Iggy would have only meant to get him away from the door but he was too crazed to gauge his own strength and shoved Simon hard enough to send him to the floor. By the time Simon got to his feet, Iggy had rushed off.

Simon stared at the empty doorway. "I thought he was going to punch me."

"Iggy's never hit anyone in his life, not that I know anyway."

"I'm going after him." He dug Seamus's number from his pocket and got the phone. He was on the line for less than a minute. "He's on his way." He thought a moment. "Where can I find Gord MacDonald?"

I wrote down the address. "Iggy won't be there."

He nodded. "But who better than Gord to point me in the right direction?"

"Be careful," I said. "They're a nasty bunch."

He hugged me. "Don't worry, I will." He leaned back and looked as if about to say something, but then he gave me a small sad smile and said, "I'm sorry, Bridge."

As I watched him go, I wondered what he was sorry for, what had already happened or what was in store. Either way, it wasn't good.

Simon called late the next morning. "We'll be there in an hour."

"So you found him?" I was relieved. And disappointed. Iggy was safe but now we had to deal with him, which begged the question, where did that leave Simon and me?

"He's not good." Background noise, like someone speaking into a loud-speaker or an intercom, made it difficult to hear. "I'll fill you in when we get there."

"Okay." Already tired from a restless night, now I felt drained.

"And Bridge, Katie got into town this morning. She and Joey are coming over to take Maggie out for lunch."

Joey was Seamus's friend. Katie was smitten. So was he.

Half an hour later, there was a tap on the door. Katie, one hand covered in a red Raggedy Ann sock puppet, tiptoed in and over to the table where Maggie sat colouring. "Is there a girl named Maggie here?" she said through the puppet.

Maggie scrambled to her feet. "Me, me," she yelled, waving her hand.

Katie's arm moved up and out in all directions so that the puppet was looking every which way except where Maggie was standing at her knees. "Maggie? Oh, Maggie?"

By this point Maggie was jumping up trying to grab the puppet, which Katie kept out of reach for a giggly minute. Just as Maggie was losing patience, the puppet swooped down and snuggled into her neck. She grabbed it off Katie's arm and hugged it to her.

"All right, Miss Maggie, it's high time I take you out for your birthday. What do you say, want to go to McDonald's?"

Maggie looked to me. "Mama come, too?"

"Auntie Katie wants you all to herself this time. Why don't you go get dressed?" I gave her a little push towards the hallway.

Once Maggie disappeared around the corner, Katie turned to me. "You okay?"

"Yeah. Kind of confused."

"When did Simon get here?"

I slumped down onto the couch. "Friday." I looked up at her. "He's been here with Maggie and me since then."

"Just the three of you." She sat next to me. "So, how did that go down?"

"It was pretty crazy." I gave her the Coles notes version, from the initial fight to Sunday morning's breakfast, and a quick synopsis of in between.

"My God. After all these years, you and Simon?"

"It all feels like a dream, or a nightmare in the making."

"And now Iggy's back in the picture, what does that mean for you and Simon?"

"I don't know. It's all about Iggy now."

Maggie came in, pants unbuttoned, sweater on backwards. We fixed her up, zipped her into her coat and put on her mittens and boots.

Katie looked at her watch. "They'll be here soon," she whispered, then louder, "Joey's waiting in the car. Hurry, Mags." With a couple of quick hugs, off they went.

Ten minutes later, the Connors brothers were at the door.

Simon and Seamus had found Iggy in jail. According to Simon, it wasn't the first time, although this arrest was more serious. He'd been caught trying to sell drugs to an undercover policeman, and whereas before he'd been picked up for being drunk or loitering and was released the next day, this time he could face a prison sentence. The possibility of being locked up had him petrified.

"Bridge, you got to help, please?" One of his eyes was swollen shut and his arm was in a homemade sling. There was a gap at the front of his mouth where one of his fine white teeth had been. "I really screwed up this time."

"What the hell happened to you?"

"The cops…I can't…oh man…"

"What? The cops did that to you?"

"No, that was before. That's why I was there."

"You're not making much sense."

"Sorry, I don't know what to do. Please," he begged. A shudder went through him and he dropped into a chair.

"Iggy, what on earth can I do?"

Simon squeezed Iggy's shoulder and looked at me. "If you could take him in so he's got a permanent address, and they can see he's got a wife and child that need him to take care of them – "

"Take care of them?" They were just words. We all knew they meant nothing. They should not have set me off. "Iggy hasn't done that in a long time."

"I know, but if the court thinks he's a family man it might make a better impression."

"And anyway, sure I always let him come back. What's different this time?"

Simon glanced at Iggy. He said nothing for several moments. "Because this time…this time he's staying. He needs to move back in."

I felt something slipping away from me, a delicacy, something good and real that had settled on my tongue just long enough to make me want more. "For how long?"

"Till he goes to court at least." He ran a hand through his hair. "That's the other thing. Would you go to court and back him up?"

"Please, Bridge," Iggy said, his hands together, shaking. "I'll stay on the meds this time, I promise."

Simon and I looked at each other for a moment, then at Iggy.

"Is that what you do?" Simon said. "Just stop taking them?"

Iggy nodded.

"So…is that why I never know who to expect when you show up, Dopey or Grumpy?" I didn't say it to be cruel. I wanted to know. "Because sometimes you were on meds and sometimes you weren't? Can you even do that?"

He shrugged. "Probably shouldn't but…I don't know, sometimes they made me feel so weird…" His face was earnest, his voice almost steady. "But I'll listen to the doctors this time, I will, I'll give it time to work, and I'll do whatever you say, please just don't make me go to jail, I can't do it, I can't. I'll straighten up, please…" He put his head in his hands, his shoulders shaking as he cried.

"See? He means it. He really does." Simon turned to Iggy. "Don't you, Ig?"

Iggy looked up at me. "I do, Bridge, and I'll get a job soon as I can – "

"And we'll help," Simon cut in. "Mom and me, we'll both chip in. We can send you money every month, anything you need, okay?"

"Money?" The word spat out of my mouth. "It's not about money. It never has been." My heart felt like it was coming up through my throat.

"I'm sorry, I didn't mean it that way. Oh Jesus, Bridge, he needs help. I can't just leave him. Please don't expect me to do that. He's my brother."

There was nothing to say to that. I felt abandoned. What was I to him?

"One more chance, Bridge. I think he means it this time."

I slumped against the counter. "I don't know if I can do it again, Simon."

"Bridge, he needs you. We both need you."

It wasn't the kind of need I needed though. In fact, no one had thought about what I might need, what Maggie needed. It had long been that way with Iggy. I had let it be that way, out of fear of being alone perhaps, coupled with a lack of confidence in myself. But that was in the past. I had changed. My life had changed.

I moved away from Iggy. Simon followed. I kept my voice low. "The truth is, I'm not sure I want him in my life anymore." There. I'd said it.

Simon looked back at Iggy then turned to me. "Okay. Then do it for Maggie."

I stared at him full on. "Really, Simon? That's how you want to play this?"

He stared back at me for a few seconds, then had the grace to look embarrassed. He didn't take it back though.

Simon made arrangements to extend his stay in Calgary and brought Iggy to his motel to stabilize before he moved back in with us. I'd insisted on that. None of us, including Iggy as far as I could tell, knew how bad it might get before it got better. We didn't know the true source of Iggy's problems, how much was due to his use of illegal drugs, how much could be helped by the legal kind. I did not want Maggie around Iggy while he figured it out.

When Maggie and I arrived home after work the next Monday, they were there. Seamus had dropped them off because Simon's rental car had only been paid for until the previous Tuesday and between the cost of the hotel and the new plane ticket, the bills were racking up. Seamus had been driving them where they needed to go ever since.

Iggy looked exhausted but he was no longer a bag of shuddering bones. According to Simon, once he'd gotten onto proper medications, which he had more experience with than either of us would have guessed, having stopped and started a number of them over the years, Iggy started to improve. Still, it would take some time to figure out what worked best and at what dosage. Simon was convinced that Iggy was a changed man, that he was determined to do whatever was necessary to get well. "I know it sounds weird," he said to me right in front of Iggy, "but all in all, it was a good week. Right, Ig?" Iggy nodded and hugged him hard.

Maggie was the only one excited to have us all together. Iggy kept dozing off on the sofa, and Simon and I did not have a lot to say to each other. What was the point? He'd chosen his brother over me, and although I understood that, I resented both of them. And I was lonely, lonelier than I could remember being. I didn't even have Katie, who had given her bedroom to Iggy for the duration. I made grilled cheese for us all for supper then went to bed early.

I left Maggie at home on Tuesday. Simon was leaving that night and wanted to spend more time with her. When I got home from work, supper was in the oven and the table was set. Maggie was sitting between Iggy and Simon watching TV. Iggy's head lay against the back of the sofa, eyes closed, mouth open, the black gap staring out.

Simon and Maggie came to meet me at the door. I picked Maggie up. She wrapped her arms around my neck and hugged me and planted kisses on my forehead like she did with her teddy bears after a day away. She reached over to draw Simon into the hug. We had no choice but to play along.

Simon caught my eye. "I'm sorry," he whispered.

Over his shoulder I saw Iggy looking at us. I set Maggie down and headed for the kitchen. Maggie ran after me.

"Smells good here." I tried to sound upbeat for her sake.

"I made chili," said Simon behind us. "Hot and spicy for a cold day."

"Thanks. Seamus still taking you to the airport?"

"He'll be here at seven."

I reached up to the cupboard just as he did. Our hands met, touched for a moment before we both pulled away. I got a glass and turned around. Iggy was watching us.

He pushed himself up and came into the kitchen.

"Hey," I said, filling my glass with water. "Feeling any better today?"

"A bit." He sat down for a second then stood back up.

"You okay?" Simon touched his arm.

"I got to talk to you, to both of you. Something I need to say."

He sounded serious. I coaxed Maggie back to the sofa with a red sucker.

"First off, I want to thank you." He held up his hand as we both started to interrupt. "You've both been so good to me. And all I've done is lie to you. I'm going to stop that, too."

Even though it was the first time he'd said anything like it, I wasn't ready to jump on his bandwagon. I wasn't ready for much of anything.

"Most of all, I'm sorry to you, Bridge. I've thought about it a lot, off and on the last couple of years." He gave a disparaging grunt. "When I could think straight. And I'm sorrier for what I did to you than anything else. You were so young, so innocent. I was older. I should have known better."

I was reminded of Simon's comment about my vulnerability that first night he was here. "You know, I'm getting a little sick of being 'poor Bridge.' It's like you guys think I'm at your mercy or something, that I can't make my own decisions."

Iggy looked from me to Simon and back. "'You guys?'"

Simon shrugged self-consciously and looked as if he felt he should say something.

"Yes, the pair of you," I jumped in. "I'm an adult, for Christ's sake. I'm not little Bridge anymore and it's time you both understood that."

Iggy sat down. "My God, you're right. Look at the three of us. You're the most responsible one of the lot. And yes, I know, Simon's going to be a doctor, and I don't even mind anymore." He looked over to the sofa where Maggie was licking the last of her sucker. "But look at our Maggie. Now there's a job well done."

Maggie had looked over at the mention of her name. She ran over and crawled up into Iggy's lap. His arms went around her. We were all still as we watched Maggie curl into him, her small hand reaching up to touch the still obvious cuts on his face. She rose up to kiss each one then snuggled back in and smiled up at me.

If there was any fight left in me, it fizzled into thin air. "Hungry, Mags? Let's get that pot out of the oven."

Simon and I served up the chili. Maggie ate sitting on Iggy's lap, chatting away, happy and content, blissfully unaware that the rest of us had little to say, except to her.

After dinner, we watched TV, Iggy, Maggie and Simon on the sofa, me in the chair. Maggie had been so excited to be home with them all day that she hadn't had a nap and fell asleep sitting in Iggy's lap. He was asleep, too. He didn't stir when I picked Maggie up and put her to bed.

When I came back out, Simon was standing at the far end of the kitchen, out of sight of the sofa on the other side of the wall. The only light was from the overhead range hood, the only sound the steady cadence of Iggy snoring in the next room. I stopped across from Simon and leaned against the counter.

"Do you know how sorry I am?" he whispered.

"You keep saying that." I kept my voice low. "What I need to know is, why? What are you sorry for? Us?"

He took hold of my hand. "No. How could I be?"

I curled my fingers into his and took a breath. "That's good."

He curled his fingers over mine. "I'm surprised you have to ask."

We stood, holding hands, quiet, fingers tickling palms.

"I'm sorry about Iggy. I'm sorry for...for pretty much forcing you into this position, for dumping this on you. I just don't know what else to do right now."

In the dim light, his eyes begged me to understand.

"I thought about trying to take him home to Mom, or to Montreal with me but I can't figure out how that might work. Once I'm back I'll see what I can do, and I'll talk to Mom, and I'll call you every – "

I pressed a finger to his lips. "Shhh, it's okay." I liked the feeling and brushed my fingers over his mouth. "If Iggy's ever going to get healthy, this is probably the best place for him. What could be better motivation than seeing Maggie every day?"

He turned my hand over and ran his thumb up and down my palm. I closed my eyes for a moment and let a warm shiver run through me. When I opened my eyes he was looking at me so intensely I wanted to fall into him.

"I have to tell you this before I go." He brought my hand to his chest. "I love you. I think I always have. I don't know what I can ever do about it, but I want you to know it." He placed his hands on either side of my face and drew me close. He kissed my eyelids and my forehead, then moved to my lips, light and tender, then harder, too hard for an I-love-you kiss but I wasn't sure that's what it was anymore.

I pulled back enough to say, "I love you, too." I let my body move into his, let his arms come around me as I lay my face against his chest.

There was a knock at the door. The snoring had stopped.

We drew apart. He went in one direction, towards the table and into the living room, I in another, to the hallway and the door.

28

Every day Iggy apologized, more than once, for being lazy, for not helping out more, for sleeping so much. Sometimes he slept when Maggie was crawling over him. As a child who easily entertained herself, who could bring teddy bears to life for hours at a time, I think she thought it was funny, that it was part of how Iggy played with her. I didn't think it was funny when she fell off the back of the sofa and cut her arm on the pointy edge of the heat register, or when I found her playing with a bottle of pills that fell out of his pocket. He didn't either. He kept his pills high up behind the medicine cabinet after that.

One week turned into two, then three. By February, the cuts on Iggy's face had cleared up, his voice was stronger, there was more white than red around the brown in his eyes. Except for the black gap at the front of his mouth, he was beginning to look like a regular guy. Most evenings he had supper ready when I got home, simple meals like soup and sandwiches or fried eggs and beans. Other than his medications, he stayed away from drugs and booze. Still, when he suggested I leave Maggie with him rather than taking her to the day home, I told him she would miss the other kids. I think he knew I was lying.

Mid-February I got a phone call from Victor. Melinda had gone home to Exile Cove at the beginning of January. She was not coming back.

"Did she call you?" he asked.

"No," I said. "Then again, she wouldn't, would she?"

"No, most likely not."

The children were doing well, he said when I asked, as was he. "Charlotte is thinking about going back to school." His voice sounded lighter, brighter.

We talked for a while and I filled him in on my situation. I was honest and up front, just as I had been ever since that first call from the Vic Park phone booth.

"I'm glad Iggy's getting help, Bridge, but don't you overdo it, okay?"

"I won't." I thanked him for letting me know about him and Melinda and hung up.

When I told Iggy about the call, he asked how I felt. I said I was glad for Victor. On impulse, I confessed Victor's part in the move from Gord's to the apartment.

Iggy chuckled. "I always thought there was more to that." Then he added, "He's a good man, Dr. Brennan."

Other than Victor's news, life was quiet, with little variation or excitement. That was good for Iggy and I tried not to be resentful. For the most part, I succeeded. Still, it was another endless February.

Except for doctor's visits and trips to the library, Iggy rarely went out. When he did leave the apartment, he looked around furtively, as if casing the area. In the old days I would have hesitated to ask him why, for fear of setting him off.

"Sorry," he said when I brought it up. "I'm just being careful."

"Of what?"

"I still owe Dave."

"Shit. How much?"

"Well, that's the thing. It's not much. That's why I'm not too worried about it."

"You're sure?"

"Yeah. If he was going to try to get it he'd have been in touch by now."

I gave that a minute. "Does he know where you are?"

He shook his head. "I never told him. I wouldn't put you or Maggie in any danger. You know that, right?"

I did know that. I also knew if Dave wanted to find him, he would find him.

Iggy's trips to the library were good for all of us. He brought home stacks of books, mysteries mostly, books by John le Carré, Ian Fleming, P.D. James, along with picture books for Maggie. I hadn't been reading as much as I used to and fell back into it easily. Reading became our pastime, especially when Maggie was sleeping, what we did to while away the dark winter evenings, the long quiet weekends. If we both read the same book, we would talk about it afterward: what we liked, what we didn't. Iggy preferred a novel that was plot-driven; I was more interested in the characters.

Occasionally, he'd check out something more serious, books on philosophy or religion or, once, a memoir of someone with mental illness. I only knew about that one because I came into the living room one day and found him absorbed, head bent, eyes unblinking. I asked him what he was reading. "Bridge!" he said, as if caught off guard. He looked alarmed. I asked him again. "It's…it's a book… it's about someone just like me." "Oh?" I sat, ready to hear more. But he stood up, book under his arm, and left the room. I didn't see him reading it again, although he might have done so privately.

We didn't have much of a social life. Katie and Joey and Seamus were pretty much it. But they were young and single and having a good time. They lived way down in the south part of the city so we only saw them every other weekend or so, although Katie would drop in on a weeknight if the guys were out of town working.

On weekends Iggy and Maggie and I would go for long walks or trips to the park, with a mandatory stop at R&B's for a treat. Ruth and Bill would fuss over Maggie, coming out from behind the counter to give her a hug, throwing an extra little something into our bag, "for later." They were the closest thing to grandparents she had.

Grace called every Sunday, Simon more often, short careful conversations where more was left unsaid than spoken aloud, where the simplest word or the timbre of his voice could send my heart into a fluttery spin or a guilty spiral.

Some days I felt like a walking contradiction. Simon's confusion didn't help. After the first few calls I could anticipate by his tone what type of conversation we would have, one of wishful musing between two lovers who missed each other, or one that was subdued, stifled by guilt. Either way, there was so much I wanted to say, most of all to respond in kind when he whispered, "I miss you" or "I love you." But my husband was sitting across from me, waiting for the phone, waiting to talk to his brother. Real conversations were impossible.

Which is not to say that Iggy and I didn't have real conversations. After years of learning to avoid one subject after another and never really saying anything that wasn't part lie or evasion, sometimes he was so honest and straightforward it was unnerving.

"Ruth doesn't trust me," he said one Sunday afternoon as we left the store.

I was laughing at Maggie, who was alternating "baas" and "roars" as she marched in front of us. It was the beginning of March. When we'd left the apartment an hour earlier, I'd stood for a moment on the step, taking in the warm spring-like day. Seeing a Chinook arch stretched across the sky, I'd said to Iggy, "In like a lamb and out like a lion, eh?" "Isn't it the other way?" he said. While I was thinking about that, Maggie started in, roaring and baaing, her hands flailing with the roars as she stomped on the concrete step, then switching, her tone softening to become a little lamb. "I guess it works either way," Iggy said, giving my hand a squeeze before scooping Maggie up in a tight hug.

"Why? Did Ruth say something to you?" I asked Iggy now.

"No, nothing like that. It's just her eyes don't smile with her mouth. But it's okay, I think she feels protective of you two."

"Aw, that's sweet. But I'm sure you're wrong," I said, even though I, too, had noticed that while Bill was friendly to Iggy, Ruth was more reserved, as if she recognized something about him, or about us, that her husband did not.

"I know the signs, Bridge. I've had some practice, you know." His voice was light, self-deprecating. He put his arm around my shoulders.

Camaraderie, I thought, then felt unsure. After a few seconds I knelt down to ask Maggie, "You tired? Want me to carry you?"

She reached out and I lifted her up, careful to stay those extra inches away from Iggy. Did he know that sign, too?

We stopped at the park near our building so Maggie could search for lambs and lions. She was soon distracted by a snowfort some budding architect had started, along with some extra "bricks" of packed snow ready for the next builder.

"I never did too many really hard drugs, you know?" Iggy said.

"I always hoped that was the case."

"Well, to be fair, I tried a couple; quite a few, actually. But I always remembered you asking me about drugs way back in St. John's."

I was touched. "'I'll never take more than I can handle,' you said."

"I meant it, then and later. It was one of the few promises I kept, to both of us."

I turned and studied his face for a second. "Why? I mean, why was it so important, especially considering everything that's happened. Why that one thing?"

"Couple of reasons, I guess. There's Maggie, of course." His eyes were bright. "There's always our Maggie. God, I can't believe how lucky I am to have her."

I nodded. "You and me both."

"I know that's all down to you. You raised her. You're her real parent."

"She loves you, Iggy."

"Thanks for that." He paused. "There was another reason, one that had nothing to do with Maggie, not directly anyhow. I'd had a run-in with a weird batch of mushrooms in first-year, at least that's what I blamed it on, but the truth was I was doing other stuff, too, God knows what the real cause was. Anyway, it wasn't pretty. I decided I never wanted to go through that again."

I didn't say anything, didn't let on that Simon had told me about it.

"In the end I didn't get to choose. After that, I could never get back to being the old me. From things I've read since, I wonder if it triggered everything that followed."

He sat on a bench and leaned forward, elbows on his knees. He looked up at me, his eyes meeting mine with absolute clarity. I had this sense that we were two friends, two adult friends, confiding, finding truth, admitting defeat.

"But it wasn't only the mushroom thing," he said.

I waited. I'd learned to do that with Iggy lately, to give him time to say what he wanted to say. He'd become introspective, thoughtful about the past, about our situation. I watched Maggie try to pick up one of the snow bricks. It slipped from her hands. She hoisted it up close to her chest and tried to plant it on one already in place in the fort. It tottered and fell. Puffing out her bright red cheeks, she tried again.

"It was you. You were the other reason."

I looked over to find him smiling softly at me, the kind of smile that would have melted my heart in the early days. "Me?" I asked gently. "How?"

"You were one good thing I'd managed to find and I didn't want to let you down. There were times when I couldn't do anything about what was happening to me, when it took hold and wouldn't let go. Even now I know I'm not out of the woods. I never will be. But I could control what I took on the street. I promised you I wasn't a drug addict and it was true and I meant it. I couldn't be a good husband or a good father or even a good friend. But I could do that, I could try to keep control over something I had some control over." He paused. "Sorry, that probably wasn't very clear."

"No, it was. It is." I had spent the last few years fairly certain that I had never really mattered much to Iggy, that our relationship was something, something *else*, that had just happened to him. I hadn't known I'd made a difference. I sat next to him and tucked my arm into his. "Thanks, Ig."

We were quiet then, both of us watching Maggie. Lips bunched in concentration, she picked up the brick and placed it on top again. As she took her hand away, it started to come too, stuck to her mitten. She stopped, took off her other mitten, and managed to detach the brick with her bare hand. She turned to us. We were all beaming.

One Sunday late in March Iggy put Maggie down for her nap and came back out to the living room. He dropped into the chair across from the sofa where I was lying down, trying to stay awake long enough to finish the book I was reading, *Catcher in the Rye*. Iggy had raved about it but I found it depressing and just wanted to be done with it. I assumed he was reading, too, until I felt his eyes on me. I'd caught him looking at me like that before, pensive, as if he was wondering about something important but was unsure how to bring it up. Worried that he might want us to go back to being married, or some new and better version of that, I had always either gotten up and left or asked some innocuous question, whatever it took to break the look. That day, I didn't. I was tired. It irritated me.

I sat up. "Why are you looking at me like that?"

My tone brought him up short. "Oh, sorry. It's...it's nothing."

"It's not nothing. You've done it before. If you got something to say, say it."

"No, it's not that. Or it is but...I'm not doing a good job of this." He joined his hands together and brought them to his mouth for a minute. "You're right, there is something. I'm not sure how to ask this, or if I should, so tell me to go to hell if you want, but have you...all this time, have you been...alone, I guess is the best way to put it?"

"Huh?" I played for time. "Not sure what you mean."

He gave me a knowing look. "Yes, you do." His saucy grin brought a younger Iggy to mind. "Have you looked in the mirror? You're after getting some pretty, girl."

"Iggy! Go on with you." I put the book back up to my face.

"Hey, come on. I'm not hitting on you."

I pretended to read.

"I'm serious, Bridge. I know we're done, you and me."

The slightest pause, after the even slighter question mark that might have ended the sentence – might have, but maybe not? Now who was paranoid?

"But you shouldn't be alone, you're too young."

"I don't want to talk about this," I said behind the book.

"Or you don't want to answer my question?"

I tossed the book onto the seat beside me. "Jesus, you're blunt these days."

"I'm just trying to be honest, say what's on my mind. You did ask." He chuckled. "Bet you never thought you'd miss the old Iggy – don't ask, don't tell."

"Not likely." I sat back. "So, all right, if we're being honest, it's not your business anymore. It doesn't have anything to do with you."

"Generally, I'd agree." He was serious now, his eyes unwavering on mine. "But I'm not sure that's exactly true. Is it?"

I tensed. Did he know about Simon? Simon – just thinking his name made me blush, which is why from the outset I'd pulled a memory-curtain around the two days we'd had together, and decided that I simply could not, would not, think of Simon that way when Iggy was in the room. Then again, maybe this had nothing to do with Simon. Maybe it was some sort of pass after all, some attempt to be the husband.

I waved my hand to release his hold on my eyes. "Come on, Iggy..."

"Okay, fine," he said, his voice light again. "Now who's being evasive?"

"You said I could tell you to go to hell." I kept my tone as light as his as I stood and headed for the kitchen. "Say hi to the devil for me."

"Fair enough." He sounded disappointed. "You're right, I suppose. But you can tell me, you know. It's not like we're really married anymore."

I was past where he could see me. I rubbed my face with both hands, wishing the heat away.

By the time Iggy had been back home a few months, he had tried several medications and dosages, determined to find the combination that would work best for him. One made him want to sleep all day. Another caused vomiting and stomach cramps. He didn't give up, but persevered with the doctor. And he had improved. We could both see that. Yet I still feared that the wild and crazy guy I'd fallen in love with had to be in there somewhere. Would he come bounding out some day and send us all whirling backwards?

One evening after supper, as he washed and I dried, he said he thought it might be time to find a job, maybe part time to begin, something to help pay his way and start him back on his feet. He patted his belly. "Get rid of this pot while I'm at it."

"Good to see a few pounds on you."

"You must feel like you got two youngsters some days. Mags is growing up and I'm growing out," he said with a wry laugh. "But I don't expect you to look after me forever. Besides, if I get a job it'll look good when I go to court next month."

Not for the first time, I was struck by how level-headed he'd become. I made a decision. I'd been planning to stay home with Maggie when her day home "nanny" went to Mexico for vacation. "Well," I said, "how about you hold off and stay here with Mags when I'm at work next week?"

"I thought you were taking it off?"

"Turns out we're short-handed right now and they're afraid the stacks won't survive without me. They didn't say no but they'd really rather I came in." I put the dry plates in the cupboard. "So? You game?"

"Absolutely. You won't be sorry, Bridge. I promise."

"You guys'll have a great week. Try not to spoil her too much."

He did, of course. By the end of the week, she was exhausted but deliriously happy. She was not going to be pleased come Monday.

Saturday evening she lay cuddled between us on the sofa, fast asleep, her feet up against Iggy's thigh, her head nestled in my lap. Although the days were getting longer it was past seven and there was little daylight left in the room. I moved to pick her up.

"Don't." Iggy's hand covered her small sock-covered foot. "Not yet, okay?"

I sat back, my finger tracing the line of her jaw.

"She's something, isn't she?" he said.

I nodded. My throat felt full watching her. "I didn't know what love was until she came along." My voice was hushed, partly so I didn't wake her, but also because it felt like something that should be said quietly, with some reverence even.

We watched her breathe, her shoulder rising and falling in seamless rhythm.

"I remember the night you told me about Melinda and your father and all that." Iggy frowned. "I was so stoned. We both were. But I remember thinking how that was so unfair, that you were such a sweet girl and you didn't deserve that."

I looked over at him. "You never said."

"I never said a lot of things I should have. I wasn't good for you, I know that."

I took a second. "I always wanted to ask you why. Why me? There were lots of girls better looking, older and more mature. Why did you ask me out?"

He gave his head a guilty little shake. "Being here this last few months, I've had time to think, time to figure out some things. And that's one of the things I've thought about, me and you, why we ended up together. To be honest, part of me wonders if it might have been because of Simon. That's where I'd heard your name, more than once, him talking about this cute girl in debate, how smart she was. He'd never spoke about a girl like that before."

This felt like dangerous ground but I needed to know more. "What are you saying?"

He sighed. "That I might have…just in the beginning, mind you…I might have been trying to get one over on Simon."

"That's ridiculous."

"That's what I thought too, at first. But the more I thought about it the more I started to question myself. Did I do it on purpose?"

"I'm not buying that. You're not underhanded enough."

"Nice of you to say but even if that were true, I wasn't exactly playing with a full deck. I did a lot of stupid things back then." He added quickly, "Not you though. And not our Mags."

"I think it's time to put our Mags to bed." I picked her up and turned to go.

"He would have been good for you." Iggy's voice was low-key, matter of fact.

I stopped. I took another step and stopped again. "What?"

"Simon. You would have been better off with him."

I took a breath. I turned around. If there was something to face, I was going to face it. "Why are you saying that?"

"Because it's the truth. He's always liked you and I know you were good friends in school. He would have been better for you than I ever was." He held up his hand as I started to interrupt. "I know, I know, I should mind my own business."

I didn't know what to say so I just gave him an odd look like he was being silly and left to tuck Maggie in. As I pulled up the covers and breathed in her little girl smell, I wondered what he'd meant, why he'd brought it up. Was this some sort of test, giving me the chance to tell him about Simon, to come clean? I shook my head. I was overthinking it. There was no ulterior motive.

I took my time going back out to the living room. When I did, the television was on and Iggy was sitting in the chair with his feet up on the stool and a Coke in his hand.

"Feel like watching the game?"

"Yeah, sure." I sat on the sofa. I would have loved a glass of wine but I only did that when we had company.

"I picked you up a bottle of wine the other day on my way home from the library. It's in the cupboard over the fridge."

I turned to stare at him. Had he read my mind?

"Go ahead. Won't bother me. I never liked wine anyway."

I hesitated, then got up and poured myself a glass.

"Cheers," said Iggy, raising his can of Coke as I walked by.

"Cheers." I sat back down and tucked my feet up under me.

29

"Maggie," Iggy called down the hall. "Let's cook cookies."

They made a lot of cookies together, Rice Krispie or peanut butter squares or snowballs, cookies you didn't have to bake. Between the medication and the sweets, Iggy's lean hard frame had gone soft and pudgy.

I had just finished getting Maggie dressed for dinner in a pretty new outfit that Katie had given her. I followed her patent leather clad feet out to the kitchen where the counter was covered with bowls and bags of sugar and flour and coconut and, in the corner, the bottle of Baby Duck I'd asked Iggy to refrigerate earlier.

Iggy was bending down, peering into the lower cupboard. A roll of fat pushed against his T-shirt and over the edge of the new jeans I'd bought him the day before. "Bridge, you got any more cocoa?"

"You two used it all up the other day," I said, reaching for the bubbly.

"Did we?" He stood up. "Oh sorry, I forgot to put the wine in."

He looked exhausted. There were bags under his eyes and crow's feet around them. He'd recently started a new medication and was constantly thirsty, then up and down all night to the bathroom. He had an appointment for Monday to see his doctor.

I pushed the bottle cork first into the crowded freezer. "It'll chill quick enough in there. And can you make cookies tomorrow? We got company tonight, remember?"

Katie and Joey and Seamus were coming for supper and I'd planned a cele-bration. The month before they'd pitched their money together and bought a duplex. They were living there while renovating it into four apartments. Katie and Joey planned to move into one of the main floor units, Seamus would have one of the basement suites, and they would rent out the others. That wasn't the best part though. The best part was the location: the house was in Charleswood, a 15-minute walk away.

"Right, right, that's tonight." He yawned. "Sorry, forgot that, too."

Some days Iggy reminded me of Dad, he was so forgetful. As I put things back into the cupboard, I made a mental note to ask Simon if that was another side effect.

Maggie's rosy cheeks puffed out. "No, I make cookies."

"Not this time, Mags. We don't have cocoa. Maybe tomorrow."

"No." Tiny feet stomped the floor. "Now."

"Maggie, that's enough," I warned, my voice stern.

Iggy lifted her up and held her high in the air. "How about you and me go to the store and get some cocoa so we can make them first thing in the morning?"

"Yeah," she yelled. "Let's go see Ruth."

He set her back down and felt his pockets. "Where did I put my wallet?" He went to the sofa and checked the cushions where he'd been napping earlier.

"Pick up some milk, will you Ig?" I leaned down to Maggie. "And you can show off your new clothes to Ruth and Bill."

"What?" Iggy turned around, wallet in hand. He looked appalled.

I laughed. "You can, too, if you want, but I was talking to Maggie."

"Oh. Good." He winked at me then, another glimpse of the old Iggy. "Come on, Missy. Maybe we'll get a yumyum for after dinner," he whispered conspiratorially.

Maggie loved yumyums, as she called them. Popsicles to share in summer, rings with candy centres so that little girls could suck their fingers all the way home, and her favourite, candy bracelets. She liked food she could wear, something she could suck and nibble on as slow as she liked, and still enjoy its prettiness in the meantime. She had a very sweet tooth, "much like the rest of her," Iggy liked to say.

At the door I leaned down and kissed her. "Mama loves you, Maggie."

"Love you, Mama," she said, reaching up to Iggy.

As he took hold of her hand, I noticed the tremor in his fingers. That was new too.

I shut the door behind them and looked around the room. Since Iggy's return I rarely had time to myself, time to sit and think without the exhaustion of the day catching up to me. When it had just been Maggie and me, I was sure to get an hour on my own after she went to bed. Even when Katie had lived with us, she was always coming and going, from work or a date or Fort Mac. Iggy had nowhere to go. For the most part I didn't mind. Iggy was my family, the closest I'd ever had besides Dad. I didn't know where he fit in, but I knew he did. Even if we had been late in coming to it, we cared, really truly cared, about each other.

I kicked off my shoes and lay down on the sofa. Caring was one thing. "Taking care of" was another. How long was I going to be Iggy's caretaker? How long would it take before he was back on his feet?

And then there was Simon. What was going to happen with Simon?

As I'd done so often since Simon left, at the end of the day, behind the closed door of my bedroom, I thought of the two nights we'd had together. I sensed something I'd never known before, something I couldn't name but that was absolute, deeper than skin. There was a sober certainty in the rightness, the inevitability, that all that had happened was a simple matter of fate. Yet at the same time, fate or not, there was something that made me swallow as I thought of him, as I tried to relive the touch of his hands, the press of his lips, my mind going over that second night again, remembering how slowly we'd made love, how sensual he made me feel, his eyes looking into mine, his hands moving –

The phone rang. I bounded off the sofa in a guilty little leap to answer it.

"Hi. It's me." Simon's voice sounded deeper than usual.

"Hi Simon," I said, savouring the sound of his name on my tongue.

He waited a second. "Is Iggy there?"

"He took Maggie to the store."

"You're alone then?"

"Yes."

"So…we can talk." I heard a light splash in the background. "I just poured a glass of wine. How about you? You have any there?"

"One sec." I went to the kitchen and poured a glass. "There," I said. "Now we're having a drink together."

"Never a good idea to drink alone."

"Hardly seems fair to all the singles in the world."

"Good point. When will they be back?"

"Could be any time now, so if I hang up that's why, okay?" I took a sip. "It's some good to hear your voice."

"You too. So good. I've been thinking about you a lot, trying to figure out what to do. All I know is that I miss you." He paused. "I mean I really miss you."

"Me too." I looked at my watch. They'd been gone quite a while.

"What are we going to do, Bridge?"

"I don't know. Wait for now, I suppose."

"That's all we can do, I guess. At least we can talk."

I heard footsteps coming up the stairs. "I should go. They're home."

"Okay. Bye. For now."

"Bye."

Seconds passed. "I can't hang up on you, Bridge." His voice was hushed. "You have to do it."

I laughed, low and throaty. "Bye, Simon," I whispered.

Katie walked in just as I was lifting my hand from the phone cradle.

"Katie…oh, it's you."

She gestured toward the phone. "What the heck was he selling?"

"Huh?"

"You're looking that hot and bothered, must've been an obscene call."

"What? That's ridiculous," I said even as my hand flew to my face.

Katie gave me a knowing look, one that said, "Hey, it's me you're talking to," and flopped onto the sofa.

"I thought you were Iggy. He and Maggie went to the store." I sounded a little breathless. "Where're the guys?"

"Held up laying carpet. Should be here in an hour." Katie sized me up. "So?"

I picked up a pillow and threw it at her. "Okay, fine. It was Simon."

She grinned. "Ooh, and what did loverboy have to say?"

"Katie!" I said, glancing toward the door before heading to the kitchen.

"Come on, girl, it's just us."

"I know, but you never know." I checked the time again as I moved the bottle of bubbly from the freezer to the fridge. "They should have been here by now."

"You know how Maggie likes to dawdle." Katie got up and poured herself a glass of wine. "Anyway, what was he saying?"

"Not much he can say, is there?"

"Oh, I don't know about that. He could say he misses you."

"Oh, well, yeah," I grinned, "he did say that. He also…" I stopped.

Hurried footsteps were bounding up the stairs. The door burst open. Iggy rushed in holding Maggie tight. He thrust her into my chest and his arms came around me to bring the three of us close. His eyes stared into mine. "Lock the door," he whispered. His lips brushed both our foreheads with one movement. Then he was out the door.

Maggie looked frightened. I held my cheek against hers and made calming circles on her back till I felt her settle. My eyes met Katie's over Maggie's dark curls.

I motioned her over. "Look who's here, Mags. Can you give Auntie Katie a hug?" I slid her gently into Katie's arms.

I shoved my feet into my shoes and opened the door.

"Are you nuts?" Katie hissed, her hand over Maggie's ear. "Don't go out there."

"Lock it," I mouthed and shut the door behind me.

I stood still and listened, then crept down the stairs to the main entrance. I glanced sideways out the small window in the north entry door. There it was, Gord's black truck, parked in the spot closest to the building. I crossed over to the south entrance and slipped outside. I heard voices but they were muffled by the wind. Heart hammering in my ears, I slid against the side of the building then ducked and scooted over behind the tall evergreen hedge. The conversation was clearer now.

Iggy: For a lousy bag of weed, what, a hundred bucks?

Dave: Fuck the weed. I'm talking about the payoff from B.C.

Iggy: I gave it to Ed. He said you told him to pick it up.

Dave: We never seen it, so you owe us, you got to do this to even up.

Iggy: That shit Ed, what's he playing at, I'll get him for this.

Dave: Nobody getting Ed no more.

A nasty snicker followed.

Iggy: What…? No, fuck no. You're kidding, right?

Gord: Yeah, like Dave's a kidder.

Iggy: What happened?

Gord: Fucked if I know. Didn't see him for a while then heard he wound up dead in Mexico, trying to pull a deal or some fucking thing.

I crouched low and peeked out. Gord sat in the driver's seat. Iggy and Dave stood by the open passenger door. The window was down and Dave's elbow rested on the ledge. He lifted his arm and began to turn in my direction. I pulled back.

Iggy: See, that's it. He took that money to score his own shit in Mexico.

Gord: That's crap. Ed didn't have the balls.

Iggy: No, think about it. He always talked about getting a piece of the action.

Dave: Look, all I know is we got nothing. Now what's it going to be?

Iggy: Listen, I started over, man, I'm clean. I got a kid to think of.

Dave: It's like this, we know where you live now, the wife and kiddie, too.

Iggy: Come on, you don't mean that.

Dave: Lucky I spotted the little missus at the post office. Hardly knew her at first. Not a fat pig anymore.

Gord: You always had a thing for her, didn't you, Dave?

Their coarse laughter made my skin crawl. Then it hit me. They knew where we lived.

Iggy: Screw off, guys, that's not funny.

Gord: Chill out, man, we're just messing with you.

Dave: So you doing the run for us or not, Connors?

Gord: Look Ig, like he says, you do this and you're off the hook.

Dave: I got no more time to be Mr. Nice here. We got to get moving tonight.

Iggy: Fine, I'll do it, just let me go say goodbye, okay?

Dave: We let you bring the kid in, so say thanks and get in.

Iggy: I'll only be a minute. I got to grab a few things.

Dave: Are you coming or not, Connors?

Iggy: Yes, Jesus, I told you I'd do it.

Dave: Then get in the fucking truck.

Iggy: Get your fucking hands off me.

The slam of a door.

Dave: Let's go. Move it.

Iggy: Five minutes, that's all I –

Whatever else he said was drowned out by the gunning of the engine.

An image of Iggy stuck in the truck between the MacDonald brothers flashed through my mind. I had to do something. I had to get upstairs. I needed to call Simon, maybe the police. I was standing, ready to act, just as the truck reversed and careened from the parking lot. Nothing remained but the roar of the motor and the screech of rubber on pavement.

Iggy was gone.

30

I didn't call the police. As Simon pointed out, that would essentially be the same as turning Iggy in. If he was running a drug deal for the MacDonald brothers, we could only hope it went okay. And in truth, Gord and Dave had not actually forced him into it. Coerced, yes, pressured, maybe vaguely threatened with respect to Maggie and me, but Iggy had agreed to it. So I agreed to wait. For now.

Simon made me promise to leave the apartment that night, to go and stay at Katie's, which I did. Early Sunday morning, however, I left Maggie with Katie and went home to wait for Iggy's call. He would not leave me worrying. He would find a way to reach me. And if he didn't call by the end of the day, I would know something was seriously wrong. Then I would decide if I should contact the police.

Seamus dropped me off with a pile of moving boxes. He offered to stay but I sent him back to work on the renovations. The MacDonald brothers were too busy with their drug business to be thinking of me and Maggie. While I waited for the phone to ring, I cleaned the apartment, working my way from one room to the next, emptying cupboards, filling boxes, clearing out the fridge. It kept me occupied, mind and body. Halfway through scrubbing the bathroom, I found Iggy's new prescription. On a hunch, I counted the number of pills, then checked the date on the bottle. There were too many left. Had he forgotten to take them, or had he chosen not to?

The call came mid-afternoon, collect from a pay phone in Vancouver.

Iggy's voice was hurried, yet low in tone with a tightly wound edge. He told me not to worry, that he had to do this, that he would be back, that everything would be fine.

"It really will, Bridge, you got to believe me, I know what I'm doing, I do, I do, yeah, you just take care of Maggie for me, give her a big hug, tell her Daddy loves her, tell her I'll be back, soon, real soon…"

When I managed to get a word in to ask was he okay, had Dave hurt him, he laughed. The high-pitched sound made my skin prickle. He said no, he was fine, that Dave was all bark and no bite and, besides, he could handle the MacDonald brothers. In the next instant, his attitude changed to alarm, and he told me to get out of the apartment, that I couldn't stay there, that I should go. "Now," he insisted. "Right this minute. Hang up and go." His voice was fierce, adamant. "Bridge, please, please, just go…" Then he was crying, "…if anything happened to you and Maggie, I couldn't stand it, you got to go, I don't trust him…"

Hearing him so distraught, I started to panic. "Iggy, listen to me. You need to calm down and get to a doctor, right now, get your medication, please, you got to…"

"…no I'm fine, Gord gave me something to tide me over, he's a good guy, Gord is, not like that fucking Dave. Jesus, Bridge, you got to go…"

"I will, I will, but listen to me, Iggy, you got to get on your meds, okay…?"

"Bridge, stop." His voice had an undercurrent of forced restraint. "I have to go now. You do, too. You have to get away from there. I'm going to hang up now so you can go. Don't stay there. I won't call this number again. I know where you'll go, okay? So don't worry, I'll call you there." I heard a sharp intake of breath and then he added, his voice breaking. "I'm sorry, Bridge. I'm so sorry."

"Iggy wait, don't hang up…"

The line went dead.

I heard nothing more until Simon called me two days later at Katie's.

"He didn't sound good, Bridge. His voice was shaky and he was begging me to look after you and Maggie, like he was never going to see you again."

"I'm worried, Simon. If he had his meds, maybe he'd be able to cope. And who knows what Gord's after giving him. Could be making it all worse."

"I know. I told him to go to a doctor but he said the cops are onto him, then went on about how he couldn't trust doctors, or cops, that they were all out to get him."

"God, sounds like the old days."

"That's what I thought."

"It's not a good sign when he gets this paranoid. He won't know who to trust."

"I know. He wouldn't even tell me where he was. When I said Vancouver, he yelled no, that I should shut up, they could be listening, whoever they are. And he kept making these weird gasping sounds, like he couldn't catch his breath. I have to go out there, I have to look for him."

"I know." I paused. "Be careful, Simon. Just, please, be careful."

Maggie and I stayed with Katie and Joey for a couple of weeks until the other apartment was ready. Seamus and Joey had already moved our bedroom furniture over so we could have a place to sleep and later stored the rest of our stuff in a corner of their garage. We didn't have much. I had called Victor to arrange for his brother to get his furniture back, if he wanted it. I didn't. It was old and ragged and I was ready for a new start. I had a few dollars saved. I would buy my own furniture.

We officially moved into Katie's and Joey's and Seamus's apartment in May in the middle of a downpour. We were all giddy from the wet, but it wasn't just that. They were exhilarated about being homeowners and landlords. I was filled with relief to be where I was compared to two years earlier, stuck in Gord Mac-Donald's basement. And even though Iggy might have been right, that Dave MacDonald was more bark than bite, I was grateful he no longer knew my address.

By day's end, except for some unopened boxes and a bit of a mess, Maggie and I were pretty well settled in. Not settled exactly, at least not me, but thankful to be safe and with good friends. Iggy's situation was a persistent weight at the back of my mind but there was nothing I could do about it. I had to leave it to Simon. No one wanted to find Iggy more than he did.

At first Maggie missed Iggy a great deal and asked about him often. When was Daddy coming home, where was he? I answered honestly – I didn't know. She was used to him being gone for weeks at a time. A month passed, then three, five, nine. Somewhere along the changing seasons, she stopped asking.

I missed Iggy, too. After spending so much time with him, I felt as if I had finally gotten to know Iggy the person, who he was, deep down. We had become friends.

Victor called every so often and we would catch up on each other's lives. We were friends, too, it seemed. I appreciated that. Grace called as well, every Sunday afternoon around her suppertime. She insisted that she phone me. She didn't want me paying for long-distance charges; she'd rather I spent the money on Maggie. The conversations were short, five or 10 minutes, her voice often sad, resigned, except when she talked about Maggie. She wanted to know everything about her, and sometimes would relate a story about when Iggy or Simon was that age. She would go quiet then, as would I. She didn't ask to speak to Maggie. I was glad of that. I didn't want to explain who Grace was.

Simon phoned us several times a week, unless he was away on the hunt for Iggy. He'd gone straight out to Vancouver after Iggy called him. He didn't find him. In between rotations at the hospital in Montreal, he kept up the search, flying to Toronto, then later, Winnipeg and Regina, Vancouver, Toronto again, with scattered overnight trips in between if he got a lead from someone, usually through Seamus, who kept his ear to the ground. He went to Mexico once, although he didn't tell me that until he was back on Canadian soil. I made him promise never to do that again, both going to Mexico and keeping it from me. Each place he went had its own haunts – homeless shelters, downtown parks and bridges, seedy druggie bars. Hospitals. Jail. No sign of Iggy.

Grace was paying for it all, with the money her mother had left her. "My father must be rolling over in his grave," she said. "Serves him right, the bastard."

Whenever Simon called he would fill me in on anything new, places he'd gone looking for Iggy, as if he needed to get that out of the way first. Once that was done, I would call out, "Maggie, it's Simon," and she would grab Bamboo and rush to the phone, babbling away, sometimes pretending Bamboo was talking. I would watch, content, or as content as I could hope to be. After a minute or so she would pass the phone to me and go back to whatever she'd been doing. Then Simon and I would talk. If it was in the evening, we would have a glass of wine while we caught each other up on all the other important and mundane aspects of our lives. Our "date nights." We both would have liked more, but they would do for now. They had to.

We seldom alluded to the future. There was no need. We each understood where the other was coming from. He needed to do everything he could to find Iggy. I needed him to do just that until he knew there was nothing more to be done, until he could look at me and say, "I'm ready," and know that he was. This would be harder for him than me. I was willing to wait until we could face the future, the uncertainty, together, with no regrets, no matter what happened. I could not settle for less than that. I would not settle for less. Not this time.

With our new place, Maggie and I had as much privacy as we wanted, but we were not alone or lonely. The two basement suites were shared amongst Seamus and other rig hands he worked with. They were all in and out of town a lot so this worked well for them. I was wary at first with so many people coming and going, thinking of Iggy's house in St. John's and Gord's in Calgary. But Katie said not to worry. "Our hard-earned cash is in that down payment, Bridge. Not just me and Joey. Seamus, too. We're not having any no-goods staying here."

A couple of times a week Maggie and I had dinner with Katie and Joey. Seamus joined us when he was in town, often bringing along a couple of his roommates who were all solid fellows. The situation was as good as any I could have hoped for at that point. I felt like I was part of some big extended family. I even got invited out on dates. Seamus never seemed all that pleased when he noticed one of his friends paying me extra attention. I didn't encourage it and I always turned them down. Unlike her brother, Katie was not happy about that.

"Bridge, get back on the horse already," she said one Saturday evening as we were prepping vegetables. "You're in the prime of your life. Just because you got a kid doesn't mean you're an old woman, doomed to sit home every night."

I heard Maggie and Joey wrestling in the living room. "Easy for you to say."

Katie tossed chopped peppers into the salad bowl. "You know me and Joey'll babysit any time. Maggie's like having our own kid without all the hassle."

I laughed. "Thanks, I think."

"I see the way guys look at you. You got to start dating, get back in the game."

I was peeling potatoes over her kitchen sink. "Get back in the game?" I gave a little snort. For a split second, Josephine came to mind. "Who are you kidding? I was never in the game."

"True enough, I guess. But don't you want to go out and have fun? Meet someone nice? Maybe fall in love?" She lowered her voice. "Or even just get laid?"

I stripped a peel off a potato. "I'm not ready for that stuff, Katie. The thought of it makes me tired."

"But Bridge, it's not good for you to be alone for so long."

I put my hand on her arm. "I'm fine. Maggie's fine. We got you and Joey and Seamus, and all his buddies who are great even if they do try to hit on me. Honest to God, that's enough, for now anyway. Unless, you know, we're in the way or you're sick of having us around so much, being stuck with us on a Saturday night – "

Katie slung her arm around me. "You know that's not it, right? Don't tell me I got to tell you that." She pulled back. "It's them damn Connors brothers, isn't it?"

"No." Then I added, "Just one of them."

"I think I know which one it isn't." Katie frowned. "What's going on there?"

"He's still searching every chance he gets."

"What's it been? A year? Where's left to look?"

"All over the place, east, west and in between. A few weeks ago he was out in the Gulf Islands. Someone said a guy from Newfoundland had a farm operation going on."

"Farm? As in…?" She brought her thumb and index finger to her mouth.

I nodded. "Hydroponics or something."

"Too bad he didn't stop over on his way back."

"He sort of suggested it. I didn't take him up on it."

She slapped the knife onto the counter. "Why the hell not?"

"He's got to figure this out first."

"What if he finds him?"

"I'm pretty sure he won't."

"Why do you say that?"

"Because Iggy didn't…he doesn't want to be found." I hesitated. "If he's alive."

Katie looked shocked. "You don't think…?"

I shrugged. "Sometimes I wonder, especially on nights that I dream about him."

"What, like you have a premonition or something?"

"No, God no, nothing like that. It's just that…" I paused, trying to figure out exactly what I meant. "The last thing I'd want is to be responsible for him again, to take that on, but in my dreams I'm so darn glad to see him. And even though he looks like the Iggy I met at that party way back when, it feels like he's someone I'm close to that I haven't seen in a long time, but more like a brother or a good friend. Not like a husband though, not like someone I'd made a life with."

Katie turned to look me in the eye. "You know why that is, don't you?"

I nodded. "Because we never really did."

Grace hadn't phoned the previous Sunday. I told myself it was probably nothing. Maybe she had been invited out for supper. She would phone the next Sunday.

Maggie and I stayed in all that day. Grace didn't call.

I phoned Simon on Monday. "Have you heard from your mother?"

I felt him hesitate. "Why? Did she call you, too?"

"No, that's just it. She's phoned me almost every Sunday for ages, except the last two. I thought I'd check with you first then I'd give her a call. How is she?"

Hesitation again. "She's okay, I guess, a little out of sorts."

"Is anything wrong?"

He didn't answer right away.

"Simon, what is it?" I kept my voice calm. "What did Grace say?"

"She said…she thinks something's happened to Iggy."

I swallowed. I waited.

"Bridge? What is it? Have you heard anything? Did he call?"

"No, Simon, he didn't call." I spoke as if he should have known that.

I heard his quick intake of breath. "Oh Bridge, not you, too?"

"I'm sorry, but you know it's a possibility."

"Mom's got herself convinced. She was out in Saint Paul for the weekend, taking a few days to herself, away from Dad and the daily trek to visit him. Sunday she woke up early and it was a warm sunny spring day and she went for a long walk in the woods. It reminds her of Iggy, she says." I heard the crack in his voice.

"He loved roaming through those woods." Past tense. I hadn't meant to do that.

"She came back and put on the kettle and made toast. She was pouring a cup of tea when the wind came up and tree branches started swishing against the window. It lasted only seconds and then it stopped and everything went still again. She said she sat down at the table with her cup of tea and all she could think of was Iggy."

"Poor Grace. How is she?"

"That's the odd bit. She's okay. It's been hard on her, not knowing, me looking and not finding anything. So yeah, she's better than I would have expected."

"What do you think? I mean, about what your mother thinks?"

"I'm a doctor. I believe in science. Facts."

I let the silence hang.

"But I'm afraid, too. And I'm tired. Tired of wondering and worrying and looking." His voice went quiet, almost a whisper. "Tired of the guilt."

He was having one of his bad days.

"Do you remember what he said, Bridge, that he was sorry, that he wanted me to forgive him? I can't get that out of my mind. Me? Forgive him? After what I did – "

"Simon, stop. He asked the same thing of me, remember, to forgive him. He was sorry, okay, sorry for putting us through everything." I paused. "All I can tell you is that if he was here, if he knew about me and you, he would forgive you – us – in a heartbeat."

"I don't know, maybe you're right. I'd sure like to think you are."

"Iggy wouldn't want you to be hurting like this. Neither do I."

He gave a small sigh. "God, I miss you."

"I miss you too. I wish I was there to hold you."

"I want to come see you. I just need to get my head around all this, figure out what I really think. Do you mind, waiting, I mean? Can you give me a little more time?"

"I've had years to get used to Iggy leaving. You take what you need."

I hung up and called Grace. "I talked to Simon," I said. "He told me."

"You mean about the branches on the window? I know, sounds crazy."

"One person's crazy is another's normal. Is that why you didn't call?"

"I didn't want to put my ideas into your head."

"Are you okay?"

"I think I am. I think I've been saying goodbye to Iggy for a long time."

"I know what you mean."

"And I'm worn out, Bridge," she said, her voice breaking. "I got nothing left. Between him and Bernie, I don't know what's real and what's not half the time."

"Thank God you have Simon."

There was a pause. Her voice, when she spoke, was stronger, determined. "When he was home he told me about you and him. I hope you don't mind."

"No, it's okay. I hope you don't mind."

She laughed lightly. "It's how they did it in the old days, you know, the brother stepping in. How's our Maggie?"

"She's real good, Grace, I wish you could see her." I paused. "Sometimes I wonder though, you know, about what might be passed down, or even for Simon."

She didn't answer right away. "I am sorry, Bridge. I feel like a lot of this is my fault. I want you to know that."

"Oh, Grace, don't say that."

"Let's be honest. I should have done something years ago, about Iggy, I mean. Maybe you wouldn't have had such a hard time of it."

I took a moment then decided honesty was a good policy. "The truth is, I did blame you at first, a bit anyway, but I don't anymore. I should have seen it. Hell, maybe I did and I ignored it. In the end it doesn't matter. There was nothing in Exile Cove for me either except Dad, and he would have died if I'd been there or not." I paused again. "Simon said he's going to go see you, make sure you're okay?"

"He's a good son. I miss him."

"I know. I miss him, too."

"He's all I've got left, you know?"

"Hey, you still got Maggie." Then I added, "And me."

Clutching Bamboo under her right arm, Maggie swung her left in time with mine as she hopped and skipped along, chatting about the peanut butter and banana crackers they'd had for a snack, the upcoming trip to the zoo, the new girl at preschool.

"And she got red hair." Maggie's brown eyes were wide and excited. "Just like Auntie Katie's."

"I can't wait to meet her," I said. "Maybe at the zoo next week."

The day was the sort fantasized about in mid-January, a blue-sky Friday in June, especially brilliant after a week of cloud and rain. Calgary had transformed from brown and dull to green and vibrant seemingly overnight. I loved the city this time of year, bursting back into life after a dark winter with never enough Chinooks.

Katie had just finished mowing the lawn when Maggie and I arrived, and the air was ripe with smells of motor oil and earth and fresh-cut grass. She pushed the mower aside and held out her arms. "Hey Mags, want to help me make brownies for dessert?"

"Yay, brownies." Maggie squealed as Katie picked her up and swung her around.

"You go in and change," Katie said to me. "Maggie and me will get started. I'm making an extra special batch."

"Not too special," I laughed. Katie and Joey were known to make some pretty good hash brownies.

"Just extra chocolate chips for our Maggie here," Katie winked.

"Okay, I'll be right over." We had a family dinner planned and I was looking forward to a fun night sitting around the fire-pit in the backyard, sipping beer or wine until the chill set in before moving inside to share whatever we'd all brought to the table.

"Sure," Katie waved at me over her shoulder. "Take your time."

I went into my apartment and hung my purse and Maggie's bag on the hooks behind the door. I turned around.

He was sitting on our new leather sofa at the far end of the living room, perched forward, hands clasped and resting on the coffee table. The sun beating through the west-facing window put his face in shadow. I had to focus an extra moment to be sure who I was seeing. He was not smiling exactly, at least not his mouth, which was closed. But his eyes held mine with an intensity that lifted my heart to a place I'd forgotten.

"Hi, Bridge." There was the voice I had longed to hear, live, unhindered by the static of phone lines.

"Hi." I wasn't sure if I'd said it out loud, or if I had, loud enough. My head was in a strange place. As often as I had imagined him before me, imagined what I would say to him and him to me, imagined reaching out and touching his face, nothing compared to the reality of having him before me in my living room.

He stood up. He was taller than I remembered. He looked older too, his eyes more deeply set in his lean face. The past year had taken its toll.

"Katie let me in."

"She never said." My heart was beating too fast. I breathed in, out, measured and deliberate, feeling the rise, fall, rise and fall, seeking a normal pace, life's normal rhythm. I inhaled and held it, enjoyed the fullness in my chest for a moment, then let it out.

Without breaking eye contact, he moved around the coffee table and began a slow walk towards me. "I hope that was okay?"

One step closer. And another.

"Yes." My eyes never wavered, never lost sight. I wanted to speak, to tell him, to hear him tell me, what we both needed to know. "You're here," was all I managed.

"I am. Finally." Another step closer. "I missed you."

I drank him in for a moment. "How are you?"

"Great, now that I'm looking at you." He shook his head. "I couldn't stay away anymore."

I waited, unsure what he meant. Was this temporary, a quick stop, then off again?

"Don't look so worried." His voice was soft, endearing. "I wouldn't do that to you, or to us."

Relief flooded through me.

"I've begun to face facts, Bridge. This couldn't go on forever. It's time to stop."

"I know that feeling. It's hard, but it's a good place to be."

He took a deep breath as if to gird himself for what he had to say. "I may never see him again. I have to accept that."

I paused. "Are you sure you're ready?"

He nodded. "Yes. Are you?"

"I faced that a while back. I had to." I walked to him. "This won't be easy, especially for you."

"We can't live our lives in limbo. I can't ask you to do that anymore. I don't want to do that anymore."

We stood facing each other, holding the moment.

I felt his hand reach for mine, take my fingers into his, bring them to his lips.

Our arms folded around each other. We held on tight.

THE END